THE
SENTINEL

GERALD PETIEVICH

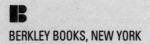

BERKLEY BOOKS, NEW YORK

THE BERKLEY PUBLISHING GROUP
Published by the Penguin Group
Penguin Group (USA) Inc.
375 Hudson Street, New York, New York 10014, USA
Penguin Group (Canada), 90 Eglinton Avenue East, Suite 700, Toronto, Ontario M4P 2Y3, Canada
(a division of Pearson Penguin Canada Inc.)
Penguin Books Ltd., 80 Strand, London WC2R 0RL, England
Penguin Group Ireland, 25 St. Stephen's Green, Dublin 2, Ireland (a division of Penguin Books Ltd.)
Penguin Group (Australia), 250 Camberwell Road, Camberwell, Victoria 3124, Australia
(a division of Pearson Australia Group Pty. Ltd.)
Penguin Books India Pvt. Ltd., 11 Community Centre, Panchsheel Park, New Delhi—110 017, India
Penguin Group (NZ), Cnr. Airborne and Rosedale Roads, Albany, Auckland 1310, New Zealand
(a division of Pearson New Zealand Ltd.)
Penguin Books (South Africa) (Pty.) Ltd., 24 Sturdee Avenue, Rosebank, Johannesburg 2196,
South Africa

Penguin Books Ltd., Registered Offices: 80 Strand, London WC2R 0RL, England

This is a work of fiction. Names, characters, places, and incidents either are the product of the author's imagination or are used fictitiously, and any resemblance to actual persons, living or dead, business establishments, events, or locales is entirely coincidental. The publisher does not have any control over and does not assume any responsibility for author or third-party websites or their content.

THE SENTINEL

A Berkley Book / published by arrangement with the author

PRINTING HISTORY
First Berkley edition / February 2003
Second Berkley edition / April 2006

Copyright © 2003 by Charles Carr Productions, Inc.
Interior text design by Julie Rogers.

ISBN: 0-425-21232-7

BERKLEY®
Berkley Books are published by The Berkley Publishing Group,
a division of Penguin Group (USA) Inc.,
375 Hudson Street, New York, New York 10014.
BERKLEY is a registered trademark of Penguin Group (USA) Inc.
The "B" design is a trademark belonging to Penguin Group (USA) Inc.

PRINTED IN THE UNITED STATES OF AMERICA

10 9 8 7 6 5 4 3

*For Robert L. Tomsic—Army Ranger,
Secret Service Agent, and loyal friend*

I wish to thank Robert Crais, who sparked the idea for this novel, and Dianne Pugh, who provided me with valuable suggestions in two drafts.

I'd also like to thank Emma Petievich for her valuable research assistance and editing, my former Army Intelligence colleague and legendary ATF Special Agent Charlie Fuller, Alice Hudson, Pam Petievich, Officer Patrick O' Hagan of the Hyattsville, Maryland, Police Department, Dr. Robert Gayles, and three U.S. Secret Service Agents (who must remain unnamed) for updating me on certain issues.

I could not have written this book without the tireless assistance of Mary Valentine, whose sound editorial advice helped me through the shadowy valleys.

I lived for the moment,
Now what can I tell,
Passion bloomed like a flower,
Until the petals fell.

The fascination drew me,
Along the shifty road to hell,
Those eyes bewitched me,
Until the petals fell.

—Melinda Troisgros,
   from *The Collected Poems of Melinda T.*

GLOSSARY

The following are U.S. Secret Service radio code terms used by the White House Detail:

Victory	The President of the United States
Valentine	The First Lady
Vigilant	National Security Advisor Helen A. Pierpont
Acrobat	Secret Service Director Larry G. Wintergreen
Crown	The Executive Mansion
Crown Control	The White House Secret Service Detail radio room

Warrior	Presidential limousine
Halftrack	Presidential follow-up car
Volcano	The President's retreat in Rehoboth Beach, Delaware
Vermont	Camp David
Shadow	Secret Service Protective Research Division
Ribbon	The Secret Service Special Operations Team (SOT)
Rabbit Hutch	The White House Secret Service command post

SECRET SERVICE AGENTS

Rip Cord	Special Agent Peter C. Garrison
Roadster	Special Agent Gilbert D. Flanagan, commander of SOT
Rolling Pin	Special Agent Ronan P. Squires
Roadwork	Special Agent Walter E. Sebastian

PROLOGUE

CHARLIE MERIWEATHER'S FEET ached as he stood post at the East Wing private quarters elevator. He glanced at his Timex. It was 8:06 A.M. He'd been on duty since last midnight, spending most of the time thinking about fly-fishing along a wide stream in Great Falls, Montana. Nineteen years in the U.S. Secret Service's White House Detail had taught him how to endure a tedious eight-hour shift.

Ronan Squires shuffled around the corner from the colonnade.

"You're pushed, Charlie."

"You're late."

"What's six minutes in the course of life?"

"Squires, you think the world revolves around you. Someday you'll realize it revolves around the Man."

"No need to get pushed out of shape."

Squires slid back an Early American tapestry on the wall, opened a gun box, and checked the Uzi submachine gun that was in it. He was thirty years old and wore a dark-blue business suit, a striped necktie, and highly shined, wing-tip shoes. Meriweather saw in Squires a younger version of himself.

"You're loaded with a thirty-round clip," Meriweather said. "The special orders remain unchanged. Or do you even know what they are?"

Squires closed the gun box. "The elevator post," he said as if reciting. "Duties: Limit access to the elevator and if an intruder breaches security, grab the Uzi and head upstairs to lock the President and the First Lady inside the Cage. How's that?" The Cage was a walk-in closet in the President's master bedroom that had been stocked with military communications gear, gas masks, and other survival items. Meriweather knew that such elaborate Presidential security precautions were necessary in the age of rising terrorism.

"You're going to go a long way in this outfit, Ronan."

"Being Irish and handsome, how could I fail?"

Meriweather coughed dryly. "Sorry I'm going to have to miss your rise to power. I'm retiring."

"No shit?"

"And don't tell me I'm too young to pull the pin. The day comes when an agent gets fed up with all the White House politics. For me that day has arrived. I've had it right up to here. As soon as I take care of a few loose ends, Delores and I are loading up the fishing poles and heading to Montana."

"You'll get bored."

Meriweather smiled. "Compared to what? The excitement of standing here from midnight to eight while some political hack catches his Zs upstairs?"

"You're really gonna do it, aren't you?"

Meriweather winked at him, ambled to the stairwell, and then jogged down the stairs to the basement level. At a door marked with a brass nameplate that read STAFF AUXILIARY OFFICE, he tapped out a six-digit code on the cipher lock. The bolt retracted with a buzzing sound and he walked into the U.S. Secret Service White House Command Post, ground zero of the White House security system; an aquarium of electronic duty rosters, alarm maps, radio consoles, computer equipment, gun cabinets, and television monitors that were transmitting color views of hallways and rooms. He moved past a digitized Protectee Locator Board that tracked each member of the First Family from room to room within the White House and around the world, and stopped at an On Duty Agents roster, a large electronic display board with color photographs of every member of the Secret Service's White House Detail. Meriweather pressed a button that transferred his name to the OFF DUTY column.

Meriweather walked outside. A clammy summer rain had been clinging to the Potomac for the last few days, and some tourists taking photographs from behind the wrought-iron fence at Pennsylvania Avenue looked wet and uncomfortable. Meriweather walked up the driveway, stopped, and looked back across an expanse of perfectly manicured lawn. The White House had once been the largest residence in the entire country. He wondered whether in those days lunatics were drawn to it like a magnet as they were now. There were at least thirty incidents of individuals trying to break into the White

House every year. During the last month agents had arrested a man who'd bolted from the White House tour line and charged the stairs, and a shrieking woman in a Superman costume who'd scrambled over the wrought-iron fence and made it halfway to the portico before being tackled.

At the Northeast guard booth, Meriweather gave a nod to the uniformed officer inside whose job it was to monitor a switch controlling the raising and lowering of the car-blocking iron beams. As Meriweather had learned in Secret Service school years earlier, the White House security system was based on the Secret Service Concentric Theory: powerful circles of defense extending inward to the President. The system included heat-sensing, infrared, foot-pressure, and sound sensors, electronic fences, agents in mufti who infiltrated the White House tour groups to detect suspicious persons, officers on the roof armed with handheld surface-to-air missiles capable of shooting down aircraft and surveillance cars that patrolled nearby streets.

Inside the White House, a fifty-man shift of Secret Service agents worked in three separate shifts, twenty-four hours a day, operating under detailed security advance plans that covered transportation, escape, and communications; every possible contingency that related to Presidential security. When the President traveled, the names of every person whom he came in contact with were checked through all national intelligence indices.

Presidential security was a science unto itself. Meriweather figured that without it, the President wouldn't last a week. But he'd had enough. Let someone else pace the White House halls and ride the running board of the limousine waiting to get blown up for the Man.

Walking along G Street, Meriweather stopped at the Margit Holakoui Flower shop, where Margit helped him pick out some orchids for Delores.

"When are you guys going to catch the terrorists who blew up the Federal Building?"

"Soon, I hope."

Terrorism was again the topic of the day for everyone in the country after five public buildings had been bombed in the last eighteen months; each incident attributed to right-wing extremists. Meriweather wrote out a card for Delores, and paid Holakoui the White House discount price in cash. There was no use running up a credit-card bill when one was retiring to live on fifty-percent pay.

He departed, and it began to rain. He held the flowers over his head as a shield. Walking along G Street, he passed some construction workers who were excavating a portion of the road. He knew that if they dug far enough, they would run into the escape tunnel that was to be used by the President in the event of a paramilitary attack on the White House. The standing orders were to evacuate the President using a secret door in the White House East Wing and the underground route to the basement parking lot of Secret Service Headquarters in the nearby Telco Bank Building. Thank God he'd never had to make that run, thought Meriweather.

At the corner was a four-story public garage where he always parked his car. Meriweather turned into the driveway, and was pleased to get out of the rain. He trotted up three flights of stairs rather than use the elevator. The third-floor parking spaces were filled. Moving along a row of cars, he heard the sound of a car door open and close, but saw no one. Reaching his Chevrolet

Monte Carlo, he took out his key and inserted it into the lock. He sensed someone behind him and turned.

A man wearing a skin-colored mask was aiming a silencer-equipped revolver at him.

Meriweather's stomach muscles contracted. Over the years, standing post for five different Presidents—at stairwells, back doors, service entries, palatial back-yards, and palace gates—there had been a thousand times when Meriweather had imagined what he would do if confronted by an armed gunman. One never really knew for sure how one would react. Meriweather reached for his SIG-Sauer 9mm automatic.

The gunman fired. The blast spun Meriweather back-ward and down.

On his back, immobilized and bleeding, he saw a childhood memory flash into his mind: missing the school bus in his hometown of Hyden, Kentucky. He was ten years old, running along the sidewalk, shouting at the bus driver. *"Mr. Osborne! Mr. Osborne. Wait!"*

The mask stared down at him.

"Sonofabitch," Meriweather said, his lips barely mov-ing.

The silencer spit fire again. Meriweather's body roiled, and as his nervous system uncoupled from his brain, his final spark of thought was of him and Delores fly-fishing in an icy Montana stream, casting into clear water. Delores was the only woman he'd ever met who liked fly-fishing.

CHAPTER 1

SECRET SERVICE SPECIAL Agent Martha Breckinridge lifted the plastic sheet and aimed a Kel-light at Meriweather's corpse. His right hand was reaching inside his jacket for his SIG-Sauer 9mm pistol. She'd known him and liked him, and seeing him lying dead sickened her. She knew the scene would stay with her forever. Some orchids wrapped in cellophane were a few feet away. The card with the flowers read:

Dear Delores:
    Thanks for putting up with me through everything. Start packing, baby. We're heading for God's country.
    Love you, sugar baby,
    Charlie

Police officers had blocked off the entire garage with evidence tape. Police detectives, crime-scene photographers, and Secret Service supervisors were milling about. To Breckinridge, it was an eerie, surreal scene.

Her partner, Rachel Kallenstien, joined her.

"A Department of Agriculture file clerk who was parking her car found the body."

"His wallet and gun weren't taken."

"Maybe the shooter chickened out."

"Rachel, a street robber isn't going to leave a gun on his victim."

"I can see some punk getting cold feet. These street types think they're tough until something like this goes down."

Kallenstien was a tall, spindly woman with a natural tan and close-cropped ebony hair.

"If a robber was going to take someone off, why would he pick a floor where there are only six cars parked?"

"Maybe a transient was sleeping in a car and just got the idea. Maybe it was a crime of opportunity."

"There is nothing to indicate that," Breckinridge said.

"If you want to get right down to it, there is nothing to indicate anything except that he got blown up."

Kallenstien was Breckinridge's best friend. They were pals and they shared everything in their lives. Breckinridge valued her ideas, as well as her support and her counsel.

"Street robbers who need a fix wait for the first victim they see," said Kallenstien. "What happens after that doesn't always fit with anything we know. You have to look at it through the eyes of the sociopath who did it. That is, unless you think Charlie was doing another agent's wife, or owed someone a lot of money. That's a different story altogether. In that case, it could be a premeditated murder."

Kallenstien was a member of a police family—the only daughter of a high-ranking officer in the New York City Police Department.

"Charlie wasn't involved in anything like that," said Breckinridge.

A flashbulb went off, the police photographer taking the millionth shot since she'd arrived.

A police detective joined them.

"What are you folks doing here?"

Breckinridge said, "We're assigned to Secret Service Protective Research Division, the division responsible for gathering information about threats to Secret Service protectees. We've been sent here to monitor the homicide investigation and determine whether Agent Meriweather's death was a simple street robbery that went bad, or something else—a security matter."

He was tall, black, and had a goatee. A cigarette was dangling from his lips, and he wore a hat with a small feather in it.

"What do you think?"

"I'm bothered by the fact that the robber didn't take his wallet or gun."

"Lady, sometimes investigations are uneven. Not everything fits a pattern. You Secret Service people probably haven't seen a lot of this kind of thing like we have."

"I spent five years on the Tulsa Police Department before joining the Service."

He wrote something on his clipboard. "Right on."

She reached in her purse and handed him her business card.

"I'd like copies of your homicide reports."

"No problem."

He dropped the card in his shirt pocket and walked toward the other end of the garage to join some other officers. The high-ranking Secret Service officials who'd been there earlier had departed, leaving the case to Breckinridge.

The elevator doors opened. Two coroner's deputies got off with a wheeled gurney. For the first time since arriving at the scene, Breckinridge felt tears. She swallowed and looked over at Kallenstien, who was solemnly staring at the gurney.

"There's nothing else for us to do here, Rachel."

Breckinridge and Kallenstien departed, and walked down the street bantering back and forth as they often did in cases, going over the same ground as if the dialogue might suddenly give them a key to the investigation. A tour bus cruised by them, heading toward the White House. Velvety clouds covered Washington, D.C., like a shawl.

At the Telco Bank Building, they entered through the lobby and rode the elevator to Secret Service Headquarters Protective Research Division (PRD) on the fifth floor. The ceiling-high shelves lining the walls in the office contained handwriting, fingerprint, photograph, and voice-tape records on people who'd exhibited an undue interest in the President of the United States. Threat calls received by the White House switchboard were transferred to Protective Research Division twenty-four hours a day. PRD gathered information from eighty Secret Service offices in the continental U.S. and five foreign countries, and from other U.S. intelligence agencies including the NSA, FBI, and CIA. Once a person was identified as violent and having an unusual interest in the President, his name was placed in the computerized PRD data-threat bank.

The phone on Kallenstien's desk was ringing. She lifted the receiver.

Across the desk from her, Breckinridge dropped her purse and sat glumly. Her feet ached from standing on the garage floor for the last four hours, and she felt like she had a piano wire cinched around her head. She took out a compact and checked her makeup. She had full lips and eyelashes, and she had worn her hair in a utilitarian French braid since the day a mental patient she'd been interviewing lunged through the bars of his cell and grabbed her ponytail. Her natural skin tone was a blithe mixture of color that matched her father's dusky, half-Cherokee complexion. She was thirty-four years old, five-five, high-hipped, and more buxom than she wanted to be. Her tight, dark skirt and an open-collar blouse had been a birthday gift from her former husband, who'd filed for divorce shortly after she joined the U.S. Secret Service.

Kallenstien made notes as she spoke on the phone, then set down the receiver.

"Three threat-call referrals: a remote-controlled glider-bomb launched at the White House from the planet Uranus, an Egyptian-led conspiracy to put rat poison in the President's toothpaste, and a brain-ray attack on the White House led by the reincarnated Nostradamus. And we have a priority message from the White House mail room. They have something for us."

• • •

At the White House Executive Office Building entrance, Breckinridge and Kallenstien showed identification to the uniformed officer. He let them in, and they walked down a highly waxed hallway to a door marked TRAVEL ACCOUNTING SERVICES. Using her Secret Service master key, Breckinridge unlocked the door, and they entered the White House mail room, where every letter and parcel addressed to the White House was X-rayed and searched for explosives, poisons, and biohazards before being distributed to the addressee. It was a large windowless, cement-walled cubicle filled with X-ray machines. The room had been engineered so that a bomb detonation inside it would collapse its floor into the basement, leaving the rest of the building and the nearby White House unscathed. On the walls hung X-rays and color photographs of known bombs, including an enlarged photograph of a C-4 bomb with an electric clock-timer that looked like the kind used in some recent terrorist bombings.

The duty agent opened a file drawer, took out a clear-plastic evidence bag, and handed it to Breckinridge. In it was a typed letter.

"This arrived here a few minutes ago by private courier."

Kallenstien looked over her shoulder as Breckinridge read:

To the President of the United States:

As loyal, God-fearing Americans we are proud to take responsibility for the execution of one of your Secret Service bodyguards. The purpose of this action was to show you how vulnerable you and all the members of your quisling United Nations-Communist-international-order-government are to the direct action of true patriots. As you have now seen, we are able to defeat your Secret Service security group. We chose the time and the place and we can do it again.

We intend to rid the United States of America of political vermin and our action today is the beginning of the end for all traitors. Let the world know that we will make the supreme sacrifice. We will risk everything to stand up for the sacred American Bill of Rights.

You, Mister Communist President, you who has besmirched the American nation and all its proud ssons, are next on our execution list. *Say your prayers.*

Long live the white race!
THE ARYAN DISCIPLES OF THE UNITED STATES OF AMERICA

"The ADs," Kallenstien said.

Breckinridge knew about the neo-Nazi Aryan Disciples of the United States of America, the most dangerous extremist group in the U.S., whose members included insane right-wing political zealots and dangerous ex-convicts. Members of the Aryan Disciples were responsible for a long series of violent acts, including the bombing of the Ronald Reagan Federal Building in D.C. that killed twenty-nine people and wounded eighty; and the bombing of the Houston and Albuquerque federal buildings that killed another forty-two people. Recent rumors had it that the Libyan Army Intelligence Service had been secretly funding some Aryan Disciples terrorist actions.

"It arrived by private courier service," the duty agent said. "The driver who signed the delivery paperwork has a route in Alexandria. There are no other clues."

Breckinridge signed an evidence receipt.

"Thanks. By the way, this case is classified from here on."

"I'll mark the file."

Breckinridge and Kallenstien crossed the street, heading back to Headquarters.

"If they figured they could get Charlie alone when he was coming off duty, they had to know that he would be carrying a gun," Breckinridge said. "Why take that risk when they could have hit him when he was off duty; at the grocery store or on a golf course when there would be a good chance that he would be unarmed? And if this were an Aryan Disciples thing, why would they murder him a block from the White House? They had to know that other agents park in that lot too. One of them could have been nearby and seen what was going on—"

"Maybe they want to throw it in our faces."

"Rachel, this is the first time the Aryan Disciples have claimed responsibility for a terrorist action—a complete change of M.O. And they've never directly threatened the President. Up to now they've always targeted Cabinet officers and lesser officials. The IRS. Federal buildings."

"They could be looking for press coverage."

"It doesn't fit. Why would they believe that killing an off-duty Secret Service agent would gain them more attention than their usual actions—like detonating a bomb in a public building?"

"Maybe they are trying to change their methods just to be clever. Just to keep us all guessing."

"We're guessing, all right," Breckinridge said after a silence.

Later, at her Georgetown two-bedroom apartment, Breckinridge unlocked the door and turned on the lights. The message light on her answering machine was flashing. She pressed PLAY.

"Martha, This is your mother. I just called to say hi, but I guess you are still working. Please make sure you eat a good dinner. Love you. Bye."

"Okay, Mom."

She pressed REWIND.

Breckinridge had chosen to enter the law-enforcement field while at Oklahoma State. After five years with the Tulsa Police Department, she decided that the nearly all-male power structure would keep her from getting promoted out of her radio car, so she joined the U.S. Secret Service. To avoid the boring ex-President and Foreign Dignitary Protection Details to which most female Secret Service agents were assigned, she maneuvered herself into the Protective Research Division, where she'd been working inordinate amounts of overtime, hoping to eventually get promoted to the White House Detail.

Her divorce was final. Ted had been the "man of substance" her mother had told her to marry: a steady, nine-to-five lawyer who'd convinced her there was no reason his career would conflict with her Secret Service aspirations. His direct, straightforward approach—the lifetime commitment—had caught her off guard. Just the word *marriage*. He'd dazzled her with his poise and uprightness. But she knew their relationship wasn't going to last. It wasn't that she didn't like the idea of having a life partner she could share everything with. But the moment they'd moved in together, he'd changed from romantic suitor to demanding prosecutor. It had become clear to her that he considered her less than an equal life partner. She'd believed his words rather than his actions, and she'd known better. She'd allowed herself to be a dreamer. Now she was alone again and much wiser for the experience.

She showered, washed her hair, and put on a terry-cloth robe. She combed her hair, leaving it wet, then went into the kitchen and poured herself a glass of wine before she walked to the sofa and put her feet up on the coffee table. She sipped wine for a while, reliving the day. Finally, her eyelids became heavy. Leaving the half-full wineglass sitting on the table, she went into the bedroom and crawled between the sheets. Closing her eyes, she pictured Charlie Meriweather dead, his hand on his gun.

CHAPTER 2

PETE GARRISON LEANED back in the passenger seat of a Secret Service limousine and gazed at the scenery along a wooded Highway 404. First Lady Eleanor Hollingsworth Jordan was in the right rear seat, reading. They were headed to the President's summer home at Rehoboth Beach, Delaware, the nearest beach to the White House. A thick, fully soundproof window separated the front seat from the rear.

Agent Walter Sebastian was driving.

"What's bothering you, Pete?" he asked.

Garrison fidgeted. "Nothing."

Sebastian was a tall, muscle-bound man with an over-sized head and hands. He'd been an Army Intelligence officer before joining the Secret Service. Garrison liked him.

"It's a change all right," said Sebastian.

"Whatsat?"

"Tagging along with the First Frau. It takes a while, but you'll get used to it. Sure, everyone knows the First Lady Detail is a dumping ground for agents from the Man's detail. It was the same when they sent me here for using the Oval Office phone to place a bet on a Redskins game. But the moment some other agent ends up in the barrel, everyone will forget. I used to tell myself I'd get back to the Man's detail someday. But then I finally realized that I was getting paid the same for going to tea parties as for risking taking rounds for the Man. Hell, we'll be at the beach all weekend while the first team is working double shifts because of the Aryan Disciples. We have it *made*."

Deep down, Garrison knew Sebastian was right. But Garrison had no choice. Three weeks earlier he'd been "promoted" to supervisor of the First Lady Detail. Disciplinary transfers were often couched as promotions. He'd blown his position in the Presidential detail, the assignment that he'd desired from the day that he'd received his badge, thirteen years earlier. Working his way up to the Presidential detail had been for naught. He'd wasted his time in the Secret Service bomb detail, terrorist task force, and PRD.

Sebastian changed lanes, following the lead car. The limousine was part of a motorcade consisting of a police escort sedan, the First Lady's limousine, and a backup limousine manned by a Secret Service automobile mechanic whose sole duty was to repair and maintain official cars. Security had been augmented as a result of Charlie Meriweather's murder two weeks earlier.

Garrison glanced at the specially designed rearview mirror extending nearly across the entire windshield.

Eleanor Jordan unexpectedly looked up and met his eyes. She was a handsome woman of Garrison's age. She was a Manhattan ice queen with high cheekbones, deep-set, green eyes, and strawberry-blond hair, a head-turner and darling of the media whose photograph appeared on the covers of the women's magazines.

Passing a sign that read DESIRE BAY, Sebastian swerved off the highway. Garrison could smell the ocean. Winding his way along a one-lane road leading toward Rehoboth Beach, Sebastian pulled up to a guard booth at a private condominium development. The gate lifted automatically and a private security officer motioned them inside. They cruised slowly past high-priced, two-story homes that all looked the same: clapboards, weather vanes, swamp-grass lawns, and bicycles on front porches. Making a left turn into a cul-de-sac, Sebastian parked in front of the President's summer home, a two-story, rectangular house with a central chimney and a steep, shingled roof. In a Mercury sedan across the street were two agents from the local field office.

Garrison and Sebastian got out of the limousine. Garrison led the First Lady inside and Sebastian followed.

A service counter separated a modern kitchen from a large living room with two pillow-covered sofas. Ceiling-high bookshelves lined a small study off the main room. Tinted-glass sliding doors led to a patio with a full view of the ocean.

Garrison cleared his throat.

"Are you expecting any visitors tonight, Mrs. Jordan?"

"No."

"If you decide to go somewhere, please let me know as soon—"

"As soon as possible?" she said wryly.

"Just a reminder. Have a nice night."

Garrison and Sebastian exited the kitchen door and walked along a short walkway to the house next door, an ad hoc command post that the Secret Service termed a security room. The living area faced sliding glass doors leading to the beach.

"I'll take the first shift," Garrison said.

"Are you sure—?"

"I feel like staying up."

"I'll get the iron out of the trunk."

Sebastian exited the front door.

Garrison checked the equipment. On the dining room table were a portable Secret Service worldwide radio console and a large, open suitcase containing emergency lights, an Uzi submachine gun, night-viewing devices, emergency manuals, smoke grenades, a complete paramedic's first-aid kit including poison antidotes and snakebite serum, surgical operating tools, and a foldable metal stretcher; the required Secret Service security equipment.

Sebastian returned carrying a leather shotgun case. He unzipped it and handed Garrison a .12-gauge Remington 870 shotgun. Garrison checked it, insuring that the safety was off and there was a round in the chamber.

"What are you gonna do for dinner, Pete?"

"Call out."

"I can bring you something—"

"I may even skip dinner."

"Suit yourself."

Sebastian walked to the glass door. "You know, it's

kind of sad to think of a good-looking woman like her sitting over there alone all weekend."

Garrison placed the shotgun on the table. "Sounds like you're falling in love, Walter."

The term "falling in love" was a Secret Service phrase that implied nothing about romance, referring rather to Secret Service agents who allowed themselves to become friends with a protectee and lost the required professional distance called for by Secret Service custom and protocol.

"All I'm saying is that it's a shame to see a good-looking woman like her go to waste like that. But after D day, her and the Man do their own thing."

Garrison joined him at the sliding glass door. Looking left, to Eleanor's beach house, he could see its patio and a solitary lounge chair.

"What's D day?"

"A few weeks ago she and the Man had a knock-down, drag-out in the solarium. I was outside the door and heard the whole argument from beginning to end. Lots of shouting and screaming. She ended up throwing a candy dish at him. Thus, the D in D day."

"What was the argument about?"

"The Man is planning to divorce her the moment he leaves office. You being in charge of her detail, I figured you should know."

Garrison was aware of how important it was to have a feel for a protectee's personal life. To be an effective bodyguard was to be able to anticipate the actions of the protectee. But Eleanor had always told him about her estrangement from the President. Even in his mind, it felt odd calling her by her first name. . . .

"Thanks for filling me in," Garrison said.

"What do you think of her, Pete?"

Garrison found the First Lady to be sensual, and captivating—a real knockout. "As long as she tells us where she is going ahead of time and doesn't give us any guff, what's not to like?"

"I wonder if she'll start dating again after she and the Man finally cut the cord."

"Probably."

"I heard that before she met him, she had plenty of guys after her. Rich playboys. Major Wall Street players, English royalty dudes. . . . like that. Let's face it. She is a good-looking woman. I'd like to jump her myself. Hell I'd like to climb her like a ladder—"

When she gets divorced you can ask her out."

Sebastian laughed. "Me? Not a chance. A woman like her wouldn't give either of us a second look."

"Why not?"

"To her we're nothing but stooges with neckties. The way women like her figure it, why get involved with a guy who doesn't drive a Mercedes Benz? Uptown broads like her don't want to just be able to order the lobster. They want to walk out of the restaurant and leave it on the plate. More than anything, they want the power and prestige. They want to be on the arm of some guy who owns the Redskins, not some defensive lineman."

Sebastian moved to the table, signed the daily report, and headed for the door. "Have a nice night."

Garrison's eyes were on the house next door.

"See you in the morning, Walter."

Sebastian departed. Garrison shrugged off his suit jacket and hung it over a chair. He checked the Uzi. It was loaded, and there were extra ammunition clips. If the Aryan Disciples terrorists came calling, he and the agents across the street would be able to give them a warm welcome.

He reached for the telephone, but stopped himself.

He sat on a sofa and picked up a copy of *Time* magazine. The First Lady's face was on the cover. Flipping pages, he scanned another breathless account of her history. He and everyone else in the world already knew the details. Eleanor Hollingsworth Jordan was the divorced daughter of political kingmaker and wealthy philanthropist Joseph Horton Hollingsworth III. When she'd begun dating California Senator Russell Jordan, everyone had wondered what she saw in an aging politician fifteen years her senior. After a marriage ceremony on the Hollingsworth family yacht, she became Jordan's campaign manager and spent millions from her father's estate to fund a campaign that carried Jordan into the U.S. Senate and later the White House.

It was going to be a long night, Garrison told himself. After a while, he dropped to the floor and began doing push-ups, counting out loud. He reached one hundred, took a five-minute break, and then started again. The phone rang. He vaulted to his feet and snatched the receiver.

"Agent Garrison speaking."

"Is Walter gone?" Eleanor asked.

"Yes."

"I don't feel like eating alone, hon."

"I never thought you'd ask."

Garrison racked the phone, picked up the Uzi, and walked across the yard. He didn't consider leaving his assigned post a breach of security. The main house was alarmed and secure. In the event of an emergency, he would be closer to her. He opened the kitchen door and went in.

Eleanor was at the stove. Her hair was down, brushed shiny after a wash and swept boldly back. She looked comfortably casual in white slacks, a black sweater, and sandals.

"I hope you're hungry, Pete."

He placed the Uzi on an empty bookshelf. "Starving."

He offered to help in the kitchen. She declined. As she worked at the stove, he admired an oil painting that hung over the sofa. He'd never noticed it before.

"Do you like it, Pete?"

"It's very engaging." He'd once heard the word *engaging* used repeatedly by an art critic at a Presidential visit to the Corcoran Gallery.

"Its called *Farmhouse in San Gabriel* by Dorothy Hibbert. It belonged to my father. He was a collector of fine art, among other things."

She pointed above the mantel to an oil painting of a svelte blonde, the wind blowing her hair as she hurried along a dark, cobblestone street with a band of sunken-eyed orphans.

"That one was painted by Carleton Phipps—a recluse who paints naked on the porch of a cabin in Idaho."

Garrison could hear the waves outside. "I'll bet that becomes a real hardship for him in January."

Her courtly laugh revealed perfect, white teeth. It occurred to Garrison that beauty was, as someone once said, in the symmetry. Nothing about Eleanor Jordan was out of balance. Nothing at all. She turned back to the stove to cook. He admired her for a moment, and then walked across the kitchen and turned off the stove.

"Pete—"

He wrapped his arms around her. They kissed, and her tongue met his. He embraced her tightly, and the sound of the waves seemed to get louder. Then, in a blurry trance, he swept her into his arms and carried her to the sofa. They devoured each other with kisses and undressed one another. He could hear her breathing. His tongue flicked her erect nipples. Then, moving lower, he kissed her abdomen, her navel. Her hips began to move. He gently tasted her sex, making love to her with his tongue for a long time, her hands grasping his head tightly. She pulled him up, kissing him hungrily, reaching for his hardness. They melded together, her legs wrapping around him. As he was locked with her in the driving tempo of sex, her deepening warmth consumed him. They kissed and bit one another feverishly until, finally, pressing her lips to the nape of his neck, she cried out in orgasm. Garrison continued to ravish her, and then, finally thrusting his hips in a paroxysm of brain-throbbing ecstasy, he too found release.

As they ate, they chatted about an upcoming Russian summit meeting to be held at Camp David, and journalist Joe Kretchvane's unauthorized biography of her, which she said he was slanting to put her in the worst possible light.

"Pete, what's being done about the Aryan Disciples threat?"

"More agents on post, more scrutiny of White House visitors, less scheduled Presidential stops. Other than that, the security plan remains pretty much the same. Don't worry. We have it under control."

"Did you know Agent Meriweather?"

"Not very well. But he was well liked."

"What was his background?"

"He used to work in the Technical Security Division before being assigned to the White House Detail."

"What do they do?"

"Electronic eavesdropping."

She nodded. "Do you miss the Presidential detail?"

He got up and walked to the slidingglass door.

After a moment, she joined him. The sea was calm and dark gray. Close to shore, a swell curved into a frosty wave, roaring from right to left, then bursting onto the beach, an arm of surf reaching out, only to disappear forever in thirsty, moonlit sand.

"The answer to your question is yes. I miss the action."

She kissed him. "I'm not trying to toy with you, Pete. I trust you. I could feel it the first day we met. I don't feel that way with everyone, but there was something about you. I don't know why, but there is an electricity between us." She nuzzled her head to his shoulder. "You feel good."

"Feelings aren't the problem. It's reality that gets people in trouble."

He knew that if the word ever got out, he would be fired. Both he and she would end up as voodoo dolls for the world press to stick pins in.

"No one will ever know," she said.

Garrison's experience, his common sense, and the discipline inculcated by his training told him that even the thought of being with her was crazy and dangerous. But he could smell her hair and her perfume. He wanted her. He wanted her and nothing else mattered. The thought flashed through his mind that he would like to stay with her all night, but that it was impossible.

She tenderly kissed his cheek. "It's my fault."

"It's nobody's fault."

"I don't care about him anymore. You don't believe me."

"Then why don't you leave him?"

"And be the only First Lady to walk out on her husband? The price is too high. No, I'm stuck in the White House for another few months. After the new Administration comes in, it's over between him and me once and for all. In the meantime, I'll put up with the charade. Pete, when you were married, were you happy?"

"For a while."

"What happened?"

"Being on the detail, I traveled with the President constantly, and my wife wanted a husband who could be home with her. It just didn't work."

"She wanted more from the relationship than you were willing to give?"

"That's probably the way she would describe it."

Garrison hated talking about himself. He considered it a sign of weakness. Gabbing about one's feelings was for TV gurus, totem worshipers, and alfalfa-sprout eaters.

"Do you keep in touch with her?"

"We exchange Christmas cards. I don't blame her for leaving. She's better off without me."

"Do you miss her?"

"It's been five years."

On the wall was a framed photograph of a well-groomed, gray-haired matron.

"Who is the lady in the photo?" he asked.

"My mom. My father turned her into an alcoholic. He was a cold man—aloof. She worshipped him. She sat in our wonderful old house in Pacific Heights and secretly drank her bottle of brandy every day—after she'd gotten her charity work out of the way, of course. She was an intelligent, talented person who never recovered from my father abandoning her. He spent my mother's last Christmas in Aruba with a twenty-two-year-old stripper. Good old Dad. He pushed me into marrying my first husband, who turned out to be a lot like him—a user. He was killed sailing drunk off Cabo San Lucas. When my father died, I took stock of my life. I'd been raised rich. I'd attended the right schools, dated the right men. What did I have to show for it? Nothing. Then a friend introduced me to Senator Russell Jordan. He had White House written all over him. I decided to make my own man. I set out to take him to the top. My inheritance money put Russell Jordan into the White House. Not his staff, not his advisors. Me. And to return the favor, he hung me on his political tree like a cheap ornament. I guess it's true that women seek out men like their father. Crazy, isn't it?"

He kissed her.

"What are your secrets, Pete?"

"I don't have any."

"You're angry about being transferred from the Presidential detail, aren't you?"

"You could say that."

"What happened?"

"I screwed up. It doesn't matter."

"Talk to me, Pete. Please."

"It happened at the State Department picnic on the South Lawn. We'd been briefed about how a radio talk-show host had hired someone to throw a pie in the President's face. I spotted the suspect. He was dressed as a waiter. When I confronted him, he spit at me. I slammed the pie into his face and it knocked him unconscious. The Director charged me with 'conduct unbecoming an agent.' I was transferred to your detail because the position was open and no one else wanted the job."

"You feel like you failed yourself."

"I got the shaft."

She kissed him. "You're not a failure in my book."

Garrison returned to the security room later, dazed and exhausted. He studied himself in a gold-framed mirror over the sofa.

"You really know how to complicate your life, don't you?" he said out loud.

He was six feet tall. He had clean features, short, sandy hair, and blue eyes. His shoulder fit his suit neatly. He'd been having an affair with the First Lady of the United States and he felt like some stupid, gawky teenager. He knew well what untoward familiarity with a Secret Service protectee could lead to. It was bad enough for an agent to allow himself to be used to perform servile chores like carrying suitcases and golf clubs for a protectee, much less getting involved sexually. He'd broken the first commandment of Secret Service protection. Though he wanted to believe otherwise, he knew, deep down that it was possible Eleanor might be using him. She was on the rocks with the President. Would she shout out his name during an argument?

He paced the security room, then plopped into a recliner and turned on the television. An anchorman droned on about the President's plans to hold a private Camp David foreign policy conference with the President of Russia. Changing channels, Pete watched a Dan

Duryea movie, thinking about Eleanor: the look in her eyes when they had sex, the curve of her neck, her hair. He told himself he should have never gotten involved. But he'd wanted her. He'd wanted the closeness. Admittedly, he was infatuated with Eleanor Jordan. He felt for her a sublimated possessiveness that one could feel for a woman who could never be his. And it was clear to him that she was his impulsive counterpart, his partner in the thrill, the buzz that came from the most dangerous of illicit relationships. But Garrison wasn't unaccustomed to danger. He'd spent his life seeking it out.

As a teenager, he'd raced motorcycles and had once nearly been killed in a crash. In the Army, he'd volunteered for paratrooper school and later for training as an Army Explosive Ordnance technician. Before his promotion to the White House Detail, he'd worked in a special Secret Service bomb detail, and had volunteered for a tour of duty on a risky terrorism task force that had required him to work undercover among killers and ex-convicts for over a year. But he hadn't allowed himself to become involved with Eleanor for a simple thrill. There was something about her. . . .

Shortly before eight A.M., Garrison stood at the glass door, staring outside, thinking about the night before. Outside, the first morning light had illuminated a grayish, endless panorama of waves and the kelpy foam lining the shore. He heard three radio transmitter clicks, the daily code for *Agent approaching*.

Walter Sebastian walked into the room carrying a box of doughnuts and a large container of coffee.

"You look like a sack full of doorknobs, Pete."

"I'll be doing better after I catch some rack time."

Using one of the field office cars parked outside, Garrison drove to the nearby Ramada Inn and went to his room. He showered and crawled into bed, exhausted and feeling discomfited about what had happened. He closed his eyes and recalled the first day he'd reported for duty at the First Lady Detail. He and Eleanor had chatted casually between her appointments and they'd had a few discussions about her schedule. He'd found her distracted, but not aloof. She was a woman under stress.

The first time he'd accompanied her jogging they'd gotten to know one another. . . .

Arriving in Rock Creek Park, Garrison climbed out of the limousine and looked about quickly, scanning the high ground. Seeing nothing unusual, he opened the rear passenger door for the First Lady. She wore a blue Nike warm-up suit, running shoes, a baseball hat, and sunglasses—an appropriate but unassuming outfit. Garrison could see how the President had fallen for her. She was attractive no matter what she wore—healthy and athletic, without the pampered, made-up look that many women had.

Under shadows cast by tall oak trees, Garrison and the First Lady jogged along the bank of a meandering stream.

"You seem familiar with the trail, Pete."

"This is the path President Clinton liked."

Garrison had chosen the route after reviewing Secret Service reports on the First Lady Detail's previous jogging activities. The Park had last been chosen six weeks earlier. He knew that, while a previously announced trip presented great danger to a protectee, an unannounced activity negated the possibility of an assassin lying in wait.

"*I see,*" *she replied.*

At a clearing that had been washed by a stream trib-utary, they began walking to avoid jagged rocks.

"*Where are you from, Pete?*"

"*I grew up in Bisbee, Arizona.*"

"*Bisbee. . . .*"

"*A onetime mining area near the Mexican border. My father liked the quiet. It was that, all right. Quiet. My dad ran the only service station in town, and my mother was a clerk at the Foursquare church. She dragged me to church every Sunday.*"

"*So you left the small town to find adventure?*"

"*Actually I saw some soldiers on a desert training mission. They were from Fort Huachuca. That's an Army post near Bisbee. I struck up a conversation. One of them told me he'd been to twenty different countries. I joined when I was eighteen. The Army put me through college.*"

"*Are you married?*"

"*Not anymore.*"

He remembered a postcard he'd received a year ear-lier from his ex-wife—a color photograph of her and her new beau, a stable, stay-at-home accountant, posing in front of an Aspen ski lodge.

"*Are you seeing anyone?*"

"*Not at present.*"

The trail turned to the right, leading them across a small meadow, then closer to the stream. Garrison de-tected the smell of wildflowers.

"*Free and unencumbered,*" *she said.* "*That's the way I was before I met Russell. I loved the single life, the parties. The White House is the opposite of that kind of freedom. It's like being stuck at a health resort where the scenery is beautiful but there is nothing to do at night. It's a four-star hotel where the other guests are waiting for you to fall flat on your face."*

"Does the President feel that way too?"

He knew the question was inappropriate. But he wanted to find out if she genuinely wanted to communicate, or whether she was just toying with him in that way powerful women sometimes do with their bodyguards.

"He relishes power and is willing to do anything to remain in control. It's part of his psyche. For me, it's like being a moving target. Maybe that's why there is nothing between us any longer. My marriage is over. Dead."

Garrison was amazed that she'd revealed such intimacies to him. On the other hand, she probably had no one else to confide in. Most of her friends were tied to the media in one way or another, and nearly everyone on the White House staff leaked stories to selected journalists.

The trail veered left, and they crossed a gravel-covered strip before jogging under a low-hanging branch and through the shade of some tall elms. In the distance, to his right, the motorcade slowly followed the street, the drivers keeping the First Lady in sight. When they reached a small plateau overlooking the District, the First Lady stopped at a public drinking fountain.

She drank water, wiped her mouth with the back of her hand, and then considered him for a moment.

"What are you going to do tonight when you get off duty?"

There was an intangible, beguiling quality about her. Admittedly, the First Lady was a woman who, under other circumstances, in another world, he would ask out.

"I'll probably stop for a drink somewhere."

"I'd love to be able to do that—to go somewhere without the paparazzi—and without a motorcade," she said wistfully, looking toward the Capitol. "It's been seven and a half years and I miss the freedom."

"You've forgotten having to find a parking spot, fighting to get a table. It's not that great."

Her eyes were on his, and he felt his face flush.

"Pete, I've noticed you looking at me. Women see such things."

"I'm not going to deny it," he said without hesitation, surprising himself.

"I've admired you too."

Returning to the limousine, he opened the door for her. Climbing in, she grasped his forearm briefly. Garrison considered the gesture to be neither a sign of clumsiness nor indecorous vivacity. It was the thing women sometimes do after they decide they trust a man—not a sexual signal necessarily, but rather, a non-verbal communication defining the first step in a friendship. Her touch sent a tingle up his arm. Eleanor Jordan was a very different First Lady.

His mind flashed over everything she'd said to him from the first moment they'd met. He'd seen loneliness in her eyes. He'd felt the vibes coming from her.

The following weekend, when the President was in New York, they'd made love for the first time in the White House, in the upstairs private quarters.

"We're going to have to be careful, aren't we, Pete?" she said as he was putting on his clothes.

"I'm glad to hear it wasn't just a fling."

"I'm not in the habit of doing things like that," she said testily.

"I didn't mean—"

"If it was just sex you were looking for, I'd say you really grabbed the brass ring."

"It was a stupid joke. Sorry."

She blinked a few times as if she was thinking about saying something. Then she shook her head.

"We'll need a way to communicate, Eleanor. The White House phones can't be trusted."

"I'll give you the number to my private cell phone. This is so strange."

"Strange isn't the word for it."

She moved close to him. *"Pete, I want us to be close. Please don't interpret that as some boundary I am setting. I understand the reality of this as well as you do. No one must ever know."*

"You didn't have to say that."

She hugged him.

"Please promise me," she whispered.

He cupped her face with his hands.

"I promise."

Garrison returned to the security room before midnight.

Early Monday morning, as he was sitting in the right front seat of the limousine on the way back to D.C. from Rehoboth Beach, Garrison's cell phone vibrated. He unclipped it from his belt and said hello.

"This is White House Operator 13. I have a Mr. Frank Hightower on the line. He says he has to talk to you— that it's an emergency."

"Put him on."

The phone clicked.

"Agent Garrison. How are things at the Secret Service?"

"About the same, Frank. Where have you been?"

"Just knocking around. Are you still looking for terrorists?"

"I'm not assigned to PRD any longer."

"Why?"

"After you disappeared, I had no more information."

Hightower laughed. "And I just saw a flying pig."

Frank Hightower was an informant Garrison had used when assigned to temporary duty at the Secret Service Protective Research Division. Hightower had provided reliable information concerning white supremacist groups involved in terrorism.

"What's up?" Garrison said cautiously.

"I have information on an Aryan Disciples plot to kill the President. Are you interested?"

"I'll put you in touch with an agent from PRD."

"No chance."

"Pardon me?"

"I'm not talking to anyone but you."

"Why?"

"I don't like talking over the phone. How about coming down to our old meeting place?"

"Okay," Garrison said after a moment.

"If I see anyone else but you, I walk."

The phone clicked twice.

Garrison wondered what Hightower was up to.

CHAPTER 3

"LONG TIME NO see, Garrison."

"Carrying any weapons today?"

"No way. Hey, it's me. I ain't changed any."

Garrison ran his hands around Hightower's waist. His clothing smelled faintly of marijuana and motor oil. It was uncomfortably muggy in the Smithsonian Natural History Museum gift shop, even with air-conditioning. Hightower had been standing near the door, like before, when Garrison would meet with him to gather information on terrorist activities. Garrison had chosen the location because it was always crowded and the windows and glass doors made it easy to detect possible countersurveillance.

"I thought you dropped off the face of the earth," said Garrison.

"I figured I would just lay low for a while. I met a

broad and moved to Texas. Shit like that. Just kicking back. Then one thing led to another. I sort of just happened back into some of the old places and faces. Then bingo."

"Let's go upstairs."

Garrison led him up an escalator to a high-ceilinged lobby where a crowd of tourists was gathered around a full-size reproduction of an African bush elephant. The museum smell was overpowering: a post-organic odor that leaked from glass display cases that were inhabited by old bones and musty cloth. They sat on a bench, their backs to the wall.

"Okay, Frank. What is this about a plot?"

"This ain't no small case. I'm going to have to have some cash to put it all together for you—"

"Cut to the chase, Frank."

"The Aryan Disciples killed that Secret Service agent the other day in the parking garage downtown. It was done as a challenge to the government."

Garrison nodded. "That's it?"

Garrison thought Hightower looked nervous, which was unlike him.

"Not really, amigo. Get this shit: They also hired a guy to kill the President. He's not a member, but was brought in from the outside. They figure that after the assassination, you people will come after them. But all their hitters will have alibis and you'll never be able to figure out how it all went down because by then, the outside man they hired will be back in Europe. He is right here in D.C. as we speak. That's all I have at the moment. But I'm working on everything you need to make some solid arrests. That is, once you tell me what's in this for me."

Hightower's appearance hadn't changed much in two years. He was about forty-five years old, tall and over-weight, with shoulder-length hair. He wore beer-bar ha-bitué apparel: Levi's, a grayish sweatshirt with chopped sleeves, and grimy, buckle-strap motorcycle boots. He looked like a creep. In fact, he was a creep: a duplicitous ex-convict who made a living selling illegal weapons and narcotics, and ratting out his neo-Nazi pals. But Gar-rison knew that one had to take informants as they came. The information Hightower had given Garrison had al-ways been reliable.

"What do you have in mind?"

"One million dollars. I ain't going to risk my sweet ass for one cent less."

Garrison looked him in the eye. "You know how it works. I can't promise you any specific amount."

"But this is bigger than anything I ever gave you be-fore. This is a real, honest-to-Christ plot to kill the King and I am sitting right on the fucking top of it. So you people gotta come through for your man. I'm out there on fucking Front Street with the boys who play for keeps."

"If what you are telling me is true and we can make a case, that amount isn't out of the question." Garrison was aware of the reasons that informants provided in-formation to the authorities: revenge, to avoid jail, money. If no motivation could be established, the infor-mant was probably lying. Hightower worked solely for money.

"I'm going to want the money guaranteed, or I'm not going any further. I'll take it in cash, twenty-dollar bills."

"Where are you getting this information?"

"Can't tell you."

"That isn't the way we used to do business, Frank. My rules are up front and no games. You remember that, don't you?"

"This is different."

"I'm going to need names and phone numbers. The works. You're not going to be able to stand back too far and earn a reward of that size. You're going to have to get in the center ring."

"I'm working on it."

Garrison studied him. "I'll arrange a lie-detector test for you."

A wounded look crossed Hightower's face, as if Garrison had violated some sacred trust.

"I never had to do that before."

Garrison smiled. "You never asked for a million dollars before."

Hightower slipped his right hand into his trouser pocket and took out a white, business-sized envelope.

"Open it," Hightower said offering it to him.

"You open it, Frank."

Hightower removed a document from the envelope and handed it to him. Garrison studied it, and the hair on the back of his neck began to tingle.

"Where did you get this?"

Astonishingly, it was a copy of the current Secret Service "Commo Card," a list of the current White House Communications Agency (WHCA) radio codes and computer passwords used by the Secret Service's White House Detail. No one but White House Detail agents and members of the military-run WHCA had access to such top-secret information. And the codes were changed weekly. The code provided access to top-secret information on the Secret Service security systems, including guard posts, weaponry, alarm systems, emergency procedures, and all Secret Service radio frequencies.

"From a high-ranking member of the Disciples. And he got it from a U.S. Secret Service agent."

Garrison wanted to say *bullshit,* but restrained himself.

"Secret Service agent helping a terrorist organization. That's a real first, Frank."

"He's doing it for the money. The Disciples are flush. They've been getting dough from the Libyans through a secret offshore account. The rugheads like what the ADs are doing. That's why they've been getting behind their action. They are getting their licks in on Uncle Sam from behind the Disciples."

Garrison had heard the rumor about the Libyan connection in a recent foreign intelligence briefing.

"I don't hear any names to go with that story."

"I'll get them for you. Don't worry."

Hightower straightened his cap. He had a tattoo on the back of his right hand: a cross with a circle of dots surrounding it. He'd once told Garrison he'd fashioned it while in prison, using a hat pin and the ink from a ballpoint pen.

"How do I reach you, Frank?"

"I'm moving around at the moment. I'll call you when I drop anchor. In the meantime, make sure you have your people approve my reward. I know that this information is going to cause a stir with your bosses. But I'm telling you ahead of time that I'm not going to stand for being passed around from agent to agent. I'm not going to meet with anyone but you. With someone on the inside of your department working for the Disciples, it's too much of a risk."

"Frank, after all the other cases you made for me, didn't anyone in the Disciples ever suspect you of . . . being the one who provided the information?"

Hightower smirked. "I noticed you didn't use the word rat."

Garrison had consciously avoided using the word. Informants didn't like to think of themselves as what they were—lepers of the underworld who were disliked by both cops and crooks.

"Why don't you just answer the question?" said Garrison.

"But I don't give a fuck what you or your pals call me. I'm in this for the money. I'm not some political dipshit who believes that the government is out to get him. I believe in the Golden Rule. *He who has the gold rules.* But to answer your question, I always made sure I wasn't giving you exclusive information—that I wasn't the only one who knew about what I was telling you. That way, when you people started kicking down doors, there was always someone else to blame. See, Frank Hightower doesn't believe in being out there on Front Street all alone. It's a survival thing. A man has to keep his wits in this line of work to keep from getting his fucking head blown off."

"Who else in the Disciples knows about this?"

"Only a couple of the heavies. That's why this is going to cost you some gold. I'm sticking my neck out for the last time. Once you move in on them, they'll know it was me. I'm going to need the combat pay to relocate. The Disciples will have the bloodhounds after my ass."

Garrison ran a hand through his hair. "Keep in touch, Frank."

"I will. Don't you worry about that."

Hightower walked to the down escalator and got on.

Garrison anxiously mulled over what he'd learned. He recalled an informant once reporting to him that a White House maintenance employee was going to smuggle in a vial of deadly anthrax to be released when the President lit the White House Christmas tree. After an intensive investigation, it turned out that the informant had made up the story, hoping to earn enough to pay for a sex-change operation. Intelligence work was frequently stranger than fiction.

Because of the Commo Card Hightower had provided and his record of reliability as an informant, Garrison knew the information given him had to be taken seriously. But an agent involved in an assassination conspiracy? Nothing like that had ever happened before. Traitors had scandalized the CIA and the FBI, but the close-knit Secret Service had, for its entire history, remained untouched by such disgrace. To Garrison, it was difficult to imagine.

Driving back to the White House, Garrison placed a call to the Director's office on his cell phone. A secretary answered.

"This is Agent Garrison, First Lady Detail. I need to speak with Director Wintergreen in private as soon as possible."

"He's booked up."

"It has to be today."

"What's it about?"

"A priority case."

"Four P.M. And it better be important."

The phone clicked.

CHAPTER 4

IN HIS PRIVATE office in the Secret Service White House command post, Secret Service Director Larry Wintergreen finished initialing some papers he'd taken from his IN box and dropped them into the OUT box. He rose from a wide oak desk and moved to a polished credenza lined with award plaques and framed photographs. He straightened a framed photo of him with the Pope, taken during a recent Presidential visit to the Vatican. Wintergreen liked the elegant people and places to which he'd been introduced by virtue of his position. He'd vacationed at Cap D'Antibes, spent weeks skiing in Aspen, and eaten at some of the finest restaurants in the world. But it had always been sponsored by whomever he'd been protecting at the time, or paid for by his Secret Service expense account.

He was a bodyguard. But he'd always wanted more.

Why not? Why should he be satisfied with half a cake? The day-to-day drudgery of standing post and trying to stay awake from midnight to eight was behind him now. He'd reached the cushy pinnacle of the Secret Service where he could make things happen. He was the Secret Service Pope—the Chief White House Centurion with duties mostly symbolic: handing out diplomas at Secret Service Training Academy graduations, fixing problems for the First Family, keeping his agents on their toes with a speech now and then, accepting and distributing awards. Wintergreen relished being Director, and still got a thrill when seeing his photograph on the cover of *Time* or *Newsweek* standing near the President.

After cleverly managing to avoid being identified with the two Secret Service Directors who'd resigned during the scandal-ridden Clinton years, Wintergreen had volunteered for the campaign protection detail of leading Presidential contender Russell Jordan. Shortly after Jordan's inauguration, Jordan had promoted him to the Directorship. Wintergreen knew that being Secret Service Director was a unique position, earned by years of balancing on the White House tightrope.

Being Secret Service Director was an unusual job in an unusual agency. Created in 1865 as a Federal law-enforcement agency, the Secret Service's mission until 1901 had been to investigate and arrest counterfeiters. Presidential protection operations began only after the assassination of President McKinley. Only since the 1950's had the Vice President and the First Lady been included as protectees. The Service was still relatively small and close-knit in those days, when every agent in the Service was a Roman Catholic and the entire upper echelon staff consisted of heavy-drinking New York

Irishmen. The agency grew rapidly after the assassination of President Kennedy, and then expanded exponentially after the assassination of Senator Robert Kennedy and the wounding of President Reagan. Wintergreen believed himself overqualified as an agent—a routine poststander—a cigar-store Indian. He'd been destined to be Director, and he thrived in the White House Secret Service. The gold-braided hallways were finally his. It was his time.

Gilbert Flanagan leaned in the doorway.

"Pete Garrison is here."

Thirty-eight years old Adjutant to the Director Flanagan was a lanky, six-foot Alabamian whose sideburns were slightly too long. He was Wintergreen's personal envoy to the rest of the Secret Service, his right-hand man, his most trusted minion and commander of the Secret Services' Special Operations Team (SOT) that Wintergreen used in sensitive Presidential threat cases. SOT had recently flown to Ethiopia to apprehend the leader of a Sudanese terrorist cell whose mission had been to kill President Jordan.

Though Wintergreen had an ample staff that included seven assistant directors, Flanagan was the one he trusted with delicate issues. Most importantly, Wintergreen used him as an executive assistant and gave him special, confidential tasks to carry out discreetly. In the Secret Service, the most political of security agencies, a man of unquestioned loyalty was indispensable.

Flanagan owed Wintergreen his allegiance. Years earlier, Flanagan had inadvertently mishandled a confidential-informant fund while working on a terrorist task force. He'd been in danger of being relieved of command by a Secret Service inspection team, but Wintergreen had whitewashed the incident and rescued Flanagan's career. And to insure Wintergreen's loyalty, Wintergreen had promised to reward him with a promotion to Assistant Director some day.

Wintergreen winked. "Send him in."

He stood in front of the trophy case, believing that being on one's feet was the best way to communicate, particularly in the White House.

"Sorry to break into your schedule," Garrison said.

"Close the door."

Garrison complied.

"How are things on the Valentine detail, Pete?" *Valentine* was the Secret Service radio code name for First Lady. The President's designation was Victory. The members of the Jordan Administration were all Vs.

"Not bad."

"When I assigned you to her, you told me you didn't want to spend your career sitting in a golf cart as she played a round with the Red Cross ladies."

"Uh, I'm getting used to it now. The reason I'm here—"

"Like I told you. Working the Valentine detail for a year certainly didn't do my career any harm, Pete. To get ahead in the Service, an agent has to be versatile. It's not just about riding the running boards. It's about diplomacy. That's the word for it. Diplomacy. I understand you have something you want to discuss—"

"A threat case."

"Shoot."

Garrison recounted what he had learned from informant Frank Hightower: that an unnamed Secret Service agent assigned to the White House Detail and a hired assassin from Europe were involved in an Aryan Disciples plot to assassinate the President. Garrison handed Wintergreen copies of a code card Hightower had given him. Wintergreen licked his lips and formed an expression of concern on his face as he studied the items.

"Frank Hightower. What can you tell me about him?"

"When I was working PRD he provided reliable information—enough to make four solid convictions. He has connections with dealers of illegal weapons and other paramilitary types both here and in Canada and Europe. He likes to think of himself as a soldier of fortune. His motivation has always been money. He wants a million dollars for the case."

"I'm glad he's not greedy," Wintergreen said facetiously.

"He's not asking for cash until after the arrests are made."

Wintergreen picked up a plastic pitcher from his desk. He poured water into a glass and took a drink. "That's encouraging."

"Hightower is reliable."

"Pete, how do you see this?"

"Going by what he has done for us in the past and the fact that he turned over a Commo Card, I think he may be telling the truth."

Wintergreen coughed. "Frankly, this sounds like a case where the information and the informant sound a little too good to be true. But we have to move on the information. I want you to stay with your normal duties but continue handling Hightower. You've worked with him in the past. You know him. If there is a demand on your time from the First Lady Detail, take vacation days and I will recredit them to you later. You'll be point man on this. That way no one in the world will know what we're up to. In case the information may fit with the Meriweather murder, bring Martha Breckinridge up to speed."

"Okay."

"Keep this top secret, Pete."

"I'll open an internal investigation file—"

"I don't want a formal internal investigation opened at this point. If we have an insider working for the Disciples, he might smell a rat and pull back into his shell. Handle this off the record until something jells. Keep me informed at every step."

"Will do."

"Any questions?"

Garrison said there wasn't, then left the office.

Wintergreen felt pleased. He sensed that time was condensed. He could handle difficult situations, while others, the brown-baggers in life, sat on the steps and ate their measly stale sandwiches, whining and crying in their beer. Wintergreen remembered an incident when he'd been a junior agent. He'd been on Air Force One returning from a Presidential trip to the West Coast, and the shift leader had told the entire shift that they were continuing on duty after working twelve days straight. When he and the others had complained, a veteran shift leader had told him: *See the President sitting up there sipping whisky with the newsies? He doesn't give a damn about how many hours you work. In fact, unless you get promoted to Director, you can stay twenty years and no President will ever know your name. Get used to it. And get used to the long hours. You're not the President, and in the White House you are lower than the lowliest appointed assistant, and only slightly higher than the steward who serves coffee in the Red Room. You're nothing but part of the woodwork.*

Now that Wintergreen had achieved the rank, he figured he owed no one. In the paramilitary U.S. Secret Service, he had the power of an Army general. He gave orders and his White House Detail agents jumped to carry them out. The White House was a good place to be.

A sign on the wall behind his desk read, "THE PRIORITY IS PRESIDENTIAL SECURITY."

He got up and straightened it.

CHAPTER 5

IN THE WHITE House private quarters dining room, President Russell Jordan sat alone at a gleaming mahogany table, sipping coffee and reading from a stack of newspapers and cables that were stacked neatly on a hand-carved maple teacart.

He glanced at a *Washington Times* headline. "President Agrees to Russian Summit Meeting." He wasn't looking forward to wrangling with the Russians at Camp David, but he had an ace up his sleeve: an aid package that had been put together by his allies in Congress. Summit meetings were always about money, and the successful ones always involved lots of Uncle Sugar's dough for the opposing sides. Jordan recognized this as a fact of political life. It had been one of many dismaying lessons he'd learned in office. No wonder that Presidents were all cynics. Previous Presidents had faced war, cold war, hostage-taking incidents, recessions, and the 9/11/01 terrorist attacks on the New York World Trade Center and the Pentagon—when terrorists of all stripes had figured out that they could gain worldwide attention by using violence for their cause.

In the Jordan Administration, the back-alley war against terror had become a fact of life. Every year of his Administration there had been federal buildings and military facilities destroyed by bombs. In the last eighteen months alone, four U.S. ambassadors had been assassinated. Nothing Jordan had ever read, no advice or counsel, had prepared him for the day-by-day stress of dealing with such violence and all its lasting ramifications while, at the same time, holding his fingers in the dikes of domestic political crises.

The door opened and Eleanor came in.

"Nice perfume," he said as she joined him at the table.

"How kind of you to notice."

Her impersonal comments had started in the last few months, but he'd chosen not to confront her. He wanted peace. He wanted to leave office with her at his side and turn the reins of government over to Vice President Cord, who was ahead of his Democratic opponent in the national polls. He wanted to give the party back what it gave him.

"How was the beach?" he asked.

She picked up a newspaper. "Sunny."

A waiter appeared to pour her coffee.

"It's good to see you taking advantage of the house," Jordan said.

"Uh-huh."

"Camp David. It would be a big help if you could

come up to help entertain. The Russians are bringing their wives."

"The *wives*," she said glibly.

After a long, annoying silence, he cleared his throat. "Have you done any more thinking about the Kennedy Center?"

"I haven't made a decision yet."

"Some of the major donors would love to see you."

"What's that play again?"

"Long Day's Journey into Night."

He'd told her a week ago. But she didn't like the party fat cats and she was playing head games again.

"Yuck," she said.

"It's an awards evening. There will be press speculation if you don't attend."

"We certainly wouldn't want to have that, would we?"

"The major money people. That guy from Texas and his wife. They need him—"

"I don't like him and I don't like his low-class wife."

"Since when do we have to be in love with people to handle our social duties?"

Here he was, cajoling his own wife into attending a function with him. It was absurd.

"Duties," she said. "White House *duties*."

"Eleanor, do you have to break my balls over every little issue?"

"Sorry," she said coldly. "Okay. I'll go to the play."

"Good. And have you done any thinking about the lawyer issue?"

"I prefer to wait."

"I thought we could have someone begin the paperwork," he said. "It would be better than to wait."

"You mean the *divorce* paperwork?"

"An amicable thing and completely discreet, Eleanor. Super-secret. I feel it would be easier than just putting it off until the end of the term. Start the ball rolling by going through the negotiating and getting all the papers ready. Then later, there could be a quick court filing that would limit the press coverage of the matter."

"Could this be some advice from your trusted National Security Advisor Helen Pierpont?"

"Keeping the legal proceedings to a minimum would be easier for the both of us."

She glared at him. "How magnanimous of you to think of the *both of us.*"

He sat back. He wouldn't press it further with her. He didn't want to enter into an endless argument. What he really wanted was to leave the White House with his head held high, take care of the divorce, and then move on with his life. He didn't understand why she didn't want to discreetly begin the divorce process now, to help simplify things after he went out of office. It wasn't logical. But sometimes women weren't logical.

The phone buzzed. He pressed the speakerphone button.

"Yes?"

"The National Security Advisor would like to know when you'll be in the office to discuss a priority matter."

"Shortly." He released the switch. "I have to run."

"What is it?"

"You don't want to know."

"I don't?"

"It's a threat thing. The Aryan Disciples is sending threat letters to me now."

"Why wasn't I informed about this?"

"I just didn't think you wanted to deal with all the negativity."

"Bye."

"Come on, hon," Jordan said gently taking her hand. "Let's don't do this to one another. We'll make it through this and life will be better." She looked up at him. "That's my baby."

He told her to have a nice day, and left the room carrying his cables. Moving along the hallway with an agent following close behind, Jordan felt relieved that she'd agreed to attend the Kennedy Center function. He'd been worried that the press would begin wondering why they were avoiding joint public appearances. Eleanor had never been able to resist the Jordan charm. And he believed that she would soon come around on his request to get the lawyers involved earlier rather than later. The entire matter was painful. He could tell that she still loved him. But it had to be done. How ironic, he thought, that his popularity rating with the women the pollsters called "soccer moms" was the reason he'd been able to win two national elections, but he would be the first President to divorce immediately upon leaving office. But irony was politics.

Jordan had only a few months left in his second term, and he would miss being President. He knew that his White House years would be the pinnacle of his life— that the accomplishments of an ex-President would pale in comparison to being in executive command. He didn't look forward to becoming a familiar face that provided the occasional sound bite on the evening news, a bystander rather than a participant in world events.

On the other hand, the concept of living without the burdens that came with the job was becoming more and

more appealing. He was tired of riding on a thorned
saddle. He'd nearly made it through two Administrations
in one piece. He'd neither been assassinated nor involved in a scandal. He was going to leave the big white
target on the Potomac with his legacy intact. There had
been no war and the stock market had recovered from a
two-year recession and was now healthy. He had nothing
to complain about.

In the Oval Office, sunlight streamed in through the tall
French doors. Jordan stood in the middle of the room
on a bordered azure carpet with the Presidential seal.
Hands in pockets, he listened intently to Wintergreen
brief him on the Aryan Disciples threat to his life. Jordan
didn't like what he was hearing. When Wintergreen finished, there was only the sound of ticking coming from
an ornate grandfather clock.

Jordan glanced at National Security Advisor Helen
Pierpont, who was leaning against an oversized oak
desk. The expression on her face meant she was concerned. He turned to the portrait of George Washington
over the fireplace.

"As I see it, the question is whether to believe the
informant."

"Mr. President, Agent Garrison believes Hightower is
reliable," Wintergreen said. "Without question. A
proven track record."

Pierpont rubbed her eyes. "The code card corroborates
his information. This can't be taken lightly."

She'd been pacing about the room, as was her habit
during such briefings. She was wearing the sleek, black
dress and the gold necklace Jordan had bought her for
her birthday. He thought she looked more like a pam-

pered New York socialite than a government bureaucrat.
Helen Pierpont stood out in a crowd. Before coming to
the White House she'd been a professor of international
relations at Columbia and ambassador to Peru. She'd
worked her way up in the second Jordan-for-President
election campaign, and he'd personally picked her to be
National Security Advisor.

Jordan made eye contact with Wintergreen.

"What's the plan, Mr. Director?"

"Agent Garrison will maintain contact with the informant."

Pierpont coughed dryly. "I think what the President
means, Mr. Director, is: What *proactive* steps are you
taking?"

"We're doing everything humanly possible."

"How about putting all your agents on the lie-detector
machine?" Pierpont asked.

"Not yet—"

"That might be a good place to start, don't you think?
Test everyone with access to the Secret Service radio
code cards—"

"And if that doesn't uncover the turncoat, then test
everyone who works in the White House—right down
to the janitors if necessary," the President said, chiming
in.

"That will take some time," Wintergreen said. "There
aren't enough polygraph experts in the Service to get
this done in anything less than a month."

"Use Army Intelligence personnel," Pierpont said.
"Bring in every polygraph operator in the military if necessary."

Wintergreen turned to him. "Can do."

"That sounds like a good place to start," Jordan said to back her up.

He liked Pierpont's style. She was a mover and shaker, a woman full of surprises in more ways than one. She could deal with men like Wintergreen. She spoke Russian and German fluently, was a scratch golfer, and could quote from Henry Kissinger's *The Age of Power and Diminishing Values*. During Wintergreen's briefing, Pierpont had been slinking about the room, stopping now and then to put a hand on her hip. She was a few years younger than Jordan. She had reddish hair, green eyes, and an athletic figure.

"Yes, sir," said Wintergreen.

"You're the expert on Presidential protection, Larry," Pierpont said. "Let me ask you a simple question: Is the President safe?"

Wintergreen coughed nervously. "The White House is a fully secure environment."

"That's not what I am asking."

"Pardon me," Wintergreen said bitterly. "I must have misunderstood."

"I think what Helen is asking," Jordan said, "is whether, if this information is true—if there is a terrorist spy, a co-opted Secret Service agent working on your staff—you can trust any part of your security operation. With all due respect, Larry, isn't a security system only as good as its weakest link?"

"Mr. President, it's possible that we have been compromised, but I am doing everything I can to rectify the problem in the best way I know how."

Pierpont turned to Jordan and gave him a nearly imperceptible nod.

"That should cover it, Larry," Jordan said to close the meeting.

"Because this is a matter of national priority, I would ask to have some leeway in the investigation," Wintergreen said.

Jordan furrowed his brow and wondered exactly what Wintergreen was getting at.

"Leeway?"

"I think Larry is asking about permission to conduct unauthorized searches and telephone monitoring," Pierpont said.

The first thing Jordan had learned, as President, was that acrimony never solved problems. Only consensus. Helen was taking the threat thing personally.

"Do what you have to along those lines," Jordan said. "We need to get this system back in order."

"Yes, Mr. President."

Wintergreen got up and left the room. Jordan left his chair to stretch.

"What do you think of all this, Helen?"

"Someone selling security information is a solvable security problem. The lie-detector tests should be able to clear it up."

The door was closed and they were alone. Jordan moved behind her and slipped his hands around her firm waist.

"Thank you for arranging that comprehensive briefing, Ms. Pierpont."

He kissed her neck.

"Will there be anything else, Mr. President?" she said wryly, looking him in the eye.

She wrapped her arms around him and they kissed. From the beginning, the sex between them had been wild and irrepressible. There was something about her, an enigmatic quality he found enthralling. It had something to do with the way she could look him in the eye. Though reserved and remote in official business, she was the most sexually uninhibited woman he'd ever met. The two dynamics acted on him electrically, and he found himself thinking about her constantly. Theirs was an affair that hadn't dimmed though an entire Administration.

"What did she say about getting the paperwork started?" Helen asked.

"She didn't reject the idea outright."

"Did you tell her that it would be so much easier to bring the lawyers in now?"

"It's not that easy."

"Why?"

"She could blow the divorce out to the press. She could ruin the party and me."

"She's not going to do anything like that."

"How can you be so sure?"

"I know women."

"Well enough for me to risk being made out to be the worst heel in the Western world?"

"Eleanor's public image is more important to her than life itself. She will eventually go along with the program. She will take the easy way."

"I'm not so sure. Please have patience." She pulled away from him. "It's no fun being in limbo like this, Russell. It makes me feel cheap. Damn it. You either love me or you don't. I've put up with all the tiptoeing, and now all I am asking is that we move forward. Please."

He'd been drawn to Helen Pierpont for the first time at a West Palm Beach political fund-raiser. She had a way of focusing her attention on him that he'd found hypnotic. When he'd appointed her National Security Advisor, the media had loved it, and had referred to her as a "think-tank star," the author of two well-received texts on foreign policy, which she had written while teaching at Yale and the Fletcher School of Diplomacy. At the time, Jordan recalled thinking how nice it was when one's personal and professional interests meshed so closely. Now, the public knew Helen Pierpont as the one who navigated a steady course through the dangerous straits of international politics.

She had also been the one who'd alerted him to a Democratic Party ambush, one that could have finished him in the election. She'd single-handedly engineered a deal with Governor Alfred Cord of California, placing Cord in the Vice Presidency and collapsing the radical right wing of the party, insuring the Jordan nomination. Without her, Jordan would have been a one-term President like Bush and Carter, politicians rejected at the peak of their power and influence, tossed aside by a fickle public. While Eleanor reminded him every day of what she had done for him, Helen stood quietly at his side. She was his support, his rock. Helen loved him without reservation.

"I'll talk to her again," he said.

"I don't know where the hell I stand."

He leaned down to kiss her neck. "Yes, you do."

"Say it."

"I love you, Helen."

"I hate lurking around like this. I can tell that the agents know. I can tell by the way they look at me. I hate the role of *other woman*—"

"I love you more than I can say."

"Honey."

Reaching behind her, he grasped her taut buttocks and pulled her to him.

"I have thirty minutes before I have to meet with the Ambassador to Iran," he whispered.

"Then you'll have to concentrate."

"Yes, ma'am."

She kicked off her shoes and moved toward a blue-and-white-striped sofa.

He pressed a button on the wall. The curtain began closing slowly, automatically, left to right, dimming the glare from the South Lawn. His heart raced and he unfastened his belt.

After she left, Jordan opened the curtain and stared through the tall windows at the South Lawn, where a workman was setting up a microphone for an awards presentation later. A stranger driving by on Constitution Avenue and seeing Jordan now might describe him as a stockbroker or a Wall Street businessman. At sixty, his features were etched with maturity lines. His hair was full, parted and graying heavily only at the temples. He was six feet tall, and watched his weight so assiduously that his personal tailor had been making custom-made business suits from the same body form since his first inauguration seven and a half years earlier.

Jordan recalled standing at the window then, believing he was at the center of the universe, the apex of unfathomable power. It hadn't taken him long to learn that Presidential authority was a fleeting wisp of smoke. It required dodging scandal, assuaging powerful egos every minute of every day, being strapped to a telephone, wheedling one's way from one crisis to another, walking a tightrope with no respite, and peddling one's ass to party fat cats. The day-to-day pressure was something he could have never anticipated. As a Senator from California he'd dealt with complex, intractable issues for years. But nothing had prepared him for the trials of the Oval Office.

Thankfully, he'd survived. He'd taken his lumps while watching his political allies and followers drop off one by one as his own popularity inevitably ebbed in the second half of his second term. There were only two Cabinet officers remaining of those appointed at the beginning of the Administration. But he'd nearly made it to the finish line.

And now terrorists were out to assassinate him.

CHAPTER 6

BRECKINRIDGE ANXIOUSLY DROVE along the Potomac River into the Old Town section of Alexandria, Virginia, a milieu of eighteenth- and nineteenth-century streets lined with brick and wood-frame buildings and wrought-iron fences encircling brick courtyards. Because of traffic, it had taken her about twenty minutes to get there from D.C. She swerved into a long driveway leading inside a newly built condominium complex. The street names were Duke and Prince.

It occurred to her that Charlie Meriweather's murder involved a succession of horrors: informing his wife Delores of his death, the funeral, and now the painful errand of interviewing her. Breckinridge parked the car, and felt a warm breeze coming from the river. She knocked on the door of a modest walk-up condo, and heard footsteps inside. Delores Meriweather opened the door.

"Hello, Martha."

"I know this is unannounced, but I couldn't get through—"

"I took the phone off the hook."

Delores was a few years younger than Charlie. She had piercing, green eyes and wore her hair in a topknot. She was a petite, strident woman, and a veteran American Airlines flight attendant who Charlie had met on a Presidential campaign flight. She often played piano and sang at the annual Secret Service holiday party. At Charlie's funeral, Breckinridge had watched her accept condolences stiffly, her eyes red, her jaw set in the anger of loss.

"May I come in?"

"Of course."

Delores motioned her to the sofa. The living room was decorated with Oriental tapestries and Spanish art that Delores and Charlie had acquired during their ten-year union. Open shelving held the knickknacks that Meriweather had picked up when traveling across the world with the President: a Russian samovar, an African ritual mask, and a Colombian figurine.

"I'm sorry to bother you—"

"I'm so tired of hearing the word sorry and tired of all the shitty, Secret Service bureaucratic, federal schmaltz. All the flowery crap."

"Delores, I know the police department has already asked you questions, but I am investigating Charlie's murder separate from the others, as a security issue—"

"No, I don't know of anyone who would want to kill

him if that's what you're asking. The others had the same question."

"Was there anything unusual that happened with Charlie during the last few months?"

"Wait a minute," Delores said with furrowed brow. "Larry Wintergreen told me that Charlie had been picked at random by a terrorist group. Is that true?"

"As far as I know, yes."

"Then why are you asking these questions?"

"I'm trying to figure out if there is some connection to Charlie—some clue as to why they picked him—the method of how they might have picked him."

"How the hell would I know anything about that?"

"Something Charlie said perhaps."

"The only thing that was different with him in the last few months was that he was fed up with the job. He was fed up with standing post and fed up with White House politics. That's what he told me. I've already told everyone this. How many times do I have to go over it? He's dead and I'm moving to Montana. They could have given Charlie a desk job, but they kept him standing post at his age. I know it had nothing to do with him getting killed, but he wasn't in love with the Secret Service any longer. That's why it is so ironic that he got killed in the line of duty. I'd finally talked him into taking his pension. We were planning to move to Montana. All that is over now."

"The White House politics you just mentioned. Did Charlie go into any detail about what was bothering him?"

"He'd been forced to take part in some investigation. He called it an 'in-house caper.' Gil Flanagan was running it. He told Charlie it had had something to do with a defense contractor getting inside information on contract bids. Or at least that's what Flanagan told him. It involved Helen Pierpont. Charlie told Flanagan he didn't want to do it—that he didn't want to get involved. But Flanagan put pressure on him and Charlie felt like he had no choice but to go along."

"That doesn't sound like Charlie."

"That's because you don't know the whole story like I do. Charlie had been arrested for drunk driving in Manassas last year. He ran into a parked car and got arrested. Flanagan saved his job by going to his pal Wintergreen. Wintergreen covered everything up for Charlie, so Charlie couldn't very well refuse to go along with what they wanted. Charlie owed Flanagan big-time. Besides, Flanagan told him the request came from Wintergreen himself. Charlie wasn't in a position to refuse."

Breckinridge rubbed her chin for a moment, and her thoughts bounced off one another like bumper cars.

"Did Charlie speak with Wintergreen in person about the assignment?"

The look that crossed Delores's face was one of bafflement and apprehension.

"I think Flanagan relayed all the information to him. But supposedly the orders were coming from the President himself."

"What did Flanagan ask him to do?"

"Bug a room at the Waldorf Astoria Hotel in New York. It was during a Presidential trip."

"Whose room?"

"I'm sitting here wondering if I should say. But it's a foolish thought, isn't it? Now that Charlie is dead, what the hell is the difference? He planted a bug in Pierpont's room and connected it to a tape recorder. He hated being used, but he had no choice. Charlie drove up to New York on a Friday and came back the next morning. He told me that Flanagan dismissed him as soon as he'd finished the installation. When he got back, Charlie was worried. He told me he thought something funny was going on—that Flanagan might be up to something. He was concerned that he was getting in over his head—that he'd allowed himself to slip into a 'trick bag' as he called it—that there might have been another reason for the investigation that had nothing to do with defense contractors at all.

"So Charlie went to Wintergreen. Wintergreen confirmed that he had asked Flanagan to bug the room. But Charlie said Wintergreen beat around the bush and avoided telling him what it was all about. All along Charlie believed that he was acting on orders from the President. But after he spoke with Wintergreen, he was convinced there was something funny about the whole investigation. He believed that Wintergreen had used him.

"Charlie and I talked about it, but I could tell he was holding back something. I suggested that Charlie go to Pierpont. He said it was too dangerous. He thought that if he told her what he'd done and the others denied ordering him, then he would end up holding the bag. That's when Charlie decided to retire. He said he was tired of being a government drone—that he was being put in the middle. There, that's all I know. Now, if you don't mind, I'd like to be alone now."

Breckinridge cleared her throat. "Did Charlie mention what he'd learned from the operation itself—what was on the tapes?"

"If he learned anything, he never told me. If you want

to know about this, wouldn't it be better for you to talk to Flanagan or Wintergreen?"

Breckinridge stood. "I apologize for bothering you."

Delores led her to the door and opened it.

"Is there something you aren't telling me about what happened to Charlie?" Delores asked.

"I'm just investigating. Really."

"Martha, have you ever been married?" Breckinridge shook her head. "If you do, don't marry a Secret Service agent."

"Good-bye, Delores."

Walking down the steps, Breckinridge heard the door close. Stopping at the sidewalk, she took a deep breath, let it out, and looked up to the sky. The clouds drifting from the east had turned metallic gray, as if drawing moisture from the Potomac. For some reason, Breckinridge found herself thinking of a similar day when she was a young girl, riding her bicycle through a public park in Tulsa, Oklahoma, and pretending she was an explorer. Her mother had called her a tomboy. That's why people longed for childhood, Breckinridge thought. They wanted to relive the freedom and lack of responsibility.

But she couldn't get on a bike and just ride away from the Charlie Meriweather case. She couldn't get it out of her mind. It had enveloped her.

Returning to Secret Service headquarters, Breckinridge took the elevator to the seventh floor. Passing by a guard at a desk, she moved along a darkened hallway to a door that was stenciled in crude black letters JC ADMINIS-TRATIVE SERVICES DIVISION. She took out her badge and held it up to a surveillance camera mounted above the door. The lock buzzed. She went inside the Secret Service wiretap room known as "Junction City." Agent Lino Palmieri was adjusting the controls on a tape recorder. He was the technician in charge of electronic eavesdropping. He was a slender man, younger than she was, with weather-yellowed hair, a close-cropped beard, and wire-frame eyeglasses.

"Lino, have you had any unusual activity on the Aryan Disciples taps?"

"Nothing but small talk. Nasty people talking about what they watched on TV; the price of motorcycles. Junkola."

All telephone lines tapped by the Secret Service, no matter their location, were routed to the room via dedicated circuit. On tall shelves lining the walls were dozens of voice-activated tape recorders and pen register machines that automatically recorded telephone-dialing impulses and conversations. Each piece of equipment was neatly marked with a case number and the name of the special agent handling the investigation. Breckinridge's name was on six recorders.

"That's all?"

"And I've been checking the tapes frequently. None of your Aryan Disciples suspects have been doing much of anything. They've been on the phone to one another, all right, but I haven't heard anyone telling people to call back from a pay phone. And none of the ring codes. Nothing out of the ordinary. There has been some general talk about the government being after them—rehashing, small talk—but nothing we haven't heard before.

"Nothing so far indicates any action being planned against the President. None of these people are even talking around anything that sounds like a planned action. You know what I mean; no verbal code. I've heard none of that. And that is always what these Aryan Disciples types do. When there is an action in the wind, they start the word games, the pig Latin. Before the Federal Building bombing, they were talking about silly putty, their code word for C-4 explosives."

"What do you make of it?"

"Overall, I'd say they aren't up to anything at the moment."

"Hard to figure."

It didn't make sense to her. The Aryan Disciples wiretaps had proved helpful in the past. Even offhand comments by the suspects being monitored could help identify Disciples bombers and their helpers and pinpoint places and times of planned bombings. And Lino had a good ear for detecting terrorist plots.

"Does this have anything to do with a case that Pete Garrison is working on?" he asked.

"Garrison?"

"He just sent me a coded E-mail and asked if I had any Aryan Disciples taps going that had mentioned the name Frank Hightower. I told him that he could come over and look through the database, but that I wasn't going to run through all that shit without a written order. My job isn't to run out investigative leads for the hell of it. It's to see that this equipment is working. Sounds to me like he might be trying to horn in on your case."

"That's what it sounds like."

The U.S. Secret Service was a competitive, cutthroat environment in which case stealing—encroaching on another agent's investigation—was common. She'd never worked with Garrison and knew little about him, other than that he'd been kicked off the White House Detail for knocking out a pie-thrower. But what was Garrison up to? And who was Frank Hightower?

The footplate alarm buzzed. Palmieri cocked his head toward the television monitor depicting the hallway. It was Garrison.

"Speaking of the devil."

Palmieri pushed the buzzer. Garrison walked in.

"What were you doing asking about Aryan Disciples wiretaps?" Breckinridge asked.

"I'm not trying to work anything behind your back, if that's what you think."

"Give me a break."

"I just left a message for you to call me."

She nodded toward the door. They walked out of the office and down the hallway to a conference room that was strewn with schematic diagrams of the Kennedy Center. Breckinridge assumed that agents had been using the room in preparing a security plan for the President's upcoming visit to the Kennedy Center. They sat at a table. Garrison told her about his case.

"Let me get this straight, Pete. The reason you were asking about the wiretaps was to see if anyone was talking about your informant."

"He refused to tell me which Disciples members he is dealing with. I thought I might be able to pick up some information at JC."

"I am up to date on the current Aryan Disciples wiretaps. None of the Disciples members we are monitoring are talking to any Frank Hightower. But his information sounds promising. This could be the first break in the Meriweather case. What else did he say about the Secret Service insider?"

"That's about it. He didn't tell me enough to identify him."

"Do you think he knows and is just trying to piece out the information out to you?"

"I don't think so. But I can't be sure. And Hightower isn't above doing something that would build up his reward in the case."

"I want to talk to him."

"He won't meet with anyone but me."

"Bullshit."

"If I was going to lie to you I wouldn't have told you anything about him. Martha, I have no objection to you interviewing Hightower, but at this point he's spooked. He says he's worried about a comeback from the Secret Service insider. Look, I'm not trying to steal your case. Hightower came to me out of the blue. I hadn't spoken to him since I worked at PRD two years ago and so help me, I'm not trying to parlay this case or any other one into a promotion."

She stared into his eyes. "Where is Hightower now?"

"I don't know."

"So if he disappeared you wouldn't know where to look for him?"

"I'm giving it to you straight."

"Did Hightower play hard to get like this when you worked with him previously?"

"No. In fact, he gave me his home phone number. That's how I used to reach him."

She nodded. "What do you think he is up to?"

"I'm not sure. He's either building a tremendous scam, or he's telling the truth and is scared that the agent he believes is working for the Aryan Disciples might find out his role and kill him. But, as of this moment, I have no other choice but to accept his information as kosher."

Breckinridge wanted to say something else, to try to drag more information out of Garrison about Hightower, but she believed him. Garrison wasn't trying to build up Hightower's reliability as she'd seen pushy agents do when it came to their own informants. She sensed that he was as skeptical as she was about Hightower's information. Garrison didn't know any more than he had told her.

"Let me give it to you straight, Pete. I know of few terrorist cases where an informant who wasn't a principal player in the conspiracy had such detailed information."

Garrison ran a hand through his hair. "That has been bothering me too."

Garrison's cell phone rang. He answered it. His eyebrows raised. Meeting Breckinridge's eyes, he mouthed the name Hightower.

"Let's get together. I'll see you there in a half hour."

He pressed OFF.

"Hightower?"

"He says he has something new."

CHAPTER 7

GARRISON PARKED AT the Smithsonian Natural
History Museum and went inside. The lobby was
filled with school-age children and a few schoolteachers
trying to herd them here and there. Hightower was standing in the corner, looking anxious and out of place.

"We have to stop meeting like this," Hightower said.

He never was any good at making small talk.

"What's the new scoop?" he went on. "Did you get
authorization to pay my reward?"

"I was waiting for authorization right when you
called."

"Is there a problem?"

"Not as long as your information is on the up and
up."

"Your people should be digging this case. One of your

own and all that. A prize like this doesn't come along every day—"

"A prize. That's a good word for it. What's up, Frank?"

"Is there any chance they would refuse to pay my price? Do you see even a remote possibility that they would back away from me?"

"Not if the situation is what you say it is, Frank. How many times do I have to say it?"

"No need to get pissed."

"Lay the info on me, Frank."

Hightower lifted his baseball hat and ran a hand through his hair.

"It's like this. The dude who the Disciples hired to do the President is registered in Room 21 at the Plantation Motel in Laurel, Maryland. He checked in yesterday. And get this: He's not an Aryan Disciples member. In fact, he has no connection with them whatsoever. He is a hit man. Like I said, from Europe. Supposedly, he is military-trained and once was a cop or a private eye or some shit like that. Supposedly, he's done this before."

"Political murder?"

"That's the word. Supposedly, he whacked some guy who ran an island. Fiji or some shit like that. And he blew someone up in Spain. He's been around. He knows what he is doing. He used phony ID to register at the motel. And he is doing some recon; casing out the area where he is going to do the hit. A source I just talked to says that he has been taking a lot of pictures. He likes to plan everything down to the last nut and bolt. He is a major professional. A Jackal type."

"I need a number where I can reach you."

"I'll have one for you tomorrow," Hightower said

glancing at his wristwatch. "But I have to get back now. I'm expecting some calls."

"Where are you staying?"

"With a friend."

"You don't trust me, Frank?"

"Nothing like that. But I have a right to protect myself. I have a right to my own security procedures. How do I know what fucking reports you have to write? Like someone reads it and pins me down."

"Frank, you and I have always been up front with one another about cases. Haven't we?"

Hightower had a quizzical expression. "Yeah?"

"You started the ball rolling, Frank. This case is bigger than the both of us. You're going to have to come through."

"That's what I am doing. Goddamn it. But I'm not going to put myself in the bull's-eye. And I don't like these face-to-face meetings."

"Why?"

"How do I know someone isn't following you? Like maybe the Secret Service guy who is in on this caper?"

As Garrison studied him, he got a strange feeling. There was something about the way the words had been coming out of his mouth. And he'd been rolling his eye now and then, as if trying to recall a script. Garrison thought back to previous meetings, to other cases. Something was different this time. He couldn't put his finger on it exactly, but something was different.

"Frank, tap-dancing isn't going to get you that big, fat reward you're looking for."

"I'm not playing hard to get. I'm just being cautious. You can't blame a man for looking out for his own ass."

"No, I guess you can't."

"What's wrong, Pete?"

"Who said anything was wrong?"

"I'm getting some weird vibes from you."

"You're reading me wrong. If you're referring to my insisting on a face-to-face, that's just the way we've always done business. Besides, for a million bucks, you shouldn't mind risking a meet."

"Look, I'm not nuts. I'm not going to pitch you a phony Presidential assassination story. I know what would happen. I know you could convict me of lying to a federal officer. You and I go back a ways. I just want everything to be cool between us."

Garrison elevated his eyebrows. "We're cool."

"I'll be in touch."

Garrison watched as Hightower turned and walked to the escalator. As he descended out of sight, Garrison looked about to see if anyone might be watching, then raised his hand to his chin and pressed his wrist microphone.

"He's coming your way, Martha."

Breckinridge pressed the transmitter button on the dashboard microphone.

"Roger, Pete. I see him."

She focused on the museum doors with binoculars. Earlier, she'd walked past Garrison and Hightower as they were talking so she could get a look at Hightower. She was sitting behind the wheel of an unmarked Secret Service sedan that was parked across the street from the Natural History Museum. The motor was running and she had a good five feet separating her sedan from the car in front so she could steer into traffic with one turn of the steering wheel.

Hightower moved briskly down the steps and then crossed the street to a late-model blue Chevrolet Malibu.

Breckinridge put the binoculars on the seat beside her and wrote down the Malibu's license number in her daily log. She was alone and she wished she had some help in the surveillance. Most Secret Service mobile surveillance operations involved ten or more cars driven by agents monitoring every direction taken by the person being followed. But she and Garrison were the only agents involved in the case. She would have to handle the surveillance without help.

After looking about furtively for a few moments, Hightower opened the driver's-side door of the Malibu and got in. He started the engine and pulled out from the curb.

Breckinridge followed him along Constitution Avenue, keeping at least one car between them as cover, praying that she didn't lose him in the traffic. With little else to go on, maybe Hightower was the key to the case. It wouldn't be the first time an informant was more involved in something than he'd let on.

Hightower turned left at Louisiana Avenue. He drove a few blocks to the Trailways bus station, where he pulled his car to the curb and parked.

Breckinridge drove by the Malibu, stopping at the end of the block to watch Hightower in her rearview mirror. She broke out in a cold sweat. Bus stations made her uncomfortable. During Aryan Disciples surveillance in Cleveland, Ohio, a year earlier, she'd followed a suspected terrorist to a bus terminal. As she'd watched him place a package in a rental locker, the package had unexpectedly detonated. The blast propelled pieces of his body and clothing all over the terminal. Luckily, only a few people had been injured, including Breckinridge, who'd had human bone fragments removed from her right buttock.

Hightower got out of his car and jogged across the street to the bus station. Breckinridge parked quickly and hurried after him. There were lots of tourists around. Hightower entered the terminal, meshing into the crowd of travelers. Was he going to meet someone? What would she do if he got on a bus?

A group of children got in her way and she almost tripped. When she looked up, he was out of sight. Cursing silently, she hurried from one end of the terminal to the other, scanning faces. Had she lost him? She moved briskly through the station, hunting for him. Passing a bank of rental lockers, she almost bumped into him. He was inserting coins into a rental locker coin slot. Her heart raced as he pulled open the locker and reached inside. He took out a thick, business-sized envelope and shoved it into this jacket. He looked about suspiciously.

She turned her head. Was he looking at her? He walked toward the door. She followed him outside and down the sidewalk. Reaching his car, he unlocked the door and got behind the wheel.

Breckinridge crossed the street and followed the sidewalk in his direction. He was opening the envelope and taking out money in what looked like banded half-inch greenbacks. To avoid drawing attention, she continued along the sidewalk. He drove off. She reached for her cell phone and dialed Garrison's cell phone number. He answered on the first ring. She told him to meet her at the bus terminal. He arrived about five minutes later, pulling up next to her as she stood outside her car.

"Your boy just picked up some money from a rental

locker," she said leaning down to the driver's-side window. "Banded green, like from a bank. What did he have to say?"

"That the shooter is at a motel in Laurel and has been doing some recon. But the way he is doling out information is bothering me. He's nervous and hesitant. He was never like that before."

She nodded. "What do you think he is up to?"

"He's known to deal in illegal weapons. But why would an informant hoping to make a million dollars from turning a Presidential assassination plot risk everything on some gun deal? Besides, if he were doing such a deal, the buyer would want to see the guns before he put the money in some rental locker. This seems like more of a terrorist thing to me."

"I have another question. If the Aryan Disciples were planning to kill the President, why would they tell Hightower? They keep their organization leak-free and compartmentalized. The members seldom use the telephones . . . much less tell a non-member like Hightower what they are up to. In the federal building bombings no one but the participants and one or two other key members knew about the plan." She believed that criminals were predictable. Whatever they did revolved around money. They seldom anticipated future events and, instead, lived life moment to moment, like animals. Hightower wasn't fitting any pattern. "Your rat is screwing us. Commo Card or not, I think he's playing a game on us."

"I agree. Something is fishy. But I find it hard to believe that he would have the guts to make up a scheme this big on his own. Not even if he thought he could make a million bucks. He's too cautious. When I worked with him before, he had plenty of opportunities to build up the information he was giving me and he didn't. He knew we would see through it."

"Maybe something changed."

"That's what we have to find out," Garrison said. "For some reason or another he thinks he can get away with this."

CHAPTER 8

A T THE PLANTATION Motel, a two-story, forty-room structure with a fenced pool and a slot in the office wall for departing guests to drop off their room keys, the motel manager removed the registration card for Room 21 from a drawer and handed it to Garrison. Garrison noticed the manager's name tag: PATEL. It had seemed to him that every motel manager had the name Patel until he'd learned that it was true. One East Indian caste owned and operated nearly all the independent motels in the United States.

"Alexander," Patel said. "Garth Alexander. He's paid up until tomorrow at noon. A cash transaction."

The card had an address in New York and a phone number. Garrison took out a pen and pad and copied the information.

"Can you describe him?" Breckinridge asked.

"I think he was wearing sunglasses and a cowboy hat when he checked in. And there was a blond fair-skinned woman with him with tattoos. But she left that day and didn't stay." Patel rubbed his stubble for a moment, then turned to Garrison. "He looks a little like you."

Garrison knew that when witnesses made such comments, it often meant that they had no independent recollection of what the person looked like. Witnesses, with the exception of those involved in crime, always wanted to help.

"We'll need a key to the room," Breckinridge said.

Patel glanced from Breckinridge to Garrison and back.

Garrison figured Patel was trying to think of a reason to decline. Then he reached into a drawer, took out a key that was attached to a plastic holder, and handed it to Breckinridge. She and Garrison left the office and walked toward the Secret Service sedan in the parking lot.

"Alexander," Breckinridge said. "The name doesn't ring a bell."

They got in the car and Breckinridge used her cell phone to call PRD on a scrambled line. She gave someone Alexander's name, waited on the line for a moment, and then began making notes.

"Thanks," she said, and then dropped the phone back in her purse. "The New York address and phone number are bogus," she said referring to her notes. "Garth Alexander is a name used by an ex-French Legionnaire who has been involved in some action jobs in Africa. He was an intelligence officer at one time. There is an entry on him from the CIA a couple of months ago. They name him as being a suspect in the murder of a businessman in Gijon, Spain, a possible contract job for the Basque separatist movement. He also may have taken part in a coup that took place on the island of Reunion, a French protectorate in the Indian Ocean. They're sending a mug shot."

"A mercenary. That fits with what Hightower told me."

"The Aryan Disciples have ties to a couple of Canadian anarchist groups and some German neo-Nazi clubs. It wouldn't be the first time terrorist organizations have traded favors."

She opened the glove compartment, slid out a tray that held a laptop computer/modem. She pressed some keys. Moments later, a booking photograph of Garth Alexander appeared on the screen. He was white, of medium weight and height. He had clean features, brown eyes, and a full head of sandy hair. In a crowd, he wouldn't stand out.

Breckinridge laughed. "He does look like you."

"Thanks."

"What now?"

"We hit his room."

"I agree."

Garrison was aware that in a Presidential assassination investigation, both evidence-gathering and general law-enforcement protocols took second place to thwarting the plot—to stopping it from going forward in any way possible. The mission, above all others, was to save the President. No matter what. The legalities could be sorted out later. If an assassination occurred, afterwards no one would thank Garrison for following the letter of the law. Instead, all the Monday morning quarterbacks of the world would crucify him for not taking action.

They returned to the motel, ascended a flight of stairs,

and followed the balcony to Room 21. They pulled guns. Garrison knocked on the door. Hearing nothing, he slipped the key into the lock and turned. He shoved the door open and they rushed inside.

No one was there. The bed was unmade. On the wall was a solitary faded print of a lakeside cabin. There was no luggage or belongings. Garrison reholstered his gun. Breckinridge pulled the door closed. Garrison opened the dresser drawers one by one. They were empty. Breckinridge checked under the bed. In the bathroom, Garrison knelt down next to a wastebasket. In it was a copy of *Guns & Ammo* magazine. He thumbed pages and a small piece of paper fell out. He kneeled down and used another scrap of paper to pick it up. It was a cash receipt for two rolls of 35mm black-and-white film, dated a few days earlier.

"Martha."

She joined him and read the receipt.

"Sandor's Camera Store, Rehoboth Beach. Your informant's information pans out again. This looks like a professional recon job to me."

Garrison tore off a corner of the magazine, and used it to pick up the receipt and place it in his shirt pocket.

"Why would a mercenary who is in town to kill the President tell anyone where he was staying?"

"Maybe they know each other."

"Hightower didn't mention that. On the other hand, he didn't mention anything except the bare facts. He's holding back on me."

"Did he ever do this before?"

"No."

"What now?"

"We send up the flag."

She nodded.

In Wintergreen's office, Garrison and Breckinridge sat in chairs in front of Wintergreen's desk as they explained what they had learned. Garrison thought Wintergreen looked visibly stunned.

"Have we done a full workup on Alexander?"

"We just came from PRD," Garrison said. "We went through every database trying to find anything else on Garth Alexander. There was nothing but the booking photograph and the bio sketch. He has the same kind of vague history as most mercenaries."

"Hightower. Where is he in this?"

"Being standoffish."

"Just what the hell does that mean?" Wintergreen asked.

"He doesn't want me to know where he is living, and I get the impression that he is holding back."

"Have you been able to verify that?"

Garrison had guessed Wintergreen's reaction. In a developing case, the informant was always the issue.

"It's just a feeling I get. But his information has panned out so far. Every bit of it."

"Unfortunately."

Wintergreen rubbed his chin.

"Maybe we should have a showdown with Hightower," Breckinridge said looking at Garrison. "Bring him in and squeeze the full story out of him."

"I agree," Garrison said. "It's time."

Wintergreen cleared his throat. "I don't want to risk alienating an informant in a case like this."

Garrison said, "If Hightower knows more than he is

telling us, we might be able to clear some of this up."

"I see where you are coming from," Wintergreen said. "Hightower has dropped a major security issue in our laps. I'm going to put the detail on full-alert status. On the other hand, we don't want to alienate the informant and end up cutting off our only pipeline into an assassination conspiracy. Then where the hell would we be?"

"He's not going to walk away from a million-dollar reward," Garrison said.

Breckinridge said she agreed.

Wintergreen formed his hands into a steeple, and then cracked his knuckles. "Informants have been known to get cold feet."

"I've had a lot of experience working with High—"

"Let Hightower do his thing for the time being," Wintergreen said. "Don't lean on him and risk blowing the case. I don't want to end up in the dark with a pro gunning for the Man. Pete, I'm going to hold you responsible for keeping Hightower engaged with us until we close this thing down. Do whatever it takes. In the meantime, surveil him. Use twenty agents if you have to. I want him followed twenty-four hours a day."

Garrison nodded. "As soon as I can find out where he is staying."

Wintergreen gave Garrison a condescending wink to close the meeting. Garrison and Breckinridge left the office and walked down the corridor.

"Talk about micromanaging a case," she said.

"I should have leaned on Hightower right at first."

"Don't beat yourself up over it. It probably wouldn't have done any good. It sounds to me like he had his plan all worked out."

Garrison liked Breckinridge's perspective. She was an

experienced investigator. She was also easy to get along with. Breckinridge would make a good partner in the field. They stopped to grab a bite across from the Treasury Building at the Old Ebbitt Grille, an establishment of wood-paneled ambiance, the oldest restaurant in the capital. Sitting at the bar, they rehashed the facts and agreed that the pressure would be on them because of Wintergreen's personal interest in the case. Then she changed the subject and asked him about the pie-thrower incident that had ended his assignment to the White House Detail. He explained it.

She shook her head. "Talk about a raw deal. How did you end up on the First Lady Detail?"

"The slot was open at the time."

"Roland Prefontaine told me he didn't want to leave, but got the boot all of a sudden."

Before Garrison, Prefontaine had been the supervisor of the First Lady Detail.

"He thought it was because he did something that pissed someone off," she went on. "But no one would say. You know how those things happen. A White House mystery."

"The First Lady has never mentioned anything about him to me."

Breckinridge shrugged and glanced at her wristwatch.

"I'd better be going." She reached into her purse.

"I'll get the bill."

"Thanks, Pete. I'll get it next time."

They went back to discussing the case.

Garrison pondered the events of the day as he arrived at his apartment in the Scott Circle Arms on Rhode Island Avenue. He'd lived in the brick-front apartment house since coming to D.C. to join the Secret Service thirteen years earlier. After dialing a code number on an electronic keypad, he walked into a stifling foyer that held the D.C. humidity like an orchid farm. Unlocking his mailbox, he pulled out bills, a fishing catalogue, and a padded envelope with no return address.

On the third floor he unlocked his apartment and hurried inside to the closet to enter the ALARM OFF code on the keypad. He'd installed the alarm system a few weeks earlier. Though no one could prove it, a teenager who lived on the first floor had been burglarizing apartments to feed his narcotics habit, and Garrison had figured it was worth investing a few dollars on the alarm to avoid the kid stealing his gun and perhaps shooting someone.

On an assemble-yourself entertainment center in the living room was a framed photograph of Garrison's father, in Army dress uniform. He had been nineteen years old when the picture had been taken. Garrison adored him. Garrison took his gun and handcuffs from his belt and placed them on the dinette table. Attached to his key ring were a duplicate White House gun box master key and the ignition and trunk keys for the Presidential limousines. Every agent was required to carry the keys so they would be able to both gain access to White House shoulder weapons and drive the President to safety even if a limousine driver were disabled by gunfire.

He walked into the kitchen and opened the refrigerator. Selecting some leftovers, he created a dinner that included a small tin of mandarin orange slices, half a liverwurst sandwich, a frozen French roll, and some creamed corn in a Tupperware container. Carrying the items to the work counter, he ate over the sink while reading his mail. In the padded envelope were a letter and a 5×7 photograph of him and Eleanor standing inside the glass patio door at the Rehoboth Beach house, kissing passionately, his right hand on her breast. Garrison felt like he'd opened a coffin and found his own corpse inside.

"What the hell?" he said out loud.

A letter attached to the photograph read:

Dear Agent Garrison:

Please tell the First Lady that the price to purchase the original negative of this photo is two million dollars, a reasonable amount considering what I could get by selling it to the tabloids. I'm sure you agree that the shot would capture a big price.

If you or one of her representatives would like to discuss an amicable settlement of this matter, come to the Mayflower Hotel Bar tomorrow at noon to discuss the arrangements. I suggest you proceed discreetly. If you try any tricks, please be advised I have taken steps insuring that the photograph will be released to the worldwide press if anything goes wrong. I am only in this for the money and once I am paid, you will never hear from me again. So I suggest you not try to get clever on me, but just go along with the program. There is an easy way and a hard way to handle certain matters. Why not the easy way?

Cordially,

A Concerned Photographer

Garrison felt suddenly overwhelmed, confused, and angry. It was as if he were standing at the edge of a great chasm, staring down. He considered the coincidence factor. Was it bad luck, fate, or bad karma? *God-damn it to hell*. He should have known better than to be near a glass door. He was well aware of the existence of cameras that could take easily identifiable photographs from more than a mile away. Could the Aryan Disciples hit man, Alexander, have been stalking the President and seen them? What were the chances that Garrison would be kissing the First Lady at the beach house at the same time it was under surveillance by an Aryan Disciples assassin? A million to one? Or could it be two separate, unconnected people? A reporter perhaps? But it had been black-and-white film he'd found in Alexander's room. Garrison knew that blackmail was always a losing proposition for the victim. During the last Administration, there had been a number of blackmail attempts on the President, and Garrison had personally handled two of the investigations. He knew that some blackmailers, once they were apprehended, inexplicably chose to reveal the embarrassing information anyway.

Garrison left the kitchen and walked to the window. Across the street, the streetlight illuminated the traffic only as the cars passed by, as if they were disappearing into the darkness. He let out his breath. He's been stupid and foolish. He'd momentarily abandoned his good sense when he'd gotten involved with Eleanor, and now he was in the worst predicament of his life. He felt like a dunce.

In the First Family quarters Garrison got off the elevator and walked down a wide, oak-paneled vestibule. Crossing an expansive living room filled with antique furniture and original American art, he moved through a doorway that led into a study. Eleanor was sitting at an antique desk, reading. She wore a yellow summer dress that contrasted with her tan.

"Pete, I have a surprise. You and I are going to have a night alone at Camp David before everyone else arrives for the Russian summit meeting. . . . What's wrong?"

Her eyes were on his as he handed her the photograph and the blackmail letter. She studied them and her mouth became a straight line.

"Oh, my God."

She stood.

"Someone mailed this to my apartment."

"Who . . . ?"

"I think this relates to the Aryan Disciples."

"In what way?"

"We believe they hired a mercenary to assassinate the President." He told her about Hightower's information. He explained searching Alexander's motel room and finding a receipt for film that had been purchased in Rehoboth Beach. "I think this is one of the shots he took."

There was a look of horror and shock in her eyes.

"I still don't get it. Why would an assassin—?"

"I think this mercenary—his name is Alexander—was scouting the beach house and just happened to see us."

"By *scouting,* you mean . . . ?"

"Planning an assassination. Looking for security weaknesses. I think the blackmail idea came to him as an afterthought. Look, if my information is correct, if the person who sent this letter is part of the assassination conspiracy, he could have figured that he could pull off both the blackmail scheme and the assassination and collect the money for both jobs before flying back to Europe. I'm guessing now. But his type would be in this for the money."

"Is that the way these kind of people think?"

"Stranger things have happened."

"Pete, isn't it possible that this assassin and the blackmailer could be two separate people?"

"Yes. For all I know the entire Aryan Disciples could be in on it. Or, it could be the work of one enterprising blackmailer, an opportunist who is taking advantage of having taken that photo. But it doesn't really matter. The point is: There is a real threat against the President and a blackmail scheme has to be dealt with."

"Does my husband know?" She had a look of fear in her eyes that he'd never seen before, and he suddenly felt sorry for her. She wasn't used to talking about assassinations and other crimes the way he was.

"I briefed Wintergreen on the threat. I assume he'll brief the President."

She handed him the photograph and walked slowly to the window.

"Is my husband safe?"

"I don't want to frighten you, but I believe this is a real threat."

She pinched the bridge of her nose with thumb and index finger in contemplation.

"And it is certainly a real blackmail scheme," she said. "It's just you and me? We are the only ones who know?"

"Yes."

"Pete, what can be done?"

"This type of man has to be dealt with."

"You mean—"

"In person. I'm going to meet with him."

"And do what?"

"Force him to turn over the negatives."

"How? How will you do that?"

"You don't want to know."

"What if he turns out to be connected with the Aryan Disciples?"

"This isn't just another case. This is all or nothing."

"The Aryan Disciples are killers."

"There is no other way. If they are behind this, I'm going to turn him against them. I am going to make him take me to the ones who killed Charlie Meriweather."

"It's too dangerous to handle alone, Pete."

"Don't you see what would happen if this photo gets out?"

"I don't like your plan. I don't like it one single bit. Something could happen—"

"If the tabloids get their hands on this photo, they'll be selling posters of us in every shopping mall in the country. It would never end."

"I would be ruined," she said staring out the window. "Humiliated for life."

"As would I."

"We could deny. We could say that the photo is doctored—"

"And the media would hire a thousand experts to prove that the photograph was true and accurate. It is a damn photograph and it is solid evidence. There is no denying the truth in this kind of thing."

"Surely this person isn't going to just sit down and talk with you."

"He might send a middleman. He thinks he has nothing to lose as long as he doesn't let me close enough to arrest him. But that's where he is wrong. I'll do whatever I have to to draw him in. And once I get my hands on him, he's not going anywhere until the matter is resolved. One way or the other."

"It's too dangerous. Something terrible could happen. I don't want you to go through this—"

"He is in this for the money. That's what I'm going to use against him."

"Pete, listen. If they want money, I will pay."

"It could take a lot."

"I have a lot. That's one thing we don't have to worry about."

Garrison thought her tone was less than confident. He joined her at the window. Below, a uniformed officer was walking to his post.

"And if you did pay, they would come back the next week for more. No, this has to be handled once and for all. Blackmailers don't go away."

"The best way is to give them money. You tell him how much—"

"The difficulty in this kind of thing is *who* to pay and *how* to pay without getting ripped off," he said. "It's not going to do us any good to give someone a suitcase full of money and then have him come back next week for more."

"I'm scared to death, Pete."

"I'll take care of this."

But he wasn't sure. He wasn't sure of anything.

CHAPTER 9

BRECKINRIDGE WATCHED ANXIOUSLY as Rachel Kallenstien adjusted the focus on a slide projector. They were sitting in the Protective Research Division briefing room with the lights dimmed. When Kallenstien told her that the Secret Service forensic division had developed a clue on the Aryan Disciples threat letter, received the day Charlie Meriweather had been murdered, Breckinridge had hurried into the room.

Kallenstien pressed a remote-control button, causing a photographic slide of the letter to come onto the screen.

"This is the letter before."

She clicked the control again. The next slide that came on the screen depicted the letter with a seven-digit number scribbled in the lower right corner.

"And this is the letter after the EDSA process—which

involves placing the letter in a vacuum frame and sprinkling it with powdered graphite. A vacuum frame makes the graphite stick to any indentations that are on the paper. The criminalists think that this piece of paper was in a stack of similar paper when someone wrote on it using a ballpoint pen, leaving an indentation."

Breckinridge had heard of the EDSA process, but had never seen it demonstrated. For the first time since being assigned the case, Breckinridge felt energized.

"Seven digits—a phone number. Too bad there is no area code."

Later, Breckinridge and Kallenstien were at Breckinridge's desk. Breckinridge typed the password DUSTY on her keyboard and waited for a clear screen.

"Dusty?" Kallenstien asked.

Breckinridge tapped the phone number onto her computer keyboard.

"My father gave me the nickname. My mother hated it."

Breckinridge's father had been an oil-rig worker who spent many months away from home each year. She had been a Daddy's girl, and had written him every day when he was away from home on the job.

The display screen flashed the message NOT IN FILE.

"Goddamn it."

"Let's try the number using the dialing codes around Washington, D.C.," Kallenstien said.

"Good idea."

Breckinridge dialed the first number. It was not in service. She dialed the second number. A woman answered in the Spanish language.

"You speak Spanish?"

Kallenstien said she did, and Breckinridge handed her the receiver. Kallenstien held a short conversation in Spanish, then dropped the receiver onto the cradle.

"That was the sister of a retired postal worker. She doesn't know anything about her phone number being on a threat letter. She's been in the country for two years and she cleans houses for a living. She doesn't know anyone in the Aryan Disciples. She sounds legit."

Breckinridge and Kallenstien used computers to verify that the person to whom the telephone was registered had no criminal record, and to query telephone company security representatives in other telephone dialing codes across the country to obtain the registered users of the telephone number in question. Of the eighty numbers they came up with, more than half were no longer in service. Of those remaining, many were registered to phone booths and business addresses. As for the few that were registered to private persons, only a few of the persons had criminal records. One was a child molester, and the other was a man who had a juvenile record for car theft. Finally, Breckinridge stood and walked to the water cooler. Kallenstien followed. They sipped water for a minute or so.

"So the phone number is like a dead lead."

"Something else will come up," Kallenstien said. "Anyone could have written down a number on some piece of paper that was later used for the threat letter. Don't let it get you down."

"The lady the number registers to. Would you interview her in person? Maybe there will be something."

"Sure."

"We don't have much else to go on."

"Martha, you look like you could use a drink."

Breckinridge nodded agreement. It had been a long day.

As they were leaving the office, Kallenstien mentioned the subject of the lie-detector tests that were being given to every agent on the White House Detail. Breckinridge didn't let on that she knew their real purpose.

"The operator said it was a routine security investigation, but I don't buy it," said Rachel. "The questions didn't jibe. I think they are trying to camouflage an internal investigation. There is no other reason for putting everyone on the box like that."

"Rach, you're a very observant person."

"Sounds like you may know something I don't."

"All I can tell you at this point is that it is a high-power investigation."

"You little tease."

"I've been ordered not to talk about what I know. But . . . thanks for the help on this Aryan Disciples case."

"The ADs?" Kallenstien asked.

Breckinridge nodded.

"If it's an internal investigation, that could mean that someone in the Service may be suspected of having some connection with the ADs."

Breckinridge nodded.

"Wow."

CHAPTER 10

IN WHITE HOUSE Room 5711, sitting in a chair next to a polygraph machine, Garrison had sensors attached to his index fingers and chest.

The polygraph operator, Army Intelligence Lieutenant Mary Nicklanovich, was monitoring the polygraph stylus as it rolled ink onto moving paper. Prior to beginning the test, she'd introduced herself to him and had told him the test was required of all special agents because of newly formulated government security regulations. Garrison hadn't believed her.

"Are you acting as an agent of a foreign power?"

"No."

"Have you lied on your daily report during the last thirty days?"

"No."

"Have you done anything to endanger the President of the United States?"

Nicklanovich was the polygrapher used in the most sensitive White House internal investigations. She was a trim, athletic woman with a pixie haircut and broad, Slavic features. Her uniform fit her perfectly.

"No."

Garrison stared at a framed color photograph on the facing wall of President Gerald Ford playing with his dog on the South Lawn. He was concerned that some of his answers might be affected by his interlude with Eleanor. What if his concern showed up as possible deception? He'd left his post in the Rehoboth Beach security room to be with her.

"Have you knowingly withheld information during this interview?"

"No."

Nicklanovich made a red mark on the chart.

"Have you violated Secret Service protection protocol during the last thirty days?"

"No."

"Are you planning to do anything that might tend to harm any Secret Service protectee?"

"No."

"Have you done anything that could harm Presidential security?"

"No," Garrison said after hesitating for a moment.

Nicklanovich frowned and used a red pen to make a note on the chart, an indication to Garrison that his answer may also have been marked red on the chart.

"Have you done anything that could harm Presidential security?"

"No."

After repeating the series of questions and noting his answers twice more, Nicklanovich turned off the machine. She stood and leaned down to unfasten the chest strap and the finger sensors, then sat back in her chair.

"How are you feeling today, Agent Garrison?"

"Fine. Why?"

"You had a problem with: *Have you done anything to harm Presidential security?* Why do you think that is?"

"I have no earthly idea."

"You showed deception every time I asked it." She shrugged, and then used a knuckle to push her eyeglasses back on her nose. "That's strange."

"I didn't sleep well. Maybe that could be playing into it."

"Maybe," she said studying him.

"So that's it?"

"Unless you have some explanation—"

"I'll let you know if anything occurs to me."

"Look, I don't know what the hell they are looking for with these questions. They haven't told me. But I can tell you that this is a major investigation and if you don't clear up whatever is on your mind—whatever is bothering you—you're going to stand out like a sore thumb in the investigation. Having said that, would you like to take the test again?"

"No."

"It's your decision. But don't blame me if you end up on the suspect list."

She stared at him as he got up and left the room.

Garrison knew a polygraph did nothing more than test one's physiological reactions to various stimuli. He also knew that most law-enforcement professionals considered such tests unreliable. Polygraphs were, by their very nature, inexact. Like most other Secret Service agents, he believed them to be pseudo-scientific nonsense. Lie-detector test results could not be used as evidence against the accused in any legal proceeding. Nevertheless, it was clear that he would be singled out for further questioning. The problem was, his concern about his affair with Eleanor had caused him to show deception, and he would probably never be able to answer security questions without showing deception. And he could never explain the truth. A hundred things went through his mind at the same time. He knew that he had just become a suspect. His daily reports, his shift schedules, and his expense accounts would be scrutinized. Such Secret Service paperwork, with its strict accounting of hours, was designed to fix blame and was a powerful tool to use against agents during internal investigations.

In the command post, Garrison found a classified E-mail message from Breckinridge on his computer. In it she mentioned that she'd come up with what looked like a telephone number on the Aryan Disciples threat letter received shortly after Meriweather's death, but that a preliminary investigation indicated that the phone number wasn't a local one and that more investigation was required. He appreciated her keeping him informed.

"How do you like the Frau detail, Pete?"

Garrison turned. "Long time no see, Roland."

Roland Prefontaine was Garrison's predecessor on the First Lady Detail. He was a natty dresser and his hair and mustache were neatly trimmed. His olive complexion seemed to match his necktie.

"So far, it's a walk," said Garrison.

"Bored?"

"I'm getting used to it."

"They put me in the Foreign Dignitary Protection Division. I just spent two weeks protecting the President of Guinea while he was traveling to power plants in Texas."

Garrison nodded. "Can I ask you a question?"

"Go."

"Why did you leave her detail?"

"You tell me."

Garrison stared. "You really don't know?" Prefontaine said coldly. "One day I came to work and I had transfer orders waiting for me. She said she didn't know anything about it. I figured Wintergreen was making room for one of his fair-haired boys. Was he?"

"If I'd wormed my way into the job, I wouldn't be asking you what happened, would I?"

"Who knows? All I know is that I got the boot. If you didn't arrange it, then the only thing I can figure is that I pissed someone off. Maybe someone figured I knew too much."

"You mean about D day and all that."

"The Frau was interested in what the Man was up to with Pierpont, and asked me a few questions about what I had heard. I dummied up because I didn't want to get involved. Later, she hinted that she would like to find out what was going on. I didn't bite. I just wasn't going to put myself in a cross between her and the man. I'm not saying that is the reason I was forced to walk the plank, but it's a possibility. But what the hell. I'm not the first agent to get shuffled off a detail because someone thought he knew too much."

"Well, I had nothing to do with it."

"The way I see it, after you got in your jam with that pie-thrower, you knew you were on your way out the door. Maybe you thought weaseling your way onto her detail was a way to stay assigned at the House until you could slide back in with the Man himself."

Garrison stood. "I just told you I had nothing to do with it," he said staring him in the eye.

"Good luck in the assignment."

Prefontaine headed for the door.

Garrison sat and mulled over what Prefontaine had said. Maybe he was right. Maybe the President had been trying to limit agents from learning too much about First Family marital problems. During the Clinton scandals, Garrison had seen both agents and supervisors go and come from the White House. But it didn't matter. He had other things to think about: like an assassination conspiracy.

CHAPTER 11

THE NEXT MORNING Garrison hurried down a White House corridor, heading for the South Lawn.

"Garrison," someone shouted from inside the press room.

He stopped. Joe Kretchvane came to the doorway, smiling broadly. He was a journalist whose unauthorized biographies of Presidents Bush and Clinton and other VIPs had caused them great embarrassment. His writing technique was to ferret out unbecoming details from his target's enemies.

"Good morning, Joe."

"Agent Garrison. The Dragon Lady's Man Friday. Do you have a moment?"

"Not really."

"What's this I hear about a big Presidential threat investigation?"

"I don't know what you're talking about."

"I hear there's a divorce in the wind."

"Mine was final months ago."

"You know what I am talking about. Do you deny the Man and his Dragon Lady are going to split the sheets?"

Kretchvane was about thirty years old. His full beard and styled hair gave him a "Wolf Man" appearance. His beard was crusty, as if it had been dunked in soup a hundred times. He wore a T-shirt, a photographer's vest, and tennis shoes. Garrison detested him. But in Garrison's position, it never paid to show anger. It was impossible to win a battle with an unscrupulous boor like Kretchvane, or any newsie for that matter. Being a Secret Service agent was about blending in with the woodwork and protecting oneself by utilizing protocol.

"News to me," Garrison said.

"You're a bad liar."

"Joe, for as long as you've known me, have I ever answered even one of your questions?"

"No. But lots of people do. In fact I have them waiting in line. And that includes federal gumshoes like you. People have to have a reason for handing someone up. You've simply never had a reason to tell me secrets. One day you will. You'll get screwed and you'll want to get back at someone."

"How's your unauthorized biography going?"

"Did she tell you to ask that?"

"Who?"

Kretchvane tugged his beard. "Fuck you too, Garrison. But since you asked, I'll tell you that my book will be a best-seller. Not that the scoop in it compares to Clinton jacking off in the Oval office or Bush making a fool of himself, but the facts I've gathered about the First

Lady are nonetheless compelling. I've got her. I've got her *down*."

"Such as?"

"Her father made his millions by being a crook. Her first husband married her for her money, and then dumped her. After he was killed in a boating accident, she told her attorney that she was glad he was dead. She once received treatment for depression. I have the medical records. But you know something, Garrison? I still haven't figured out exactly what makes her tick."

"Who knows what makes any woman tick?"

Kretchvane smiled. "You sound like Jay Leno."

"Do you ever have trouble going to sleep at night, Joe?"

Garrison moved to go by him and Kretchvane stepped in front of him, blocking his way.

"Not at all. You can tell the Dragon Lady that I know about the counterattack against me that she has planned."

"What counterattack is that?"

"She's hired someone to ghostwrite an autobiography for her. She figures that publishing it at the same time my book comes out will soften the effect my book will have on her public image. She's a clever bitch, the Dragon Lady. But you tell her that I'm going to sell a lot of copies anyway. That's what the First Amendment is all about."

"Joe, may we speak off the record?"

"Certainly."

"If you don't get out of my way, I'm going to knock you on your ass."

Kretchvane smiled lewdly. "When are you going to get off her detail and go back to protecting the President?"

"Who knows?"

"Don't you think protecting the President's wife is below you?"

"No. Do you?"

"What do you think of her? Off the record."

"I'm not paid to think."

Garrison shoved by him and continued down the hall.

"Have fun at Camp David," Joe called.

Garrison found Walter Sebastian on the South Lawn, standing near the Presidential helicopter, directing some White House stewards in the process of loading the craft for the trip to Camp David.

"We're loaded up," Sebastian said. "This chopper will shuttle up and back twice, then stand by at the Camp for the Man. We will have another chopper for our detail."

"Can you handle the trip up for me?"

"You're not going?"

"I have to take care of a couple of errands," Garrison said. "I'll take a chopper up later today. I already ran it by the First Lady."

Sebastian nodded. "No problem. By the way, that asshole Joe Kretchvane has been asking questions about you."

"What kind of questions?"

"There's a rumor going around that you may have to take the lie-detector test again and that you showed deception on one of the questions. I heard it from one of the secretaries in the travel office."

"Like they say, there are no secrets in the Secret Service."

"You okay, Pete?"

"It's nothing. I botched one of the questions and

someone is probably trying to make a big deal out of it. You know how they do."

"As I see it, lie detectors are nothing but witchcraft anyway," Sebastian said. "Hell, I've seen guilty crooks pass polygraph examinations one after the other." Sebastian furrowed his brow. "The lie-detector tests are probably a ruse. Wintergreen is telling everyone he is testing every member of the detail because of some routine security matter, but I think it's much bigger than that. I think it's a major case. An internal thing. Why else would they bring in every polygrapher on the East Coast?"

"Who knows?" Garrison said, and his words didn't sound believable.

"Yeah, who knows?" Sebastian said studying him. "What is this errand you have to take care of?"

"Huh?"

"The reason you are missing the flight."

"Uh, a neighbor has one of her old boyfriends stalking her. I told her I would go with her to Metro to make a report."

"What does she look like?"

"Why, you looking for a date?"

Sebastian smiled. "Ask her if she knows how to make decent chili."

"I'll do that."

Garrison anxiously departed the White House by the Executive Office Building exit.

He told himself he had to be flexible, ready for anything. He was alone and would be dealing with a blackmailer. It wasn't going to be easy without backup. Anything could happen in Washington, D.C., an unusual city with hidden agendas, middlemen, procurers, espionage dead drops, and a murder rate that was higher than all the cities of Europe added together. Lacking the sophistication of New York or Paris, D.C. had its own established rituals, cliques, and secrets.

Walking in the direction of the Mayflower Hotel, he could feel the humidity on his face and clothing. It was tangible and onerous, a portent of a summer downpour that could ripple the Potomac, cleanse the Capitol dome, cause a thousand bureaucrats to fight over taxis, and cancel reservations at the Old Ebbitt Grille. It could release pent-up lightning, burst the storm drains along Massachusetts Avenue that would take the inefficient D.C. bureaucracy weeks to repair. It would also lower the District's daily crime rate by more than half because dope dealers would stay inside and have fewer business disputes.

At the Mayflower, a friendly doorman in a white uniform said hello to Garrison and opened a shiny, brass-framed door.

In a high-ceilinged lobby accented with elaborate flower arrangements, a group of Japanese tourists milled about near the front desk. In the lounge area across from a marbled check-in counter, two well-dressed young women sat at a small table, a middle-aged man was reading a book, and three businessmen huddled over some papers. Garrison thought no one looked suspicious. He moved past the elevators to the restaurant, a spacious, open room with white pillars among a sea of linen-covered tables, nearly all of which were occupied. He checked his wristwatch: 11:50 A.M.

Returning to the front desk, he turned right and entered the dimly lit Town and Country cocktail lounge, a wood-paneled replica of an English gentleman's club. On the walls hung framed prints of pointing beagles and setters. Two well-dressed men sat at the bar conversing. At the opposite end of the room some college-age men and women lounged on a sofa. To their right, glass doors led to the street. Garrison slid onto a bar stool. A white-coated young bartender placed a linen napkin in front of him. Garrison wondered if the bartender might be working with the blackmailer. But it was just a thought. Garrison's best guess was that no one in the place had anything to do with the extortion letter. He ordered a Coca-Cola.

At precisely noon, the telephone rang. The bartender walked to the other end of the bar and picked up the receiver.

"Hello . . . Hold the line." The bartender turned. "Is there a Mr. Garrison here?" Garrison motioned to the bartender. The bartender pointed to an extension phone on the wall. "Line one, sir."

Garrison picked up the receiver.

"Hello?"

"This is your concerned photographer," said an electronic voice. "To whom am I speaking?"

Garrison turned toward the wall so he could speak without being overheard. He figured the caller was probably using a handheld electronic voice-changer device. Originally developed for spies, such devices were now commonly available in security-product stores. Garrison strained to hear any background noise coming from the phone. There was the sound of eerie music—a Wagnerian opera? He wondered whether the caller was playing the music to drown some other identifiable background noise.

"I represent the subject of the photo."

"Who is with you?"

"I'm alone."

"Walk across the street to the Sperling Finance Building at 1140 Connecticut. Wait in the coffee shop."

"Wait for what?"

"I'll meet you there."

"What's wrong with this place?"

"Are you refusing to meet me?"

"No. But I'm not going to play games all day either. Why don't you just come here? I'll buy you a drink and we'll straighten this out man-to-man." Garrison wanted to see how far the man would go.

"I'll be at the coffee shop. If you're not there, then I might change my mind and phone the *National Enquirer.*"

"What do you look like?"

"Just sit near the window. I'll find you."

The phone clicked. Garrison hung the receiver back on the hook. He turned to study the faces in the bar. No one was paying any attention to him. He paid for the drink and departed by a door leading to the street.

Garrison moved briskly along the sidewalk, making his way through a bustling afternoon crowd. He walked to the corner and crossed the street, heading toward the Sperling Finance Building. He darted into a candy shop and looked out the display window, waiting for someone on the street to stop suspiciously as surveillants do when their prey suddenly changes course. Nothing untoward occurred. As far as he could tell, no one was following him.

"Can I help you, sir?" said a female clerk.

"No, thanks."

Garrison exited the shop and continued down the street to the Sperling Finance Building, a multistory commercial structure of tinted glass. He went inside and walked across a tiled lobby to an information counter where a bored-looking female uniformed guard sat.

"Where are the pay phones in this building?"

She gave him a puzzled look. "In the basement and the coffee shop."

"Thanks."

As the guard stared at him, Garrison headed across the lobby. The coffee shop was next to a door that read: MOUNTAIN ESCROW INC. Walking into the coffee shop, Garrison was met by the heavy odors of coffee grounds and potato salad. There were about ten tables and not so much as a framed print on the wall or a plastic flower for decoration. The only customers were a young man and an older man, business types, sitting at different tables. *Cafe Drab.* A middle-aged woman stood behind the cash register. Could she be the blackmailer's lookout?

Garrison purchased a cup of coffee. He sat at a table close to the window. He thought it unusual that a blackmailer who was daring enough to extort the First Lady would choose a coffee shop in an office building for a risky face-to-face meeting. The coffee shop provided no ready avenue of escape. It didn't fit with the ruse meeting at the Mayflower and an electronic voice-changer to hide his identity. On the other hand, Garrison knew that, in the end, criminals were screwy, that their actions were often inexplicable.

For the next hour, he diligently studied all those who entered. For a while he thought everyone who came in looked suspicious. But after thirty or so customers came and went, the feeling dissipated. He got up, walked to the hallway, and paced about for a few minutes to stretch his legs, then returned inside. The woman at the cash register kept eyeing him suspiciously. He purchased a hamburger and sat again. The hamburger tasted like potato salad.

By 1:30 P.M. those who'd eaten lunch or purchased takeout food had returned to work. Only Garrison remained. Tired, exasperated, and disappointed, Garrison decided that the blackmailer was being cagey and had set up the meeting just to determine whether he was walking into a trap. Garrison decided to head back to the White House.

Exiting the front door of the office building, he turned left and walked north to Dupont Circle. Crossing the park, he reversed course and headed back the way he came. In front of a clothing store, he studied the reflection in the window glass to determine if he was being followed.

Across the street, a heavyset man slowed his pace, then stopped. Holding a cigar in his teeth, he knelt to tie his shoe, and in doing so glanced in Garrison's direction. Unless Garrison's memory was playing tricks on him, he had seen the man in the Sperling Finance Building coffee shop. If he remembered correctly, shortly after Garrison had arrived, the man had entered, purchased something, then left. As Garrison had trained himself to do long ago, he described the cigar-smoker in his mind as if writing on a chalkboard: forty years old, five-eleven, two hundred pounds, olive complexion, black hair, and eyeglasses. He wore Levi's, white sneakers, and a green T-shirt with the word NASHVILLE stenciled across the front. Garrison figured the cigar-smoker was either the blackmailer himself or an accomplice sent to detect whether Garrison was alone.

Garrison continued on, walking to the corner, where he joined a group of pedestrians waiting for a red light.

Across the street, the cigar-smoker stopped and waited.

Garrison considered the alternatives. He could ignore the man and return to the White House to wait for another blackmail letter. Or he could do something. The mission was to stop the blackmailer from playing his game and to seize the photographs and burn them.

Garrison headed across the street toward him.

The cigar-smoker turned and walked north on Connecticut Avenue.

Garrison followed.

The cigar-smoker began walking faster, dodging pedestrians. He turned the corner at N Street.

Garrison ran after him. Reaching the corner, Garrison saw the cigar-smoker was out of sight. To Garrison's left, a bank building covered the entire block. On the other side of the street was a multistoried parking structure with open walls and a ground-level entrance/exit. He walked to the bank's entrance, where a tall, dark-haired woman was smoking a cigarette. She had a bank-employee photo identification card pinned to her suit jacket. Garrison held out his badge.

"Did you see a man in a green T-shirt and Levi's come by here just now?"

"He went in there like he was in a hurry," she said with a nod toward the parking garage.

"Is that the only entrance and exit?"

"Yes. What'd he do?"

"Shoplifter."

"Wow."

The way Garrison figured it, Mr. Cigar-Smoker was

laying low in the parking garage. And he was probably watching Garrison.

Garrison turned and walked back the way he came. Turning right, out of sight of anyone in the parking garage, he ran back to Connecticut Avenue and rounded the corner. Making his way to an alley at the rear of the parking garage, he crawled over a retaining wall into the lot's ground level, filled with cars. Moving cautiously, Garrison scanned the entire level, glancing into cars. Then he walked up the ramp to the second level. It was full. He walked slowly along the perimeter, checking cars.

"Looking for someone?"

Garrison turned. The cigar-smoker was holding a gun on him, a Beretta automatic. Garrison felt his face and hands tingle.

"Yeah, you," Garrison said.

"Face the street."

Garrison estimated the distance to the gun. It was just out of reach. If Garrison made a move for his own gun, he would get shot.

"I came here to talk."

"We can talk after I search you."

The stogie was clenched in his teeth. Garrison figured he wasn't bluffing.

"Put the piece down," Garrison said. "Relax."

"Turn around, Goddamn it!"

Garrison reluctantly turned away and raised his hands. Sensing the man moving closer, he considered how to disarm him. He could drive his right elbow backward to catch him in the solar plexus. . . .

Garrison felt a powerful blow at the back of his head,

and all at once, he was overwhelmed by a black wave of pain, heat, and cold.

Garrison heard thunder and rain spattering on something near him, sounds from his childhood. He was lying in bed, dizzy and feverish with pneumonia. There was no money for a doctor and Garrison wondered if the illness, like the recent death of his father, was part of some horrible curse being visited on him—a punishment.

"I'm sick, Mom," Garrison said to his mother, standing at his bedside.

She knelt and placed her hands on his chest, palms down. She looked up to the ceiling with that look on her face.

"Lord, please heal this boy!" she prayed. "Send down your healing angels and set him free of this affliction. Glory be to the King of Kings and the Savior of mankind, healer of the sick. You took his father, but please don't take him. He is an innocent boy and he doesn't deserve this punishment. Forgive him, Lord, and rid him of this fever and sickness."

"Mom, did God make me sick?"

"The Lord is putting you through a trial, son. Like the trial of Daniel in the lions' den. Close your eyes and pray. The Lord will cleanse you."

As his mother continued to pray for him, Garrison lay there weak and dazed. But rather than hope or resignation, he felt only anger. If God had killed his father, then the hell with God. Garrison didn't care any more. He had no fear because all God could do was kill him too.

Garrison had recovered, and his mother witnessed to the divine largesse in front of the congregation of the

Bisbee, Arizona, Foursquare Tabernacle Church with the boy Garrison standing at her side. But when other parishioners asked Garrison to testify about his healing, Garrison said nothing. He didn't believe God cured him. He didn't trust a God who would kill his father. And he no longer trusted his mother. Money or not, she should have gotten him to a doctor.

"You're a man now, Pete," she said a few months later as she prepared to leave town in an Airstream trailer with a man she met at church. "There is no way you can go with us. I love you, son, but you're a man now. You can live with Uncle Travis until you graduate. You'll do just fine."

After she'd left, Garrison took a long walk along the train track at the edge of town. With tears streaming down his face, he'd pondered how his mother could have done this to him.

"Are you okay, mister?"

Garrison opened his eyes. It was raining. He was lying on the parking garage roof.

A uniformed parking lot attendant, a young man wearing a baseball hat, was kneeling next to him.

Garrison saw double and tried to focus his concentration. Had someone fired a bullet into his skull? He struggled to sit up. He touched the back of his head. There was a painful bump, but no blood. He tried to focus on the attendant.

"Did you see what happened?"

"Some guy in a beige Jaguar. He raced out of here like a bat out of hell after he hit you. I got the license number. YFD 927. The ambulance is coming."

"No ambulance. I'm okay."

"You're sure? You're hurt, mister."

"I have to get out of here."

"You ain't thinking right, mister. You got knocked out."

With the attendant's help, Garrison unsteadily came to his feet.

"Thanks."

Garrison reached inside his suit jacket. His gun and wallet were still there. He took out a pen and wrote the license number on a business card in his wallet.

"Where you going?" the man said as Garrison hurried down the ramp. *"You gotta wait for the police!"*

Garrison's head throbbed, and he broke into a full run. He'd been conducting an unofficial investigation for the First Lady and there was nothing else to do but get the hell away. Rounding the corner onto Connecticut Avenue, he heard a distant siren. Seeing that no one was following him, he slowed down to a jog and pondered the situation. The cigar-smoker's use of countersurveillance techniques indicated an unusual degree of sophistication. Changing locations like he'd done wasn't the work of an amateur. But why hadn't the blackmailer wanted to talk to him about money?

A block away, Garrison took out his cellular telephone and reached the White House Secret Service command post. He asked for the duty agent. The line beeped.

"Duty agent speaking."

"This is Garrison. I need you to run a license plate for me."

"Shoot."

"Yankee Foxtrot Delta 927, a Virginia tag."

The agent repeated the license number, then said: "Hold the line." After a silence, he came back. "YFD

927 is a Jaguar registered to someone named Lydell Catering, that's L-Y-D-E-L-L, 1402 Tynan Place, Apartment 133, Northwest."

Garrison wrote the address on the palm of his hand.

"I hear you had some trouble on the lie detector, Pete."

"You know the lie box."

"Very well. When I was on the Bush detail, they sat us on the lie box to find out who wasn't turning in their airline mileage points. We all got ten-day suspensions."

"Too bad. I gotta run. Thanks."

"You bet."

Garrison pressed the OFF button, and then clipped the phone back onto his belt. He had an unsettled feeling as he walked a few blocks to his apartment. He picked up his car, a ten-year-old Ford Taurus he'd purchased after the divorce.

Garrison turned left on Tynan Place and parked his car across the street from 1402, a three-story apartment house with a blue canvas awning over the front entrance. The Northwest D.C. neighborhood just off Wisconsin Avenue was a onetime slum that had been reconditioned by yuppies a few years earlier. Now, fed up with having their bicycles and Volvos stolen by D.C. street people, the yuppies were packing up their replica antique doorknobs and returning to the Maryland and Virginia suburbs where they'd come from.

He got out of his car, locked it, and walked down a sloping driveway to the gated entrance of an underground parking area. He craned his neck to see inside. There was no Jaguar. He walked to the front door, lifted a telephone receiver, and following printed directions, dialed the manager's apartment code. The phone rang.

"Who's there?" a woman said in a shrill voice.

"Federal officer. May I come in?"

"What's it about?"

"Someone who lives here."

A minute later, the door was opened by a middle-aged woman wearing a white dress, white-frame eyeglasses, and a matching scarf wrapped tightly around her skull. Garrison held out his badge.

"Who lives in apartment one-thirty-three?"

"There is no one-thirty-three in this building. In fact, there is no apartment with a thirty-three in it."

"Does Lydell Catering ring a bell with you?"

"No. And I've been manager here for fifteen years."

"How about a white man, about forty years old, with an olive complexion. He smokes cigars. Today he was wearing a green T-shirt with the word Nashville on it. He may drive a late-model, beige Jaguar."

"There are no white men living here and never have been. And no Jaguars. What did that badge of yours say?"

"U.S. Secret Service."

"That boy must have really done something nasty to have the CIA after him."

"Sorry to have bothered you, ma'am."

Stopping at the command post, Garrison sat and tapped computer keys trying to trace Lydell Catering and the beige Jaguar. He checked the multi-agency index, the FBI trace file, and a dozen other indices. Nothing. The Jaguar license plate was phony and Lydell Catering was probably a figment of the blackmailer's imagination.

Garrison felt that he was struggling to swim with an anchor tied to his foot.

CHAPTER 12

IN MARINE ONE, the Presidential helicopter, Garrison sipped coffee from a mug emblazoned with a Presidential seal. As the craft descended slowly toward Camp David, Garrison looked out a window. The sky was clear. Below, Camp David, nestled high in Maryland's Catoctin Mountains, was barely visible from the wooded environment surrounding it, a mixture of bright greens and reddish browns. As protection against airborne attack, giant camouflage tarps covered the roofs of the six cabins, the Secret Service Command Post, and the helicopter-landing pad when they weren't in use. During the flight he'd been trying to make sense of what had happened earlier. He had a dull ache at the back of his head.

"Check your seat belts," Marine pilot Captain Thad Delgarian said.

The passengers were seated against the fuselage, facing in. There were three White House communications technicians and two State Department protocol aides. When the President was at Camp David, the helicopters of the Presidential fleet shuttled back and forth carrying aides and Secret Service personnel. The helicopter bounced slightly as it touched down. After the chopper blades stopped turning, the copilot opened the door and lowered the boarding ramp.

Garrison descended the stairs. Walter Sebastian was waiting with an electric golf cart, the usual mode of transportation around the camp.

"The First Lady wants to see you," Sebastian said. "What do you think it is?"

Garrison dropped his overnight bag on the rack behind the golf-cart seat.

"She asked me to get her some information about travel in—uh—Africa. A possible State Department trip."

"The Man is in the conference cabin with some of the State Department pinheads."

"He's here?"

"He and Wintergreen hopped on the chopper at the last minute. Something about wanting to go over something with the State Department people. The Russian President is in his cabin with his pinheads. The Russian agents are playing cards with our guys who are on break. The Russkies are winning."

Secret Service protection protocol called for each head of state to bring his own bodyguards when traveling. But the responsibility for protection was on the host country's agents. In this case, the Secret Service was in charge of protecting not only the U.S. President, but also the Russian President.

"What's Wintergreen doing here?"

"He made a quick run-through of the posts, then took a staff car and headed back to the house. He said he just wanted to make sure everything was going okay with the Russians."

Garrison nodded.

"Pete, this is the job I want. Camp David resident agent. Think of it. Hunting and fishing every day except when the Man comes up. It's the only job better than the First Lady Detail."

"You'd go stir-crazy."

Leaving Sebastian at the helipad, Garrison drove the golf cart along a narrow macadam road that led past the Command Post and two guest cabins, one that served as a military communications unit. Camp David, a U.S. Navy facility, was used solely for Presidential recreation. Its security system included a camouflaged electrified fence that ringed its uneven perimeter and a platoon of highly trained U.S. Marine sentries manning hidden bunkers equipped with night-vision devices. In more than thirty trees, remote-operated cameras in all-weather boxes scanned the countryside, transmitting continuous images to the state-of-the-art Secret Service Command Post inside an innocuous-looking ranch-style house near the front gate.

After passing through some shadowy spots, Garrison swerved left into a dense forest. Passing three cabins with wide front porches cluttered with lounge chairs and tables, he stopped at the Presidential cabin, a rustic, one-story, three-thousand-square-foot notched-wood structure with a porch overlooking sloping woodland.

Garrison knew that though the cabin looked like a rugged shanty found at ski lodges and other mountain areas, it was different in many ways. The half-log exterior was only a facade covering an inner wall of solid cement reinforced with bomb-and-weapon-resistant Kevlar plugs. An emergency generator and a generous stock of supplies could be found in its basement, which had been reinforced to ground-zero specifications in case of nuclear attack. Garrison was aware that, per the Camp David Manual of Operations, no agent was allowed to venture near the cabin without first obtaining permission from the Detail Leader. Due to the multiple layers of security, there were no fixed guard posts near the cabin.

Inside, Eleanor was sitting on the sofa reading. Garrison shoved the door closed, pushing the dead bolt closed. She got up.

"What happened?"

Garrison briefed her on the phone call he'd received at the Mayflower Hotel, his wait in the Sperling Finance Building coffee shop, the cat-and-mouse with the man in the Nashville T-shirt, copying the license plate, getting hit over the head, and determining that the license plate was fictitious.

"My God. Are you okay?" she said with a look of concern.

"I'll be all right."

Framed cowboy art, landscape photographs, and Western-motif tapestries covered the walls. On a burnished wood dining table was an extravagant arrangement of fresh roses and a large, overflowing fruit basket. Two large overstuffed sofas were burdened with a dozen textured pillows. To Garrison, it was a dream house, the kind of place he would like to build in New Mexico after he retired.

"But the phone call—could you determine anything?"

"He was using an electronic voice-changer. And he had opera music playing during the call—probably to cover some identifiable background noise. Either that or he likes mood music."

From her expression, it became obvious that she saw no humor in the remark.

"I don't understand why he followed you from the hotel."

"He probably wanted to determine if I'd set a trap for him. That's par for the course in extortion cases."

She walked to a bullet-proof window that overlooked a sea of pine trees.

"What now?" she said after a moment.

"It's just a matter of waiting for him to work up the courage to make a second contact. This is about money, and he believes we're ready to pay. He'll call back."

"I'm not so confident," she said wistfully.

"Try not to worry."

"This whole thing makes me sick," she whispered. "It's the not knowing . . . waiting for the press office to call and tell me that the photograph has appeared in one of the tabloids. Sometimes I wish I could live here. Away from everything."

The sound of static came from his Secret Service radio.

"Command Post to Valentine Supervisor."

It was Sebastian. Garrison picked up the radio and pressed the transmit button.

"Go, CP."

"Victory en route to three."

"That's a Roger."

"What is it, Pete?"

"The President is on his way here."

Garrison stood on the front porch as the President drove up in a golf cart with the Presidential seal on the right fender. The President stepped out of the cart. He wore a blue double-breasted sport jacket and Levi's. Garrison thought he looked like a gray-haired model in a men's clothing catalogue.

"Good evening, Mr. President."

"Mrs. Jordan tells me you're doing a fine job, Pete."

"Doing my best, sir."

The President climbed the three steps to the porch.

"She deserves a high-quality agent like you. Of course, no disrespect intended to the other agents who have been assigned to protect her. None whatsoever. Wintergreen did a fine job years ago, and so did Roland Prefontaine. The stewards are bringing dinner over. Will you to join us?"

"I really shouldn't."

The last thing in the world Garrison wanted to do was sit through a dinner with the Man. But how could he decline a Presidential invitation. *What the hell did the Man want?*

The President swept an arm toward the door. "I insist."

Eleanor came to the door.

"Yes, please join us," she said.

Garrison heard tension in her voice.

"Pete, I have a bone to pick with you," the President said after they were all seated in the dining room and the Navy stewards were serving a meal that had been prepared in the Navy mess and brought over in three golf carts.

"Yes, sir?" Garrison said, and felt his eyebrows elevate. There was a buzzing in his ears. He assumed it was blood rushing toward his brain at a hundred miles an hour. Survival-adrenaline blood. High-stress blood. The President conspiratorially leaned forward.

"Early in the Administration, you tackled a man with a knife—at the UN Plaza. The man you saved, the Iranian Prime Minister, is the one who later double-crossed me in the Turkish accords. *You moved too fast.*"

Garrison smiled. "If I would have known, I could have looked the other way."

The President threw his head back in an open-mouth, Bohemian Club laugh. "Thataboy! Let him get the gaffe. Let that pipsqueak get what's coming to him!"

"Russell," Eleanor said reprovingly. "Agent Garrison might think you're serious."

"Pete knows I'm joking, dear. A man has to have a sense of humor in this place, right, Pete?"

"No doubt about that," Garrison said with a glance at Eleanor.

The dining room had oak-paneled walls and was filled with antique American furniture: a mahogany serving cart with marble top, a polished rosewood dining table with legs of exaggerated rounded shapes. An enormous bouquet of flowers in the middle of the dining table matched the yellows and greens of a French Beauvais tapestry on the wall. The silverware and the gold-rimmed china bore the Presidential seal.

A coffee-skinned Filipino steward of singular presence and bearing served prime rib from food trays.

"The President seldom gets a chance to tell a joke," Jordan said. "The damn press distorts everything."

Garrison had been avoiding eye contact with Eleanor. He considered Jordan nothing more than a political hack who would still be begging for contributions to his Senate campaign if it weren't for his wife's money.

After a while, as if he could sense that Garrison wasn't impressed, Jordan began dropping the names of the Secret Service Directors he'd known over the years. To politicians, men who spent their lives unashamedly gauging reaction, anticipating behavior, and making connections, name-dropping was both language and religion. Garrison felt a pang of jealousy, and wondered if Eleanor had told him the truth when she'd mentioned she didn't sleep with him.

"I've often thought the job of a Secret Service agent to be like that of a politician—a lot of split-second decisions," the President said.

More like few decisions after maximum procrastination, thought Garrison.

"Makes sense to me," he said.

"Good decisions are based on values. That's what's been wrong in this country. Old-fashioned American values have been on a downhill slide. People don't think anything is worth standing up for any longer. American malaise is a product of television. It's degraded the thinking process of the nation. People don't know how to think for themselves any longer. That kind of brainwashing has half the people in this country wearing their baseball hat backwards because they've seen it on a sitcom."

"Never thought of it like that."

"Let's change the subject," Eleanor said coldly.

"Certainly, dear," the President said, his eyes cast downward.

Garrison mused that it was when couples were behind closed doors that the truth came out. Eleanor was dominant in the relationship.

A waiter entered the room.

"Excuse me, Mrs. Jordan. You have a priority call."

Eleanor rose to leave. Garrison and the President stood.

"Will you two please sit down," she said on her way out. "I'll just take a second."

The President picked up his wineglass and took a swig. Pursing his lips, he swallowed. "A wonderful woman, the First Lady. I'm a very lucky man."

"It's a pleasure working for her."

Garrison's words sounded absurd. But what the hell was he supposed to say?

The President offered wine. Garrison declined, though he felt like chugging down the entire bottle. The President was tipsy, but he always held his liquor like a true political professional, betrayed only by a slight rosiness high on his cheeks. The President's every action exuded that mixture of magnetism, ambition, and adroitness that people call leadership.

Garrison recalled the President's unique ability to make his voice crack when he wanted to show emotion—a trait often mimicked by Secret Service comedians. Once, when standing beside him at a St. Patrick's Day party in the Diplomatic Reception Room, Garrison had noticed a distinct Irish brogue creep into the President's voice.

Garrison and the other members of the White House Secret Service Detail judged Presidents by their manner and accessibility rather than by any political standard. They regarded President Jordan as a lightweight. Aloof and insensitive, Jordan allowed the members of his youthful, immature staff to tromp on Secret Service agents whenever they pleased. Like President Lyndon Johnson, being the most powerful man in the world still wasn't enough to satisfy his ego. Jordan relished *demonstrating* his power. Once, at an official dinner in France's Elysee Palace, Garrison had watched him stub his cigar on a gold-plated Louis XIV antique dinner plate, then smirk as his hosts squirmed silently in anger.

"When I ran for President she put me over the top," he now said. "I owe that to her. But in politics, Pete, there is always a price to pay. Little favors, little price. And the big favors? They require endless payments. Sometimes the price is too great. Eleanor has had to put up with a lot since we came to D.C. It's not easy when I'm on the road half the time. Her being alone so often when I travel . . . the media pressure. It takes a toll. The White House can be a real House of Pain—a pressure cooker. The reporters have been after her since we got here. Slime merchants, digging up shit from the past. Oh, I have a hundred friends. The big operators—network anchors. I'm talking about the so-called *muckrakers*. Like that prick reporter Joe Kretchvane."

"No one likes newsies—"

"Not even their own damn mothers." The President set his fork down on his plate, sat back, and looked Garrison in the eye. "You know, Pete, the strain the press puts on the First Family can lead to errors of judgment . . . even by those who are otherwise strong and self-reliant. The First Lady and I are a team. If I found out someone was trying to take advantage of her, I'd bury him. You understand what I mean, don't you, Pete?"

Garrison forced a guileless smile. "You're saying that person would suddenly be in a world of hurt."

The President set his glass down. "How do you feel about that kind of thing? A user, a maggot who would take advantage of a woman's weakness?"

"I feel the same way."

Garrison read the President's expression as general suspicion rather than animosity. He might suspect something, but he didn't know for sure. Otherwise, even the President, with his practiced political nature, wouldn't have been able to mask his feelings so fully. The most shocking revelation Garrison had learned since entering the Secret Service was that whether Presidents were former football captains, Rhodes scholars, or business executives, the only thing that distinguished them from other men was the strength of their will to prevail. Garrison had sworn to give his life for Russell Jordan, a second-rate Rotary Club lunch orator.

"That's what I'd thought you'd say, Pete."

Eleanor returned to the room.

"Everything okay, dear?" the President asked.

"Just a minor scheduling problem."

The President left a few minutes later after mentioning something about getting back to the conference center before his aides gave away all the gold in Fort Knox. Garrison followed him outside. As the President went out of sight, Eleanor joined Garrison.

"Pete, did he say anything when I was gone?"

Garrison stared down the road. "He suspects something."

"Pardon me?"

"I told him we were having an affair."

"You *what?*"

Garrison smiled.

"Very funny." She paused. "I hate him."

Her tone surprised him. It was both strident and distracted, as if she were speaking to someone else.

"Eleanor, look, you can't—"

"He's sneaky. Pete, I deserve to be happy too. I've earned it. I've earned it the hard way by putting up with him. "Pete, tell me we can handle this blackmail thing. We can deal with it, right? It's not going to blow up in our faces is it?"

"We can handle it."

But he didn't believe what he was saying. Getting involved with her had been a mistake, an error in judgment, and now there was no easy way out of it. The blackmailer would come back. They always did. It was the nature of the crime.

"Pete, I want to go back to the White House."

"Tonight?"

She took a deep breath and let it out. "I can't stand being here with him."

Later, as the helicopter lifted off the Camp David pad, Garrison sat across from Eleanor as she busied herself making telephone calls. He had the feeling that he'd forgotten something, that there were last-minute errands he couldn't recall.

Arriving at the White House, Garrison led Eleanor inside to the private elevator where Agent Ronan Squires was on duty.

She looked troubled as she stepped into the elevator.

Garrison wanted to ask her if she was okay, but said nothing because of Squires. She said good night, and the elevator doors slowly closed.

"I hear you're riding some kind of a lie-detector beef," Squires said.

"It's nothing."

"Whatever it is, I wish you luck on it."

Garrison said thanks.

"Wintergreen was looking for you a few minutes ago."

Garrison headed down the hall.

CHAPTER 13

BRECKINRIDGE PULLED UP to a guard booth near the front entrance of Fort McNair in southwest Washington. Rolling down the window, she held out her badge to a military police officer.

"Can you direct me to Building 46?"

"The Military Intelligence Corps building is to the right after you pass the Post Exchange, ma'am," the MP said before saluting.

She drove inside. The rain had subsided a few minutes earlier and she'd turned off the windshield wipers. But there was still electricity in the air, indicating to her that a heavier rain might start at any minute.

Kallenstien was eating sunflower seeds from a cellophane package.

"Mr. MP has a Class A butt."

"Go back and tell him."

"No way. But sometimes I wish I was a major slut."

Following the MP's directions, Breckinridge drove past the general officers quarters—brick Colonial homes nestled among drooping elms—and a wide lawn extending to the edge of the water. There is a well-kept, olive-drab uniformity to military installations, no matter where they are in the world.

She parked in one of the marked spaces in front of Building 46, a prefabricated structure with a large air-conditioning unit on its metal roof. A sign read: 511TH MIC—RESEARCH. She and Flanagan got out of the car and walked to the door. A peephole opened. They held up badges. Lieutenant Mary Nicklanovich opened the door and led them inside. Breckinridge had called her earlier and asked for a briefing on the polygraph tests.

"So far we've completed polygraph examinations on about ninety percent of the agents assigned to the White House Detail," Nicklanovich said opening a notebook. "I've had six operators going hucklety-buck night and day to get through the list. The long and short of it is none of the agents showed deception to the questions relating to terrorism or espionage. On the questions relating to protection work, the only deception to any question was shown by Agent Garrison." Nicklanovich turned a page. "He had a problem with two questions: *'Have you violated Secret Service protection protocol during the last thirty days?'* and *'Have you done anything that could harm Presidential security?'*"

Breckinridge was secretly stunned. "How experienced are your operators?"

Nicklanovich took off her eyeglasses. "All are warrant officers with at least ten years' experience on the polygraph machine. Three have actually taught polygraph at Military Police School."

"Is there any possibility that it could have been something in the machine?" Kallenstien asked.

"I'll be happy to show you the charts."

"That's not necessary," Breckinridge said. "What was Garrison's reaction?"

"He had no explanation for the deception—nothing he wanted to clear up anyway," Nicklanovich said. "I got the impression that he had something to hide. Whether it's about what you are investigating remains to be seen. But one thing is for sure. He wasn't comfortable with the questions."

"Sounds like your pal Garrison does have something to hide," Kallenstien said when they returned to the car.

"He isn't involved in any assassination plot."

"Stranger things have happened."

"He once was recommended for the Medal of Valor. Pete Garrison isn't an assassin and he's not involved with the Aryan Disciples."

"I hope you're right."

Breckinridge told herself to ignore the test as she mulled over the facts of the case. Surely Garrison had some explanation for the deception. Hell, everyone in security work had seen false results from the polygraph at one time or another. The test itself was nothing more than modern witchcraft based on the assumption that telling the truth had something to do with one's fingertips perspiring. But why did Garrison fail the test?

CHAPTER 14

GARRISON SAT IN Wintergreen's office, facing him across a shiny desk and wondering why Wintergreen called him in.

"I understand you had a one-on-one with the Man."

"Not exactly. He asked me to join him and the First Lady for dinner."

"What did he have to say?"

"Nothing more than small talk."

Wintergreen tapped a pencil on the desk. "He didn't have to invite you to dinner to do that."

"It was a spur-of-the-moment thing. He just asked me to join them."

Garrison figured Wintergreen was being mindful of the power of a bureaucratic end run. He wanted to make sure he wasn't being left out of anything—that Garrison wasn't plotting to take his job. Wintergreen required agents to write a memorandum to him delineating any non-official contact with a protectee. The policy was ostensibly to discourage problems that came with fraternizing with protectees, but Garrison knew the real reason. Wintergreen wanted to monitor agents who might be trying to ingratiate themselves with a protectee to help them get a promotion in the same way Wintergreen had maneuvered himself into the Directorship by getting next to President Jordan. Wintergreen swiveled his chair to the right, stared out the window for a moment, and then swiveled back.

"It's unusual for the Man to want to break bread with an agent like that, wouldn't you say?"

"I didn't feel I could decline his invitation without being rude."

"Sometimes, when an agent gets assigned to a Family detail, when he comes in close contact with the First Family, he forgets his role is nothing more than bodyguard. When that happens is when problems start. I call it the *disease of distorted self-image*."

"As far as the job goes, my self-image is that of a barking seal."

Wintergreen stopped glaring at him, and the edges of his mouth rose in mirth.

"Barking seal. I like that." Then Wintergreen abruptly stopped laughing. "The Jordans, just like the Bushes and the Clintons and before them, are nothing more than politicians who convinced the right fat cats to bankroll their campaign. A few months from now, they'll be on a golf course and two other sets of capped teeth will arrive to take their place. In the meantime, you and I will still be here. We outlast these people, Pete. Keep that in mind."

"I read you loud and clear, Mr. Director."

"Thanks for stopping by, Pete."

Garrison walked out the door and moved past desk partitions labeled with government-issue brass name-plates designating members of Wintergreen's staff: Assistant Directors Houlihan, Kennedy, O'Keefe, and Shanahan.

After stopping at Blackie's Lounge for a martini and a hamburger, Garrison walked to his apartment and went to bed. The booze and food had been exactly the right mix. He closed his eyes and immediately dropped into sleep.

CHAPTER 15

IT WAS TWO A.M., and the woods surrounding Camp David loomed as a vast blackness, lit only by an occasional security light.

"Circuit breakers."

"Checked," said Marine Captain Thad Delgarian responding to his copilot, Lieutenant Fernando Gomez, as they went through the preflight checklist in the cockpit of Marine One, the President's personal helicopter.

"Controls."

Delgarian moved the stick. "Cleared."

"I don't know about you, but I'm tired of sitting around here all damn day and night."

"Just one more day toward twenty, Fernando."

Having received word that the President had decided to motorcade back to the White House with the Russian President rather than fly, Delgarian had charted a flight to Andrews Air Force Base. Delgarian was glad to be wrapping up the mission after shuttling passengers back and forth from the White House all day and being on standby since eight P.M. the night before waiting to fly the President back to D.C. Delgarian's chopper was the last craft at Camp David and he would have left earlier, but the overly cautious Secret Service had ordered that a chopper remain on standby in case the Presidential motorcade broke down. Now, Delgarian had finally been released from duty.

"Fuel."

"Check."

Finally, the checklist was completed.

"Start the auxiliary, Fernando. We're outta here."

The engine started. After going through another checklist, Delgarian maneuvered the controls to develop airspeed. After liftoff, he waited a few moments before pushing the stick forward. Marine One swept in an upward arc over the tree line, heading nose-down south into blackness. Delgarian glanced back at Camp David, its perimeter security lights giving off an eerie, greenish glow. He was proud to be a Marine and proud to have been chosen as one of the pilots of Marine One, also known as Angel One, the President's helicopter. He'd been flying the President for seven years, and had chosen his pal Gomez to be his copilot. As far as Delgarian was concerned, he had the best job in the Marine Corps. He was part of the elite of the elite. The benefits definitely outweighed the inconveniences of submitting to a complete Secret Service physical examination every four weeks and undergoing a background investigation every year. He was on his own, and didn't have to put up with the inspections and other routine bullshit he'd experienced during his last assignment, running back-to-back training missions at Parris Island.

"I'll bet that bride of yours will be happy to see you home, Fernando."

"That is, if she hasn't filed for divorce."

Because of a recent crisis in Albania, Fernando had had to cut short his honeymoon to fill in on the White House helicopter squadron. They'd been on flight duty, away from home for two weeks.

Delgarian laughed. "You'd better buy you some posies and a box of Almond Roca."

Delgarian had been married for more than twenty years and his wife, Harriet, was used to him being gone for long periods of time. But Fernando and his spouse had a lot to learn about the military life.

"I'll tell you one thing. The *second* time I'm going to make love to her is *after* I put down my suitcase."

"I roger that."

Delgarian looked below into a blue and black forest and could see stretches of Interstate 270, a fuzzy glow-worm cutting through inky black. On either side were the lights of farmhouses. There was nothing better than being a chopper pilot—except, of course, being a Marine. He was tired and he would be glad to get back to Andrews Air Force Base and catch up on his sleep. Nothing was more tiring than long days at Camp David killing time on standby flight duty. And he hadn't even gotten to fly the Man back to the White House.

Suddenly, there was an explosion. The craft rocked violently to the right.

Delgarian fought the stick as the helicopter spun out of control.

"Fernando!"

Delgarian struggled to manipulate the controls. Fernando was bleeding and unconscious, slumped forward in his safety harness. And there was smoke in the cabin and a spray of red on the windscreen. The radio . . .

"Marine One to Control! Declaring an emergency five minutes southwest of Camp David. Explosion on board."

"Roger your emergency, Angel One," someone said.

Blood gushed from Delgarian's left leg. There was a hole in the fuselage and cold air blew into the cabin. The craft spun wildly, pulling him back and forth. He was going down.

Delgarian flashed back to the Gulf War—trying to land with shrapnel damage to his craft. The throttle hadn't worked for a while then; finally, he'd regained control and managed to land safely. He'd been spared. But nothing was working now. This was it. He'd used up his luck.

As the craft turned fully upside down, carrying him toward earth as military wreckage, he heard himself shouting. . . .

CHAPTER 16

IT WAS DARK as Martha Breckinridge sped north, through an unlighted, wooded area with little traffic. She was about fifty miles from Washington, D.C., on Highway 194. Director Wintergreen had awakened her an hour earlier with a telephone call, informing her of the helicopter crash.

"I want you to assume control of the investigation, classify it top secret, and make sure the press is kept away," he'd said.

"194 near Le Gore, Maryland," Kallenstien said referring to "Mr. Grid," the specially marked Secret Service world map book that was open on her lap. "We should be close. I guess it was too much for Wintergreen to give you the coordinates. But that's assuming he knows how to read a map. . . ."

Breckinridge nodded. Having awakened from a sound

sleep, she was still trying to will herself awake. She needed a cup of coffee.

"They must think this is an Aryan Disciples thing if they called you," Kallenstien said.

Kallenstien pointed to the right of the highway, toward flashing red and yellow lights. As they drove closer, the scene came into view: A police light truck was aiming its heavy candlepower at a jumble of twisted, blackened helicopter wreckage surrounded by a grayish pool of fire-retardant foam. Breckinridge slowed and then swerved onto an unpaved road that followed the edge of a furrowed field that was indented with tire tracks from the three fire engines and four police cars parked nearby. At the edge of the foam, yellow ponchos covered two bodies.

Breckinridge stopped the car and turned off the engine. They got out. They trudged across the field toward the destruction. A uniformed police officer stopped them. They showed badges and the officer led them to a man wearing Levi's and a leather jacket who was making notes on an illuminated clipboard. The officer told him they were Secret Service agents.

"I'm Ernest Santovecchia, National Transportation Safety Board. I'm in charge here."

Breckinridge introduced herself and Kallenstien. Santovecchia didn't offer his hand.

"Whatayahave so far?" Breckinridge asked.

"I'm not able to share that with you without authorization."

"Mr. Santovecchia, have you ever met the Director of your agency?" Breckinridge asked politely.

Santovecchia furrowed his brow. "Once."

Kallenstien took out her cellular phone and dialed a number.

"Would you recognize his voice?" Breckinridge asked.

"I think so."

Kallenstien handed the phone to Breckinridge.

"White House Signal Board," a female operator said.

"This is Agent Breckinridge—Protective Research Division. I need the Director of the National Transportation Safety Board on a secure line. Authorization Blue Sunday. Flash priority."

"Blue Sunday?"

"Roger."

"Stand by, Agent Breckinridge."

Less than a minute later, the phone beeped and a man came on the line.

"Agent Breckinridge? This is Leo Whitehall, Director of the National Transportation Safety Board."

"You're aware of the Marine One incident?"

"Yes—"

"I'm standing here with Mr. Santovecchia, who works for you. I want you to instruct him to cooperate with me."

"You are invoking Blue Sunday?"

"Correct."

She handed Santovecchia the phone. Blue Sunday was a code word for Standing Executive Order 350-8, requiring every government agency, including all branches of the military, to cooperate with U.S. Secret Service agents in the performance of their protective and investigative responsibilities relating to the protection of the President.

"Sir? Yes, sir."

Santovecchia looked dumbfounded as he handed Breckinridge the phone.

"All I have at this point is that the helicopter had transported the First Lady and some other officials to Camp David yesterday and was scheduled to fly the President back to the House last night," Santovecchia said. "The President wasn't on board this flight because, at the last minute, he decided to motorcade back to D.C. with the Russian President. The pilot had orders to return to Andrews Air Force Base as a deadhead, and reported an explosion in the aircraft before he went down."

"Have you established that it, in fact, was an explosion?" Breckinridge asked.

He led them to the wreckage and shined his flashlight on a large hole in the starboard side. The metal was twisted from inside out. There was faint whiteness on the shards.

"That's bomb damage, all right," Kallenstien said.

Breckinridge knelt close. "The bomb was planted inside."

"Sounds like you people had a security problem," Santovecchia said.

"That white substance," Breckinridge said. "Have you ever seen anything like that before?"

"I tested it with a field kit. It's military C-4. The whiteness is because it has a slow burn rate, unlike black powder—"

"You have experience investigating bomb incidents like this?" Kallenstien asked.

"Dozens of them."

Breckinridge stood. "Have you told anyone else about your findings?"

"Absolutely not. And there have been no press inquiries. The public safety agencies here still have no idea that this is Marine One."

"Let no one else approach the wreckage," Breckinridge said. "Move the police line back and stand by here for the FBI and ATF forensic teams. I want everything humanly possible done to insure that we extract every bit of physical evidence from this wreckage—without regard to cost or manpower. That means, if necessary, I can provide you a hundred agents or anything else you need. And I am ordering you not to tell anyone except your Director what I just said. This investigation is now classified top secret. Agent Kallenstien will be working with you."

"Yes, ma'am."

"I want you to put out a cover story through your press-relations people that it *wasn't* foul play—that you are sure it is something else."

"Am I to take that as an order under your authority?"

"Yes."

"A rotor problem," Kallenstien said.

"That should fly," he said making a note on his clipboard.

"Sounds good to me."

Santovecchia moved toward a group of officers standing near a fire engine.

Breckinridge dialed the White House Signal Board emergency line.

"This is Agent Breckinridge, Protective Research Division," she said to the operator. "I'm calling a K-3 Special Incident. Have the Agents-in-Charge of Liaison Division and Forensic Division meet me on Tac Four at—"

"Grid 13 Yankee One," Kallenstien said.

Breckinridge repeated the grid designation.

"Wilco, Breckinridge," said the operator. Breckinridge pressed OFF.

"It had to be an agent," Kallenstien said softly so the police office standing nearby wouldn't hear.

Breckinridge nodded. Kallenstien was right. No one else except the pilots and the Secret Service, and a few communications technicians and State Department employees, had been in the Presidential helicopter.

A sedan swerved off the highway onto the dirt road and drove to the officer standing at the perimeter. Wintergreen got out of the car and trudged through the dirt to join Breckinridge and Kallenstien. Breckinridge introduced him to Santovecchia.

"I'd like to speak to Breckinridge alone," Wintergreen said.

Kallenstien and Santovecchia moved away.

"Is it sabotage, Martha?"

"Yes."

"What is your theory?"

"It had to be someone with access."

"What is your investigative plan?"

"I'll develop suspects from the helicopter access list. It could be someone in the Marine maintenance crew."

"And if those leads don't pan out?"

"Then I'll start interviewing the agents who had access to the chopper."

He nodded. "Pete Garrison had problems with the polygraph test. No one knows except the polygraph examiner and me. Garrison showed deception when asked about Presidential security. It was her opinion that he was definitely hiding something. She gave him a chance to clear up whatever it was, but he declined. I consider it odd. Very odd."

"Garrison? It could be a mistake on a polygraph—"

"He is a bomb expert. U.S. Army trained. His first assignment in the Service was to the bomb detail."

"I'm aware of that, but—"

"But what?"

"I know him. He doesn't . . . He couldn't—" Wintergreen was actually naming Pete as a suspect, and she was astounded.

"Do you agree it's possible he might be involved?"

There was a silence as Breckinridge ruminated over what he was saying. "I guess anything is possible."

"I was doing some thinking on the drive out. It occurred to me that maybe this thing with Garrison's informant—Hightower—could be a scenario he created to cover his tracks. He could be trying to make it look like there is some other agent working for the Aryan Disciples, when in actuality it's him. Garrison is clever enough to realize that part of a Presidential assassination attempt would be a veil to cover up the ones who did it—some disinformation planted here and there to throw us off. This would be common."

"Let me get this straight, Mr. Director. Are you saying that you believe that both Garrison and his informant Frank Hightower may be in on the assassination attempt?"

"Yes. But I'm not making any direct accusations at this point. You and I are speaking in confidence. But I believe the Garrison angle needs to be fully explored. The chopper blew up. It goes without saying that the person who did it had to have special access. No outsider got into one of our choppers—or into Camp David for that matter."

"What would be Garrison's motive?"

Wintergreen stared at the wreckage, and the emergency lights danced across his face.

"That's for you to find out. That is, unless you would rather be removed from the case. I should have asked this before. Are you a close friend of Garrison?"

"No, but—"

"What is it, Martha? Tell me what is on your mind."

"Frankly, I don't think Garrison is the kind of person who would ever get involved in anything like that."

"That's the way it is in these kinds of cases. It's always an insider *who no one suspects*. Would you rather have me assign someone else to handle the investigation? If so, tell me now. I certainly won't hold it against you."

"I'll handle the case."

"I'm looking for a full-court press—taking the case wherever it goes. I want you to pull out all the stops."

"I'll handle it."

"I don't see Garrison falling for any extremist line. If I were you, I'd concentrate on money as a motive. The Aryan Disciples have plenty of it. Maybe Garrison wanted to get rich."

"I'll look into it."

"If we have someone operating us from the inside, we have no time to waste. Not one second. Cut Garrison out of the loop in your investigation from here on. Avoid him. He is to be considered a suspect. Is that clear?"

"Yes."

But she couldn't see Garrison as a turncoat. It just didn't fit with what she knew about him.

"Keep me informed at every step."

"Okay."

As he walked back toward his car, the sun was coming up. Breckinridge turned her head from the brightness.

"What was that all about?" Kallenstien asked.

Breckinridge told her what Wintergreen had said.

"Goddamn."

"Rachel, I don't think Garrison is guilty of anything like this."

Breckinridge shifted her weight from one foot to another. There was dirt in her shoes.

"I don't either," said Kallenstien. "As far as I am concerned, lie detectors are baloney."

"Once, when I was in the police department, they called me in to the Internal Affairs office and told me that an informant had named my partner as having been involved in a series of on-duty burglaries. There had been no question then. I'd had a feeling he'd been up to no good for a long time, but I just couldn't prove it. But Garrison doesn't fit with being involved in terrorism or, for that matter, being compromised at all. Unless I'm missing something, unless Garrison has some evil part of his personality that is completely hidden, Wintergreen is barking up the wrong tree. Garrison isn't good for this. Someone could say the same thing about you or me."

"On the other hand, there is always the unknown about people. You think you know someone, and then all of a sudden the truth comes out."

"I have a funny feeling about all of this." Breckinridge knew there was no end to disappointments in law enforcement and security work. But it didn't matter. "What happened to Charlie . . . and now this. Nothing like this has ever happened before in the Service. Something is wrong."

"Garrison being in with the bad guys could wreck our operations. There is no doubt about that."

Kallenstien nodded. "And what if it isn't him? What then?"

"Then someone else—"

"Someone in headquarters. Someone high up in the chain. This isn't some junior agent who planned this one out."

CHAPTER 17

THE TELEPHONE RANG. Garrison awoke, and reached to the nightstand and picked up the receiver.

"Hello."

"This is White House Signal Operator 23," a woman said. "I just got a call from someone named Frank who was trying to reach you. He wouldn't give his last name and said he wanted to talk to you about a Presidential threat. He said it was an emergency. He left a phone number."

"Hold on."

Garrison dropped his feet to the floor, opened the nightstand drawer, and took out a pen and pad. He wrote down the number she gave him.

"Thanks."

He pressed the cradle, and then dialed the number. Hightower answered on the first ring.

"What's up, Frank?"

"We need to meet."

Garrison glanced at the clock radio. The display showed 6:03 A.M.

"The museum is closed to the public right now."

"How about, say, K Street and Connecticut?"

"See you there in a half hour."

Garrison put the receiver down and rubbed his eyes. It wasn't unusual for Hightower to reach him through the White House operator. During Garrison's PRD days, he'd met Hightower often on his way to work. Hightower knew Garrison walked, rather than drove to work every day. Garrison ran a hand through his hair. He'd come to believe that Hightower was trying to put something over on him. There was no one issue on which he could base his suspicion, but rather a combination of things, including Hightower's tone of voice and body language, his omission of certain relevant facts, and the way he was doling out information. All of this was nothing like when Garrison had dealt with him in the past. It was as if Hightower might be working from a prepared script. Garrison told himself that it had gone on long enough. He was going to confront Hightower and insist that he take a polygraph test. It had come to that. Garrison knew that informants were indispensable to both intelligence and security work, but they were also dangerous.

Garrison dressed and put on his gun and handcuffs. Locking his apartment, he departed.

As he walked along Rhode Island Avenue toward M Street, the commuter traffic was beginning to pick up. Garrison worried about the lie-detector test he'd submitted to. He hoped the operator had chalked up his problems with some of the questions to an anomaly. If not, he was going to be in for more questioning.

A brown late-model Honda with tinted windows slowly drove by. The driver wore dark glasses and a baseball hat. Maybe the driver was lost, Garrison told himself. After all, though Washington, D.C., was the best-planned city in the U.S., tourists often had trouble finding their way through its labyrinth of one-way streets. As Garrison neared the middle of the block, the Honda drove past again. Was the driver eyeing him? People lost in traffic usually focused on street signs and landmarks rather than pedestrians. What was he up to? Garrison crossed the street to an outdoor newsstand adjacent to St. Matthew's Cathedral. He picked up a copy of the *Washington Post.*

"Don't look now," Garrison said to the seller, a young dark-skinned man. "But is there a Honda across the street?"

The man focused across the street. "Yes."

"The driver. What's he doing?"

"Looking this way. Is everything okay, mister?"

"I'm not sure."

Garrison paid for the paper, then tucked it under his arm and continued along the street. At the corner, he headed south on Connecticut Avenue.

The Honda drove by.

Reaching De Sales Street, Garrison saw the Honda again coming north on Connecticut. About a half block up the street, it pulled to the curb in a no-parking zone. If Garrison continued the way he was going, he would have to pass by it. He knew that a trained surveillance agent would never park facing him. They would park farther away and use binoculars to monitor him. But if

the driver wasn't a Secret Service agent assigned to surveillance duties, who was he? Garrison knew he'd made
enemies working against terrorist groups. And he knew
that terrorists frequently talked about how they'd like to
kill a federal agent. Could the Aryan Disciples have targeted him? He decided to find out.

South of K Street, he turned left and walked into an
office building. Crossing the lobby, he asked a young
woman stepping out of the elevator for directions to the
rear exit. She pointed. Making his way out the back
door, he followed an alley east to 18th Street, then
turned south to K Street. Heading back to Connecticut
Avenue, he circled behind the Honda. Garrison pulled
his SIG-Sauer. Holding it under the newspaper, he
walked into the street. Remaining in what he believed
was the driver's blind spot, he approached the Honda
from behind, moving toward the driver's door. Reaching
the car, Garrison held his badge out. The man reacted
with an audible "uh" sound.

"Why are you following me?"

"I'm just waiting for someone."

Garrison's danger radar alerted a sixth-sense alarm
that activated when the right stimuli reached the brain's
danger-survival center. The driver was wearing skin-
colored latex gloves. He had a thin, red scar under his
left eye. Garrison pictured him without the cap and sunglasses he was wearing. Could he be Garth Alexander,
the mercenary whose room Garrison and Breckinridge
had searched at the Plantation Motel? Garrison recalled
that in Alexander's mug shot that Breckinridge had
shown him, Alexander had had black hair. But now his
hair was reddish. It was a wig. Garrison hadn't recognized him earlier because of the tinted window glass.

"Turn off the engine and put the keys on the dashboard."

"Whatever you say, Officer."

Alexander's expression unsettled Garrison. It could best be described as between anger and desperation; a trapped appearance that Garrison had seen before. As Alexander complied, his carotid artery pulsated abnormally and his hands trembled. Alexander was going to do something. He was going to *commit*.

Garrison fingered the trigger on his SIG-Sauer.

"Now get out of the car and keep your hands where I can see them."

"Take it easy," Alexander said. "I'm getting out."

Alexander opened the door with his left hand. As he climbed out of the car, his right hand dropped just for a moment and he whirled toward Garrison with a revolver in his hand.

Garrison fired twice, his right hand jerking upward with each deafening shot. Alexander flew back into the car door and slumped down, his revolver clattering onto the pavement. Both hands gripping his SIG-Sauer in the combat-firing position, Garrison moved closer and kicked Alexander's gun away. Alexander was dead.

Standing at the curb, next to a police car, Garrison had the feeling that everything was happening in slow motion. A small crowd of gawkers had gathered on the sidewalk to stare at Alexander's sheet-covered corpse. The curb lane had been blocked off with police evidence tape, and uniformed Metro officers and detectives were moving about.

Two black Mercurys swerved around the corner and pulled to the yellow-tape line. Wintergreen got out of the first car. Wintergreen's adjutant, Gil Flanagan, and Agent Ted Beatty got out of the second car. Beatty was a member of SOT, the Secret Service Special Operations Team of twelve handpicked agents headed by Flanagan.

"You okay, Pete?" Wintergreen asked.

Garrison nodded. He detected an edgy lilt in Wintergreen's voice. And the man was slightly pale. Wintergreen was shaken.

"It was Alexander. The mercenary Hightower told me had been hired by the Aryan Disciples."

Flanagan and Beatty were staring at him. "How did it go down?"

"I spotted a car following me. I ordered him out of his car. He drew down on me."

Wintergreen coughed dryly. "I've assigned Flanagan to take over the investigation of this shooting."

"Why would SOT handle this rather than the police department?"

"This incident and Marine One going down. I've already spoken with the Chief of Police—"

"Marine One?"

"It crashed a few hours ago coming back from the Camp. The pilot and copilot were killed. It looks like sabotage. We're exerting our authority under the Federal Anti-Terrorist Statute."

The law empowered the Secret Service to assume control of any felony investigation involving possible terrorism. Congress had passed it as a response to a wave of terrorist incidents.

"My God—"

"Pete, I'm relieving you of duty. I'll have to ask for your gun and badge."

Garrison tried to comprehend what was going on. He felt coldness around his lips.

"You've got this all wrong—"

"I order you to surrender your weapon."

Flanagan and Beatty moved closer.

"You think I had something to do with the sabotage?" Wintergreen held out his hand. "The gun, Pete."

Garrison studied him for a moment, then reached inside his coat and handed over the gun. Wintergreen handed it to Flanagan.

"Go with Flanagan. He will take your statement and he will handle any follow-up investigation."

"Do you know something that I don't?" Garrison asked.

"There are a lot of things in the air right now, Pete. Until we get them ironed out, it's going to be somewhat confusing. I suggest you tell the complete truth."

"Someone just tried to kill me and I am being treated as a suspect. I deserve an explanation."

"My orders are that you be interviewed concerning possible sabotage and other crimes."

"You consider me a suspect?"

"Yes. Now, if you'll excuse me."

Wintergreen moved away and began conferring in whispers with two police detectives.

Beatty frisked Garrison.

"Get in the car," Flanagan said.

CHAPTER 18

"WHERE ARE WE going?" Garrison asked.

He was sitting in the backseat of Flanagan's Mercury with Beatty as Flanagan turned off Connecticut Avenue.

Flanagan cleared his throat. "Eight-Two-Nine."

"Why a safe house?"

"That's our choice."

"What the hell is this all about?"

"We can talk when we get there."

"Oh, am I bothering you?" Garrison asked.

Flanagan and Beatty exchanged a glance. Surely they wouldn't be treating him like this unless they had some evidence against him. Something was up. Something big.

In Georgetown, Flanagan turned off Wisconsin Avenue onto Westboro Avenue, and veered into the driveway of a two-story, Georgian-style house with high columns, an attached garage, and a towering oak tree in the middle of the front lawn. It was a quiet neighborhood: a suburban cul-de-sac lined with rose-red brick-front dwellings. Though there was no address plate on the house, Garrison knew the address: 829 Westboro. He'd once spent three days there debriefing an Iraqi defector about a terrorist plan to bomb the President during a dedication ceremony at the Washington Monument.

In the dining room, the musty smell and the spider-webs against the baseboards stimulated Garrison's memory. He wondered if anyone had so much as vacuumed the place since he'd last been there. The house was one of three Secret Service safe houses in Washington, D.C., all leased, single-family homes in quiet, middle-class neighborhoods where foreign intelligence agents or terrorist spies would be readily detected if they tried to surveil. The safe houses were used for debriefing intelligence sources and, occasionally, to hide some foreign dignitary whose life was in jeopardy. When the Secret Service received specific, credible information about a threat to a protectee, the security plan often included what was known as a "Veil" operation: making it appear the protectee was residing in a particular hotel when, in actuality, he was ensconced in a safe house. Agents actually stood post at the empty hotel room as if the protectee were there. "Veil operations," as they were known in Secret Service lingo, were popular with the agents assigned to protect the empty hotel room. Other than the one agent posted at the door to make it appear like the dignitary was present, they could play poker all day without supervision.

"I'll open some windows," Beatty said.

He left the room, and there was the sound of his footsteps on the stairs. Flanagan sat across the table from Garrison. Opening his briefcase, he took out a clearplastic, laminated three-by-five card and read:

"Special Agent Pete Garrison, Secret Service Badge Number 961, be advised that you are the subject of an official investigation concerning the attempted assassination of the President of the United States. Any refusal on your part to answer questions will be deemed a violation of a direct order given you by the Director of the U.S. Secret Service and will result in the immediate termination of your federal employment. Do you understand what I have just read to you?"

Garrison nodded.

"I didn't hear you," Flanagan said.

"Yes. I understand my rights."

Garrison assumed what he was saying was being recorded. Beatty had gone upstairs to the listening post in the second-floor bedroom where he could monitor the sound and video recorders that were installed in every room. Garrison knew the microphones and "pinhole" video cameras hidden in the walls were invisible to all except trained technicians.

"You know the routine," Flanagan said.

"You're talking to a fellow agent, Flanagan. What's going on?"

"A post-shooting interview."

"Then why the warning of rights and the recorders?"

"This is a suspect interview."

"What is the charge?"

"Murder and possible sabotage."

"You're out of your mind."

Flanagan opened his briefcase, took out a sheet of

paper, and then placed Garrison's gun inside before closing it. He handed the paper to Garrison.

"That is a copy of the Marine One flight manifest."

"And?"

"Read it."

"Okay," he said impatiently. "There were two State Department protocol types and three White House communications technicians in the chopper when I came up. The chopper made two trips. On the first trip the Director was on board with the First Lady, the Man, Junior Sebastian, and two military aides. Would you like me to read off the names?"

"For your flight. Did you see anyone on board who isn't listed there?"

"No."

Let Flanagan ask his questions so he could figure what the hell was going on, Garrison thought. Flanagan sat back in his chair.

"Did you notice anything unusual during the flight?"

"No."

"Would it be possible for someone who was a passenger on the flight you were on to plant a bomb?"

"Anything is possible."

"Who do you think planted the bomb in Marine One?"

"I have no idea."

"Dangerous people in those right-wing extremist groups. Wouldn't you say?"

"What are you getting at?" Garrison said.

Flanagan stared at him. "The Aryan Disciples."

"Why don't you forget the roundabout questions and just come out with it. *What about the Aryan Disciples?*"

"Someone just tried to kill you. I wonder why."

"Are you telling me you have information that the

Aryan Disciples sent Alexander to kill me? Is that what you are saying?"

"The Disciples have vowed to kill the President, Garrison. If they wanted to plant a bomb in his chopper, they'd need an insider to help them, wouldn't you say?"

Garrison straightened his chair. He felt like the world was swirling out of control, as if the room itself was off-kilter, like some sleazy, county fair fun house.

"Let me get this straight. Are you trying to connect me to the chopper bombing?"

"I'm just asking questions."

"Other than the fact that I am a trained explosive ordnance technician, what leads you to believe that I had anything to do with the bombing?"

"I'm not here to answer questions. Just ask them."

"Then ask away and let's get this over with because you are on a major, wild-goose chase and you are wasting my time."

Flanagan formed his mouth into a sideways smile. "Has any terrorist organization approached you and asked for favors?"

Garrison swallowed the anger bubbling up in him. "No."

Flanagan exhaled loudly. "No need to take things personal. Other than as part of your official duties as a U.S. Secret Service agent, have you had any contact with the Aryan Disciples?"

"No."

Flanagan stood, adjusted his trousers, and walked to the door. Tilting his head toward the stairs, he shouted.

"Dwight, come down here!"

Who the hell is Dwight? Garrison heard footsteps descending the stairs.

The man who'd followed Garrison from the Sperling Finance Building—the man who'd knocked him out in the parking garage—walked into the room smoking a cigar. Instead of the NASHVILLE T-shirt, he was wearing a charcoal-gray business suit. Garrison felt like he'd just been tossed off a boat into the Arctic Sea.

"Garrison, meet FBI Special Agent Dwight Catherwood," Flanagan said.

Holding the cigar between his teeth, Catherwood reached inside his suit jacket, took out a black leather folder, and opened it to display a gold FBI badge with picture-card identification.

"Sorry about having to down you."

"Try it sometime when I'm not looking the other way."

Catherwood puffed the cigar and shoved his badge back into his pocket.

"Thanks, Dwight," Flanagan said. "I'll give you a call later."

Catherwood walked out of the room. Moments later, there was the sound of the front door opening, then closing. Flanagan tapped his pen on the table.

"What were you doing at the Sperling Finance Building?"

Garrison knew his choices were limited. He could say he'd been at the Sperling Finance Building conducting an unofficial investigation for someone on the White House staff. But experience told him that an answer involving a partial truth would lead inevitably to other, more probing questions that would eventually unravel the lie. The other alternative was to reveal his interlude with Eleanor and his desire to keep their affair secret as the reasons he'd been at the Sperling Finance Building.

To do so would violate his scruples and destroy both Eleanor's reputation and his Secret Service career. The course was clear. FBI or not, he was innocent and the investigation would surely clear him. He told himself that no matter how unusual it might seem to others that he had been at the Sperling Finance Building, there was nothing else that would tend to incriminate him. In the end, after the investigation was completed, Flanagan and everyone else would see that they had made fools of themselves by considering him a suspect.

"Having coffee."

"Took you quite a while to answer that."

"So what? Next question."

Flanagan took a paper from his briefcase and studied it for a moment, then thumbed to the second page.

"This FBI report shows that you were in the coffee shop for over two hours. Do you often sit in a coffee shop that long?"

"I don't know."

"When people get involved in things they shouldn't, sometimes they have bad luck—like when some little old lady who is looking out the window happens to see a bank robber climbing into his getaway car and writes down the license number. It's the luck of the draw— sheer misfortune. That's what happened to you. Hell, you had no way of knowing that the FBI had been staking out the Aryan Disciples' front office in the Sperling Finance Building. Its called Mountain Escrow Incorporated, and the coffee shop next door to it is where the deals are done. For payoffs, they send someone into the coffee shop to leave an envelope on the table. You walked into an FBI stakeout."

Garrison's throat felt dry. "Being in a building where

terrorists rent an office isn't evidence of anything. And in case it may have slipped your mind, I just killed an Aryan Disciples hit man. Do you think *killing* them is evidence of *being in* with them?"

Flanagan stood and shrugged off his suit jacket. "Maybe that was part of the plan they didn't tell you about. Maybe they had to get rid of you because you planted the bomb on Marine One and are the one who could hand them up. They certainly weren't planning on you getting the drop on the guy they sent to kill you."

"You're barking up the wrong tree, Flanagan. You're wasting your time with me. You are following a false lead and the President is in danger because of it. What would be my motive, for God's sake?"

"The Aryan Disciples have money. They could have offered to make you a rich man. You wouldn't have been the first—"

"That's horseshit and you know it."

Flanagan leaned back in his chair, and Garrison hoped he would fall over.

"I have a proposition to make," said Flanagan. "If you'll help us make a case on the others involved, the Director is willing to intercede with the Attorney General on your behalf—to cut a deal for you. If you'll tell us everything you know, a judge might look at you as the guy who made one mistake in his life and was willing to step up to the plate to rectify it. On the other hand, if you sit here like a stiff prick and deny everything, things could go the other way. You will end up being the new Lee Harvey Oswald. Everything you've ever accomplished—your entire life—will be ruined. There will be no way back for you."

"Flanagan, you are being *used*. Can't you see that?"

"We're going to find out the whole story. One way or the other, with or without you, now or later, we will get the ones who are behind this. The Director will assign every agent in the Service to work on this case if he has to. Be reasonable, Garrison. Time is running out. The sooner you come to terms with what you have done, the sooner you can help yourself."

Garrison had the feeling that he'd been abandoned at a train station in a foreign country whose language he didn't speak. He knew there was nothing he could say to convince Flanagan that he was innocent. Someone had framed him. Was it the Aryan Disciples? Had they sent the blackmail letter?

"Flanagan, you're wasting your time."

"Don't take it personal, Pete. I'm just doing my job," Flanagan said coldly.

Garrison gritted his teeth. Talking to Flanagan was like trying to communicate with granite. They were focusing on him. He was the number one suspect in the helicopter bombing.

At the Riggs Bank on Madison, Breckinridge and Rachel Kallenstien sat at a desk as the bank operations officer leaned close to a computer and tapped keys. Acting on Wintergreen's orders, Breckinridge had provided the operations officer with a photocopy of a release form signed by Garrison, giving permission for the Secret Service to review his financial records. All Secret Service agents signed such paperwork when they first entered on duty. The releases were a permanent part of every agent's personnel file, and were used to facilitate the gathering of evidence against the agent if the agent became the subject of an internal investigation.

"Got it," the operations officer said.

She pressed a key and the printer activated. She tore off the page that came out and handed it to Breckinridge.

Breckinridge read it and was utterly astonished. She offered it to Kallenstien.

"For the record," Breckinridge asked. "Does this mean that two hundred thousand dollars was wire-transferred into Garrison's account this morning?"

"Yes. From a bank in Antigua. It's definitely unusual, considering that Mr. Garrison has never had a deposit to the account more than the amount of his government pay-check. The bank sent this from a general account, and then closed the account immediately afterwards, which means that we may never know the exact source of the money. Offshore banks don't give out such information. They make their money from the fees they receive from the sender. Will you be needing anything else?"

Breckinridge shook her head. "No, thanks," she said softly.

"If you'll excuse me, I have a customer waiting."

Breckinridge nodded. The operations officer walked toward a desk where a man and woman were waiting. Breckinridge sat in stunned silence as she considered the import of what she had found.

"There is no way Garrison is going to be able to ex-plain his way out of two hundred grand being deposited into his personal account on the day the Man's chopper is sabotaged," Kallenstien said.

"Rachel, I don't believe he is guilty."

"You think someone spent two large just to falsely incriminate him?"

"I don't believe he is involved in any Presidential as-sassination conspiracy. I just don't see it."

"How well do you know him?"

"Not that well. But I haven't seen anything so far that would lead me to believe that he is involved in something like this. No clue whatsoever."

"Were not psychics, Martha. If you got involved in defending someone from this kind of a charge and it turned out that he actually was guilty, you could be cutting your own throat. You know how the Service treats agents who go against the grain."

Breckinridge had a heavy feeling in the pit of her stomach. There was something wrong and she couldn't put her finger on it. "And if Garrison is innocent?"

"Don't get angry at me. I'm just trying to figure out where you are coming from. I'm just pointing out some issues—"

"I know I'm not explaining my doubts clearly, but it's not just Garrison. There is something about this that is all too pat. It's as if someone is tying Garrison up in a nice big package for some prosecutor. This isn't the way the average assassination case comes together."

"It did for Lee Harvey Oswald."

"Oswald was a psycho, a screwball. Garrison has undergone every test and trial that you and I have. He's not a nut case. Its possible that someone could have set him up."

"Who, for God's sake? Who could it be?"

Breckinridge rubbed her temples. "I don't know."

"Martha, you and I both know that it had to be an agent. No one in the Aryan Disciples got inside that helicopter and planted a bomb. That is a given. Don't you agree?"

"Yes. But that doesn't mean I think it is *him*." Breckinridge stood, took out her cell phone, and dialed Wintergreen's number. He answered. "Breckinridge here.

I've completed the bank records search." She told him the result of the records check.

"Very interesting," he said. "Now head for the courthouse and get a search warrant for Garrison's apartment."

"Shouldn't he be interviewed first?"

"That's being handled. Call me the moment you have the warrant."

He gave her Garrison's address, and she wrote it down. The telephone clicked.

"What now?" Kallenstien asked after Breckinridge set the phone down.

"It's search-warrant time."

At Scott Circle, Breckinridge steered her sedan to the curb in front of Garrison's apartment house. Wintergreen was already there, standing on the sidewalk, waiting.

"Never seen Wintergreen out on a case," Kallenstien said.

"Neither have I."

Breckinridge nodded agreement, and she and Kallenstien got out of the car. Breckinridge showed Wintergreen the search warrant. She and Kallenstien had written it with the help of the duty officer at the U.S. Attorney's office, and then had taken it to a federal judge for signature. Wintergreen read it quickly.

"Let's do it," he said.

At Garrison's apartment, Breckinridge tried the door. It was locked. Peeking through the crack in the door, she determined that there was a dead-bolt lock above the handle. She returned to her car and got a pry bar from the trunk. Returning to the apartment, she pried the door open. An alarm sounded. They went inside and began hunting for the alarm box.

A middle-aged woman came to the door with a base-ball bat in her hand.

"Hands up!"

Wintergreen had his badge out. "Federal officers."

"I'm the manager here. What's going on?"

"We have a federal search warrant."

"Pete Garrison lives here and he is a U.S. Secret Service agent."

"We know," Breckinridge said, and gently took the bat from her. "This is an administrative matter."

"Is Pete in trouble?"

"You'll have to ask him," Breckinridge said.

"I live next door and heard the alarm."

"Ma'am, I'll have to ask you to leave. I'll give you your bat back later."

"I hope Pete is okay," the woman said before departing.

Kallenstien opened the closet door. "Here's the alarm." She turned it off.

"Are you going to participate in the search, Mr. Director?" Breckinridge asked.

"You two go ahead. I'm just here to monitor the investigation."

He took out his cell phone and began dialing as he walked toward the kitchen.

"I'll take the bedroom," Kallenstien said.

Breckinridge began searching the living room, lifting sofa cushions, moving furniture. She heard Wintergreen on the phone, telling someone that they were inside the apartment. It felt strange searching Garrison's home. She knew him, if only casually, but nevertheless it was a personal, invasive thing to do to someone, a violation. She went through Garrison's fishing and hunting mag-

azines and some copies of the *Journal of Explosive Ordnance,* a professional publication for U.S. Army bomb
experts. There was nothing in his entertainment center
but some Jerry Vale and Elton John CDs.

Wintergreen joined her. Seeing that there wasn't much
to search, he walked into the bedroom.

With the living room search completed, Breckinridge
walked into the kitchen, which she thought was relatively clean and neat considering that most men were
pigs when it came to cleaning. She opened drawers and
cupboards. Nothing but dishes and glasses. One drawer
was filled with bill receipts and other home miscellanea.
She opened the refrigerator. On the top shelf was a flat,
rectangular piece of yellowish, putty-like material about
an inch thick and a foot long. She touched it. It was
malleable. She'd first seen it in Secret Service training
school, and over the years she'd found it more than once
when searching the homes of suspected terrorists. It was
military-grade C-4 explosive material, also known as
plastique. She was aware that in its inert form, it was
completely safe.

"Rachel," she said loudly.

Kallenstien hurried into the kitchen. "My God. He
was keeping it right here."

Wintergreen joined them. Breckinridge shoved the refrigerator door closed. Wintergreen stared at the bomb
material. He turned away, took out his cell phone, and
began dialing.

"No wonder he put an alarm system in," said Breckinridge.

"Garrison could get the death sentence," Kallenstien
said softly.

Breckinridge nodded. She felt dizzy.

Wintergreen departed a few minutes later, still making calls on his cell phone. A Secret Service forensics team arrived about twenty minutes later. For the next few hours Breckinridge supervised them as they took photographs and lifted fingerprints. Finally, as they began to leave, Breckinridge felt enervated.

"Rachel, you know Garrison," Breckinridge said. "Would you ever think that he could be involved in something like this?"

"No. But I've been surprised before. Maybe it's one of those things. Maybe there are secrets in his life."

"But *assassination*?"

"I'll admit it strains the imagination."

Breckinridge nodded agreement, but she felt as if she was in a forest and had just heard something, someone walking among the trees, hidden in the darkness. It was there, but what was it?

"Have you ever seen Wintergreen out in the field like this before?" Breckinridge asked.

"Not on even the most serious internal investigations in cases involving the most credible Presidential threats. He's never been known for dirtying his hands. Not even before he was Director. He was always the one who arrived early at the press conference after the case was over."

"He's definitely taking a personal interest in this one, isn't he?"

"He must really believe Garrison is good for this. He must figure this case is different than the others."

"It's different, all right," Breckinridge said.

"What are you getting at?"

"I don't know. But there are a lot of funny things going on."

CHAPTER 19

GARRISON RESTED HIS elbows on the dining table as he waited for Flanagan to finish making a phone call. The call had been a welcome break from the questioning. During the last couple of hours, Flanagan had asked him every question anyone could possibly think of. Garrison was fed up and angry at the whole absurd process, and he has having trouble keeping his patience.

Flanagan said "Okay" to the party on the telephone. He set the receiver down, looked Garrison in the eye, and then smiled.

"Gotcha."

"What's that supposed to mean?"

"A search team just found two pounds of C-4 in your apartment."

As Garrison tried to come to terms with what was

happening, poisonous bile of anger rose in his throat and spread to his temples, to the top of his head.

"What the hell are you talking about?"

"What do you want me to do, draw you a diagram?"

"Someone is trying to frame me. I ask you. What would be *my motive?* Why in God's name would I want to kill the President?"

"We have motive covered. We know about the two hundred thousand dollars transferred into your bank account from an offshore account. They have the bank ledger."

Garrison's hands felt cold. "If I was involved in a Presidential assassination plot, would I be dumb enough to put money into a *bank account?*"

It was now clear. He, Garrison, was in the middle of a sophisticated assassination conspiracy. He was the scapegoat. Now it was no longer a matter of waiting for someone to clear him, of letting the system take its course. The cards were stacked and who knows how many Secret Service insiders were involved. Could Flanagan be one of them? He'd always been on the outskirts of the Secret Service, gravitating to the special quasi-legal SOT unit, and remaining there when he could have requested a transfer to a protective detail or some other normal line assignment.

Flanagan spoke. "Lee Harvey Oswald had photographs in his home of him posing with the rifle he used to assassinate President Kennedy. It's like this: You never thought anyone was going to find out. And the offshore bank is one of those that doesn't cooperate with the authorities. Someone opens an account, transfers money into your account, then closes the account."

"Flanagan, even you should realize that by focusing

on me, the heat is being kept off the real conspirators. Don't you see? Whoever is responsible for the helicopter bombing is using me as a patsy. They must have decided it was worth two hundred grand to divert the investigation, so they dropped cash into my account. And they planted C-4 in my apartment. You can't just go along with this. Whether you realize it or not, you are playing a part in a frame-job that someone spent a lot of time planning."

"Let me tell you a little story," Flanagan said, scowling at him. "There once was a Secret Service Agent who stepped on his dick and ended up getting transferred off the Man's detail. The agent is resentful, confused, and angry with the Director, the President, and the system. So, the agent decides to do something about it—to get back at the system. He makes contact with the Aryan Disciples and offers some inside help to kill the Man. They like the idea, and the agent cuts himself a nice, fat deal. What do you think of that story, Garrison?"

"I think you are an imbecile and a donkey."

Flanagan tapped his pencil on the table. "Whoever hired you used you to plant the bomb, then sent a hit man to shut you up."

"Thirteen years as an agent, someone plants evidence in my apartment, and suddenly I'm a Presidential assassin? How utterly absurd."

"If the explosion had killed the President and Alexander had gotten away with killing you, it would have been the perfect caper. But you saw the hit coming. I give you credit for that. But why sit there and take the rap for the goddamn Aryan Disciples? Why not take advantage of the fact that they screwed up? We can do a deal for your cooperation. You might be able to save your life. I ask you. Why take the fall? Why walk the plank for a group of terrorists?"

"I'm not taking the fall for anybody—not now or later. No matter how much phony evidence someone has dropped on your doorstep, I am innocent. I'm asking you to use your head. I'm asking you to believe me."

Flanagan smiled. "But I don't."

"Am I under arrest?"

It was no use talking. No use whatsoever. Flanagan was narrow-minded and stupid.

"The U.S. Attorney has ordered you held as a material witness under the authority of the Anti-Terrorism Statute. I'm sure you're aware that the AT statute—"

"I know as much about it as you do."

And he did. He knew that the statute had created a special federal court with the power to authorize U.S. agents to hold suspects without bail during "priority terrorism" investigations. Congress had passed the law as a reaction to the Aryan Disciples bombings of federal office buildings.

"Then why fight City Hall?" said Flanagan.

Garrison's lips and face tingled apprehensively. "I want to make a phone call."

"To?"

"That's none of your business."

"Under the AT statute, material witnesses aren't allowed to communicate with anyone until a U.S. District Judge gives his permission."

He knew Flanagan was right. "Then I want to talk to a judge."

"The AT judges aren't available. It's like this, Garrison. Either talk to me or I book you into the federal lockup. Unless you're ready to roll over, you're finished."

Garrison stared sullenly at the carpet. He wasn't going to be able to convince Flanagan of anything. The man's mind was made up. Garrison knew that he was the fall guy in a sophisticated plot under way to kill the President of the United States—a scheme that probably involved a Secret Service agent. The time for talking, for trying to reason, was over. Garrison had to change the course of events. No matter what the cost, he wasn't going to allow Flanagan to book him into the D.C. federal lockup. He wasn't going to sit in limbo hoping that some court-appointed attorney would clear him while Flanagan was out busily collecting other spurious information planted by the Aryan Disciples that could be used against him. That would allow the real conspirators to complete their assassination plans. In a wave of controlled fear and deadly resolve, Garrison made a decision he knew would change his life forever.

"Okay."

Flanagan looked genuinely surprised. *"Okay what?"*

"I'm ready to make a statement," he said softly.

Barely able to conceal his satisfaction, Flanagan stood and walked to the door.

"Beatty, come down here!" There was the sound of footsteps. Beatty walked into the room. "Garrison is going to tell us his story and you're going to write up what he says."

"No problem."

Beatty pulled back a chair and sat across the table from Garrison.

"I'm thirsty," Garrison said.

"Get him a drink of water," Flanagan said.

Beatty got up, walked around the table to Garrison's right, and then pushed open a swinging door that led to the kitchen. The moment Garrison heard the sound of the water faucet he dove across the table and ratcheted his arm securely around Flanagan's neck. Flanagan made frantic grunting sounds. Adrenaline surged through Garrison's veins, and he held the choke hold and yanked Flanagan's SIG-Sauer from his cross-draw holster

"Don't make me do it," Garrison whispered, and pressed the barrel to Flanagan's right temple. Flanagan stopped struggling. Garrison released him, and motioned him back to his chair with the gun. Flanagan complied. "Move from the chair and I'll kill you."

Garrison aimed the gun at him under the table, and Flanagan returned to his chair.

The door opened. Beatty walked in carrying a glass of water.

Garrison swung the gun in his direction.

"Hands on top of your head." Beatty raised his hands, dropped the glass. "Face the wall."

Beatty turned. Garrison moved to him and took his gun. Shoving it in his waistband, he moved to the other side of the table, grabbed Flanagan by the collar, and shoved him toward Beatty.

He forced Flanagan and Beatty into the kitchen at gunpoint.

"We're just doing our job," Flanagan said as Garrison cautiously used handcuffs to lock both of them to the drainpipe under the sink.

"If I'm a real Presidential assassin, what do I have to lose?"

"Don't shoot, please."

Garrison took Beatty's car keys.

"Shut up."

Returning to the dining room, Garrison dropped Flanagan's gun on the table, grabbed Flanagan's briefcase, and departed from the kitchen door.

As he climbed into Flanagan's car, Garrison's temples were pulsing. He sped away, feeling as alone as he'd ever been in his entire life.

Garrison pulled into an office-building parking lot on L Street. He parked the car, turned off the engine, and used his cellular telephone to dial 911.

"Police emergency," a woman said.

"There are two people tied up in the kitchen at 829 Westboro Avenue, North West," Garrison said. "You'd better send a car."

"May I have your name, sir?"

"Gilbert Flanagan."

Garrison pressed the OFF button.

Garrison opened Flanagan's briefcase, took out his gun, and reholstered it. He opened a folder in the briefcase containing a copy of the PRD file on Garth Alexander.

CONFIDENTIAL

NAME: Alexander, Garth Clement AKA: Ronnie Roberts, Carl Bronkirk, Ray Waters

ADDRESS: 29 Rue La Boetie, Paris

AFFILIATION: Aryan Disciples of the United States— associate

DESCRIPTION: Male, Caucasian, 6' 1", 210, 41 years old.

SCARS, MARKS, TATTOOS: Tattoo mermaid nailed to a cross covering full chest, panther on right upper arm, dog with army helmet on left forearm, "Corsican Boy" on upper back.

HANGOUTS: Paris Cocktail bars in Pigalle and Belleville quarter, Montreal: Chez Alain, in U.S.: The Scene and The Corral Club in Bakersfield, California

ASSOCIATES: Unknown

RELATIVES: None living

MARITAL STATUS: Divorced from Helene Lorraine

PROPENSITY FOR VIOLENCE: Alexander is a former sergeant in the French Foreign Legion. He has contacts with neo-fascist groups in Canada and the U.S., including the Aryan Disciples of the U.S. He may have been involved in the plans to bomb the Chicago Federal Building and the Montreal City Hall. Unsubstantiated information from various Spanish government sources has it that Alexander may have acted as a hit man for the Basque Separatist Organization (BSO) on two separate occasions. Alexander is wanted for murder in Sierra Leone as a result of a barroom fight, but because of his dual Canadian and French citizenship cannot be extradited. Alexander is familiar with weapons and should be considered armed and dangerous.

ASSOCIATES: Leroy P. Vincent AKA Spike Vincent. Vincent served time with Alexander in prison in Spain. Vincent and he were involved in collecting debts for a seller of illegal weapons in France. As of January of this year, Vincent was released from prison and is residing in Bakersfield. He frequents the Corral Club in Bakersfield, a known hangout for ex-convicts and right-wing extremists.

SOURCE OF ABOVE INFO: Reliable informants, sister agencies, INTERPOL SECRETARIAT GENERAL, ST. CLOUD, FRANCE.

Garrison was disappointed. The information in the file was too general to be of any real use, except for the information on Alexander's American associate, Leroy Vincent of Bakersfield, California. Bakersfield was a hotbed of Aryan Disciples activities, and if the information in the file was up-to-date and reliable, it was possible that Vincent could be the connection between Alexander and the Aryan Disciples.

Garrison sorted through the issues in his mind. He had to investigate Alexander and find out who hired him. But first, he had to convince the President that he, Garrison, was innocent—that someone else in the Secret Service was betraying him. Garrison decided to talk to Eleanor. He glanced at his wristwatch. It was too dangerous to try to reach her by telephone. He recalled her schedule, which he'd recently reviewed. If he remembered correctly, this evening she would be having dinner at the Chez Doucette restaurant on K Street.

Garrison stopped at a small hardware store on I Street, where he purchased a screwdriver, then walked briskly to the corner of K and 14th Streets. The First Lady's motorcade was parked in front of the Chez Doucette, at the corner on the ground floor of a three-story office building. He couldn't approach along the sidewalk because the agents outside on K Street would spot him.

Garrison knew the standard Secret Service security plan for the Chez Doucette from having done advance security duties there in the past. The plan included a police car parked in the alley at the rear of the restaurant and an agent posted at the front door, inside. He assumed Walter Sebastian would probably be posted there. Because the alley at the right of the entrance was blocked off at either end, no agent would be posted there.

When the President visited the restaurant, agents were positioned on all the nearby rooftops. But unless there was specific information concerning a threat to the First Lady's safety, the Secret Service protective manual did not require the same elaborate security precautions for her. Unless something had changed, Eleanor would be seated in the restaurant's private dining room, reserved for members of the First Family and a few other White House insiders. Chez Doucette catered to the rich and famous, and its private dining room had one entrance and no windows. There were private washrooms for VIPs in the basement down a short flight of stairs from the private dining room.

Garrison walked into an office building down the block from the Chez Doucette and took an elevator to the penthouse floor. Exiting the elevator, he found a stairway leading to the roof. The door was locked. He used his screwdriver to jimmy the lock. On the roof, he walked to the edge and gauged the distance to the adjacent building. After some quick calculations, he moved to the middle of the roof. He took a deep breath and let it out. Breaking into a full sprint, he traversed the roof to build up speed and leaped across the chasm, landing on the roof of the adjacent building and breaking the fall with his hands.

CHAPTER 20

H E MADE TWO more such leaps, moving from rooftop to rooftop to reach the roof of the Chez Doucette building. He stopped there to catch his breath and brush off his hands and trousers. His palms stung. He walked to the edge of the roof and peeked below. A police car and what he figured was a Secret Service sedan were parked in the alley behind the restaurant—the standard "security package" as it was called in Service argot. His problem: He had to get to the main floor of the restaurant without being seen.

Catty-corner from where he was standing was a rooftop hatch. Using the screwdriver, he pried it open. Climbing down a ladder into a utility closet, he opened the door that led to a hallway, and walked quietly down the hall to a stairwell. Descending the steps to the second floor, he followed a hall to an office with a VACANCY sign on the door. Using the screwdriver on the lock for what must have been two full minutes, he managed to get in. He hurried to the window. Hoisting his leg over the sill, he crawled down a drainpipe to the window below. Hanging on with one hand, he used the screwdriver to shim the lock. With some difficulty, he crawled inside a room whose walls were lined with wide shelves from floor to ceiling. He was in the kitchen pantry of Chez Doucette. Being careful to not make noise, he closed the window and walked to the door.

He heard footsteps. He wanted to hide, to run, but there was nowhere to go. A young man in a white uniform opened the door and was startled.

"Sorry to alarm you," Garrison said pulling his badge from his pocket and flipping open the leather case. "U.S. Secret Service. Just conducting a security check. The First Lady is downstairs." His mouth felt dry as he stood there, unsure whether the man was going to call for help or accept the story.

The man shrugged. "They told us you guys would be everywhere."

"The First Lady has had some threats recently."

"I guess you can't be too careful," the man said grabbing two boxes from a shelf.

Garrison followed him out the door into the kitchen. The chef was busy at the stove. Garrison introduced himself as Agent Flanagan.

"Weren't you here with the President a few months ago?" the chef asked.

"Yes. The President was here with Helen Pierpont and some Russian diplomats."

"I'm having sandwiches made up for the agents outside."

"Thanks."

Garrison walked across the kitchen and through a doorway leading to an elegant, frescoed dining room filled with customers. The walls were lined with oil portraits of Washington power brokers, including Clark Clifford and Henry Kissinger. Praying that neither Sebastian nor the other agents had changed the usual procedure and decided to come inside to eat, Garrison walked across a floral carpet past the door of the private dining room where a young waiter stood. Garrison hurried down a flight of nearby stairs to a plushly carpeted basement hall where there was a pay telephone and private rest room facilities reserved solely for the use of private dining room guests. He entered the men's room, and held the door open about an inch to keep an eye on the stairs, waiting for Eleanor to come downstairs to check her makeup before leaving, as was her habit. If she chose not to do so, all of his trouble would have been for nothing. The other question in his mind was what he would do if she panicked when she saw him. For all he knew, someone might have convinced her that he was an assassin. If so, agents would come rushing down the steps to arrest or shoot him. As time passed, he glanced at his wristwatch repeatedly.

He heard footsteps. Eleanor descended the steps looking polished and elegant in a beige business suit, designer scarf, and high heels. He needed her now to survive. As she reached the bottom of the stairs, he opened the door and pulled her inside.

"Pete—what are you doing here?"

Garrison touched a finger to his lips. "What did they tell you about me?"

"Wintergreen told me they found evidence in your apartment," she whispered anxiously.

"It was planted there. What else?"

She stared into his eyes, and he wondered what he would think if he were she. "Your bank account—"

"There are ways to transfer money from an offshore bank and cover up the source of the funds. People do it by opening an account, transferring the money, then closing the account and paying off the bank to destroy the records. I am being framed.

"You believe me, don't you?"

"I don't know what to think," she said looking down.

"You know me, for God's sake. I would never do anything like that. You have to believe me."

"I started to think about our . . . uh . . . relationship."

"That has nothing to do with all this—"

"I wondered if maybe you thought that I wanted to be free of him—"

"Eleanor, think about what you are saying. I haven't changed. I'm not some raving lunatic."

"Then I wondered if the blackmail thing had spooked you. I wondered if you'd lost your judgment and were so afraid of losing everything that you'd . . . uh . . . lost your mind."

"Do I look crazy?"

She looked into his eyes. "Maybe all this makes sense to you," she said "But I am confused and frightened. I don't know what the hell to think about all this."

"Please listen to me. I don't know what is going on. I don't know who is behind this. But I swear to you that I am not involved." He took her hand. "We don't have much time, Eleanor. I need your help. There is a plot to kill the President involving one or more Secret Service agents, and they have gone to a lot of trouble to frame me for the helicopter bombing. They needed a scapegoat to steer the investigation away from them. It's obviously part of their plan. You have to believe me."

"I have to protect to my husband. No matter what our differences—"

"If I meant him any harm, why would I be here?"

She stared at him, and he could see the fear in her eyes.

"You would never have come here like this, would you?" she said, as if thinking out loud.

"I'm here because I am trying to save his life. And because someone has put me in the middle."

She nodded and looked away. "If you were culpable, there would be no reason for you to come to me."

"Exactly."

"What do you want me to do?"

"Tell the President he needs to replace the entire Secret Service White House Detail immediately. Tell him not to waste any time."

"What about Director Wintergreen? Can't he be trusted?"

"I don't know who to point a finger at. That's the problem. The Secret Service security system is useless with a turncoat inside. But the President is in danger from within and something has to be done. Now. I want you to tell him to bring in the military to take over his protection until this is resolved. And he needs to appoint outsiders to investigate the bombing. You can trust Sebastian. No matter what happens, keep him with you. He's not involved in any conspiracy."

"Have you talked to him?"

Garrison shook his head. "No. I don't want to force

him to side with me and put his career on the line. There's nothing he can do to help at this point."

"Okay."

"Eleanor, the President's life is in danger. You are in danger. I am in danger."

"He thinks it's you—"

"This is a sophisticated conspiracy involving someone in the Service and possibly a terrorist connection or a foreign power."

"What am I to say?"

"Tell him I contacted you. Don't tell him I was here because it will frighten him. Tell him that I managed to get through to you on a White House phone—that I impersonated some official contact to get through your secretary. Tell him what I said. You have to try. Will you do that for me?"

She nervously fingered her scarf.

"Pete, this is a plot to take over the government, isn't it? A coup d'état?"

"I don't know."

"Please don't take this the wrong way, but . . . do you . . . do you have anything that would tend to prove your innocence?"

"No. And I know the President may not take my word. I know the evidence is stacked up against me. But you have to try or we are all done for. Look, you'd better go back to your guests before people start to worry."

"I'm afraid, Pete. I'm afraid for my husband and I'm afraid for you."

"You have to calm down. We have to keep our wits about us."

"I know."

"I once had a premonition that when Russell was

elected to a second term, I wouldn't survive it."

"Don't worry. I'm going to get to the bottom of all this."

"How?"

"There are some things I have to investigate."

"They're after you, Pete."

"I know. But I'll be all right."

"Where will you stay?"

"I'll find somewhere."

She thought for a moment, and then said, "I can arrange for a room at the Watergate for you. I'll call the management office and tell them my cousin Jonathan Hollingsworth will be staying there. The name will be familiar to them. He was scheduled to use the place a couple of months ago, but couldn't make it and had to cancel. They will give you a key. Do you need money?"

"I'm sure that by now they have placed stops on my checking account and credit cards."

She opened her purse, took out her wallet, and handed him all the money in it, at least twenty hundred-dollar bills.

"Take this."

"I don't need this much—"

"Take it," she insisted. "I want you to call me the moment you learn something."

"From here on, the phone is too dangerous. So are pagers. Everything can be traced. You'll have to be very careful with the White House phone. If you need to speak with me, call the apartment and ask for Jonathan. If I say he is at work, that means it's okay to come over. If I say anything else, just hang up. If I need to speak with you, I'll leave a red chalk mark on the curb directly across the street at Lafayette Park: three circles. You'll be able to see them from Bedroom Three. If you see my signal, tell the agents that you are going over to your cousin's place. When you get there, insist that the agents remain at the first-floor elevator bank. Tell them that your cousin doesn't like seeing agents around. They won't like it, but they'll go along because it's an un-announced visit and they will believe you are safe." Garrison knew that agents were aware of the difference between a risky, public First Family visit and one that was unexpected. The unannounced visit neutralized the greatest danger to a protectee . . . the assassin lying in wait.

"I understand. Be careful."

"Sure."

He watched anxiously as she hurried upstairs. A few minutes later, he heard footsteps and conversation at the top of the stairs as Eleanor and her guests exited the private dining room and walked to the front door. He waited until he was sure she had departed, then walked up the stairs and peeked into the main dining area. He crossed the room to the kitchen and moved toward a side door.

"Sir?"

Garrison stopped and turned. A waiter was standing behind him with a brown paper bag.

"Did you get a sandwich? The chef made some up."

"Thanks, but I've already eaten."

Outside, Garrison looked both ways, then crossed between buildings and began walking up the street praying no one would spot him. His mind was short-circuiting and he wouldn't allow himself to feel what was going on. He was in the middle of a whirlpool with no time to mull over options and he was reacting from an inner place in the back of his brain. He neared the middle of the block as a Mercury sedan pulled around the corner and parked at the curb, facing in his direction. The driver turned off the headlights. Because of the darkness, Garrison couldn't make out the faces of the two people in the front seat. He glanced behind him.

At the other end of the block, another Mercury sedan pulled to the curb. Its headlights went out.

Garrison felt a chill. Could the Chez Doucette chef have recognized him and mentioned his name to one of the other agents? Or maybe Flanagan had ordered PRD teams to keep an eye out for him at every location on the President and the First Lady's itineraries. Could Eleanor have betrayed him? Garrison quickly surveyed the situation. He knew the alley to his left was a dead end.

He ran across the street and darted down another darkened alley. Frantically, he tried a door on his left. It was locked. He continued running. At the end of the alley was a large industrial trash container. He jumped atop it and struggled to crawl over an adjacent fence.

Shots rang out from the mouth of the alley and red tracer fire, the standard Secret Service-issue ammunition, ricocheted off the trash container. Garrison stopped, pulled his gun, and fired twice in the air, hoping his pursuers would believe they were under fire and would deploy rather than run headlong into the passageway, giving him time to get away. God knows he didn't want to kill an agent who was simply carrying out orders. But *they were trying to kill him* and he wasn't going to allow anyone to shoot him down in the street. He reholstered the gun, dove over the fence, ran to his left, then turned right, running along a narrow passageway between buildings. He sprinted across the street and a sedan barely avoided hitting him, its brakes squealing. Reaching the sidewalk, he ran right, then left at the corner.

At a Metro stop, he glanced behind him, and then ran down the steps. A large crowd was waiting on the platform. He walked into the middle of the group, keeping his eyes on the stairs leading from the street as he waited for a train to arrive. He was breathing so hard that people were looking at him. Finally, he heard a train approaching. He turned. Two agents were standing at the top of the escalator. Garrison remained in the middle of the crowd until a train pulled into the station. Then he hurried inside a car, looking back only after the doors closed. The train pulled away from the station. He felt confused and angry. His mind flashed back to years earlier in Munich, Germany, when, half-asleep after working all night, he'd boarded the wrong train. Realizing his mistake only as the train pulled out of the station, he hadn't known where he was going and had no idea how to get back.

Garrison entered through the glass doors of the administrative office at the Watergate apartment complex. A young female desk clerk standing behind the counter looked up at him.

"May I help you, sir?"

"I'm Jonathan Hollingsworth. The First Lady's, uh, staff person told me there would be a key here for me."

She smiled.

"We just received a call from the First Lady's office, Mr. Hollingsworth." She reached into a drawer and handed him a key. "If you have any questions, just call."

"I'll do that."

He crossed a lobby flanked on either side by an atrium. He pressed the elevator button and looked back at the woman behind the counter, now busy at a computer.

In the sixth-floor condominium, Garrison walked through the four rooms, admiring the expensive furniture and wall hangings. The living room walls were painted a deep mocha that accented the rattan furniture and marigold patterns on the sofa and pull-up chairs. There were mirrors in bamboo frames and bamboo legs on a round, glass-topped dining table. Everything in the room indicated comfort and relaxation. The kitchen was a showcase of butcher block and stainless steel—a gourmet's workplace with an exit leading to a service elevator. In the bedroom, he walked to the window.

Across the street was the Kennedy Center for the Performing Arts, the hub of D.C. culture where the city's upper crust went to be seen by other members of the upper crust as they sat through music recitals. Garrison knew the interior of the imposing structure inch by inch, having been assigned as Presidential advance agent there three different times in the last two years. He preferred a boxing match or a basketball game. For a moment, he had the feeling that he was in the middle of a dream. He was hiding out in an apartment owned by the First Lady and he had few options. It was only a matter of time before agents found him—before the conspirators moved again to assassinate the President.

At the living room table, Garrison opened Flanagan's briefcase and went over the paperwork on Alexander again. He took out a pen and began making notes, random notations about what he knew, hoping that the simple act of writing itself might guide him. Such doodling had helped him in other investigations. After a few minutes, he was staring at a name he had written: SPIKE VINCENT. In the file, Vincent was the only listed associate of Garth Alexander, the Aryan Disciples mercenary to whom Frank Hightower had directed him.

With Alexander dead, Garrison had little else to go on. He had to trace Alexander and determine who had hired him.

CHAPTER 21

IN THE WHITE House Situation Room, Wintergreen anxiously described the evidence against Garrison to the National Security Council: the President, National Security Advisor Helen Pierpont, Cabinet members, and the Chairman of the Joint Chiefs of Staff. Wintergreen was standing at the far end of a long mahogany conference table. He could tell by the eye contact he was getting that he had everyone's undivided attention.

"You're saying Garrison did this because the Aryan Disciples gave him money?" the President asked.

"That's what his motive appears to be at this point, Mr. President."

Finally, Wintergreen finished his talk and turned deferentially to the President, who was tapping a pencil on the table, an irritating habit that had been getting on Wintergreen's nerves. The President glanced toward

Pierpont, to whom he often looked for advice in such matters. Wintergreen had known all along that it was Pierpont he had to convince. Few Presidents went against the advice of their National Security Advisor. And with Jordan, Pierpont had special influence.

"What in the name of God made this agent think he could get away with something like this?" the Secretary of the Treasury asked.

"Targeting the executive is a psychological syndrome—a psychopathology," Wintergreen said.

"It's psycho, all right," Pierpont said.

"To hell with all the gobbledygook," the President said, and a hush spread across the room.

"I have a question, Mr. Director," Pierpont said, doodling on a yellow pad. Then, with upturned palms and her thin lips formed into an O, she continued. "As we sit here, is the President of the United States safe?"

Wintergreen had anticipated Pierpont digging into the Garrison issue. Making others look bad was her way.

"Garrison is not going to be able to make it through our security if that's what you mean. No way."

Pierpont stood and walked to a formidable array of the latest in military communications equipment.

"How can you be so sure?"

"I certainly don't mean to imply that we're taking this lightly."

"Nor did I mean to imply that."

"I've ordered every working shift beefed up. We've launched a full-scale, nationwide manhunt."

"What I mean is: Wouldn't a veteran Secret Service agent assigned to the White House Detail—an agent with Garrison's experience—be able to defeat all your security plans if he so chose?"

"He knows we are looking for him," Wintergreen said.

He'd anticipated the question, and had already decided to lead her on with the incomplete answer.

Pierpont pensively rubbed an index finger along her upper lip.

"All your agents are fully knowledgeable about all your security arrangements and plans, are they not?"

"Yes."

"And Garrison had a supervisory position, did he not?"

"My point is: The plot has been uncovered. He's not going to continue on now that he has lost the element of surprise. The Aryan Disciples is a crazy, extremist organization, but they are not suicidal."

"How can you be sure he won't try some kind of kamikaze attack to finish me?" the President said. "Isn't that what these kind of fanatics do? The helicopter bomb missed, so they try something else? Garrison is at large. He is out there."

Wintergreen swallowed. "I really don't anticipate anything like that in this case, but I can only surmise—"

"Surmise?" the President interrupted. "I surmise that I am in danger of getting my ass blown off. And who was the damn mastermind who allowed Agent Garrison to escape from custody?"

"Agent Beatty. But I take responsibility, of course."

Wintergreen recognized the risk in making such a self-evident remark. But what else was he to say?

"That's admirable," the President said. "But it doesn't change the situation, does it?"

Wintergreen felt drawn and enervated. He had the feeling he was watching himself from afar. But he was

confident that at the end of the meeting he would have
what he wanted. As he saw it, it was why the other
Cabinet members were being silent. They knew that ex-
traordinary measures were about to be imposed. They
knew that the President of the United States wasn't going to sit back and allow someone to assassinate him.
He was going to defend himself. Pierpont would lead
him to making the decision.

"I have a team of handpicked agents on the street as
we speak, Mr. President. Agent Flanagan is in command.
He will get results."

"What results?" Pierpont asked.

"We will apprehend Garrison," Wintergreen said. "We
will throw him in a federal lockup." He knew what Pierpont wanted to hear, but he would force her to get the
President himself to say it. Wintergreen was stimulated
by the exchange. He was in control and he liked the feeling. "I have a major effort out there to recapture him."

"And then what?" Pierpont asked.

"He'll stand trial in federal court. My agents have
gathered plenty of evidence to use against him."

"The judicial process might be a problem in this
case," Pierpont said.

The President coughed dryly. "Please explain, Helen."

She turned toward the President.

"Every passing day means a greater risk of the story
getting out to the press. When it does, the Presidency
will be hurt. The country won't just roll merrily along
with a government-trained stalker lurking out there,
waiting to kill the President. I can see it on the six
o'clock news: *President in Danger*. The issue would
build by the day. It would be another Iran hostage crisis.
The stock market might even nosedive. Can you imagine

what this town would be like with an assassination conspiracy trial going on? If it turns out that Garrison is connected to the Aryan Disciples, he could even become a hero to the neo-Nazi movement. The reports that I get indicate that these people are out there. More of them than we like to think."

Wintergreen loved how power freaks like Pierpont thought they could foretell events. He felt like asking her to predict the winner of the Kentucky Derby.

"What is your take on that, Mr. Director?" the President asked.

Wintergreen fidgeted. "I agree. If the press gets this story, we will have to worry about behavioral contagion."

"What's that?"

"I'm referring to insane people getting the same idea. Our studies have shown that even talk of assassination causes kooks to come out of the woodwork. It creates instability and can frequently rouse them to action."

"Let's not forget that Garrison is a trained federal agent who has the expertise to defeat Presidential security," Pierpont said. "His file shows that he is also an explosives expert. He is a walking time bomb."

The President licked his lips.

"Is there anyone who doesn't believe that this is a matter requiring special action?" he asked. The others shook their heads.

Wintergreen waited for someone to disagree. But because of the President's tone of voice, indicating that he was for such an action, the others said nothing. To Wintergreen, it was always fascinating to watch the pack mentality at work. Even at this level, the bureaucrats invariably went along with whatever they thought the President wanted. During the Yugoslavian crisis, Wintergreen had attended a National Security Council meeting and watched with interest as everyone in the room had concurred with the President's decision to cluster-bomb civilian areas. Hungry sled dogs. He noticed Pierpont place a pencil on the yellow tablet in front of her, and Wintergreen wondered if it wasn't a code she'd worked out with the President beforehand.

"Then it's my firm opinion that if a decision was made to reach outside normal channels, it would conform to precedent," the President said. "Thanks, everyone," he added to close the meeting. "I'd like Ms. Pierpont and Director Wintergreen to remain."

The others departed. A military aide closed the door.

"Mr. President, as of this moment, no one outside a few people in the Secret Service and some staffers know about the Garrison matter," Pierpont said. "It could be brought to an end swiftly. Even if some of the facts later leaked, it would be manageable."

"How would it . . . sound?"

"People have mental problems," she said. "A bump-in-the-road thing. People have been known to commit suicide. Afterward, the President appoints a blue-ribbon commission to investigate. I would be happy to chair such a commission."

The President rubbed his chin. He rose from his chair and walked slowly to an electronic map of Russia. He absentmindedly pushed a button on the projection. Moscow lit up.

For a moment, Wintergreen wondered if the President would balk. But he knew the President didn't like messes. He believed in anticipating future events, in taking action *now* rather than *later*. Wintergreen could almost see the goal line. Wintergreen had taken the horse to water and he was about to drink. *Come on and say it, you fucking blowhard.*

The President returned to the table.

"I find the facts clear as to what has to be done to put things back in order without any more commotion—to neutralize the problem." He sat, picked up a pen, and made a note on the writing pad in front of him, then tore off the sheet of paper and shoved it in his pocket. "Are we all on track with that?" the President asked looking at Wintergreen.

As Wintergreen was aware, the President's use of the words *find* and *neutralize* had a special meaning when used in a national security context. He was issuing a Presidential finding, in which the word *neutralize* was a euphemism for murder. A CIA lawyer, authorizing Garrison's murder under Presidential executive authority, would now prepare a legal document. Wintergreen revisited the urge to release his breath in a gesture of relief, but he held back.

"Mr. President," Wintergreen said. "If you would . . . I don't want to make a mistake on this. I want to make sure I'm reading you correctly—"

"Catch Garrison and kill him. Is that clear enough for you?"

"Yes, Mr. President."

"Put together a team," Pierpont said. "People you trust. We want this done right."

"Roger that."

After the President and Pierpont left the room, Wintergreen stretched. He imagined Garrison as a miniature cloud in the room, floating toward the ceiling to be sucked out of the room by the air conditioner to join the ghosts of others who'd gotten in the path of the wrong people.

CHAPTER 22

GARRISON WAITED ON a crowded sidewalk outside the arrival baggage area at Dulles International
airport, watching a line of arriving passengers waiting
in a taxi line. He was headed for Bakersfield, California,
where he hoped to be able to find out more about Garth
Alexander. But to get there he needed someone else's
identification. By now Flanagan had probably placed his
name in every law-enforcement and travel-security database in the world.

A man at the end of the line had a foreign passport
protruding from his shirt pocket. Garrison studied him.
He was about Garrison's height and age. Figuring that
with some luck he might be able to impersonate him,
Garrison got in line behind him. When the man walked
toward the trunk of a taxi to put in his luggage, Garrison

intentionally bumped into him, deftly snatching the passport.

"Pardon me, sir," he said.

"Entshuldigen sie mich."

Garrison moved away briskly. Meshing into the crowd, he looked back. The man got into a taxi and it pulled into traffic. Garrison looked about to see if anyone had seen anything, then checked the passport. The man's name was Joachim Porzig. In the passport photograph he wore eyeglasses and his hair was brushed forward.

In the airport departure-terminal gift shop, Garrison purchased a pair of reading glasses and a comb. In the men's room, he stood at a mirror and combed his hair to approximate Porzig's forward sweep. Satisfied that the style was the best he could do to match Porzig's appearance, he put on the reading glasses. He didn't look like Porzig's twin, but no one expected passport photographs to be precise, particularly a harried ticket clerk who looked at ID photographs all day.

At the United Airlines ticketing area, Garrison checked the flight-departure schedule. There was a United Airlines flight leaving for L.A. in forty minutes. He waited in line at a ticket counter, telling the clerk that his destination was Bakersfield, California.

"You have to fly through Los Angeles."

"Yes."

He purchased a ticket using some of the cash Eleanor had given him. He knew that flying across the country to follow up the lead he'd found in Flanagan's briefcase was a dangerous exercise, a long shot, and might end up being a waste of time. But he had to try.

"May I see some identification, Mr. Porzig?"

"Certainly."

He handed her the passport. She opened it and looked up at him to compare the photo with his appearance. After entering the passport number into her computer, she handed him the ticket and the passport.

"I love Salzburg," she said, having noted the address in the passport.

"My hometown."

"You have no accent."

"I'm a language teacher."

"No wonder. You'll be departing from Gate 23A. Have a nice trip."

Relieved, Garrison moved cautiously toward the boarding area, staying close to groups of people, using them as camouflage. Reaching the jet way, he checked in at the gate, then sat and waited.

Two uniformed police officers emerged from the escalator and began walking past the boarding gates.

Garrison hurried into the bus and moved anxiously into the corner, facing away from the door as other passengers filed in. After a few minutes, the bus pulled away from the terminal and drove toward the waiting aircraft. Garrison looked back at the terminal receding into the distance. He felt numb, as if some strange magnetism was holding him in its grip.

During the flight to the West Coast, Garrison tried to plan his moves and went over what he knew a hundred times. Garrison had to do more than just shoot holes in the evidence against him. He had to come up with something solid. To convince the President that he was innocent, he actually had to solve the case. Nothing less would suffice.

CHAPTER 23

A T ROBERTS FIELD, the airport north of Bakersfield, Garrison got off a commuter plane from Los Angeles. Inside a small arrival terminal, he rented a car.

The weather was as hot and dry as Washington, D.C., was humid. It was hellish Central California evangelist-tent heat that turned necks into red leather, melted asphalt on drag strips, and brought a steady stream of refrigerated beer trucks crossing the ridge route from L.A. each day.

Garrison knew about Bakersfield from having been there during the last Presidential campaign. Its growth in the 1920's stemmed from the migration from the Dust Bowl by people looking for farm labor. It had been a harsh desert that had eventually been transformed into agricultural farmland for as far as the eye could see. He'd learned that Bakersfield was an unusual place, made up of wealthy farmers, stoop laborers, and a suburban class that owned boats they stored in their garages until the weekend, when they launched them in the Kern River, the lifeblood of the flatland city. Up until the 1950's, there had been Ku Klux Klan activity and reports of lynchings in the city. Even today, Bakersfield's politics was kooky, with right-wing city prosecutors in the District Attorney's office and KILL THE IRS stickers on pickup truck bumpers all over town.

He drove to a downtown clothing store and purchased Levi's and a white crew-neck T-shirt. Having changed clothes in the rental car, he used a city map he found in the glove compartment to find the Corral Club, the establishment mentioned in the file folder he'd taken from Flanagan as being a hangout for Garth Alexander's associate Spike Vincent.

Cruising slowly on a road just off Highway 99 at the Norton Boulevard turnoff, Garrison spotted a sign: CORRAL CLUB—DANCING. Above it was a martini glass. Inside, it would be bucking bronco. Garrison parked his car in a gravel-covered parking lot.

The dimly lit bar was deceptively larger than it looked from the outside. Half of the room was a horseshoe-shaped cocktail bar of the red padded-leather variety. The other side was a pool table and some booths. The only other customers in the place were three men attired in motorcycle leather and two hefty women at the pool table. An overpowering odor of beer-soaked wood reminded Garrison of a hundred such places he'd been to during investigations.

Garrison straddled a bar stool. Everyone stared at him. It was the kind of place the local police officers would refer to as a "toilet," which, translated, meant a bar frequented by ex-cons and other white underclass creeps with tattoos, bad teeth, and long, greasy hair. It wasn't the kind of place where he was going to be able to identify himself, ask questions, and hope to get truthful answers. He would have to wing it.

The bartender placed a cocktail napkin on the bar in front of him. She was in her late thirties and had stringy-blond hair and an ingratiating smile.

"Haven't seen you in here before,"

"I'm a first-timer."

"Remind me not to sleep with you."

"I have a bad memory."

She smiled. She wore jeans and an olive-drab tank top stretched tightly over rigid, silicone-filled breasts. She was tall and thin with alabaster cheeks, a narrow nose, and high forehead: classic Nordic features that without the conspicuous tattoos that ringed her arms and neck might have allowed her to have been a fashion model.

"What can I get you?"

He ordered beer. She walked to the other end of the bar, whispered something to a customer, then brought Garrison's beer and placed it in front of him. For the next few minutes, Garrison alternated between staring out the window, glancing at his wristwatch, feigning making calls on a cellular phone, and chatting with the bartender. She told him her name was Tammy.

More customers began to come in and there were more whispers about him, the stranger. Finally, Garrison figured it was time to make his move. He picked up a book of Corral Club matches and walked into the men's room. He took out his cell phone, wrapped a handkerchief over the mouthpiece. He dialed the Corral Club and heard a distant ring in the bar.

"Hello," Tammy said.

"Is Spike there?"

"Who's calling?"

"Bobby."

"Bobby who?"

"Bobby Toland from Fresno. I'm supposed to meet him and another guy there. Just tell him I'll be a few minutes late. Gotta run."

He pressed OFF, shoved the phone in his pocket, and returned to his seat at the bar. Tammy was conferring with two men at the end of bar who looked like ex-cons.

"Another beer," Garrison said.

She reached inside a cooler, and took out a Miller High Life and set it in front of him.

"You a cop?"

"No, but I like guns."

She studied him.

"You waiting for Spike?" He didn't answer. "Because if you are, Bobby Toland from Fresno just called and said he'll be late."

Garrison feigned concern. "The Bobby Toland I know is an FBI rat."

"Just relaying a message, hon."

Garrison took out cash and put money on the bar to pay for the beers. "When you see Spike tell him about the call."

"You'd better tell him yourself."

"He and I are doing a deal. I don't talk on phones when there is the possibility of heat. If you know what I mean."

"You can catch him at the tow yard. If he's not there he'll be out on a call."

"How do I get there?"

"Next to the McDonald's. Wasco Tow Service."

Garrison felt like cheering. "Thanks."

"Catch you later, first-timer."

Garrison stood under a streetlight on Stockdale Highway in an undeveloped area near an abandoned drag strip. He glanced at his wristwatch, and a tepid, dusty wind that was blowing east to west made him blink.

A tow truck came into view. The sign on the truck door read: WASCO TOW. He waved. The truck slowed to a stop on the gravel soft shoulder, then backed up to him, creating a large cloud of dust. A man with massive arms and neck got out of the truck. He was about Garrison's age but heavier, about the same height, and had a diminutive chin and a weathered, ocher complexion that matched the color of his uniform shirt. The skin under and around his eyes was cracked like streambed adobe.

"You the guy who called for a tow?"

"Are you Spike Vincent?"

Vincent stared at him suspiciously. "I was the last time I checked."

Garrison took out his badge.

"I'm a special agent, U.S. Secret Service. I need to ask you a few questions."

"What is this shit? Calling me out here for nothing?"

"I thought it might be easier for us to talk with no one else around."

"Talk about what?"

"Garth Alexander."

Vincent blinked rapidly. "Who's he?"

"He was killed in a shoot-out."

A revealing expression crossed Vincent's face—a brief twitch of the left upper lip and jaw that told Garrison Vincent was hearing the news for the first time.

"You feds don't impress me any. Don't ever stiff me with a bad call again or I'll squeeze your neck until your heads pops off."

"All I want is what you know about Alexander. No one has to know that you and I are talking."

"I can't believe this. You actually got me out here on a stiff call."

"I understand you served time with Alexander in Europe. You and he were involved in collecting debts for a French gunrunner and got tagged. All I want to know is what has been going on with Alexander recently."

Vincent smirked. "If he's dead, what do you give a fuck?"

"Alexander got himself involved in something that is a lot bigger than breaking legs and gunrunning. That's how he ended up getting smoked. This isn't a routine case. This is as big as it gets and I'm not just going to go away. I promise that what you tell me will be kept in confidence. No one has to know that we talked. Just tell me what you know about Alexander and you have my word that you can get back in your rig and drive off. That's not a lot to ask it, is it?"

"Let's put it to you like this, federal shine boy: Even if I did know the motherfucker, I wouldn't tell you."

Anger welled from deep inside Garrison. He detested men like Vincent, a member of the great American white, angry underclass that blamed their perceived misfortune on everyone but themselves.

Vincent opened the driver's door of his truck. Garrison slammed the door shut and Vincent got a wild look in his eye.

"You think you're a real big man standing there with your badge and piece, don't you, cocksucker?"

"I didn't fly across the country to have you walk away from me."

"You want to fight? I'll whip your ass here and now."

Garrison lunged and delivered a straight right punch that caught Vincent squarely on the nose and slammed his head against the truck door. Vincent made an animal-like grunt and began fighting back. Deflecting two of his counterpunches, Garrison leaned into a powerful body blow, striking Vincent sharply in his swollen torso. Garrison punched savagely—a left and a right combination, then a slashing uppercut. Vincent went down, sliding on the gravel, then scrambled to his feet and dove at him. Garrison threw a right, striking him on the jaw and stopping his forward motion. Vincent dropped solidly to his hands and knees. Garrison snap-kicked him, lifting Vincent's jaw and knocking him unconscious.

Garrison looked about, and then searched the tow truck cab. In the glove compartment he found a loaded .45 automatic. He shoved it in his waistband, returned to Vincent, and then slapped him awake.

"No more," Vincent said.

"Now I'll explain it in language you understand, hillbilly. Either tell me what you know about Alexander or I put your ass in jail."

Vincent spat blood. "What's the charge?"

"All the things you got away with in the past."

Vincent rubbed his chin with both hands. "You'd really do that, wouldn't you? You'd frame my ass just because I'm on parole."

"Watch me."

"I can't be going to jail."

"Then start cranking those jaws, tough guy."

"About what? I don't know anything."

"Let's start with the Aryan Disciples."

"I know a few members but I ain't into any of that political shit."

"What do you know about them killing a Secret Service agent in Washington, D.C.?"

"Not a damn thing," Vincent answered without hesitation. "I swear on my mother's grave. Nothing. If that's what you're here about, you got the wrong dude."

"When did you first meet Garth Alexander?"

"In Spain a few years ago. I was doing some time in a Malaga prison. The police said I had a hand grenade in my luggage and they said I was connected with a bunch of Basque rebels. But it was bullshit. Alexander and I were the only Americans there and we got to know each other. We knew some of the same people."

"Aryan Disciples people?"

Vincent struggled to his feet and wiped his mouth with the back of his hand. "Yeah. But I didn't know him for very long. He escaped. Alexander was good at that kind of shit. He used to be in the French Foreign Legion. Look, I know what you're here about. It's because I put him together with someone a couple of weeks ago, right?"

"Who are you talking about?"

Vincent shook his head. "I ain't going to commit suicide."

"No one is asking you to. All I want is some guidance

on this. No one will know. You have my word."

"Feds lie."

"Yeah, and you are a donkey," Garrison said. "Either sing or put you hands on the truck so I can package you up."

"All I did was steer him to a guy."

"Who?"

"A guy named Timmons. That's who I put him together with. Timmons was looking for someone to handle a job. He asked for him by name. He knew that I knew him."

"Timmons. What's his game?"

Vincent stared blankly at the highway. "Explosives. He's with the Disciples."

Garrison took out a cell phone and offered him the cell phone.

"What's this for?"

"Call Timmons and tell him you have a buyer for C-4."

"Are you nuts?"

"Either you help me put a case on him or it's back to the pen."

"You're trying to put a twist on him, aren't you? You want to put him in a position where he will snitch for you."

"Duh."

Vincent stared at him for a moment, and then took the phone. During the next hour, Vincent made a number of telephone calls—leaving messages on answering machines and with bartenders. Finally he reached Timmons.

"Hello . . . Spike. Who the hell do you think? I have a man I want you to meet. He's interested in buying some sewing machines. . . . What do you think? . . . The river. We'll be there."

Vincent pressed OFF and handed the phone back to Garrison.

"What did he say?"

"He'll meet you but only if I come along."

"Let's go."

"He's gonna know it was me. He's gonna know I set him up. He'll kill me."

"Not if he's in the joint."

"Timmons is in with the Aryan Disciples. I can get killed over this."

"You wouldn't have set up the meeting if you were worried about him or them. So cut the sob story and let's get on with it."

The corners of Vincent's mouth elevated into a smile. "I like your moves."

Night fell as Garrison rode in the passenger seat of the tow truck and wondered if he had bitten off more than he could chew. Vincent was driving.

"Timmons will put us through some changes—security procedures—he's super-cautious when doing a deal. Particularly when he is selling explosives. He and some of his boys broke into an Army base down in Texas and stole the shit. He's been making a living off it ever since."

Garrison was driving to God knows where to attempt to buy explosives from a known terrorist and he had no buy money. He was alone and he didn't trust Vincent. Admittedly, Garrison was afraid. To him, fear was an emotion to be controlled, to utilize to his best advantage. He'd realized this for the first time in the Army, when he'd learned to disarm bombs. It was a matter of detaching oneself from the reality of fear. Overcoming the natural instinct to flee a perceived danger put one into another zone; one that he'd become accustomed to after years in the Secret Service.

Garrison recalled being in Cartagena, Colombia, riding on the running board of the Presidential convertible limousine as the President waved at the throngs of onlookers lining the street. As the motorcade turned the corner, a man had emerged from the throng and sprinted toward the limousine. Without thinking, Garrison had jumped from the moving limousine and tackled him. Afterwards, Garrison realized that he hadn't been afraid, that he'd mastered the fear of dying for the Man. But tonight was different. He was in a strange place trying to investigate terrorists and he didn't trust Vincent. Garrison was over his head with no one on his side and he knew that he could get killed.

In northern Bakersfield, Vincent swerved the tow truck off Highway 99 onto an adjacent road and threaded his way to the tree-lined Kern River.

"What's this?" Garrison asked.

"Take it easy. I know what this looks like, but it's just part of Timmons's security act."

Vincent turned left and cruised slowly along the riverbank. They were out of sight of cars passing on the highway, and Garrison wondered if Vincent was leading him into an Aryan Disciples trap. Stopping at a boat shack, Vincent turned off the engine. The truck windows were down and the eucalyptus trees rustled with a warm breeze. A full moon mirrored itself on the shiny, black-glass water. The night heat reminded Garrison of the Persian Gulf War when he'd hiked ten miles at night to

lay mines near an enemy fuel depot. Vincent's hands
were shaking.

From behind the boat shack came the sound of a motorcycle engine turning over. Garrison pulled his automatic and touched it in Vincent's rib cage.

"If anything happens you'll be the first one to die."

"Easy, man."

A man wearing a cowboy hat drove a motorcycle
from behind the shack, revving the engine. Moving to
the passenger side of the tow truck, he turned on a flashlight and aimed its narrow beam at Garrison's face.

Garrison aimed his gun at him.

"Get the light out of my eyes."

"Everything okay, Spike?" the cowboy asked.

"We're cool."

"Your boy here has got the jumps, doesn't he?"

"He don't know you."

"Where'd you get that black eye?"

"My old lady threw a pan at me."

"You're lucky it wasn't full of hot grease. Follow
me."

The man revved the engine and slowly drove toward
the highway. Vincent turned the ignition key.

"Who's he?"

"One of Timmons's people. He's taking us to Timmons. He has other people here. If any cops had followed us, they would have wasted us for sure."

They followed the motorcycle onto the highway.

"Where are we going?"

"To one of the three pads that Timmons uses for his
deals. Don't forget. We knew each other from L.A. I
told Timmons you had money and you wanted military-

grade C-4. When I told him I wanted sewing machines, he knew I meant C-4."

"How can you be sure he has the stuff?"

"He didn't try to put off the deal, so he must have it. I've bought from him before."

They followed the motorcycle along Highway 99 for about a mile, and Garrison could feel sweat soaking through his T-shirt. The motorcycle swerved onto an off-ramp and got off at Bakersfield's Oildale section, comprised of run-down tract homes and apartment houses. He made a few turns, and ended up in a deserted area lined with abandoned factories and empty lots. Passing an automobile junkyard, the motorcycle turned left into a gravel-covered driveway and crossed an empty lot covered with weeds to a single-story, wood-frame house that was next to a chicken coop. There was a light next to the front porch. A handwritten sign on a post next to the door read: NO PEDDLERS—RING BUZZER. There was a Ford Thunderbird parked in front of the house.

"That's Timmons's car."

The motorcyclist pointed toward the door, then turned and drove past them, heading back toward the road. Vincent turned off the engine and they got out of the truck.

Garrison could sense someone watching them in the darkness, a lookout probably. But he figured that if they were going to kill him, they would have done it at the river.

Vincent knocked on the door. "Timmons?"

"Come in," a man shouted.

Vincent turned the handle and shoved the door open. Garrison followed him inside. A sofa and lounger were arranged around a large-screen television tuned to a talk show. The dingy living room reeked of stale cigarette smoke and beer. A bearded, overweight Timmons was sitting at a dinette table in front of a .38 revolver. He wore a black leather vest and white T-shirt. He had a leathery complexion. A splash of dark freckles extended from his cheeks upward across his baldness.

"You sure you weren't followed?"

"Positive," Vincent said.

Timmons smirked. "You must have eyes in the back of your head."

"This is my man," Vincent said to introduce Garrison.

"Spike says you need some clay."

"Right."

"Who you going to blow up?"

"Your mom."

Timmons glared at Garrison, and then turned to Vincent.

"This cat is a friend of yours, right, Spike?"

"He's good people. And I've seen his buy money. Every dollar."

Timmons lit a cigarette and coughed. The walls were covered with what Garrison would describe as American fascist kitsch; racing flags, a luminous painting of John Wayne, a saddle, a hand-painted WHITE POWER sign and swastika, deer hooves, an antique rifle.

"Yeah, now I want to see it," said Timmons.

It was sweltering and Garrison felt like he needed air.

"It's in town."

"So go get it."

"Not until I see the stuff."

Garrison had to give himself time. He could sense other people in the house. Garrison had to get Timmons away from this house. For all he knew, people were hiding in the other rooms. In a fight, he would be out-numbered.

"What's wrong, funnyman?" Timmons asked.

"I'm the one with the money. I went through your security games. Now it's my call. I don't know you."

"Spike does."

"For all I know, you and he might be planning to rip me off. Maybe you're planning to kill me and bury me in your chicken coop."

Timmons studied him with a practiced look of disdain. "If we could get away with it we probably would." He laughed, and Vincent joined in. "Where you from, man?"

"Beverly Hills."

"Yeah, and I'm from the wonderful land of dog dick."

"You look like it. So what's it gonna be? Do you want to sell some clay or should I head back over the grapevine?"

Timmons coughed richly and turned to Vincent.

"Okay. You pick the spot to do the deal. Call me in exactly one hour."

Garrison followed Vincent toward the door.

"What happened to you, Spike?"

"Huh?"

"Your eye."

"Oh, that—"

"I punched him because he talked back to me," Garrison said.

Vincent laughed. "My wife threw something at me."

Timmons smiled sardonically.

Garrison followed Vincent outside. They got back in the truck.

"You got a lot of balls," Vincent said as they drove off.

On Buck Owens Boulevard Garrison saw a neon sign: MARTY'S BAKERSFIELD INN—CABLE TV, FREE ICE. He motioned to Vincent and they drove into the parking lot.

Garrison stared through the window down at a dimly lit Buck Owens Boulevard. He glanced at his Timex, and had the peculiar sensation that he was trapped in the motel room with its rattling air conditioner and cowboys-on-horseback-chasing-Indians prints on the wall. Vincent had been pacing the room and it was getting on Garrison's nerves.

"It's been an hour since you made the call," Garrison said. "Where is he?"

"He's cagey. But he'll be here. Look, man. What the hell are you going to do when he delivers the C-4?"

"Arrest him. Then you can leave."

"Where are the rest of your people?"

"Nearby."

"Why haven't you been talking to them, telling them what the hell is going on?" '

"Relax, Spike."

"Relax? My ass is on the line here."

Garrison knew he was right. But Timmons was the one who'd sought out the hit man Alexander. Garrison had to find out why and there was no other way. A man like Timmons wasn't going to tell him anything unless he had something to hold over his head. Could Timmons have been the one who sent Alexander to kill the President? What was Timmons's role? Garrison needed a case to hold over Timmons's head if he was going to get him to tell what he knew about Garth Alexander.

A Ford Thunderbird veered into the parking lot. Garrison leaned close to the glass.

"It's him."

Vincent joined him at the window. They watched as Timmons slowly cruised past the motel office and pulled into a parking space. Garrison felt his pulse quicken.

Timmons got out of the Thunderbird, looked about, then took out a handkerchief and wiped his neck and brow. Then a blue, late-model pickup truck drove into the parking lot and maneuvered into a marked space next to the Thunderbird. Two men with shaved heads climbed out and began talking to Timmons. Garrison leaned close to the venetian blind. He'd wondered whether Timmons would come alone. The men wore loose-fitting shirts, which Garrison assumed meant that they were carrying guns.

"He didn't say anything about bringing muscle with him."

"They work for him," Vincent said, looking worried. "What's going on, Spike?"

"This means Timmons didn't like your looks. He'll probably demand to see your money before he delivers anything."

Garrison knew he was at the reward-risk intersection that comes in every undercover case—that moment when all the maneuvering was over. Outnumbered or not, he'd succeeded in getting Timmons away from his home turf. Now the trick was to get him to show the C-4, establishing a possession case that Garrison could use to make him talk. He had to go through with it as is.

Timmons opened the driver's door of the Thunderbird and took out a shiny aluminum briefcase.

"That must be the C-4," Vincent said. "Look. Once he gets here, I'm gonna split—"

"You're not going anywhere."

"I done my part—"

"It'll make him suspicious if you want to leave. I'll do the talking and you will go along with what I say. Get it?"

"Okay. Okay. But I don't like it. I don't want to be involved."

Timmons and the skinheads began walking across the lot in their direction, and Garrison had the instinctive urge to pick up a two-way radio and notify other Secret Service units. But there was neither a radio nor any Secret Service units to help him. Garrison drew his SIG-Sauer and checked the clip, then reholstered. He closed the venetian blind.

There was the sound of knocking on the door.

Garrison checked the peephole, and then opened it. Chino Timmons was holding the briefcase in his left hand. The skinheads were behind him.

Garrison opened the door.

"I thought you got lost."

"Me pass up a deal? Not on your life, funnyman. Aren't you going to invite us in?"

Garrison nodded toward the skinheads. "Who are they?"

"You didn't think I was going to show up alone, did you?"

"What are you worried about?"

"There are two of you and I have the shit. What's the damn problem? What are you afraid of?"

Garrison reluctantly stepped aside. There was nothing else to do. He had to know for sure that Timmons had the explosives. He had to see the C-4 or he would have no hold on Timmons.

Timmons walked in, followed by the skinheads. They reeked of motor oil, tobacco and marijuana, the stench of losers who hated the police and the federal government and believed black helicopters filled with FBI agents, an evil White House, and greedy Wall Street bankers were out to destroy them. The skinheads, though trying to look poised, had a flushed appearance that reminded Garrison of paratroopers waiting to jump. That was the way it was in contraband cases: strangers meeting strangers to commit crime. It was a zero-sum game where each side suspected the other of planning to rob them. Garrison knew half such undercover meetings ended in robbery.

"Let's see your cash," Timmons said.

Garrison closed the door. "Not before I see the C-4."

Timmons stared at Garrison and nervously chewed his bottom lip.

Vincent moved toward the door. Timmons's eyes darted toward the skinheads. They moved in front of the door, blocking Vincent's exit. Garrison could feel the tension in the room.

"Where are you going?" Timmons asked.

"I have to get back to work. You guys go ahead and do your thing. Hell, you don't need me."

"You ain't never let a deal scare you before, Spike," Timmons said.

"We don't need him," Garrison said. He felt like choking him.

Timmons's right hand dropped to his side. "What's wrong, my man?"

"I'm on parole," Vincent said. "I gotta be careful."

Vincent tried to push past the skinheads. They stopped him.

"Don't let him screw up a solid deal," Garrison said. "Let him go."

Timmons's eyes were wide. He pulled a .45 automatic and aimed it at Garrison. The skinheads drew guns.

Timmons moved to Vincent and slapped him across the face with the .45. Vincent went to his knees.

"What's up, Spike?"

"Nothing. I swear."

"Where's the buy money?"

"It's close by," Garrison said.

"Shut up, motherfucker," Timmons said, pressing the barrel of the .45 to Vincent's head.

"Go get it."

"Let's go, Spike," Garrison said.

"Spike is gonna wait right here with us until you get back," Timmons said.

At that moment Garrison knew that the time for talking was over. Garrison felt suspended in time, as if he were looking down into the room from afar, waiting for the inevitable violence to explode. There was no talking his way out. Vincent was going to crack. Garrison could see it in his eyes. Now it was a matter of survival.

"He don't have any buy money," Vincent said. "If he leaves he won't come back. He forced me to introduce him to you."

Garrison's head throbbed as they stared at him.

Timmons pulled the slide on the .45.

"Who is he, Spike?"

"A fed," Vincent said. "He said he would kill me if I didn't introduce him to you. He has a gun. There was nothing else I could do."

Timmons moved to Garrison.

"So you came here to do me, eh, fed? Did you, rotten motherfucker?"

Garrison snatched the barrel of Timmons's gun with both hands. The gun fired searing Garrison's neck. He yanked Timmons in front of him as a shield, shoving the gun into his back.

"Tell them to drop the guns," Garrison said.

The skinheads looked panicky and unsure of themselves as they aimed their guns in Garrison's direction, unable to fire without hitting Timmons.

"Do as he says," Timmons said.

The skinheads looked at one another, just for a split second. The man on the left began lowering his weapon slowly. The man on the right edged slowly toward Garrison's right, and there was no doubt in Garrison's mind that he was trying to line up Garrison for a head shot.

Garrison pulled Timmons tightly in front of him and shot the skinhead. The room erupted in rapid, deafening gunshots, muzzle-flashes, shouts, and breaking glass. Timmons dropped like a puppet with severed strings and Garrison went down with him, instinctively firing the .45 at the skinhead still standing. As the windows and the mirror shattered, what flashed through Garrison's mind wasn't his *life,* as those who'd never experienced such terror imagined, but his death—the final destination a cheap room at Marty's Bakersfield Inn. *Garrison, Peter* would be written on his toe-tag and a bored attendant would roll his corpse into the back of a coroner's wagon parked under the blinking neon downstairs.

Then, suddenly, everything was quiet. A haze of acrid gunsmoke hung in the air. Timmons was lying in the middle of the room, holding his side and moaning. Vincent was on his back next to the bed. The skinheads were in a jumble next to the door, unmoving. Garrison held his gun in the two-handed combat position as he moved forward to check the skinheads. They were dead, as was Vincent. Garrison touched his own neck. His skin was creased, burned. A bullet had missed killing him by millimeters.

"Get up," Garrison said to Timmons.

"My side . . . I've been shot."

Garrison grabbed Timmons by his shirt collar and pulled him to his feet.

"Give me your car keys."

"What?"

Garrison reached into his trouser pocket and took out car keys. He picked up the briefcase and dragged Timmons out of the room and down the stairs. Forcing him across the lot to the Thunderbird, Garrison opened the passenger door and shoved him inside and across the seat to behind the wheel. Keeping the gun on him, Garrison climbed in and pulled the door closed. Motel occupants began streaming out of their rooms to see what was going on.

"Drive."

"I'm bleeding, man."

Garrison shoved the gun against his neck.

"Okay. Okay."

Timmons shoved the key into the ignition and started the engine. He backed out of the parking space and drove onto Buck Owens Boulevard.

"Head for the river."

Minutes later, Timmons pulled off the road and drove to a spot near the boathouse, where Garrison had been earlier.

"I need a doctor."

"Turn off the lights."

Timmons complied.

"Now get out."

Timmons opened the door and climbed out, holding the right side of his abdomen. Garrison got out on the passenger side, walked around the car, and aimed the gun at him. Keeping his eyes on Timmons, Garrison opened the briefcase, took out the C-4.

"What are you gonna do, man?"

"Give me a match."

Timmons looked at him strangely as he searched his pockets. He handed him a book of matches. Garrison struck a match and lit the C-4. It began burning, slowly.

"What the hell?"

"Don't worry. It won't blow without a blasting cap. We used to light campfires with it in the Army." He dropped it in a metal trash can. He moved close to Timmons. "Now listen closely. A couple of weeks ago you asked Vincent to find you a hit man. Why?"

"I ain't no rat."

Garrison pointed the SIG-Sauer at Timmons's right leg.

"Don't shoot!"

"Talk."

"I went to Vincent as a favor. A guy I know offered me ten grand to find him a hit man. Supposedly there was some paper out on some guy who'd ripped someone off for a lot of money. The contract was for two hundred and fifty thousand dollars. He wanted a shooter from outside the country—someone reliable, a professional. All I did was make a few calls. I knew Spike Vincent had connections across the pond, so I asked him if he knew anyone who fit the bill. He told me about this Alexander; some dude he'd served time with. Vincent gave me his E-mail address and I passed the information on. I'm not guilty of any crime. I'm bleeding, man. You got to get me to a hospital or I'm gonna die."

"The guy who was looking for the hit man. I didn't hear a name."

"You ain't no cop. Who the fuck are you?"

Garrison slapped him across the face with the gun, knocking him down. As he tried to get up, Garrison kicked him. Timmons fell backward, into the shallow river.

"Eddie Richardson," Timmons said after spitting water.

"Where can I find him?"

"I met him in a bar called the Corral Club. He seemed like a together guy. I know he's done some time. That's about it. All I did was give him some information. A pass-off kind of thing. What happened after that, I had no control over. I'm an innocent bystander. Why should I get screwed behind something like this? I'm going to bleed out, man."

"I'll take you to the hospital just as soon as you tell me what you know about Richardson."

"Medium build, brown hair. He weighs more than you."

"Where can I find him?"

"Look, dude. I can't tell you something I don't know. This Richardson is a secretive-type person. That was one of the reasons he and I didn't hit it off after a couple of weeks. He was a damn liar. I don't know where he is staying. And I just didn't trust him."

Garrison raised his gun and took careful aim.

"What the hell are you doing? I told you everything I know. I swear I'm telling you the—"

Aiming the SIG-Sauer slightly to the right of Timmons, Garrison fired. Timmons shrieked and fell into the shallow water as the fire flash momentarily lit the river. Timmons struggled to his knees and patted his chest to see if he had been hit. Garrison aimed at his head.

"Richardson is staying in a motel—at the Viking Ship Residence Inn in Vienna, Virginia. That's near Washington, D.C. I talked to him day before yesterday. He said he wouldn't be coming back for about a week. But if you tell him I ratted him out, he'll kill me."

"If I get back there and I find out that you called him and told him I was looking for him, then all bets are off. I'll be back to finish you."

"I won't. I swear."

Garrison drove Timmons's car to Bakersfield Mercy Hospital and left him at the emergency entrance.

Garrison cruised south to Highway 99, ascending from the Central Valley flatland up the Grapevine, a steep grade leading through the mountainous Tejon Pass toward Los Angeles. His mind was filled with what he had learned. It was a jumble of facts that barely fit together, leading to someone named Eddie Richardson. The case reminded Garrison of other investigations where the facts were disparate, like blackbirds that swooped down now and then, wings fluttering, only to fly away again. Some of the cases remained unsolved to this day. But something about this investigation was different and, for the life of him, he couldn't put his finger on it.

About forty minutes later, he reached the bottom of the grapevine, where two main L.A. freeway arteries led into the smoggy Los Angeles basin. He took Highway 210, leading south and east to Interstate 10, leading toward Ontario Airport, east of Los Angeles. He would depart from Ontario rather than the Bakersfield or Los Angeles International Airport, where he assumed agents might be monitoring outgoing flights, looking for him.

At the Ontario Airport he parked his car in a pay lot and used his cell phone to make a reservation under the name Joachim Porzig on a flight from L.A. Airport to Mexico City. He believed that the Porzig passport that he'd used to fly from D.C. had probably been reported stolen by now, and the reservation would create a false trail for his pursuers that would give him more time.

In the departure terminal, Garrison roamed about a ticket counter until he spotted a man similar to him in age and description. He got in line behind him. The line moved to the ticket counter, where the man purchased a ticket. The clerk asked for his driver's license and the man took a wallet from his inside jacket pocket, displayed the license, and paid for the ticket. Garrison departed the line. The man left the counter and walked to a departure area, where he shrugged off his jacket and hung it over the back of a lounge seat. He sat down and began reading a magazine. Garrison sat next to him. When the man rose to make a call from a pay telephone a few feet away, Garrison looked about quickly to see if anyone was watching, then reached into the jacket and pulled out the wallet. He walked to an American Airlines ticket counter, hoping that no one had seen him.

Garrison asked a harried young female clerk for a one-way ticket to Washington, D.C. She filled out a ticket. She asked for his identification. He handed her the driver's license that was in the wallet.

During the flight back to D.C, Garrison gazed across the wing at a wide ledge of rain clouds far in the distance: shimmering gray cotton painted in the sky. He wondered about Martha Breckinridge—what she'd thought after hearing that he'd escaped from custody—and about Eleanor. Was she working to clear him? Or had someone in the White House convinced her he was an assassin? Garrison felt alone and abandoned. Experience had taught him that the answer to most cases—the key that opened the lock—was invariably found not just in assimilating the relevant facts, but in the way one looked at them. He had to find that way. There was no turning back. He knew that he had crossed the point of no return.

CHAPTER 24

GARRISON SHOWED HIS badge to the motel clerk at the Viking Ship Residence Inn in Vienna, Virginia.

"Do you have a Richardson registered here?"

The motel was a forty-room establishment that was next door to a supermarket. Fearful of renting a car, Garrison had taken the Metro from Dulles Airport to Vienna and then walked from the station to the motel.

"What's this about?" the clerk said.

He had a deep accent that Garrison guessed was East Indian. He was fiftyish and morbidly overweight. He wore a white Guayabera shirt with ink marks on the pockets and his eyeglasses were coated with dandruff flakes.

"A security matter."

"Mr. Richardson is in Room 785."

"May I see the registration card?"

Reaching into a file box behind the counter, the clerk thumbed through a few dividers, then handed Garrison a registration card. Garrison read it. Eddie Richardson had registered a week earlier, listing his address as a post of-fice box in Bakersfield. There was neither an automobile license number nor a telephone number listed on the card.

"Has he made any telephone calls from his room?"

The clerk let out his breath as if exasperated, and checked another file. "No telephone calls."

"Have you seen him today?"

"There are too many guests staying here for me to keep track. I am not their father and mother."

"I'd like you to call his room to see if he's there. If he answers, just make up some excuse—"

"I know what to do." The manager dialed the phone and held the receiver to his ear for what must have been a full minute. "No one answers." He set the receiver down.

"I'll need the key."

"Do you have a search warrant?"

"No. But if I get one, it gives me the right to kick in the door and tear up the room. Handing over the key for a few minutes could save you some repair bills."

Garrison wasn't going to wait. He had to get inside the room to see what Richardson had in there.

The manager opened a drawer, took out a key, and handed it to him.

Garrison glanced at some room numbers to figure out the location of Richardson's room. On the second floor, he put his ear to the door of Room 785. He heard a radio inside, playing loudly—a talk show? Garrison drew his gun. Using his left hand, he slipped the key into the lock and shoved the door open. The light was on. He walked inside with gun at the ready, his finger on the trigger.

There was a body on the floor next to the bed, curled in the fetal position. Garrison moved closer. It was Hightower and he was obviously dead. His grayish pallor and the expression of frozen anguish on his face would have made a startling Halloween mask. Garrison stepped back.

"What the hell—?"

Garrison holstered his gun. Kneeling down, he touched Hightower's arm. Stiff. He'd been dead for a few hours. Hightower was wearing a white T-shirt and jeans. On his chest were three bloodstains that had melded together and dried into fuzzy, uneven red circles. What had Hightower been doing in Richardson's room?

Garrison stood and returned to the door. Taking the key out of the lock, he pulled the door closed. He began searching the room. A half-full bottle of Yankee Clipper whiskey was on the dresser table. The drawers held only socks and T-shirts. A small garment bag on the floor next to the bed had nothing in it but men's clothing. He lifted the mattress and pulled it away from the bed to check behind. Nothing. Garrison picked up a wallet on the bed. It contained a few hundred dollars and a Florida driver's license in the name of Eddie Richardson. The identification photograph on it was of Frank Hightower. Garrison felt a chill travel down the back of his neck.

Richardson was Frank Hightower.

What the hell is going on? Garrison asked himself. It didn't make sense. Hightower, using the fictitious name Richardson, had hired the hit man, Garth Alexander, and then reported the assassination plot to Garrison. Hightower's information had been a ruse to lead Garrison and the rest of the Secret Service away from the real con-

spirators. Someone had used Hightower to throw up a
smoke screen. And whoever it was had just made sure
that Hightower wouldn't be able to tell what he knew.
It was a sophisticated plot that reeked of insider's knowledge of both the Secret Service and the White House.

In a trash can next to the dresser Garrison found a
copy of yesterday's *Washington Post,* some empty cigarette packages, coffee shop receipts, chewing gum
wrappers, orange peels, a receipt from a Pizza Hut restaurant in Beltsville, Maryland. Someone had written,
"MEET—9 PM—EVERY OTHER DAY," on it.

"Beltsville," Garrison said to himself.

Beltsville, Maryland, was where the Secret Service
Training Academy and SOT, Flanagan's special unit,
were located.

The phone rang, startling Garrison. He let it ring again
before picking up the receiver.

"Yes?"

"This is the motel manager. Uh, I found some more
telephone records. Would you like to see them?"

"I'll be right down."

"Very good."

The phone clicked.

Garrison knew something was wrong. He could feel
it. He moved to the window and peeked through the
venetian blinds. The manager opened the motel office
door and waved in the direction of a four-door Mercury
in the corner of the parking lot, then went back inside.

Flanagan and Beatty got out of the Mercury.

Garrison realized that Flanagan had been waiting for
him. How did he know he would come here? Garrison
ran to the bathroom and peeked out the louvered window. To the right, a black, late-model Mercury was

parked blocking the alley. The two men in it looked like
Secret Service agents. To the left, the alley ended behind
a tire store. A chain-link fence separated the alley from
a supermarket parking lot. Garrison stood frozen for a
moment, thinking about what to do, then grabbed his
cell phone and dialed 911.

"Police Department emergency," a woman said.
"What do you wish to report?"

"A kidnapping. I was looking out the window of my
motel room and I saw two men grab a young girl and
shove her in the trunk of a black Mercury. They're
parked in the alley behind the Viking Ship Residence
Inn. The girl was screaming. Please hurry."

There was a sound of three electronic beeps.

"A car is on the way, sir. What is your name?"

"Alexander. Garth Alexander."

"Stay where you are, sir. The officers are on their way."

"Please hurry."

He pressed OFF, and then slid panes of glass one by
one from the louvered bathroom window, placing them
in the bathtub. Hearing the sound of distant sirens, he
looked down the alley. Police cars were screeching to a
halt on either side of the Mercury. Officers jumped out
and leveled guns at the agents.

"Driver!" a uniformed officer shouted. "Turn off the
engine and get out of the car!"

Someone knocked on the motel room door.

Garrison's heart pounded wildly as he stepped onto the
edge of the bathtub and manipulated his feet into the window opening. Slithering out, he dropped to the alley,
landed feet-first and rolled to the left as he landed, the
way he'd been taught in Secret Service school. The police
officers and the Secret Service agents were shouting at

one another. The diversion had worked. He ran across the alley and the soles of his feet stung from the drop. He vaulted the fence and ran through the supermarket parking lot. Crossing the street at a full sprint, he turned left and ran down the sidewalk to a two-story shopping mall down the block, where he jogged into a driveway. He rode the elevator to the roof and walked to the edge. Below, there was no sign of police or Secret Service activity. Garrison needed a car. On the other side of the lot, a man was getting out of a Chevrolet Malibu. Garrison pulled back his suit jacket to reveal his gun to the driver.

"All I want is your car."

The man's eyes widened and he raised his hands. "I don't have any money."

Garrison took his car keys. "If you value your car, don't call the police for an hour."

The man backed away. Garrison pulled open the driver's door, climbed in, and started the engine. He sped down the ramps to the street. Turning right, he drove at the speed limit.

Spotting a service station, he got an idea and pulled the car into the service bay. A bearded young man with a long ponytail was working under a car on the next hoist. Garrison got out of the car.

"I need an oil change."

The man pulled a rag from his back pocket and wiped his hands.

"I can't have it done until five-thirty."

"Take your time."

In the service station office, Garrison wrote a fictitious name and address on a work order sheet, and then used the telephone to call a taxi. He remained in the office, keeping his eyes on the street as he waited.

CHAPTER 25

BRECKINRIDGE WALKED OUT the front door of Secret Service headquarters and took a deep breath. Even with the mugginess, being outside felt good. She'd been at her desk for hours, making phone calls and following up leads, none of which had panned out. Still mulling over the confusing Garrison situation, she began walking.

At the end of her shift, Breckinridge left headquarters and walked to her regular parking space on the fourth floor of the District Auto Park. Ambling to her car, she took keys from her purse and unlocked the driver's door. Something poked in the back.

"Don't turn around, Martha."

Her stomach contracted. Garrison moved close, reaching inside her jacket.

"Pete."

He took her gun, shoving it in his waistband. He took her purse. Opening the door, he tossed the purse in the backseat.

"Get in."

"Where are we going?"

"Just get in."

He was holding the gun close to his side in case anyone else in the lot was looking. She climbed behind the wheel. He walked to the passenger side of the car, and for a moment she considered jumping out and running. He got in.

"Stop aiming the gun at me."

"I will if you'll give your word you will listen to me for five minutes."

She studied him.

"Okay."

He holstered the gun.

"Martha, nothing you've ever heard is as important as what I'm about to tell you. I had nothing to do with the helicopter bombing. I'm being framed. Someone picked me to be the fall guy."

"Then why did you escape?"

"I wasn't going to sit in jail on a no-bail hold while Flanagan took his time building a phony case on me."

"Are you telling me that you believe Flanagan is knowingly framing you for an attempted assassination?"

He looked her in the eye.

"I'm not sure. All I know at this point is that someone chose me to be the scapegoat."

"If what you are saying is true, don't you see that running away plays right into their hands?"

"What the hell was I supposed to do?"

"Come on, Pete. Did it ever enter your mind to follow

standard procedure and go to the Director?"

"You know Wintergreen as well as I do. Do you really believe he would go against his right-hand man?"

Breckinridge studied him. He looked disheveled, but he was making some sense. He hadn't gone crazy. He was the same Garrison she knew and the expression on his face was without duplicity. He looked desperate, but she saw no indication of guilt.

"Martha, someone has gone to a lot of trouble to put me in the kill-zone. They've planted more evidence against me than there was against Lee Harvey Oswald for killing President Kennedy. They are protecting themselves by throwing up a smoke screen. This is a sophisticated frame-job using inside knowledge. Whoever is behind this knows full well that no conspiracy would be able to stand up to a full-scale post-assassination investigation. That's why they needed a scapegoat. You don't believe me, do you?"

She stared at him as she tried to assemble the facts that were bobbling about at the back of her mind in some logical, reasonable order. If he was guilty, why would he be risking contact with her rather than, say, trying to flee the country? What did he have to gain by trying to convince her of his innocence? Garrison wasn't dumb.

"Pete, how did you end up at that Aryan Disciples accommodation address in the Sperling Finance Building?"

"I . . . I can't tell you that."

"Then I don't believe anything you are telling me."

"If I told you it would violate a confidence."

"Bullshit."

"You're just going to have to trust—"

"You just pulled a gun on me. That violated a confidence. What the hell is going on, Pete? This isn't a game. Level with me, for God's sake."

"There are certain things I can't go into."

"Pete, you just told me you believe that there is a plot against the President and your life is in danger. If that is true, there should be *nothing* you would hold back to convince me of what you are saying. The time for secrets is over. This is it. It's all or nothing for you. And as of right now, I don't believe you."

"I'm asking you to trust me."

"Put yourself in my place. What if I came to you with this same story and then refused to tell you everything— if I told you I didn't want to *violate a confidence*. Would you believe me?" Garrison rubbed his temples. He looked pale. "If you didn't think you could trust me, why the hell are you here?"

Garrison let out his breath.

"I went to the Sperling Finance Building to investigate a blackmail attempt on the First Lady." He told her about finding evidence in Garth Alexander's motel room, then receiving the blackmail letter and the photograph.

"Who was in the photograph?"

Garrison licked his lips.

"The First Lady and me."

"You mean—?"

He looked embarrassed and lost. "Yes."

She told herself that he either was, in fact, fully insane, or telling the uncomfortable truth.

"You dumb shit."

"It was just something that happened. It wasn't planned—"

"Go ahead. Let's hear the rest of it."

He told her the following: that he'd shown the black-mail letter to the First Lady; that he'd subsequently gone to the Mayflower Hotel; that he'd been directed to the Sperling Finance Building but the blackmailer had never arrived; that a man he'd suspected of being the black-mailer had gotten the drop on him and knocked him out, and later had turned out to be an FBI agent; that the informant Frank Hightower, responsible for reporting the assassination conspiracy, had been murdered.

"What?"

"I found a driver's license in the name of Eddie Rich-ardson on Hightower's body."

"Hightower . . ." she said.

"Someone was using him. Hightower was nothing but a rat. He was in it for money. But he's no extremist and he wasn't heavy enough to have engineered this whole thing on his own."

"Exactly what was he up to?"

"For one thing, making it appear that the Aryan Dis-ciples were involved in the assassination of the Presi-dent."

"Which means they probably aren't."

"Yes."

Breckinridge ran a hand though her hair as she con-templated the facts.

"And the same unnamed conspirators sent Alexander to kill you. . . ."

"Because it was obvious that an agent had to have been the one who planted the C-4 on Marine One," Gar-rison said. "They had to have an agent scapegoat to cover the tracks of the agent who actually did it. They wanted to make it look like the Aryan Disciples had used me and then gotten rid of me. Look at it like this: If

Alexander had succeeded in killing me, all that would have been left was a trail of evidence leading straight to me and I wouldn't have been there to counter it—the way the evidence trail died with Lee Harvey Oswald. I was set up to be the Secret Service agent who sold out to the Aryan Disciples."

Breckinridge ran a finger along her upper lip. What Garrison was saying was both bizarre and terrifying. But, admittedly, there was an undeniable logic to it all.

"You don't believe the Aryan Disciples are behind this, do you?" Breckinridge asked.

"Why would they hire a hit man whose connections led back to them? Have they done that in other cases?"

"Then who is trying to kill the Man, for God's sake? Who are we talking about?"

"I found a receipt for the Pizza Hut in Beltsville in Hightower's room. It had some writing on it that I believe were contact instructions. Flanagan and OFCO operate out of Beltsville—"

"Surely you're not going to hang your hat on that."

"Flanagan showed up at Hightower's motel. He must have had the place staked out before I got there. How did he know where Hightower was staying? Hightower had refused to tell me."

"Pete, Hightower must have realized that getting involved in something like this was risky—that it would fly back in his face."

"That's my point exactly. Hightower was two-faced, but he wasn't dumb. He would have realized his role would eventually surface. But he took the chance because he thought he was backed up. I knew Hightower. He would never have gone along with something like this—with double-crossing any other agent or me—unless backstopped by someone in authority. I can see Flanagan selling Hightower some phony story about me being involved in something. He could have offered him a lot of confidential-fund money to go along with an internal investigation. And being in charge of SOT, Flanagan has access to all the informant files. He could gain access to them without going through the normal headquarters records process. He would have been looking for an informant who was reliable, had some connection with the Aryan Disciples, and who knew me."

Her thoughts were at the back of her mind where the big decisions are formed.

"Flanagan," she said softly. "Flanagan would never do anything without Wintergreen's approval. They're tied at the hip." Garrison met her eyes. She went on. "They certainly are. But it's a major leap to believe that they are involved in a conspiracy—"

"Martha, I'm not imagining all this."

"But what would be Wintergreen's motive?"

"He's not acting on his own. For all we know, a hostile foreign power could have bought Wintergreen. Or maybe the CIA. Both he and Flanagan were CIA case officers. Jordan is an unpopular President. Wintergreen took Marine One to Camp David. He could have planted the bomb—"

"If it's a plot to take over the government, why launch it at the *end* of a Presidential Administration? Why not just wait a few months when Jordan will be out of the White House?"

"I don't know. But the bottom line is that whoever is behind the assassination attempt owns someone in the Secret Service. If it is Wintergreen and Flanagan, it means that while every agent in the Service is out looking for me, they can be pulling strings to set up the next assassination attempt."

She realized that Garrison was winning her over. Not that anyone could ever tell for sure whether someone was lying. She knew it was always a judgment call, tempered by one's experience. She had learned from investigating other conspiracies that the facts were often hazy. She would have to make a decision by what she felt in her gut. But there were other issues she needed to clear up.

"Pete, I'm the one who searched your apartment. What was C-4 doing there?"

"Someone planted it."

"How did they bypass your alarm system?"

An expression of surprise crossed Garrison's face. "I didn't even think of that . . . my alarm."

"And the landlady came over immediately. If someone had broken in earlier to plant the evidence, it would have set off the alarm and she would have heard it too. Pete, this doesn't jibe. No one broke into your apartment."

"Who was there during the search?"

"Rachel Kallenstien and Wintergreen."

"I've never heard of Wintergreen going into the field. After the Cleveland assassination attempt, he stayed in his office and let PRD handle the whole investigation." Garrison was referring to an incident that had occurred months earlier. A man in a Cleveland tavern had shot out of a tavern window as the Presidential motorcade passed by. There had been a Presidential security uproar, with rumors of assassination plots and foreign agents, but in the end, the investigation had revealed nothing more than a drunk who thought taking a shot at the Presidential motorcade was a good idea.

"This is a major Presidential threat case involving an agent," she said. "Maybe Wintergreen wanted to make sure that the investigation was done right."

"Where did you find the C-4?" he asked.

"In the refrigerator."

"You walked into the apartment and went straight to the kitchen?"

"We walked in. The alarm went off. Kallenstien found the alarm wire and disabled it. We began searching."

"Right then?"

Breckinridge closed her eyes and concentrated. "Come to think of it, Wintergreen went into the other room to make a phone call. Rachel and I checked the bedroom and bathroom, then we decided how we were going to conduct the search."

"You and she were together?"

"Yes?"

"Where was Wintergreen?"

"I told you. On the phone."

"In which room?"

"The kitchen."

"Then you and Kallenstien began to search. You went in the kitchen and opened the refrigerator?" Garrison sounded far away to her.

"And there it was." The thought that flashed through her mind was of Cape Cod. She'd been yachting through a fog bank with Rachel Kallenstien and some other friends. Breckinridge had seen something through the grayness—a glimmer of metal in the distance—that had turned out to be a tugboat. She'd narrowly averted a collision. But at first there had been only a glimmer.

"There is something else," she said in a distracted mono-tone. "I didn't think anything of it at the time, but later . . ."

"Yes . . . ?"

"It's about the C-4. I took it out of the refrigerator. The first thing that came to my mind was how could you be involved in something like that? I was over-whelmed and sad . . . disgusted actually. But later, when I got home and went to bed, I was thinking about the search and something occurred to me. It was about when I took the C-4 out of the refrigerator. It wasn't cold. I thought that maybe I was so tired I had imagined it. But thinking back—"

"Wintergreen planted it. It had to be him. That's why he wanted to come along on the search. He wanted to salt me. And there is something else. Shortly before Charlie Meriweather was killed, Flanagan asked him to handle an off-the-record investigation. Delores Meri-weather told me it bothered Charlie so much that he decided to retire.

"Martha, will you help me?"

"Count me in."

"If you get caught helping me, you could end up in the bag—"

"I know."

"Dig up everything you can on Hightower. There has to be something that ties him to Wintergreen and/or Flanagan, or someone else in the Secret Service. High-tower is known in Bakersfield as Eddie Richardson."

She took out a pen and pad and wrote the name.

"How will you and I stay in touch?"

"I'm staying at the Watergate, Suite 1303. Ask for Jonathan Hollingsworth."

"How did you that arrange those digs?"

"The, uh, First Lady took care of it for me."

"The First Lady is so convinced of your innocence that she helped you come up with a hideout?"

"I went to her and asked her to speak with the Man, to try to convince him to replace the detail with military agents until this is resolved. The problem is that the Man is convinced of my guilt."

"Understandable—"

"Martha, other than me, you're the only one who knows about this. If something happens to me, you'll have to carry the ball."

She nodded. "Be careful, Pete."

"You too." He reached for the door handle.

"Pete, you forgot something."

"Sorry," he said, and handed her the gun.

Breckinridge shoved it into her holster.

Garrison got out of the car, and she watched him as he hurried toward the stairwell. She felt a chill as she assimilated what he'd told her. She didn't know where the danger might come from, but it was there. It was someone in the Secret Service. She still found it difficult to imagine Wintergreen and Flanagan being involved, but if she'd learned anything as an investigator, it was to be guided by the facts. If she hadn't been the one to find the C-4 at Garrison's apartment, she would have never believed Garrison. Now it was only she and he and the First Lady against Flanagan, Wintergreen, and God only knows who else.

She got out of the car and walked back to Secret Service headquarters replaying the conversation. By the time she arrived, she'd accepted what it all meant. Her

initial confusion and dismay at the jumble of facts and
events had transformed itself into cold fear.

At her desk in Protective Research Division, Breckinridge found a pink envelope with a D.C. postmark. It
was addressed to her and marked PERSONAL AND
CONFIDENTIAL. She opened it. It was a letter from
Delores Meriweather. Her handwriting was clear—a
nearly perfect cursive style—and written in blue ink
with what Breckinridge guessed was probably a fountain
pen. Delores apologized for having been rude to Breckinridge, and explained that her life had turned into a
confusing mix of feelings and memories but she believed
she would survive.

At the bottom of the letter, Delores mentioned that
she had finally gone through Charlie's papers, a task that
she'd been avoiding because she didn't think she had
the inner strength to face reading them. She'd discovered
that there might have been more to the White House
"politics" that had been bothering him before his decision to retire from the Secret Service. She enclosed a
copy of a letter Charlie had written two days before his
death.

MEMORANDUM FOR THE RECORD

To Whom It May Concern:
When Gil Flanagan first recruited me to plant a
transmitter and voice-activated recorder in Helen
Pierpont's room at the Waldorf Astoria Hotel in New
York, I believed the investigation to be legal and
proper. Flanagan assured me that Director Winter-
green had given him the assignment and that it in-

volved a defense contractor getting inside information on contract bids. Flanagan also told me that the President had been briefed on the matter. I planted the bug in Pierpont's room believing that I was acting legally, as part of a sensitive investigation.

After the President's New York visit was over and the Presidential party was on its way to the airport, Flanagan told me to retrieve the transmitter and tapes from Pierpont's room. Her suite was situated between the Presidential suite and a staff room. Adjoining doors interconnected all three rooms. I retrieved the tape and listened for a few minutes. It was of the President and Pierpont spending the night in Pierpont's room, having sex and discussing the President filing for divorce from the First Lady the moment he left office.

I confronted Flanagan and told him I didn't appreciate being lied to and drawn into what was obviously an illegal operation under false pretenses. He said it was all a mistake and he would set up an appointment for me to talk to Director Wintergreen, who would explain the other details of the case.

When I returned back to the White House, Wintergreen avoided me. I'm writing this because I may find myself in front of some Congressional committee asking questions about why I bugged the President. At any rate, yesterday I sent a memo to Wintergreen telling him that if he didn't want to meet with me, I was going to ask for an appointment with the White House Chief of Staff.

(Signed)

Charles Meriweather

Breckinridge read the letter a second time, then picked up a file folder and found Delores Meriweather's number in it. Breckinridge dialed the number. The phone rang twice.

"Hello."

"Delores, this is Martha Breckinridge. I received the letter."

"What does it mean?"

"I don't want to talk on the phone, Delores. But I am on top of it. Whatever you do, tell no one about the letter. No one. Will you promise me?"

"Does this mean that Charlie may have . . ."

"It's too early to make any assumptions. But I am going to get to the bottom of it. I'll call you the moment I come up with something. You have my word on that."

"I won't say anything."

"Thanks, Delores."

"Okay. You know something, Martha? I . . . I always hated this town."

"Good-bye, Delores."

Breckinridge put the receiver down. The next person she called was Kallenstien. She found her eating dinner and asked her to return to the office.

Kallenstien arrived at the office about twenty minutes later, and Breckinridge showed her the letter.

"This letter is dynamite, Martha. Major dynamite."

"Do you agree that this means something is wrong? Something inside the Service?"

"Yes. Without a doubt."

Breckinridge nodded.

"Rachel, I'm about to tell you something that is going

to knock your socks off. Something about Pete Garrison. Can we speak in confidence?"

"Meaning what?"

"That after I tell you something about him I am going to ask you a question, and all I ask is that if you choose to not go along with my theory, you will forget everything I have told you. Forget it forever."

"Okay. Drop it on me, sister."

Sitting at her desk, Breckinridge reiterated what Garrison had told her, fact for fact. As Kallenstien listened, her eyes got wide. When Breckinridge had finished, Kallenstien left her desk and walked to the coffee machine, where she made a pot of coffee and put it on the burner. She walked back across the room and plopped down in a chair.

"If anyone else had told me this I would have thought they were crazy," Kallenstien said.

"Rachel, I know this is risky and that things could turn the wrong way. We could end up on trial . . . or worse. I can use some help, but if you don't want to throw in with Garrison and me, I'll have no hard feelings."

"You know what I was thinking just now?"

"How nice it would have been if you would have been on vacation this week."

CHAPTER 26

AT MIDNIGHT, BRECKINRIDGE was still in her
PRD cubicle, engrossed in doing computer records
checks: extensive, detailed record examinations that involved examining every case file in which Frank Hightower was mentioned. She had been cross-referencing
each case to his Secret Service informant file.

"The federal and state databases for Hightower's arrests have nothing in them to connect him to anyone in
the Secret Service, other than Garrison," Breckinridge
said.

"And all the entries in his informant file were written
by Garrison—all generally favorable, by the way," Kallenstien said poring over some paperwork. "Hightower
was a reliable informant. There were entries for up to
two years ago; then the entries stopped."

Breckinridge stood and stretched.

"I checked the name Eddie Robinson through the indices and found nothing. There was one data entry that mentioned an Eddie Robinson fitting Hightower's description. But the file wasn't on the shelf. I checked the master file index and it showed that the file had been destroyed routinely because of age." She handed Breckinridge a printout of the file card.

"Martha, there is a J in the file number. Judicial cases aren't destroyed for fifteen years."

"So I noticed. It wouldn't be the first time some clerk screwed up the destruction schedule."

"Strange . . ."

"Someone cleaned up some files. They wanted to get Robinson's name out of the system."

"If so, they did it the right way. Just stamp the file for destruction." Kallenstien ran her hands through her hair. She looked tired. "Then they didn't have to worry about getting caught tearing up a file by one of the security cameras. It looks like we're out of luck on the Robinson angle."

"You look tired, Rach."

Kallenstien rubbed her eyes. "I could use some sleep."

"See you in the morning."

"You're going to stay?"

"I have a few things I want to finish up."

"If you want me to stay—"

"Get out of here. And thanks, friend."

Kallenstien smiled. "I'm in this for the glory."

After Kallenstien departed, Breckinridge sat at her desk and put her face in her hands to think. She recounted in her mind everything she knew, all the records checks they'd made concerning Hightower and his alias

Richardson. There had to be something. . . .

Recalling the fail-safe administrative procedure for deleted and destroyed files, she walked to a record room on the floor below where files scheduled for destruction were kept before being sent for final destruction. Hoping that the clerk responsible for records destruction was behind in her work, Breckinridge spent the next two hours looking through old files, checking the file number on each file folder one by one until her eyes began playing tricks on her. She sat back and closed her eyes and nearly fell asleep. She told herself she would finish one more pile of folders before leaving. It was then that she found the Richardson file. Oddly, its date indicated that the file was less than a year old—that it should have never been marked for destruction in the first place. In it was nothing but two sheets of blank paper and an unlabeled computer compact disk.

She took the CD to her office and inserted it into the CD port in her MacIntosh computer. *OPERATION BLUE VELVET* appeared at the top of the screen.

She typed the word SYNOPSIS. The screen displayed:

Secret Service joint operation (with, ATF, U.S. Customs, and RCMP) investigating arms smuggling to possible terrorists. Five arrests for possession of illegal weapons resulting in four convictions. Reports and photographic arrest data.

She typed PHOTOFILE.
A camera icon appeared. She double-clicked it.
A digital video presentation began with the title AR-REST—(1534 hours) U.S. CANADIAN BORDER, then

switched to a grainy film clip showing three men in the
front seat of a Cadillac parked in a parking lot. Four
men came into camera view running toward the car
wearing raid jackets. They had guns out and were holding badges. Pulling open the doors of the Cadillac, they
yanked two men from the front seat at gunpoint, forcing
them to put their hands on the roof of the car. One man
struggled with the officers, and was wrestled to the
ground and then handcuffed. The other suspect put his
hands on the side of the car and spread his legs. The
man in the backseat got out of the car.

He was Frank Hightower a.k.a. Eddie Richardson.

As the two prisoners were led toward a police van on
the right of the screen, Flanagan entered camera-view
and began speaking with Hightower. The film stopped.
There was nothing else on the tape.

"Flanagan," she muttered. She typed the words CASE
AGENT, then tapped the ENTER key. In the middle of
the screen, appeared:

Flanagan, Gilbert
SS Badge # 9236

Flanagan had been using Hightower as an informant.

She covered her eyes to think. She knew that the secret to solving a case was to concentrate on known clues
and avoid getting bogged down in too much supposition.
She knew that Hightower had been involved with someone in the Secret Service; and that the person who'd
written the Aryan Disciples threat letter received in the
White House mail room the day Charlie Meriweather
had been murdered had left a latent impression on it that
resembled a telephone number. Was there some way she

could tie the two clues together? Then it hit her. Breckinridge hurried to her desk and rummaged through the Meriweather case file until she found what she was looking for.

An hour later on the tenth floor of an apartment building on Wayne Avenue in Silver Springs, Maryland, Breckinridge knocked on a door. There was a lingering odor of cooked food in the hallway.

A woman in a blue chenille bathrobe opened the door. Breckinridge showed her badge. "I'm Agent Breckinridge, U.S. Secret Service. I apologize for coming here so late."

"Are you the lady who called my sister the other day?"

Breckinridge nodded. "One of my colleagues asked you about your phone number being written on a letter that had been sent to the White House."

"Don't you people ever sleep?"

"This will just take a second. During my investigation I've come up with a name, Gilbert Flanagan. Does that ring a bell with you?"

"I don't think so."

"Are you sure? Someone you may have had contact with in the past? It's very important."

"Flanagan," she said, pondering. "Wait a second."

"Yes?"

"My sister . . ."

"What about your sister?"

"She just got here from Mexico last year and she's been cleaning houses to make a few dollars. She has no car and sometimes I pick her up from where she is working. She has a customer with a name like that."

"Flanagan?"

"I think she cleans his house on Tuesdays and Thursdays."

Breckinridge swallowed. "What do you know about him?"

"She told me he works in Beltsville at a government training place. My sister told me he has a picture of him with President Jordan in his living room. She thinks he is a White House bodyguard for the President. His first name is Gilbert—Gilbert Flanagan. That's it. . . ."

"Thank you. Thank you very much."

"Next time come during the day. I have to go to work in the morning and I need my sleep."

Using her cell phone, Breckinridge anxiously reached Pete Garrison at the Watergate and told him she was going to stop by. As she drove along 23rd Street making her way to the Watergate, the car radio was playing softly, a familiar tune that for the life of her she couldn't name—probably because she was exhausted. The day before, her life had been going along normally, and now she was sneaking around in the dark trying to figure out which one of her colleagues was trying to kill the President.

Suddenly, a wave of trepidation came over her. She checked the rearview mirror. It didn't appear that anyone was following her. But she knew that if one was the target of a sophisticated surveillance, there was no way to detect it. She'd been around long enough to know that Washington, D.C., was a place where people played for keeps, where individuals like her got steamrolled every day of the week. She told herself to stop thinking about what could happen.

At the Watergate, she knocked on Garrison's door. Moments later, she heard footsteps and assumed he was looking out the peephole.

"It's me."

He opened the door with a gun in his hand and let her in. She told him how she'd established a connection between Hightower and Flanagan and about Flanagan's part-time housekeeper's sister's telephone number being on the Aryan Disciples threat letter.

"Flanagan," he said. "That sonofabitch. This is a breakthrough. A real breakthrough."

"Is that coffee I smell?"

"I figured you could use a cup about now."

In the kitchen, Garrison poured cups from a steaming pot and seemed extremely pleased, animated actually, as she told him the details of her investigation.

"The CD," he asked. "You have it?"

She patted her purse. "Exhibit A."

"But it's not enough, Martha. In fact, it's a long way from proving anything. Flanagan can just cop to it—he could say that he worked with Hightower on a case and knows nothing about him after that. As far as the phone number on the letter, it's evidence, all right, but it doesn't tie him directly to anything. It won't be his handwriting. It sounds like the housekeeper just wrote down her sister's phone number on a piece of paper and Flanagan ended up using the sheet of paper under it to create his phony letter. I could see a defense attorney making the case that the phone number could be anywhere, because it didn't have an area code with it. We need more. A lot more."

"What we need is a statement from Flanagan," she said. "A nice, long, written confession."

"I'd like to have a heart-to-heart with him—"

"Pete, I'm going to confront him."

"Too dangerous."

"Not if I do it in a public place. He's not going to kill me unless he thinks he can get away with it. Look at the way the rest of this case has played out."

"I feel like I should go with you—"

"Won't work. You're wanted. And we can't be letting the other side know what we're up to."

"Then you should take Rachel Kallenstien with you."

Breckinridge shook her head. She'd already gone over it in her mind. "No."

"Why not?"

"If I have any chance of getting Flanagan to either cooperate or say anything that would incriminate him, I'm going to have to be alone with him. He's not going to talk when I have an independent witness there who he knows could corroborate everything he tells me."

"That is if he says anything at all."

She sipped coffee and it warmed her throat. "I have to take the chance. If the roles were reversed, you would do the same and you know it."

. "Look, you know as well as I do that once you question him, you're going to be in danger."

"Pete, if I can get him to swing, we can wrap up this case. We can take him straight to the President."

But even hearing her own words, she got the feeling that it wasn't going to be that easy. She could tell by Garrison's expression that he was concerned.

"I wish there was some other way," he said.

"But there isn't. Leave here and you'll end up dead. Then I'll be carrying this weight alone. . . . Did anyone ever tell you that you make great coffee?"

"Thanks."

Breckinridge thought he had a nice smile. They spent the next two hours going over possible ways that she could approach Flanagan. She knew that getting any suspect to talk against his own interests was an art. And dealing with a trained Secret Service agent, she would need some luck as well as skill, but there was a chance. Flanagan was a yes-man. Everything he'd accomplished in the Secret Service was a direct result of his connection with Wintergreen. Flanagan wasn't a man of great inner strength. They came to the determination that she would have to play the interview by ear.

Finally, she could barely keep her eyes open. Garrison showed her to a well-furnished guest bedroom, where she caught a few hours sleep. When she awoke, Garrison had prepared her a big breakfast of eggs, toast, and sausage. They went over the interrogation plan again before she before departed.

"Pete, I know how you feel about having to sit here while I am out working the case. But there is no other way."

"Promise me you'll call me the moment you finish the interview."

"I promise."

Breckinridge sped along Highway 1 north from D.C., passing through College Park, Maryland, the car radio tuned to a jazz station featuring a series of cabaret singers. Breckinridge liked melancholy songs, those that had a sense of rueful destiny and failed opportunities. One tune was called "Lament," about the pain of a woman who married a man she'd met at an elegant party who romanced her, then told her he had a sweetheart.

> *I remembered him in the sun*
> *Because my eyes couldn't see*
> *A dream in tears*
> *When I savored love's destiny*

Destiny, she thought. Was it destiny that she had ended up with the Charlie Meriweather case?

At a sign that read NATIONAL AGRICULTURAL RESEARCH CENTER, she turned left and drove down a short road to a security booth at a compound surrounded by a tall chain-link fence topped with razor wire. After displaying her credentials to a uniformed guard, she drove along a one-way road that led into a wooded forest, spotted with cleared areas. Hidden from view of the highway, the U.S. Secret Service Training Center was in a large cleared area dotted with modern-looking prefabricated government buildings that contrasted with the wooded surroundings.

She parked her car in a gravel-covered parking lot, and walked past a block-long replica of a city street where Secret Service recruits practiced live fire at mechanical assassins who popped up in windows and doors. From the range areas beyond the buildings, she heard the sound of submachine-gun fire. She continued along the trail, passing a special firing range where a utility van raced along a line of targets as agents inside fired submachine guns out of its windows and open door. Three trainees walked by her dressed in orange T-shirts, Levi's, and hiking boots. Two of them were holding Uzi submachine guns, the U.S. Secret Service weapon of choice, chosen for its firepower, simplicity, reliability of operation, and the fact that it was small enough to fit inside a briefcase.

At the corner of the cleared area was a one-story building with tinted windows, the headquarters of OFCO, the Secret Service's special counterthreat unit headed by Flanagan. The sign on the door read: SPECIAL TRAINING UNIT—RESTRICTED ACCESS. She straightened her blouse and suit jacket, then knocked on the door. Moments later, Agent Beatty opened it.

"Breckinridge. What are you doing here?"

"Looking for Gil Flanagan."

"What do you want to talk to him about?"

"What, are you his secretary?"

"He's busy at the moment. We're running a priority internal investigation at the request of the Director."

"Just tell him I want to see him."

He shrugged, left her at the door, and walked down the hall. Breckinridge glanced into the squad room. There were three radio consoles. On the wall was a large map of Washington, D.C., that was crisscrossed with lines that divided it into squares of equal size—the type of map used for surveillances. There was a stack of photographs of Garrison spread about on a desk—copies of his official photo, the one that was on his identification card and passport. Seeing them gave her an eerie feeling.

Flanagan came down the hall. "What's up?"

Breckinridge told him she had to speak with him privately. He looked puzzled.

"I'm kind of busy—"

"This won't take long. I was running out some leads on the Charlie Meriweather case."

He led her outside, and she thought it strange that he hadn't invited her into his office.

"What about the Meriweather case?"

"Your name came up."

"In what regard?"

"Have you ever heard of Operation Blue Velvet?"

"No."

Breckinridge felt her spine tingle. "Are you sure?"

"What's this about?"

"I just told you. Have you ever had any dealings with an informant named Frank Hightower?"

He cleared his throat. "Who sent you here?"

"No one. You didn't answer my question."

"We'll have to do this later. I'm in the middle of a manhunt."

"I'm investigating Charlie Meriweather's murder."

He cleared his throat. "Catch me tomorrow." He walked toward the door.

"I'm not afraid to follow you inside and to ask you the same questions in front of everyone in there."

He stopped. "Look, I don't know anything about the operation you mentioned," he said angrily.

"Blue velvet. Operation Blue Velvet. An illegal weapons caper."

"Never heard of it."

"It took place on the Canadian border."

"Do you want me to say it again? I know nothing about it or the fucking Canadian border."

"The informant was Frank Hightower."

He swallowed. "Never heard of him."

"Are you sure, Gil?"

"One-hundred-percent positive. Jesus. What do I have to say to get you to understand?"

"I have a copy of the arrest videotape, Gil. You're on it."

He stared at her and all the color left his face, leaving

his lips slightly bluish. He stood there a moment, and she imagined his mind racing at a hundred miles an hour and ending up in a cul-de-sac. A look crossed his face that told her that he was furious at himself for having spoken to her. He cleared his throat.

"I don't remember every case I've ever worked on—"

"It shows you and Hightower together. You were using him as an informant. And there is something else. There was a telephone number on the Aryan Disciples threat letter—the latent impression developed in the crime lab—that registers to someone indirectly connected to you—your housekeeper's sister. It looks like she may have written the number down on a stack of typing paper that was in your house, leaving an impression on the sheet of paper that had been under it. Then someone happened to type the threat letter on that same piece of paper. What do you think about that, Gil?" He turned away from her. She moved in front of him and looked him in the eye. "Allow me to translate that for you. When I finally put the pieces of this case together, you may end up as one of the major players. You might be in some real deep shit."

He glared at her. "Be careful that you don't get involved in something that you can't handle, Martha. Something way over your head."

"That sounds like a threat, Gil. Is that a threat?"

"It's just you and I standing here. You have nothing. I strongly suggest that before you go any further with this, you head straight back to headquarters and talk to the Director. You need to talk to him."

"What is he going to tell me?"

"I'll phone him. He'll see you the moment you get

back into the District. Go straight to his office. He will explain everything."

"Why don't you save me the trip? What's going on?"

"I'm . . . uh . . . under orders . . ."

"On this Hightower thing?"

"He'll brief you on what you need to know. But if you go off half-cocked before you speak with him, you might find yourself in a real bind. That's all I can say at the moment. It's a classified matter."

She wasn't sure what to do. She needed time to think. But letting him think that she was going to talk to Wintergreen before telling anyone else wasn't going to harm her position. She nodded.

"Okay, Gil. You make that call. I'll head back."

He turned and walked away.

Striding briskly along the walkway toward the parking lot, Breckinridge anxiously went over in her mind every word Flanagan had said. She unlocked her car and climbed behind the wheel. She realized that she was breathing hard. She looked about. There was no one else in the parking lot. She unbuttoned her blouse and unclipped a miniature microphone from her brassiere. Reaching her right hand to the small of her back, she pulled a miniature Nagra tape recorder from inside her panties, along with the wire and mike. She pressed R, and then waited. The tape began to play. Both her and Flanagan's voices were clear. She turned it off and shoved it in her purse. Finally, she had something concrete. She knew it was no smoking gun, but it was evidence. It was more than she had expected to gather. Flanagan had been foolish to speak with her. Breckinridge dropped the tape in her purse and started the engine.

At the security booth at the main gate, the guard was holding the phone to his ear. His eyes were on her. She beeped the horn. He set the receiver down.

"Uh, do you have your gate pass, ma'am?"

"You didn't give me a gate pass."

"You're Agent, uh . . . ?"

"Martha Breckinridge."

"Right." He picked up a clipboard and slowly thumbed pages. "Let me see if I have your name here somewhere."

"I'm in a hurry."

"Just a moment."

The guard furtively glanced back toward the parking lot. She figured Flanagan had called and told him to stall her. Flanagan was going to make a move on her. He was going to try something. She could feel it.

"Open the goddamn gate before I drive right through it."

Glancing toward the lot again, the guard pressed a button. The gate rose. Breckinridge stepped on the gas.

Reaching the access road, she turned left. Before reaching the highway, she swerved into a service station and parked, watching the road for a minute to see if anyone was following her. Seeing nothing untoward, she drove out of the station.

Entering the highway, she thought about the day she had graduated from the Secret Service Training Academy. If someone had told her then that one day she would be investigating an assassination conspiracy involving the Director of the Secret Service and his adjutant, she would have laughed out loud. But somehow, here she was. Cruising at the speed limit, she picked up her cell phone and dialed Garrison's number at the Watergate. The phone rang, and then stopped.

"Pete?"

"What happened?"

"If I was some kind of a jerk, I might say that I had both good news and bad news."

"Meaning?"

"I have Flanagan on a nice, clear tape recording right here in my purse. It's not a confession by any means, but it's incriminating. It's enough to put the clamps on him. He told me to go talk to Wintergreen—that he would explain everything. But I'm convinced it's nothing more than a stall. Pete, I think they are both in on this conspiracy. It's them. Flanagan must think Wintergreen can talk me into keeping my mouth shut, to stall until they figure out what to do with me. I'll see you in a few minutes and we can go over it. I don't trust this phone."

"Martha, they know you're on to them now—"

"I'm aware. But I don't think he has the guts to try anything with me. On the other hand, the guard tried to stall me when I was leaving, as if someone might have needed some time to set up a surveillance on me."

"I don't like the sound of that, Martha. Where are you?"

"Highway 1 passing Hyattsville."

"Keep your eye on the rearview mirror."

"And my hand on my purse?"

"Right."

"I'll see you in a few, Pete."

She pressed OFF and dropped the phone on the seat beside her, and stepped on the gas. The highway traffic was light. She mused about what Flanagan had told her, about what she now knew. She couldn't wait to go over everything with Garrison in person—to hash out the facts with him so they could plan their next move.

She glanced at the rearview mirror. A utility van was a few car lengths behind her. She activated the right-turn signal, and then changed lanes.

The van pulled into the right lane.

Waiting until the last moment, she cut onto an off-ramp and sped up. In the rearview mirror, she watched as the van swerved to follow her. Reaching the end of the ramp, she slowed to a stop, then accelerated across a street and onto the next highway on-ramp. Returning to the highway, she checked the rearview mirror. The van wasn't in sight. She realized she was speeding, and slowed down to the speed limit.

A few moments later, she saw the van behind her again. It pulled closer at high speed.

Garrison stood at the window of Watergate Condo 1303 staring outside at the Kennedy Center. He'd spent the last hour pacing the living room, waiting for Breckinridge to call back. She should have arrived by now.

The phone finally rang and he picked it up on the first ring.

"Hello," a man said. "This is Sergeant Chester Maxwell of the Hyattsville Police Department. I need to speak with someone concerning a lady named Martha Breckinridge—"

"How did you get this number?"

"Are you related to her?"

"I'm . . . Martha's husband."

"You got a name to go with that, sir?"

"Pete—Pete Breckinridge. What's wrong?"

"Sir, I'm sorry to report that your wife has been in a

serious traffic accident. I know this is going to sound
strange, but I am at the scene of a traffic accident—a
hit-and-run—and she had no identification. I found a
credit card receipt in her pocket with her name on it and
a cell phone. I pressed the redial button—"

Garrison closed his eyes. "Martha. What is her condition?"

"She is unconscious, Mister Breckinridge. She is being transported to Prince George's County Hospital
emergency trauma center—"

"I'll be there in a few minutes."

Garrison racked the phone and hurried toward the
door. He had a horrible feeling of guilt. He should have
gone with her. He could have waited nearby, until she
finished interviewing Flanagan. . . .

In Hyattsville, Garrison sped off the highway 1 and
drove up a hill to the Prince George's County Hospital,
a red-brick structure overlooking Washington, D.C. Inside, he moved through a crowded waiting area to a long
counter where he asked a nurse about Martha Breckinridge. The nurse tapped keys on a computer.

"Intensive Care Three. Down the hall and to the left."

Garrison walked briskly along corridors. The odor of
hospital cleaning chemicals and the bright fluorescent
lights made him recall other crises. For everyone except
doctors and nurses, being in a hospital was to feel help-
less. In the intensive care room, he moved close to a
gurney surrounded by doctors and nurses.

Seeing Breckinridge in a hospital bed gave him a start.
Her eyes were shut and she had clear, plastic tubes entering her nose, throat, and arms. Her skin was a ghastly,
fishy pale. There were bloody bandages on the shiny,

tile floor next to the table. Garrison felt like someone had shoved a hand into his guts, into his heart.

A doctor who was treating Breckinridge looked up at him.

"How is she doing?"

"Please don't bother us now."

Garrison didn't move.

"Sir, did you hear me?" she said angrily.

Garrison backed away.

The doctor turned to a nurse who was standing nearby and told her to make a note on the chart about two broken ribs and to call the ENT and tell him that she had a patient with a ruptured sinus.

"Mr. Breckinridge?" someone whispered. Garrison turned. "I'm Detective Maxwell, Hyattsville City Police."

Maxwell cocked his head toward the door. They walked out of the room into the hallway. Maxwell was fiftyish and of medium height. Maybe it was because of his florid complexion and sagging belly that Garrison thought he looked like the quintessential police detective.

"The hit-and-run. What happened?"

"Mr. Breckinridge, at first it sounded like your wife was in some kind of a traffic argument; a road-rage thing. But one of my people just interviewed a truck driver who was a few lanes behind her when it happened. He saw a white delivery van force her car off the road—possibly a Dodge. But he said that as far as he could tell, her car and the Dodge hadn't been close enough earlier to have had a traffic dispute."

"Someone ran her off the road?"

"That's what it looks like. A Dodge truck hit her car

on the right rear bumper while accelerating—sort of turned right into her. Her car hit the edge of a ditch and rolled at least three full times. It's almost like the driver of the Dodge seemed to know what he was doing. Like he was trying to kill her. Then, here's the zinger: He stops and, from what we've been able to establish, searches her car. A truck driver who stopped to help sees a guy crawling out of the car carrying a woman's purse, then get in the Dodge and speed away like a bat out of hell. He said the Dodge didn't have license plates."

Garrison felt a rush of anger. "Did the witness get a look at him?"

Maxwell cupped his chin. "Unfortunately, he wasn't able to provide more than a general description: a male wearing a baseball hat. That brings me to the million-dollar question: Do you have any reason to believe someone would want to harm your wife—to steal her purse?"

It was then that Garrison saw the suspicion in Maxwell's eyes. And why shouldn't he suspect him? Most murders involved family members. But should Garrison tell him the truth? Could he tell him that there was a conspiracy to kill the President of the United States and someone involved in the conspiracy had tried to kill Breckinridge? Because her purse had been stolen, Maxwell didn't know Breckinridge was a Secret Service agent. But he would surely find out when he ran the car registration. This would cause Maxwell to notify his superiors, who would, in turn, call Secret Service Headquarters, thus putting Breckinridge in jeopardy. Garrison cleared his throat.

"Yes."

The expression that crossed Maxwell's face was one

familiar to Garrison. It was the probing, intense stare all police detectives get when an investigative lead suddenly pops into view like a well-lit road sign. Garrison reached inside his suit jacket, took out his Secret Service identification card, and handed it to Maxwell.

Maxwell's eyebrows elevated slightly.

"U.S. Secret Service?"

"Martha Breckinridge and I are special agents. I'm not her husband. She and I have been working on a sensitive federal case—an internal investigation targeting a person suspected of crimes against the U.S. I can't tell you any more than that at this point for reasons of national security."

Maxwell studied the identification card, then handed it back to him.

"Sounds like I'd better phone my captain—"

"If you do, it will hinder the investigation and endanger lives."

"This is an attempted murder. I can't sit back and do nothing because you think it's a good idea."

"Would you agree that proving a case would depend on having a victim?" Garrison asked.

Maxwell furrowed his brow. "Generally."

"In order to protect Agent Breckinridge's life, I'm asking that you hold off doing anything for the moment—except to take steps to protect her. She needs to be re-registered under an assumed name and an officer should be posted at the door of her room twenty-four hours per day."

Maxwell rubbed his chin. "Lemme see that ID again." Garrison complied. Maxwell studied it. "We all have a boss. I'm going to have to report this up the chain—"

"Did you know Charlie Meriweather when he was in your department?"

"As a matter of fact I did," Maxwell said after a moment. "We worked in the same patrol division."

"I take it you heard about what happened to him?"

"A damn shame."

"I believe the same people who ran Breckinridge's car off the road may be involved in Charlie's murder."

"Is that so," Maxwell said as a statement of fact rather than a question.

Garrison assumed that Maxwell was trying to decide whether he was telling the truth. He was using his police officer's sixth sense; the lie detector of singular police judgment based on having listened to ten thousand lies during his career.

"I know this must all sound incredible to you, Maxwell. But it's true, so help me."

"You're asking me to protect Agent Breckinridge and to delay reporting a crime. I can't do either without risking my ass."

Frustrated, Garrison turned away from him and let out his breath angrily.

A uniformed officer joined them and asked to speak with Maxwell privately. They walked a few feet down the hall and held a short conversation. The officer turned and headed back down the hall. Maxell rejoined Garrison.

"I need your help, Maxwell."

"Why don't you have Secret Service agents protect her?"

"I can't at this point. This is an internal investigation involving one or more agents who may be working for a terrorist organization."

The way Maxwell squinted at him, as if he was in deep thought, led Garrison to believe that Maxwell was considering what he had asked. Garrison asked himself what he would do in the same circumstances, and became depressed.

The door opened. A tall, middle-aged woman in a hospital scrub gown and cap walked in the room. She had black hair streaked with gray. Garrison recognized her by her eyes. She was the doctor who had been treating Breckinridge.

"Ms. Breckinridge is stabilized," she said to Maxwell. "She's suffering from chest and head injuries, but I believe she will recover."

Relieved, Garrison audibly let out his breath.

"Thanks, Doctor," Maxwell said.

"Have you located any relatives?"

Maxwell turned to Garrison. Their eyes met and Garrison waited for him to speak.

"This is Mr. Breckinridge, her husband."

She nodded. "There are some hospital forms—"

"I'll take care of them," Garrison said.

"Doctor, I've established that someone was trying to kill her," Maxwell said. "I'm going to have Mrs. Breckinridge's name changed in the hospital records."

The doctor stared at Garrison. "Who would do that to her?"

"She works for a high-level government agency, Doctor," Maxwell said. "I've agreed not to say more about the situation at this time."

"I see."

"May I speak with her?" Garrison asked.

"She's not fully out of the anesthesia yet, but you can go in for a few minutes."

"Thanks, Doctor."

"I take it you're going to post a guard on her room?" the doctor asked Maxwell.

"As we speak."

"I need a cup of coffee," she said leaving the room.

Maxwell turned to Garrison.

"My story is that you and I have never met," Maxwell said. "I will stall things as long as I can. At that point I'm going to have to trace the registration and officially notify the Secret Service."

"Fair enough. In the meantime, make sure she is protected."

"Anyone coming here to look for her will never be able to find her. If they do, they'll have to face me and my men." Garrison thanked him and they shook hands. Maxwell left.

In the intensive care unit, Garrison stepped behind a draped curtain and a nurse said: "Please don't stay longer than a minute or two."

Breckinridge was frighteningly pale from loss of blood. Garrison put his hand on hers.

"Martha, can you hear me?"

Breckinridge's eyes slitted open. They were nearly swollen shut. The right side of her face was black and blue. She stirred slightly, wincing with pain. He winced along with her. She pursed her lips, struggling to speak. Her mouth opened slightly.

"Pete?" she whispered.

Garrison leaned close.

"Everything's going to be okay."

"I saw . . . I . . ."

"The driver of the car who ran you off the road?"

"Yes."

"It was Flanagan."

Garrison's stomach felt as if someone had slugged him. The anger started as a slow burn within his heart, moving up, gaining intensity, until his face was flushed and his hands trembled. He clenched his fists to stop them, then released them when he realized he was squeezing her. She closed her eyes and took deep breaths.

"Hang on, Martha," he said touching her forehead. "It's not going to be easy, but don't give up. We need you. I . . . need you . . ."

Her head nodded almost imperceptibly in agreement. Her breathing became deep and heavy.

Garrison straightened. The blips on the electronic monitor next to the bed seemed to be measuring his life too—every heartbeat.

CHAPTER 27

AT THE FEDERAL Station metro stop, Garrison got off the train car and walked to Lafayette Park hoping that there were no Secret Service agents around. He was across the street from the White House. He was wearing a baseball hat and sunglasses he'd purchased in a drugstore. The only people in the park were two transients squatting on the grass sharing a bottle of wine. They eyed him as he walked past.

At the curb visible from the White House's Bedroom Three, Garrison feigned tying his shoe, and quickly used a piece of red chalk to draw three circles on the curb. Garrison got up and headed back toward the Metro. One of the transients, a tall man with a torn T-shirt, moved toward him.

"You got any change you can spare?"

"I was just gonna ask you the same thing."

"Very funny, motherfucker."

Garrison kept walking.

At the Watergate, Garrison took the elevator to Condominium 1303. He paced the living room, checking the window often, and wondered when Eleanor would spot his chalk signal.

The phone rang. He cautiously picked up the receiver.

"Hello . . . is Mr. Hollingsworth there?" Eleanor said.

"He's at work."

"Thank you."

Garrison set the receiver down on the cradle.

A few minutes later, he stared through the window down at the street as a lead car pulled to the curb followed by the First Lady's limousine. Walter Sebastian got out of the limousine and opened the rear door for Eleanor. She got out and he led her toward the entrance. A minute later, Garrison heard footsteps and conversation in the hallway. Someone knocked on the door. He crossed the room, used the peephole. She was alone. He opened the door and she came in.

"I'm on my way to a dinner in Georgetown," Eleanor said with a look of anxiety and fear on her face. "I was relieved when I saw the chalk marks. I've been worried about you."

"Did you talk with him?"

"He's convinced that you are guilty."

"That's what they want him to think."

"I can't help that."

She sat on the sofa.

"Eleanor, talk to me."

"They have evidence that you planted the bomb."

"I told you it's a lie—"

"—And that you killed a Secret Service informant and another man."

He could see it in her eyes. She had doubts about him. It was understandable. He had to look at this situation from her point of view. He moved to the sofa and sat next to her.

"Someone else planted the bomb. The first man . . . It was self-defense. He was an ex-convict, a hired killer. And I didn't kill the informant. So help me."

"Agents chased you from the scene of the murder."

"You're talking about Flanagan. He is in on it."

"They can't all be lying."

"Hightower was part of a conspiracy to assassinate the President and frame me. I went to the motel to interview him and found him dead—"

She furrowed her brow. "If you know about this High-tower person being involved, then you should have some idea who is behind this conspiracy. Who is it, for God's sake? What is this all about?"

"Gil Flanagan, who is Wintergreen's adjutant, showed up at Hightower's motel just after I arrived. I don't think it was a coincidence. I think he killed Hightower and he wanted to finish me there—to make it look like I killed Hightower and he found me with a smoking gun. The conspirators still need a fall guy."

"Pete, are you—are you telling me the complete truth?"

For a moment, he felt angry that she would question him. Then the anger was replaced by a sense of frustration as great as he'd felt in his entire life.

"You don't believe me?"

"The target is the President of the United States. Not

to mention that he is my husband. If I am wrong, I could be killing him."

Garrison got up and walked to the window. "Everyone else in the White House believes I'm guilty. Why shouldn't you?"

"Put yourself in my place, for God's sake."

"Eleanor, as God is my witness, I am not involved in this. I'm a victim. Someone in the Secret Service is trying to kill the President, but it isn't me. You have to believe me. I need your help to save the President from them. They're not going to stop."

"I have a bad feeling about all this."

"Please believe me."

Everything that had happened so far was fully out of his personal control. Garrison wasn't sure about anything and he was worried. He felt like a bystander at some terrible, claustrophobic barroom brawl, waiting to be inevitably drawn in. She stood and walked to him.

"I'm sorry. I know in my heart that it's not you. It's just that . . . so much has been happening. All this cloak-and-dagger stuff has me completely confused."

"Eleanor, I need to speak with him."

"The President?"

"In person. Alone. With none of his advisors present. I know it sounds crazy, but there is no other way—"

"You're asking him to meet with someone he believes is trying to kill him? Think about what you are saying."

"It has to be alone because I don't know who is involved in all this. It could be anyone. I want to tell him what I know man-to-man. If I can convince him, he can take it from there. He'll know what to do. This can't wait. Every hour we delay puts him in greater danger. Don't you see?"

"His advisors will never go along with such a thing—"

"He's gone against them in the past—"

"They blame you, Pete. They all think you are guilty. Don't you understand what I'm saying?"

"Unless I can convince him that it's not me—that the investigation is on the wrong track—he is a sitting duck. That's what the conspirators want: for him to sit in the Oval Office thinking it's me until they can pull off a surefire assassination. And have no doubt they can get it done. For an assassin, there is nothing like working from the inside, knowing the ropes. This isn't some hallucinating screwball trying to kill him. There is someone on the *inside*. Someone with access to his every move."

"Helen Pierpont spent years helping her CIA pals with their dirty tricks. God knows she could be taking orders from a foreign power. For all we know, she might have seduced my husband for the sole purpose of finding out secrets."

"Flanagan has a recording of her with the President."

"You mean—?"

"He tricked Charlie Meriweather into wiring her room at the Waldorf Astoria when they were in New York for a UN social function."

She gave him a puzzled look. "Maybe she was trying to blackmail my husband. Maybe Flanagan was working for her."

"And now she wants to kill the President? It doesn't make sense."

She looked away. "Maybe you should speak with my husband," she said softly.

"What's on his schedule for the rest of the day?"

"Meetings in the House. He and I are scheduled to

attend a stage play at the Kennedy Center tonight."

"Tell him it's too dangerous for him to leave the White House."

"You know how he is when it comes to public appearances. The Kennedy Center is prime-time national TV—"

"And tell him to put Wintergreen and Flanagan on the lie detector immediately. I'm sure they'll show deception if asked about being part of a conspiracy. That will give the President enough to have them relieved of duty."

"I'll try—"

"If it's going to happen, it's going to happen in a public place. The Kennedy Center is too dangerous."

"In the past, I've heard him say no terrorist was going to stop the President of the United States from going where he wants to go."

"And JFK said something like that before he went to Dallas. Eleanor, this isn't a security matter any longer. It is a *survival* matter. It's up to you now. You have to put your foot down. They will kill you if you are with him. This isn't a goddamn game."

"I hear you, Pete."

She glanced at her wristwatch. "I'd better get going. Will you be here if I have to reach you?"

"I'm not sure."

"I'm terrified that you're going to go out there and something will happen. Please stay here where it's safe."

"Be forceful with him. Don't take no for an answer."

"I'd better go before Walter gets worried. I almost had to get in a screaming match with him to convince him to let me come up here alone. I told him my cousin didn't like agents." She took out a compact and checked her makeup. "I'd better get going."

"Will you—"

"Yes. I'll talk with him."

"Tell him I phoned you—that I got through to your office on a signal line. I'll call the Oval Office tonight at exactly four P.M. Have him tell his secretary to put me through."

"But they'll trace the call."

"I'll call through the signal board on a scrambled line. I have the code so I can get in that way. The signal will show I'm calling from New York. Eleanor, you have to convince him to listen to me with an open mind—that assassins don't call the people they are trying to kill. I know all of this sounds outrageous and weird. But the President is a reasonable man. I believe he will listen. He is in mortal danger and so are you."

She had a faraway look. "I was just thinking. If you and I hadn't . . . I wouldn't have believed you. I would think you were guilty."

"And you would have been justified by the facts. But you would have been completely wrong."

"Pete, how is this going to end? How are things ever going to get put back into place now that all this has happened?"

"I don't know."

"Pete, it's too dangerous for you to be on the street. I want you to stay here until I can get you in to see my husband."

He nodded agreement.

"I'm not going to stand by and let some traitor do his thing," she said.

She brushed her lips against his cheek and left the apartment.

Garrison walked to the window. Below, she walked to the limousine with Sebastian at her side. He opened the door and she got in. The motorcade pulled away, turning the corner with a wide sweep. Wispy clouds extended west for as far as he could see. In the distance, the Washington Monument pointed toward the sky, a shiny, gray spear glimmering in sunlight.

CHAPTER 28

AT PRECISELY FOUR P.M., Garrison picked up his cellular phone and anxiously dialed the White House signal number. An operator came on the line. Garrison asked for the Oval Office. The President's secretary answered and he told her who he was. The line beeped twice.

"President Jordan speaking."

"Good evening, Mr. President. This is Agent Garrison."

"Good evening. Director Wintergreen and National Security Advisor Pierpont are here with me. I'm going to put you on the speakerphone."

"I need to speak with you in private."

"I want a witness to our conversation," the President said impatiently.

"This is about a threat to your life—"

"That's non-negotiable. You and I aren't going to have a private telephone conversation."

"Very well."

There was a brief humming sound as the President activated the speakerphone.

"Can you hear me, Garrison?"

"Yes."

"Agent Garrison, this is Helen Pierpont. Are you all right?"

"I don't have any bullet holes in me if that's what you mean."

"We want you to come in, Pete," Pierpont said as if she knew him.

"So you can lock me up without bail under the Anti-Terrorism Statute?"

"It's time to end all this foolishness," she said condescendingly.

"That is a meaningless statement," Garrison said. "And you don't have to talk to me like I am a child. I'm not insane and I am not an assassin. I'm being blamed for something I didn't do. Framed."

"I didn't mean to imply—"

"I have great interest in what you have to say, Pete," the President said. "But for security reasons we shouldn't be talking on the phone. If you expect me to believe you, you should be willing to look me in the eye, man-to-man."

"Mr. President, I will surrender if you will give me a half hour of your time so I can explain what I have learned concerning a threat to your life. Just you and I. Face-to-face."

"Surely you can't expect the Secret Service to abdicate its responsibility for Presidential security," Pierpont said. Garrison remained silent. "Pete?"

"I heard you."

"Well?"

"I will accept any and all security precautions the President deems necessary. I had nothing to do with the Marine One sabotage."

"I agree to meet with you if you will come to the White House unarmed," the President said.

From the President's tone of voice, Garrison tended to believe that he was telling the truth: that it wasn't just a ruse. But there was no way to know for sure. It all depended on Eleanor—on how successfully she had fought for him. Garrison told himself that from what he knew about their relationship, the President wasn't going to agree to accede to Eleanor's request to meet with him and then coldly ensnare him. At least he hoped not.

"Considering the situation as it stands, Mr. President, how do I make it there without getting killed?"

"I'll send an intermediary to escort him in, Mr. President," Wintergreen said. "How about Walter Sebastian, Pete? You trust him, don't you?"

Garrison closed his eyes to consider the offer.

"And he can accompany me to the meeting with the President?"

"Yes," the President said.

Garrison didn't trust either Wintergreen or Pierpont. But he was sure that Walter would never double-cross him. He realized he was at the point where his options were limited. He had the President's attention and he certainly wasn't negotiating from a position of strength.

"I'll agree on one condition: that Walter gets his orders directly from the President, not through any intermediaries."

"I will speak with him in person," the President said. "You have my word on that."

"I won't be arrested?"

"I give you my word that you and I will be able to talk alone," the President said after a brief silence. "If you aren't involved with the bombing, you have nothing to worry about. I will clear you."

Garrison shifted his weight from foot to foot.

"Mr. President, if you're thinking about setting a trap for me, think again. What I have to say involves a mole in the White House who is involved in a conspiracy to assassinate you."

"If you convince me of that, I will personally take over the investigation," the President said.

Garrison's temples throbbed. The President could be lying. They could all be lying. But if he refused the offer and got caught, Garrison could end up dead or spending the rest of his life in prison for something he didn't do and the President might get assassinated.

"Okay. Let's do it."

"Be at the service entrance behind the Woodley Park Marriott Hotel exactly one hour from now," Wintergreen said. "Sebastian will meet you there."

Garrison wondered whether the two-hour wait was to give Wintergreen time to insert surveillance agents into the area.

"If I see anyone other than Walter there, the deal is off," Garrison said choosing to believe the President.

"Neither you nor I have anything to gain by playing games, Pete," the President said. "Stay cool. We'll resolve this."

Garrison pressed OFF. He dropped the phone on the bed and reviewed the conversation, mulling over every word, trying to detect a double cross. He decided he had to take the President at his word. Besides, Garrison knew the layout of the Marriott Hotel by heart from having written an advance security survey for a Presidential visit there. If the President or Wintergreen were laying a trap for him, he would be able to detect it.

In the Oval Office, Wintergreen lifted a two-way radio from his belt and pressed the transmit button.

"Wintergreen to Crown Control. Have Agent Sebastian report to the Oval Office ASAP."

A radio voice said: *"Crown Control, Roger."*

Wintergreen felt energized. He relished the middle of a crisis, the heat of battle.

The President stood at the window gazing out, looking distracted. He turned to Pierpont.

"What do you think?"

"If Garrison was innocent he wouldn't have run from the safe house," she answered.

"He could be telling the truth," the President said.

"We have mountains of evidence stacked against him," Wintergreen said, and clipped the radio onto his belt. "Mountains." Wintergreen considered the President to be the picture of mediocrity—a field commander frozen in the midst of battle.

"If he's guilty," the President said, "if he is responsible for the bombing, why would he go through this charade?"

"Maybe he figures he has nothing to lose," Pierpont said. "Maybe he figures it's just a matter of time. He probably wants to save his life. He'll try to convince you, then later he'll ask for a deal."

"I could flood the area with agents—drop a net on him," said Wintergreen.

"He'll have taken precautions," the President said. "I have the feeling that if we do anything untoward, he might pull the rip cord. And once he goes under again, you might never find him. No, we're going to go through with this."

"As you wish, sir."

Wintergreen felt stimulated at the President's words. It had been the reaction he'd anticipated.

"I wonder what he has to say," Pierpont said.

"Don't worry," Wintergreen said. "Whatever it is won't negate finding C-4 in his apartment."

The intercom buzzed.

"Walter Sebastian is here, Mr. President," a secretary said over the speaker.

"Send him in."

The door opened. Sebastian walked into the room. He had a troubled expression.

"You wanted to see me, Mr. President?"

"Thanks for getting here so promptly, Walter. Please sit down."

Sebastian complied, sitting hesitantly at the table. The President nodded at Wintergreen.

"Walter, listen closely," Wintergreen said. "We don't have much time." He explained that a bomb believed planted by Pete Garrison brought down Marine One and that shortly after the bombing, Garrison killed a member of the Aryan Disciples who might have tried to silence him for his part in the assassination conspiracy. Further, while being questioned, Garrison escaped and killed

Frank Hightower, a listed confidential informant who was working on the case. Finally, Wintergreen related the contents of Garrison's telephone call to the President.

"The President has agreed to meet privately with Garrison," Pierpont said. "Garrison balked at surrendering to Wintergreen or me."

"He has agreed to accept you as an intermediary," the President said. "I want you to go out and escort him here."

Sebastian looked pale. His eyes moved from the President to Wintergreen, then to Pierpont.

"Any questions?" Wintergreen asked.

"Just one. *Are you shitting me?*"

"We couldn't be more serious," Pierpont said.

"Garrison isn't a bomber," Sebastian said.

"That remains to be seen," the President said.

"I know him. He isn't a killer. Anyone who says he is is out of his goddamn gourd. Somebody must be framing him."

"That's what we'd like to think," the President said. "You're going meet Garrison and bring him safely here. Others are hunting for him as we speak, and it's not safe for him just to come strolling in."

"Does that mean that you have paper on him?"

"That doesn't matter at this point," Wintergreen said.

"The hell it doesn't," Sebastian said. "If you have people on the street trying to kill him, I have the right to know—"

"Of course it matters," the President said. "Walter, you can assume the worst. Garrison may be a target. You'll need to use precautions bringing him here. But I have confidence in you to handle it for me."

"Mr. President, with all due respect, if you're looking

for someone to help you trap him, maybe you'd do better to find some other agent."

Wintergreen cringed.

The President cleared his throat.

"This isn't anything like that. I have given Garrison my word that he will not be arrested and that he will be allowed to speak with me alone when he arrives here. I'm telling you the same thing. You are to encourage him to come in. Encourage him. I'm ordering you to handle this for me."

"Yes, sir," Sebastian said reluctantly.

The President said he had to get to another meeting and departed.

"When you get back here with Garrison, search him thoroughly and run him through a magnetometer," Wintergreen said. "Enter using the Executive Office building entrance and bring him to the Situation Room. You will remain with him when he meets with the President."

Wintergreen followed Sebastian out of the office. Wintergreen had always felt uncomfortable around Sebastian, who he sensed didn't like him.

"The Man has the dogs after Garrison, doesn't he?" Sebastian said.

"I'm following orders just like you are."

Sebastian stopped. "Translation: *Yes, Walter. Garrison has a price on his head.*"

"It wasn't my doing."

"Well, let me tell you something, Mr. Director. You and I both know Pete Garrison is not a damn murderer. You know him as well as I do. He's flat out not involved in any shit like that. Did you tell the Man that?"

"Walter, I like Garrison as much as you do," Wintergreen said focusing on Sebastian's eyebrows, a technique he'd developed over years of dealing with the rich and powerful. "All this makes me sick. But what am I supposed to do? The cards have been stacked against Garrison and there is nothing I can do. I say let Garrison convince the Man that he isn't involved. There is nothing I can do but let this play out."

"The way I read it, Pierpont is in there pulling the strings and no one could give a rat's ass about Garrison."

"Tell Garrison I'm on his side. Tell him that if he'll go through the hoops, I'm sure this whole thing can be washed. Put him at ease and let's resolve this."

"If you are using me as bait to bag Garrison, you and I are going to have a problem. Man-to-man, outside the House and off duty."

"Don't threaten me."

"I'm not bullshitting. I can always get myself another job."

"I've given you my word. There is nothing else I have to say."

Wintergreen stepped into the elevator. Sebastian stared at him, nodded, and then followed. Wintergreen felt uncomfortable.

CHAPTER 29

SITTING IN A Metro train car on the way to Woodley Park station, Garrison imagined what he was going to say to the President. Without the CD and the tape recording Breckinridge had obtained, he had no solid evidence to give the President. All he had was some supposition and the fact that Breckinridge had seen Flanagan run her off the road. It wasn't going to be easy. And that was if the President had been leveling with him, rather than drawing him into an arrest trap.

The train slowed as it pulled into Woodley station. He walked off the car and mixed into the crowd on the platform. He knew that if they were trying to trap him, the area could be flooded with agents. As he scanned faces, looking for Secret Service agents and telltale gun bulges, he considered what he would do if he were in charge of the Garrison case. He would allow the suspect

to take the escalator up to the street before making the
arrest, eliminating the danger of a shoot-out in a
crowded subway station and the opportunity for him to
jump back on a train and escape.

A young man standing near the wall glanced at him.
Garrison knew that agents who'd been assigned to surveil and arrest him would be from outlying Secret Service field offices—agents who'd never met him. The
young man opened a newspaper as if to read. A newspaper was the sign of an inexperienced surveillant. A
six-year-old moved to the man, and he tousled the boy's
hair in a familiar manner. They were probably father and
son. Garrison felt relieved. Agents didn't bring their kids
on surveillance duty.

Garrison strolled to the other end of the station, casing
the other passengers. A woman in her thirties sat alone
on a bench. She looked trim and fit like most female
agents. She wore a business suit under which, he imagined, she might be carrying a gun. He kept an eye on
her for a while. A minute later, a train roared into the
station. She boarded it.

Moving through the crowd, he reached the escalator.
Riding it to the first level, he stopped and looked back,
allowing passengers to pass him. He spotted no one paying any attention to him.

He emerged from the escalator onto Connecticut Avenue. The multilevel Marriott Hotel next door was built
on a corner lot overlooking the fashionable Adams-
Timmons suburb. To his right, Connecticut Avenue followed a moderate downgrade through Rock Creek Park
toward D.C. proper. Garrison stood at the curb for a few
minutes, trying to spot signs of surveillance. There were
people sitting at outdoor restaurant tables across the

street, the perfect cover for agents on stakeout. After studying faces, people and cars, looking for anything untoward, any signs of people using two-way radios, Garrison walked across the street.

Ambling along the sidewalk, he passed funky shops and hip cafes. No one seemed to pay any attention to him.

At the corner, he looked across the street at the Marriott, focusing his attention on the edge of the roof. If he'd been setting up surveillance there, he would have used an agent on the roof with binoculars. He saw none. But for all he knew, there could be a dozen agents staring at him from rooms inside the hotel. He might be the subject of remote-operated cameras installed in car headlights and hollowed-out trunk locks.

He went across the street to the hotel. Rather than going directly to the service entrance where he was to meet Sebastian, he walked around the corner and entered the side door. Inside, he crossed a breezeway, opened a door near the bellman's station, and moved down a stairway to the basement. Hurrying down a hallway, he made his way to a door at the end. He tried the handle. It was locked. He took a credit card from his wallet and, after a few tries, managed to shim the bolt back into the frame. Shoving the door open, he moved into a darkened utility room. Closing the door, he hurried past furnaces and air-conditioning equipment to the window. Garrison leaned close. There were no signs of agents on surveillance in the service alley. A truck and a delivery van were parked at the hotel's loading dock. He glanced at his wristwatch. If Sebastian didn't arrive in a minute or two, he wasn't going to wait. He would assume the proposed meeting was nothing but a trap and would make a run back to the Metro station.

A black Mercury sedan entered the driveway and cruised slowly up the service road from the street. Walter Sebastian was behind the wheel. He parked his car next to a commercial trash container and got out. Standing by the driver's door, Sebastian nervously straightened his necktie. He looked troubled. Garrison trusted Walter Sebastian. He would never agree to participate in a scheme to trap him. Garrison went upstairs.

Crossing the lobby, he walked outside to the alley, his eyes darting back and forth, seeking out anything that looked unusual. He was ready to run for his life.

"Walter, is this a trap?"

"No."

"You sure about that?"

"All I can tell you is it comes from the President's lips. As far as I know, there is no one else around. And I've been looking."

"I assume they filled you in on the details," Garrison said keeping his eyes on the alley leading to the street.

"If you could call it that. My orders are to convince you that everything is cool and escort you to the House."

Garrison met his eyes. "Someone's trying to frame me, Walter. The reason I have to see the Man in person is that there is a mole in the Service. I couldn't trust anyone else."

"Could Wintergreen be involved?"

"Why?"

"I think he's playing some kind of a game."

"Walter, don't hold back on me. If you know something, spit it out for God's sake."

"There have been some funny things going on."

"Such as?"

"To start with, Wintergreen didn't take the lie-detector test—him or Flanagan."

"Are you sure?"

"One of the polygraph operators told me that Wintergreen and Flanagan were the only agents on the detail who weren't tested. Wintergreen discontinued the tests. After the operators headed back to Fort McNair, I checked the lie-detector schedule. Someone had penciled in their names to make it look like they had been tested and had shown no deception. And there is something else. Wintergreen and Flanagan have been like two peas in a pod since all this started. And yesterday, Steve Paulk, who works the day shift, told me that he was having lunch in Smokey's coffee shop on G Street and saw Wintergreen walk in and use the pay phone. Paulk just happened to be leaving and he saw Wintergreen walk straight back to the White House. Tell me that doesn't mean Wintergreen is up to no good."

Garrison nodded agreement, then something caught his eye; the white delivery van that was parked in the driveway, facing away from them. It had tinted windows.

"What's wrong, Pete?"

"That van. There's movement inside."

"You know something, you're right."

Garrison began moving away.

"I swear I had no idea—"

The delivery van's tailgate door flew open and the deafening rattle of submachine-gun fire bit the air. Sebastian was hit and flew backward.

Garrison drew his SIG-Sauer, fired back, and dove for

cover behind a trash container as bullets ricocheted off the pavement.

Emerging from the van, a man wearing a ski mask and a bullet-proof vest advanced toward Garrison, firing an Uzi submachine gun from hip level. He was a professional, a military-trained shooter. Rounds sparked violently against the trash receptacle.

Outgunned, Garrison fired two quick rounds, then ran to the hotel furnace-room window, slammed his SIG-Sauer through the glass, and plunged inside headfirst, landing on the cement floor in a shower of glass. Rolling to the right, he fired twice at the window before scrambling behind a large air conditioner. The bullets stopped. Garrison heard someone's footsteps move away from the window.

Garrison sprinted to the door and yanked it open. Launched by all the adrenaline in his body, he ran up a single flight of stairs at full speed. Emerging into a hotel hallway, he dodged his way through a large group of tourists heading to the hotel's main entrance. He burst through the doors and ran outside.

The van was speeding down the alley toward the street.

Dropping to one knee, he aimed his SIG-Sauer with both hands. Holding his breath, he aimed and squeezed the trigger repeatedly firing. *One, Two* . . . The van turned right, into the flow of traffic, and disappeared down Connecticut Avenue. Garrison ran to Sebastian and kneeled beside him.

"Walter . . ."

Sebastian had been hit in the chin and the chest. The back of his head was bloody. There were no signs of life. Garrison rose and backed away in horror, his ears buzzing from the gunshots.

People streamed from the hotel. A woman shrieked.

Garrison ran down a service road to Connecticut Avenue. Flagging down a passing taxi, he climbed in the backseat. The driver pulled into traffic.

"Where to, sir?"

Garrison stared back at the hotel, his mind filled with the sight of Sebastian dead in the alley. Closing his eyes for a moment to repress his emotions, Garrison felt his heart throbbing wildly.

"Just head down through the Park."

As the taxi drove south toward downtown, two police cars sped past in the opposite direction, sirens blaring. As the taxi entered the shaded Rock Creek Park, Garrison leaned back in the seat. The driver slipped a CD into the player. The dissonant, twangy sounds of what Garrison assumed was Pakistani music filled the car.

"Is that too loud for you, sir?"

Garrison stared straight ahead, his fists clenched.

"No."

He told himself to calm down, to take *responsibility* rather than blame himself for Sebastian's death. He willed himself to remain calm. He now knew that the conspiracy reached the highest level of the White House.

Garrison made his decision. He had the driver drop him at a hardware store. Garrison went inside and purchased a screwdriver. For the next few minutes, he walked along Nineteenth Street looking in cars until he found one that had a window down. He looked about, then got in. Using the screwdriver, he hot-wired the ignition and drove out of D.C. at the speed limit.

CHAPTER 30

IN THE SUBURB of McLean, Virginia, Garrison drove to Flanagan's residence: a Spanish Colonial revival sandwiched between other similar houses with three-car garages and second-floor balconies. Cruising slowly past, he saw that the shutters were closed and there was no car in the driveway. Across the street was a man-made lake whose water was an unnatural blue.

Garrison turned the corner, pulled to the curb, and turned off the engine. He took out his wallet and looked up Flanagan's telephone number on the White House Detail telephone list. Using his cell phone, he dialed the number and allowed it to ring ten times. Flanagan's voice came on the answering machine. Garrison pressed OFF.

He dropped the screwdriver into his suit-jacket inside pocket and then got out of the car. Looking about to make sure no neighbors were staring out the window at him, he walked around the corner to Flanagan's house. He rang the doorbell. Hearing nothing, he tried the handle. Locked. He moved to a window at the side of the house. Using the screwdriver, he pried off the screen. The window was locked. Shrugging off his suit jacket, he wrapped it around his right hand and punched the glass, shattering it. Praying no one had heard the sound, he reached inside and turned the lock.

Lifting the window, he crawled over the sill into the living room. The furnishings were tasteful: custom-made sofas and chairs, original oil paintings, a large faceless glass bust on an oversized driftwood coffee table. On the walls hung framed photographs of Flanagan with various dignitaries, including shots of him with former President of Russia Vladimir Putin, the First Lady, and the President. An elaborate sound system and dozens of jazz CDs were sitting on the shelves of a floor-to-ceiling entertainment center.

Garrison's investigative experience told him that when people hid things, they usually hid them in their bedroom. Garrison searched dresser drawers, removing each drawer from the chest to make sure nothing had been taped under the drawer. In the closet he found nothing but clothing. It was the same with the other two bedrooms. In a room Flanagan used as an office, Garrison began to feel frustrated and angry as he rummaged through some cardboard boxes. Without something to prove Flanagan a conspirator, Garrison had few options left.

He searched the kitchen. On the refrigerator was a Secret Service White House Detail weekly duty schedule. In the space for today's date was a notation that

read, "Kennedy Center—POTUS (Tux)." POTUS was
the Secret Service acronym for "President of the United
States" and "Tux" was for tuxedo, the required agent
duty uniform when accompanying protectees to the Center.

In the garage, there were some gardening tools in the
corner, a stack of used brick, a bicycle suspended from
a rafter, a collapsed lounge chair hanging on a wall
hook. On a wooden workbench were nails and screws
in old coffee cans, a hammer, a roll of duct tape, pliers,
electrical wire, wire cutters and other tools, and something else that caught Garrison's attention: two photographic developing trays, some developing solution.
Flanagan must have developed the film taken at Rehoboth Beach.

Garrison pulled open a wooden drawer under the
bench. It too was filled with garage litter: string, paraffin,
and hacksaw blades. Something at the back of the
drawer, an inch-long narrow copper tube with a wire
extending from it, caught his eye, a blasting cap of the
kind used to detonate explosives. Blasting caps were
supposed to be stored in a secure facility. If handled
improperly, the resulting detonation, even without a
main explosive charge, could prove fatal. A blasting cap
was probably what had detonated the C-4 explosive in
Marine One. Flanagan had probably assembled the bomb
he planted in the helicopter here. But Garrison knew that
a blasting cap alone wasn't enough to convince the President. He needed incontrovertible evidence. There had
to be something else.

He went back to the master bedroom and then ripped
the covers off the bed. He flipped over the mattress.
Nothing. He slid open the closet door and dropped to

the carpet. Recalling a case he'd worked on early in his career, he shoved shoes out of the way and hunted for any uneven spot. Finding a square ridge in the carpet, he grasped the carpet at the wall and pulled it back. There was an opening in the hardwood floor about two feet wide. He reached inside and lifted out a black metal box.

He opened the box and held the light close. Inside was a Nikon camera with a long-distance lens and a bankbook of the Credit Suisse bank, Zurich, Switzerland. He opened it. The account was in Flanagan's name. The ledger indicated that four hundred thousand dollars had been wire-transferred into the account from a bank in Panama a few days earlier. It occurred to Garrison that no person, no group would give Flanagan that much money and not demand that he perform. Flanagan was on the hook, Also in the box was an unmarked audio-cassette tape.

Returning to the living room, Garrison inserted the cassette tape in a tape player. He pressed ON. There was a static-like sound as the tape began to play, then faint jazz music playing in the background.

"I just want to make sure that we understand one another," Flanagan said.

"We've been through this over and over, Gil," Wintergreen impatiently said. *"I'm beginning to think you're getting cold feet."*

"This isn't like we're talking about buying a used car here. Jesus H. Christ . . ."

"Okay. Let me go through it again for you. You will get two million dollars once it is done, deposited into a Swiss account."

"In my name."

"*Of course.*"

"*And you are sure that the money is no problem?*"

"*She's worth hundreds of millions. Her father owned half of San Francisco. She'll just go on the Internet and transfer money from one account to another. No one will ever know. You pick up the money when you want.*"

"*What are you getting?*"

"*More than you, my friend. But rank has its privileges.*"

"*What's in it for her, Larry?*"

"*She's crazy.*"

Garrison had the feeling that the floor had fallen away from beneath him.

CHAPTER 31

WALKING ALONG A White House West Wing hallway, Wintergreen had the butterflies-in-stomach feeling. He recognized the sensation as part of being in the arena, the fast lane that had characterized his life.

In the reception area of Helen Pierpont's office, a secretary told him Pierpont had been expecting him. She asked him if he wanted coffee or water. He declined. She smiled, and he moved toward the inner office. Pierpont was sitting behind a massive desk.

"Thanks for getting here so promptly. First, has anything been determined at the Marriott?"

"I've been out there with the agents interviewing witnesses. It appears that Garrison had a backup man with him, possibly a member of the Aryan Disciples. From what it looked like to me, the Disciples may have tried to kidnap Sebastian. The theory we are working is that Garrison was cooperating with the Disciples in a kidnap operation. Sebastian put up a fight and got killed. A witness saw Garrison run down the street and get in a taxi. I tired to trace the taxi myself and came up with nothing. It appears that a Disciples member was driving the taxi."

"This is terrible."

"There is only so much—everything possible is being done—"

She motioned him to a chair. "I want the rundown on the security at the Kennedy Center."

He sat. "With all due respect, it's somewhat unusual to have Secret Service security plans reviewed by—"

"An outsider?"

He graciously smiled. "The Secret Service does have sole jurisdiction for protecting the President."

"Being defensive aren't we, Mr. Director?"

"Nothing personal."

He reached in his inside jacket pocket, took out a copy of the Kennedy Center advance security report, and handed it to her.

She thumbed a few pages.

"The President arrives in the underground garage . . . and then takes the elevator to the lobby floor—"

"Of course the garage, the elevator, and the lobby will be fully secured and posted."

She cleared her throat. "Then the President goes to a holding room?"

"A different holding room than the one we normally use. Anyone who has noted his movements at the Kennedy Center in the past will not know where he will be tonight."

She dropped the report on the desk. "Go ahead."

"The President remains in the holding room until five minutes before curtain time, when he is led to his box—"

"The Presidential box?"

"I've arranged for Box 12 on the other side of the balcony."

"Very good."

Wintergreen coughed dryly. "During the first inter-mission, the President and the First Lady return to the holding room to place some international phone calls."

"First Lady will be attending?"

"Last I heard."

"Please continue."

"Then the President and the First Lady will move from the holding room to different balcony seats."

"It sounds like you have made very thorough prepa-rations, Mr. Director."

"I've had my best advance security team at the Ken-nedy Center for the last two days. With what has been going on, we can't be too cautious. In fact, I'm heading over there to double-check every part of the security plan."

She picked up a pencil, made a note on a yellow pad, and then sat back in her chair.

"The inspection sounds like a very good idea. But looking at the overall situation, the question before us might be posed as whether it's safe for the President to go to the Kennedy Center tonight at all. Whether he should be in any public place until this security situation is fixed."

Wintergreen knew exactly where she was going with this, and he was enjoying the exchange. He knew that she wouldn't have called him in unless the President had already decided to go to the Kennedy Center, probably against her recommendation. People like Pierpont always underestimated others. She'd called him to her office not for a cheerleading session to make sure that all security procedures were in place for the visit, but to get him to recommend to the President that he cancel the visit to the Kennedy Center altogether. She was *standing by her man.*

"Garrison is at large and he knows all about Secret Service security procedures," she went on. "One might assume he has both the unique ability and the inside knowledge to defeat those measures and possibly kill the President. Is that not true?"

"Like I said, everything is being done—"

"What, precisely, are you doing to insure that Garrison cannot defeat your security plan . . . any Secret Service security plan?"

"I thought we went through this with the President."

"Well, now we're going to go through it again."

"Yes, ma'am. No one is taking this lightly. I have confidence in the agents I have assigned—"

"You had confidence in Garrison too."

"Did you call me here to rub my nose in the Garrison issue? Is that what this is all about?"

She folded her hands on the desk. "Are your bomb procedures adequate?"

"Our bomb dogs search every square inch of the Center. The moment an area is searched, agents are posted and the area is secured all the way to the end of the Presidential visit. No one has access except Secret Service agents. When the guests arrive, they are put through magnetometers. We do this every day at every location the President visits, Ms. Pierpont. As I said, I was just on my way to the Kennedy Center to inspect the security setup. I'm going to double-check every part of the security, hands on."

"What would you think about recommending to the President that until this Garrison issue is resolved he remain in the White House?"

"Not much."

She glared at him. "Why?"

"My job isn't to help him make up his schedule. It's to protect his life in any and every situation. He has approved the Kennedy Center visit and it would be inappropriate for me to get involved in such matters."

Pierpont studied him for a moment.

"Thanks for stopping by," she said coldly, her eyes riveted to his.

Walking out of the office, Wintergreen felt a rush. He was in the middle of the most important day of his life and the first half had gone well. His careful steps along the path had taken him nearly all the way, and his time had finally arrived.

At the Kennedy Center, Wintergreen swerved off the road onto a long driveway leading into the underground parking lot.

The Center was a sterile, conservative block of white stone with flags at the entrance; a building that belied its history, built with funds donated by American bluebloods, the elite of Boston and New York and Washington, D.C. He parked his Secret Service sedan in an open parking space among a line of police sedans, K-9 sports utility vehicles, and Secret Service cars. He adjusted the rearview mirror and straightened his necktie, an original Armani silk he'd purchased recently. He climbed out and took a zippered leather briefcase from the trunk. Carrying it under his arm, he walked to the employees' entrance.

"Afternoon, Mr. Director," said the Secret Service uniformed officer posted at the door.

Mr. Director. Wintergreen had always liked the sound of the words. The years of playing politics had been worth it to him. Soon, he would be rich.

"Where are the bomb dogs working?" he asked a uniformed officer at the entrance.

"They've finished here. They're in the main hall upstairs."

He took the elevator to the main floor.

"Find the advance agent and tell him I want to see him," Wintergreen said to a Secret Service uniformed officer whose hair was reaching his collar.

To Wintergreen, untrimmed hair was a sign of innate weakness and sloth.

"Yes, sir."

Wintergreen ambled inside the lobby, where dozens of plainclothes agents and uniformed officers were going about the business of carrying out the security plans for the Presidential visit that evening.

He walked across the lobby, passing through an open doorway into the main auditorium. Below, four bomb-detection teams comprised of one military officer with a bomb-sniffing dog were moving from row to row in a crossway pattern, examining every seat for explosive material. Once the auditorium and stage had been thoroughly searched, agents would be posted at every entrance and exit, sealing the room. Later, when guests began arriving, they would be required to pass through magnetometers to insure that they were carrying neither weapons nor explosives. Only then would they be allowed to take make their way to assigned seats.

"You wanted to see me, Mr. Wintergreen?"

Wintergreen turned. Ronan Squires was one of his best advance agents.

"Run it down for me, Ronan."

"The bomb types have already finished with the holding room, the parking area, and the hallways. I have agents posted. We'll be done in here in a few minutes, including the dressing rooms and the backstage area. The staff advance man tried to set up a photo opportunity outside and I talked him out of it. Once I lock it down, we're ready for the Man. I'll have full security in effect two hours before the President arrives. The magnetometers are in place. All guests will have to go through. When the Man is in the Presidential box, I have agents on either side of him and a look-back."

The look-back agent was designated to squat at the edge of the balcony or bandstand during the performance, keeping his eye on the people in the rows behind the President in the event an assassin popped up.

"As someone once said, if the President were to be saved from assassination, it would be by an advance agent rather than the White House Detail working shift," Wintergreen said.

"Yes, sir."

"I'd like to inspect the posts."

"Follow me."

They walked along the route the President would take when he arrived. Squires pointed out the post locations, and Wintergreen noted that the agent whose duty was to guard the holding room area was down the hall, away from the holding room.

"What do we have worked out in case of bomb threats?"

"With the area already secured, telephonic bomb threats will be nothing more than a nuisance. The President will be entering a bomb-free, assassin-free Kennedy Center."

"Very good, Ronan."

Wintergreen stopped and looked up at the Presidential box.

"Any significant intelligence information I should know about?"

"Nothing other than the Garrison thing," Squires said somberly, lowering his voice.

Wintergreen raised his eyebrows in acknowledgment.

"Ronan, may we speak in confidence?"

"Of course, Mr. Director."

"I realize that you and the others consider Garrison to be a friend and colleague. It may be hard to believe what he's done, but I don't want that to get in the way of what we may have to do here. Garrison killed Walter Sebastian in cold blood."

"I'm aware. Every agent has been briefed."

"Garrison knows this game, Ronan."

"I've taken that into account. I've doubled the security posts. Hell, I have half the Washington Field Office augmenting the detail."

"I'm certainly not implying that you aren't on top of this. But I can't emphasize enough that Garrison is coming for us. For whatever reason, he's turned into a killer. Make sure every agent knows he or she will be backed up from the top if anything goes down. I believe we owe Garrison a bullet in the brain. If he shows up here,

I don't want him to leave alive. Let the word go out that the sonofabitch Garrison is free game."

"Yes, sir."

"By the way. I'd like to see the holding room."

"Sure."

Squires led him down a corridor lined with doorways and into a comfortably-furnished holding room that was furnished with two sofas, an entertainment center, and a desk on which were two White House telephones, a red Pentagon radio-telephone, and a portable computer. At every location the President visited, a holding room was designated for him. Wintergreen knew that part of the job of protecting him was shielding him from potential embarrassment. The President could not be forced by circumstances to stand in a hallway or be confronted by members of the general public. And security considerations required that the President be near White House communications at all times. Whether the President was at a baseball stadium, a military airport hangar, or a convention hall, he had a place where he could make telephone calls in private, confer with aides without being disturbed or overheard, or simply kill time.

"The President will spend some time here before he goes to his assigned box, and then will return here during the first intermission. The First Lady has to make some international calls."

"Fine," Wintergreen said. "The bomb dogs have been through here?"

"Over an hour ago. The agent posted at the end of the corridor has secured this room."

"Sounds to me like you're on top of this advance, Ronan."

"Without a doubt, Mr. Director."

They left the holding room and walked down the hall. Squires got a call on his radio, and told Wintergreen that he had to go to the other side of the center to meet with some police officials.

Wintergreen slapped Squires on the shoulder.

"Go get 'em, tiger."

"Let me know if you see anything you want changed, Mr. Wintergreen."

"Ronan?"

He turned.

"The uniform at the front door needs a haircut," Wintergreen said tapping the back of his neck.

"Yes, sir."

Wintergreen gave Squires a wink. Squires turned and headed toward the theater. Wintergreen watched a dog handler for a minute or so. He could feel tension at the back of his brain. His lips were numb. Detaching himself from thoughts of failure, he returned to the holding room, went inside, and locked the door. He had to move fast.

He opening his zippered briefcase and took out a pair of white surgical gloves. His hands shook as he slipped them on. He took a deep breath. Climbing onto the table, he reached up and carefully removed one of the fiber-board panels from the ceiling. He climbed off the table and placed the panel on it. Then he took out a sheet of plastic seven inches by seven and one half inches in size. The sheet was reinforced with thin steel mesh and was curved in two places, like the hull of a boat. Affixed to its middle was a putty-like chunk of military-grade C-4 explosive that looked like flattened, yellowish clay. Over it was stapled three pieces of cheesecloth bristling with roofing nails. Flanagan had built the bomb using Aryan

Disciples bomb-building techniques as described in a forensic briefing book, taking care to insure that there was nothing about it that would make anyone think that it wasn't an Aryan Disciples device.

He carefully inserted a blasting cap into the center of the C-4. A small radio receiver and a timer switch had been taped down next to it, which consisted of two AA batteries connected by wires and a small digital clock with its alarm set for 9:15 P.M. He then took a piece of rubber sheeting from the briefcase and pulled it tight around the surface of the entire device. The construction allowed the nails to spread out in post-detonation flight in a planned pattern, downward and out, killing everyone in the holding room. He attached the bomb to the unfinished side of the fiberboard. Climbing back onto the table, he picked up the fiberboard and shoved it back into place in the ceiling. He got down, removed his gloves, and shoved them back into the briefcase. Done.

Wintergreen felt perspiration on his forehead and upper lip. Using a handkerchief, he wiped his face, then the table. After looking around to make sure everything was back in place, he closed his eyes and took a couple of deep breaths. Before leaving the room, he shot one last glance at the ceiling panel.

"Go, baby, go," he said softly.

Wintergreen smiled and nodded at the agents who made eye contact with him as he departed the Kennedy Center, but his mind was on the future. He pictured himself on the prow of a yacht, sailing in clear, blue water.

CHAPTER 32

GARRISON STARED GLUMLY out the window of Watergate Condominium 1303 as Eleanor's limousine pulled to the curb. Agent Steve Paulk got out of the limousine and opened the right rear door.

As Eleanor climbed out, rage stirred in Garrison's gut. He wondered if she'd been able to detect the seething anger that he'd tried to keep out of his voice when he'd called her a few minutes earlier and told her they had to talk, that she needed to come to the Watergate.

A minute later, there was a knock on the front door. He opened it and she came in.

He closed the door.

"Did you speak with the President?" he asked.

She stared at him, her brow furrowed with concern.

"Yes. But he wouldn't listen. Pete, what's wrong?"

"It's you."

"Pardon me?"

"You're the one behind the assassination."

"Pete, do you feel okay?"

"You can stop the con-game act. You're trying to kill your husband."

"Surely you can't believe that—"

"*What I believe?* That is the question, isn't it? *What do I believe?* Well, let me tell you. I believe you hired Larry Wintergreen to kill the President. You offered him millions, including a load of dough for his bun-boy Flanagan. And, although it's difficult for even someone as cynical as me to comprehend, Wintergreen actually went along with what you wanted."

"Pete—"

The look that crossed her face was one of hurt and compassionate sincerity; an expression she must have developed growing up with the rich and powerful. It was the countenance of deep perturbation people had when dealing with the immediate family at funerals or when offering a shoulder to someone whom had unexpectedly broken into tears—sympathy—the merciful hand of friendship and understanding. But he could tell the expression was false. It was the practiced facial cast of a manipulator.

"It all started when you asked Wintergreen to find out about the President and Helen Pierpont. Wintergreen coerced Meriweather into bugging Pierpont's room when in New York because you asked him to. You were checking up on your husband. When Meriweather figured out he was being used and threatened to go to the President, you and Wintergreen decided to silence him. You couldn't afford to have him telling tales. Flanagan took care of that little job for you. Then you needed a fall guy to blame for the assassination. You knew that, afterwards, it would be obvious that a White House insider was involved. I was chosen because I had experience on the bomb detail."

"Pete, I swear I know nothing about any of this—"

"Flanagan recruited Hightower to drop some phony information to me about an Aryan Disciples assassination plot. And you? You got next to me for only one reason: to gain my confidence. So you could manipulate me. I was your fall guy, your scapegoat—"

"Someone has steered you wrong. Please believe—"

"After you were convinced you could talk me into conducting an unofficial investigation for you, Wintergreen had Flanagan plant the phony blackmail letter. That was to get me on FBI videotape near an Aryan Disciples drop-off point. He knew the FBI had it under surveillance. Yes, Eleanor, if the President hadn't chosen to drive back from Camp David and had taken the chopper as originally scheduled, you and Wintergreen would have gotten the job done. But something went wrong. That's when you started having some problems."

"Pete, what can I do to convince you I am not involved? Please tell me. I can see that you are completely off base and—"

Garrison walked to the entertainment center. Reaching into his pocket, he took out the cassette tape he'd found in Flanagan's house. He pressed POWER, and then shoved the tape into the port.

"And you are sure that the money is no problem?"

"She's worth hundreds of millions. Her father owned half of San Francisco. She'll just go on the Internet and transfer money from one account to another. No one will ever know. You pick up the money when you want. . . ."

He pressed OFF.

"Flanagan made that tape as an insurance policy. He figured that if he got caught, he would be able to make a deal by handing up Wintergreen and the First Lady. He was thinking ahead."

"Tapes can be doctored."

"You know, Eleanor, somehow I figured that's what you were going to say."

She moved to him. There was an unusual rosiness high on her cheeks. Her hands grasped his waist.

"Please believe me," she said looking him in the eye. Her hands touched his cheeks. "You have it all wrong. I swear."

She kissed him, and he felt her tongue touch his. But he didn't move. She stopped. Realizing she was having no effect on him, she stepped back.

"You almost got away with it, didn't you?" he said.

"A tape isn't enough to convict me," she coldly said after a silence.

"Federal prisons are filled with people who've said that."

"You can try. But you will fail."

"I hope you're not banking on Wintergreen. He'll cut a deal behind your back."

She glared at him. "No jury will believe him over me. And my husband won't listen to you. I'll tell him you came on to me—that you've been acting strange."

"Go ahead. And I'll go straight to the press. I'll tell Joe Kretchvane everything I know and he'll call the biggest press conference that's ever hit this town. Let the games begin."

She nervously smoothed her skirt, and then glanced at her Baume Mercier.

"What do you want, Pete?"

"Now we're getting down to it."

"I can make you rich. Richer than you ever dreamed. You name the amount. There is a whole new life out there for you. I can bring you out of the wilderness. I can show you what it is like to be powerful—to have no worries. You'll be able to drive a Rolls-Royce."

"Why, Eleanor? Why did you do this?"

There was a long silence and she walked to the sofa and sat.

"Russell was nothing but a second-rate political drone when we met. He'd still be fishing for votes in San Francisco without me. I gave him everything. I carried him. He wouldn't have gotten off first base without my help— much less make it to the White House. I paid his bills. I cleaned up his goddamn messes just like I did for my first sonofabitch of a husband. *And what did I get for it?* That low-class bitch Helen Pierpont making a fool of me . . . everybody knowing about it, making comments behind my back, treating me like I was some second-rate house-frau. Oh, I could have handled the fact that Russell was running around on me. I'd accepted that. But when I found he was planning to divorce me the moment we leave office, I decided I wasn't going to stand for it. All the years I gave him to end up tossed away. Don't you see what the bastard is doing to me? He's humiliating me, like my father did to my mother. It's evil and it's rotten."

"So that's what Meriweather learned by the bugging. He learned about the divorce plans. That's what got the ball rolling. You confronted the President and he had to admit it—"

"I'm sorry about what happened to others. I didn't

mean any of that. But my husband deserves to die—"

"Eleanor, you're sick."

"At least Jackie Kennedy could hold her head up. No one pushed her out the door like some goddamn one-night stand. Some two-bit, 14th Street whore."

She got up and walked to him. They were standing close and he could smell the perfume—the roses scent—and Garrison thought about the night they'd been together. Her smell had been on him.

"Please don't go against me. You and I can be together. I love you. I know you don't believe that, but I really do."

Garrison's chagrin and guilt had turned to anger, seething, cold anger that seeped from every pore in his body and consumed his thoughts.

"You provided me with this condo to keep me alive long enough to fulfill my role as scapegoat. I can see the clerk downstairs testifying how I impersonated your cousin to get in here. You make a great undercover agent, Eleanor. Class A. You also turn my stomach."

"Do you really think you can take down the First Lady of the United States? Do you believe you can pull it off?"

"Watch me."

"Think about what you are saying. Experts will testify that the tape is doctored. My lawyers will turn it all against you. In the end, no one will believe you." She took a long look at him, as if she wanted to say something—as if she might know some magic words that would fix everything, make the past dissolve away like some ethereal image. "Don't you see? *I'm giving you a chance*. This could all be over and you and I can be together. I don't want anything to happen to you. *What we had can be real.*"

"That's an interesting way to put it."

"Please don't be a fool."

"You're responsible for people being killed. And I'm going to see that you pay for it."

"Oh, are you now? Well let me tell you something. There is *nothing* you can do. You have *nothing*. You can't arrest me and you'll never be able to convince anyone of my guilt. Use your head. The best thing for you to do is join me. I will get you out of the country. I can see to it that you are taken care of for the rest of your life."

The faraway look in her eye was one Garrison had seen before, but he couldn't remember exactly when. Had it been when they'd been in bed together? Or was he imagining it?

"Eleanor, you're actually out of your mind. I pity you."

She stared at him during a long, uncomfortable silence. "Well, I guess there isn't much left to say, is there?"

She walked to the door, looked back at him, and then departed. He wanted to rush after her, to arrest her. He wanted to march her into the Oval Office and tell the President. But he knew it wasn't going to be that easy. Moving to the window, he watched her get in the limousine and depart.

Something hard touched the back of his head.

"Move and I'll shoot," Flanagan whispered.

Garrison went numb. Keeping the gun in contact with Garrison's head, Flanagan reached around and pulled Garrison's SIG-Sauer from its holster. He backed away cautiously, aiming a .38 revolver at Garrison. Flanagan was holding the gun with both hands.

"I should have known you'd have a key to the service entrance," said Garrison. "You have this place bugged, don't you? You had to keep tabs on me."

"Bugging the Watergate. Ironic, isn't it?"

"Getting me to go to the Sperling Finance Building so you could tie me to the Aryan Disciples. That's promising for a dummy like you."

Flanagan moved to the tape player and slid the cassette tape from the tape recorder. He dropped it in his jacket pocket.

"She and Wintergreen will eventually put you out front," said Garrison. "Can't you see that?"

"Turn around."

Garrison studied him carefully because his life depended on it. Flanagan was nervous. His gun hand was trembling and his lips were lacking color. Garrison assessed his chances for survival. Flanagan was about eight feet away, and if he rushed him he was going to get shot. For a split second Garrison imagined a bullet tearing into his flesh, but swallowing the pain, imagined surviving and being able to disarm Flanagan. But it was a dream; the kind of optimistic fugue he figured that victims of premeditated murder had had throughout the ages. If Flanagan had intended to simply arrest him, he would have handcuffed him.

"Wintergreen told you to kill me here, didn't he? So you could claim I'd been stalking the First Lady. Everyone will hear the gunshot. You'll never be able to get away. They have private security officers all over this place."

"I told you to turn around. *Now!*"

Garrison's mind raced and he turned slowly away from Flanagan. There was a narrow vertical mirror on the facing wall, and he could see Flanagan's image. Flanagan reached into his jacket pocket and took something out—a shiny cylindrical object that was about six inches long—a silencer. He began to screw it onto the barrel of the .38. Flanagan was going to shoot him. He had planned it.

Garrison whirled and ran straight at him, grabbing the gun. Flanagan tried to shoot, but Garrison slammed a right forearm across Flanagan's face and took him down to the carpet. Wrenching the gun away from him, Garrison shoved the barrel between his eyes.

"For a moment there I thought you were going to shoot me."

"No . . ."

"Waiting to put a silencer on can be a real problem when you don't have a backup man, right, Gil? Now, get up."

Reaching to Flanagan's waistband, Garrison pulled out his own SIG-Sauer and scrambled to his feet. Flanagan came to his feet slowly, keeping his hands raised.

"I'll give you the money."

Flanagan's right eye was swollen and he looked confused, his eyes darting back and forth as if looking for some avenue of escape. Garrison moved behind him, lifting Flanagan's suit jacket to check for a backup gun. There was none. He took the handcuffs from Flanagan's belt and dropped them in his trouser pocket.

Garrison said, motioning to the dining table, "Sit down."

Flanagan sat. His face was red from exertion. "What are you gonna do?"

"Sit here and listen as you tell me what the hell is going on. You're going to tell me everything about the assassination plan. I know you have one. That's why you kept me alive. That's why she set me up here."

"There isn't any."

"She didn't promise you three million dollars for a college try. You have something planned right now."

"I don't know anything."

"You wouldn't have gone to the trouble of keeping me on ice here unless you had another assassination planned."

Garrison studied him for a moment. Then, being careful to keep his SIG-Sauer trained on Flanagan, he placed Flanagan's .38 on the table.

"What are you doing?"

Using one hand, Garrison slipped the silencer onto the barrel and with his other hand, kept the SIG-Sauer trained on Flanagan. With the silencer in place, he hefted the .38 in his left hand and aimed at Flanagan.

"I found a blasting cap in your garage and I want the plan. I'm not going to ask you again. I want it all, right now."

"I'm telling the truth. So help me. This isn't my thing."

Garrison aimed the .38 at the edge of the upper sleeve of Flanagan's jacket and pulled the trigger. With the powerful *whoosh-thump* of the silencer, Flanagan shrieked and whirled backward grabbing his upper arm.

"You shot me! You shot me!"

Garrison aimed at Flanagan's upper chest.

"The Kennedy Center," Flanagan said. "Wintergreen planted it. He told me to set the timer for 9:15 tonight." Flanagan's eyes were wide. He didn't look well. "He told me he was going to plant it after security was in place, after the bomb sweep. That way no one would do another check even if you called in."

"Now I get it. That's why she put me here at the Watergate. To make the plan work, she needed to have me kept alive until the bomb had been planted. And she wanted me near the Kennedy Center when the bomb detonated. You were going to shoot me and make it look like a suicide, weren't you? The headline: 'Assassin found dead in his hideout across the street from the Kennedy Center.' "

"This wasn't my idea."

Garrison shoved the .38 in his waistband. He lifted the cellular phone from his belt and dialed the White House number.

"What are you doing?" Flanagan asked, holding his upper arm.

"Calling the advance agent at the Kennedy Center. You're going to tell him where you put the bomb and how to disarm it. Either that or I kill you."

There was a sudden, loud knocking on the door.

Garrison stopped dialing.

"Who's there?"

"Housekeeping. Is everything okay in there?"

Flanagan dove across the table and grabbed Garrison's gun.

"Help!" Flanagan shouted.

They struggled away from the table to the wall. They crashed into a glass bookcase, knocking vases to the floor. The gun fired. A dull pain pierced the left side of Garrison's head, but he still managed to keep his hands on the gun. They struggled back and forth, locked together in a death contest. Flanagan almost turned the barrel around on him, but Garrison maintained his grip, straining with every fiber in his being. They slammed against the table, and then fell to the floor. Garrison fought savagely. He could hear Flanagan's breathing as they struggled to their feet.

Flanagan snapped his head forward, head-butting Garrison on the bridge of the nose. Garrison saw black for a moment. Dazed, Garrison twisted powerfully, using every ounce of his strength.

There was a muffled pop sound, and he felt the shock wave of the bullet as it hit Flanagan. Releasing his grip on the gun, Flanagan fell forward, his body causing a sickening thud as it hit the floor. There was hole in the back of his shirt from a through-and-through wound to the chest. His eyes were open. Garrison dropped to his knees.

"Where is the bomb planted?" Garrison asked. Flanagan's eyes closed involuntarily. Garrison slapped his face. He was dead. "You bastard."

The pounding on the door continued.

"Open the door or we'll kick it in!" a man shouted.

Garrison frantically searched Flanagan's pockets as Technicolor images flashed through his mind: Meriweather lying on the floor of his motel room; Walter Sebastian in the alley behind the Marriott Hotel; Breckinridge in the hospital room. In Flanagan's inside jacket pocket, he found the cassette tape and a folded six-page Secret Service Advance Survey report. He shoved the items in his pocket, unclipped the Secret Service radio from Flanagan's belt.

"I'll be right there!"

He ran through the kitchen to the service entrance. Using the peephole, he saw there was no one there. He opened the door and ran to the stairway. Descending steps three at a time, he ran down all six flights to the garage. There was a taxi parked in front.

"Are you the one who called, sir?"

"Yes," Garrison said getting in.

"Where to?"

"Uh, the Lincoln Memorial."

The driver pulled into traffic.

Garrison took out Wintergreen's advance security report and thumbed pages. It contained a detailed map of the route from the White House to the Kennedy Center and depictions of every building, storm drain, and manhole cover, including schematic diagrams of the rooms in the Kennedy Center. There were also lists of contact names, including the names and posts of the agents and uniformed officers posted along the route and at the Kennedy Center. Garrison found the list of daily radio codes, and the designations for both the assigned posts and Secret Service supervisors. As a precaution against an intruder breaking into the official radio net, every time the President left the White House and went to another location, special radio codes were assigned to every Secret Service supervisor solely for use at the site to be visited.

The first page of the report read:

ADVANCE SECURITY SURVEY

Visit of the President to the Kennedy Center for the performing arts to attend a performance of the stage play "Long Day's Journey into Night."

ADVANCE AGENT: SA Ronan B. Squires
SUPERVISOR: SAIC Wintergreen

SYNOPSIS

From CROWN, taking route 3 designated by Director Wintergreen, Victory will arrive via limousine 300JX at KCPA at approximately 1840 hours. Victory will be led to Holding Room 1343 where he will await word from Press Secretary that all guests have been seated. Victory's entrance to the Presidential box is a photo opportunity—national coverage. Shift agents are to remain out of camera view as President enters.

During the first intermission (9:00–9:20 P.M.) Victory and Valentine will move to the Holding Room Alpha where Victory will make previously scheduled telephone call to Beijing and Jakarta on secure line.

Victory will return to Presidential box, then depart KCPA shortly before the end of the last act and return to CROWN.

LIMO PARKING SPOT—469
HOLDING ROOM—1343
RADIO FREQUENCY—BRAVO LIMA
COMMAND POST—ROOM 661

There were plenty of places in the Kennedy Center where one could hide a bomb. The schematic showed a door at the rear of holding room A leading to a large closet, and another door to an adjoining lounge. It bore the Secret Service designation "S" for safe. This meant that its corner location and reinforced walls made it the best place to be in the event of a bomb detonation. Trying to get into the Kennedy Center would be suicide.

He took out his cellular phone and dialed information,

obtaining reporter Joe Kretchvane's telephone number
from the operator.

"Kretchvane Incorporated," a woman said.

"Is Joe in?"

"May I say who's calling?"

"Special Agent Pete Garrison, U.S. Secret Service."

"Hold the line."

A moment later, the phone beeped.

"What can I do you for, Agent Garrison?" Kretchvane
said.

"Just get out a pencil. I'm going to give you a story."

"Go, man."

"There is a conspiracy to assassinate the President—"

"Is this a joke?"

"No."

"Where are you?"

"In D.C."

"We need to do this in person."

"That's a problem for me."

"Come to my place. The Promenade Towers on E
Street in Capitol Hill."

"I'd prefer to do it over the phone."

"For all I know, you might be someone impersonating
Garrison. Stranger things have happened."

"I don't have much time."

"Look, I know you. You wouldn't be calling me if it
weren't important—if this weren't for real. But I can't
do anything with a story whose source I haven't nailed
down."

Garrison thought about it for a moment. He didn't
trust Joe Kretchvane. But his contacts with members of
the press were limited, and he believed the best way to

save the President was to expose the plot to the world press. Besides, Kretchvane knew he wasn't crazy—something he would have to prove to any other reporter who didn't know him.

"I'll be there in a few minutes. Joe, don't contact anyone in the Secret Service about me."

"Why would I do that?"

"Because I know that is the kind of thing writers do to check out stories. I'm telling you that if you do, you'll lose out on the biggest story of your life."

"I like the sound of this."

Garrison pressed OFF and told the driver he'd changed his mind and gave him Kretchvane's address.

The driver made a U-turn.

Garrison glanced at his wristwatch. He had three hours to warn the President, enough time for Kretchvane to call a press conference and get the attention of the President and the entire White House staff, forcing them to cancel the trip to the Kennedy Center.

Arriving at the Promenade Towers a few minutes later, Garrison had butterflies in his stomach. He paid the driver and got out of the taxi. On a pole turning slowly in the middle of the fountain was a PROMENADE TOWERS sign in silver, three-dimensional letters. The apartment house was a sterile-looking multistory place with a quadrangle and a small fountain in front.

Inside, Garrison found Kretchvane's name on the first-floor resident index and dialed his apartment number.

"Hello?" Kretchvane said.

"It's Pete Garrison. I'm downstairs."

"Wait there."

Garrison looked about. There were few cars parked on the street.

A minute later, the elevator doors opened.

"I told you someday you'd have a story for me," Kretchvane said.

"Let's go up to your apartment."

"What's this story you have?"

"You want to stand here and talk about it?"

"Just a few questions, then we can go upstairs."

"What's wrong, Joe?"

"I don't want you to think I'm inhospitable, but I can't take the chance that you might plant a listening device in my apartment. Frankly, I don't trust the government. For all I know, the First Lady sent you over to see what you can find out about my book."

Garrison blinked a few times in frustration.

"Listen carefully, Joe. I don't have much time. I'm ready to tell you some facts that involve a problem with Presidential security. A danger to the President. I'll give you the information on one condition: if you promise to spread information across the news wires immediately—like within minutes. I give you my word I won't talk to any other reporter. You'll have the exclusive. But I have to get the information out. Now. The President is in danger of being assassinated and there is no other way I can get him to listen."

Kretchvane stared at the tiled floor. "Why?"

"Because someone is trying to frame me."

"For what?"

"For the planned assassination. I've tried to warn them but they won't listen to me."

"They don't believe you?"

"Exactly."

"Then why should I?"

"You know I'm not crazy. You know I would never make something like this up."

"Do I?"

Garrison let out his breath. "The Marine helicopter that went down near Camp David was sabotaged. There is a plot to kill the President involving Secret Service Director Wintergreen—"

"You're talking about Wintergreen?"

Kretchvane glanced over Garrison's shoulder, toward the street.

"Right."

A car was parked down the street, in the direction Kretchvane had been looking.

"Let's take a walk, Pete."

Garrison got a sudden chill—a tingling sensation at the back of his head that spread through his body like ice water being flushed into his veins. Kretchvane was just going thorough the motions with him. He must have called someone in the Secret Service the moment after they had talked on the phone. Someone must have convinced him that Garrison was either guilty or crazy or both.

"You double-crossed me, Joe."

"I don't know what you're talking—"

Garrison drew his gun.

"I don't have a lot of time, Joe. What did they tell you to do?"

Kretchvane stared at the SIG-Sauer.

"They told me that you were wanted for murder—"

"I asked you a question, Joe."

"They asked me to get you to walk out to the street. To the curb. They were afraid you would see them—"

"Where is your car?"

"The underground garage." Kretchvane's voice was hoarse with emotion. "They told me to do this. It wasn't my idea—"

"Give me the keys." Kretchvane complied, his eyes on the street. "We're going to your car."

"It wasn't my fault, Garrison."

"Don't think I won't kill you."

Following him to the elevator, Garrison pressed the down button. The elevator doors opened.

From the street came the sound of running. Agents with guns out were heading in his direction.

"Help!" Kretchvane shouted.

Garrison pulled his gun and straight-armed Kretchvane into the elevator. Grabbing Kretchvane's hair, he put the gun it to head.

"Hit the wrong button and you're a dead man."

"I don't want to die, man." Kretchvane touched a button, and the doors closed and the elevator began to descend.

The doors opened into a large underground garage parking area. Holding Kretchvane in front of him, Garrison walked out of the elevator. To Garrison's right was a wide driveway that led to the street. The security gate was open.

"Which one?"

Kretchvane pointed to a sports car. "There, the Porsche."

Garrison got behind the wheel, reholstered his gun, and started the engine.

"You're going to kick yourself when you find out I was telling the truth."

The stairwell door opened and agents streamed out, running in his direction with guns out.

"There he is!" Kretchvane shouted.

Garrison sped toward the exit and onto the street. Rounding the corner at a high rate of speed, he pressed the pedal to the floor. He sped to the Capitol Center South Metro station. Looking behind him, he saw no pursuers. Parking the car in a red zone, he jumped out and ran down the steps to the station as a train was pulling in.

He hurried into a crowded car and stared at the station as the train pulled out of the station and into a tunnel. He took a deep breath and let it out. There was little time to warn the President, and nothing he could do to get him to cancel the Kennedy Center visit. Eleanor would see to it that he was there.

Considering the time and the overall situation, Garrison decided that he would disarm the bomb himself. He knew the Kennedy Center and he had a copy of the advance security report. With a little luck, he would be able to make his way through security. And with a little more luck, he would be able to find the bomb. As he saw it, it had to be planted somewhere in the holding room, the only place where the President would be alone while he was at the Center. He got off the train at the McPherson Square station.

CHAPTER 33

AT THE STATION, Garrison walked up the steps to the street. Victoria's Cleaning and Laundry was across the street. He went inside. Victoria stood behind the counter. She was a middle-aged Syrian woman, short and rail-thin, whose lined, prunish complexion was the result of years of exposure to presser steam.

"Nick Torricelli asked me to pick up his uniform for him."

Garrison figured Torricelli, a uniformed officer who worked the White House Northeast Gate, would have at least one uniform in the shop that he hadn't picked up. The shop was a couple of blocks from the White House, and Garrison had patronized it for years. He recalled seeing Officer Torricelli in the shop. Many Service Uniformed Division officers frequented Victoria's to take advantage of her Secret Service discount, a welcome help in defraying the cost of the freshly cleaned and starched uniform shirt required for every White House shift.

"You got his laundry ticket?"

"I lost it. Sorry."

"Ever lose your gun?" she said facetiously.

"Not lately."

"Maybe someday I can't find the ticket and Torricelli won't get his shirt."

"He's standing at the east gate right now wearing only his trousers."

She chuckled, opening a small wooden file box, and thumbed through laundry receipts. She pulled out a receipt, then turned and pressed a button. As the overhead clothing rack began moving, Garrison glanced toward the door again, fearing Torricelli or some other Secret Service officer or agent might walk in and see him.

She stopped the rack, reached up, and took down a Secret Service Uniformed Division shirt and trousers.

"You got some ID?"

Garrison took out his Secret Service identification, holding it out as she copied his name on the laundry receipt. He paid the bill, said thanks, and headed for the door.

"Hey, Garrison."

He stopped and turned. "Yes?"

"What do you think the President will do about Albania?"

"I'm not sure."

"Ask him for me."

"Sure."

• • •

At a police equipment store on New York Avenue, Garrison showed his Secret Service badge and identification card to purchase a Uniformed Division hat and a black leather gun belt. He paid with his credit card.

Carrying the items and Torricelli's uniform, Garrison walked down the street to a cafeteria. In the men's room, he locked the door, changed into the uniform, and then put his suit jacket on over the uniform shirt and gun belt. Carrying the uniform, hat in the store bag, he departed.

Down the street at 13th and H Street, Garrison darted into the Metro Center subway station. He boarded the first train that arrived and took a seat facing forward. As the car pulled out of the station, he found himself thinking about Martha Breckinridge. He wanted to call the hospital to check on her condition, but forced himself to put his concern for her out of his mind to concentrate on his plan.

Minutes later, he disembarked at the Dupont Circle station. Taking the escalator to the street, he turned right and walked to the White House garage at 21st Street near R, an aging two-story brick building where all the limousines and other Secret Service vehicles were housed and serviced. To avoid being filmed by the surveillance cameras he knew were on the garage roof, he approached the entrance by walking along the wall and ducking behind tall bushes adjacent to the building. Reaching the garage's roll-up door, he stopped to wait for the Presidential limousine.

The Secret Service manual required that all motorcade vehicles be serviced shortly before they were used. He knew that it was customary for one Presidential limousine to be brought to the White House garage, where it would be switched for a newly serviced limo. There were eight identical Presidential limousines, enough so that they could be used for Presidential transportation even on multiple-stop foreign trips. After picking up the newly serviced limousine, the driver would then return to the White House, parking it near the South Portico, where the motorcade would be formed.

As Garrison hid next to the building, behind some tall cypress trees, the lawn sprinklers came on. With water spraying his shoes, socks, and trousers, he tried not to think of how slim his chances were of succeeding with his mission.

A few minutes later, a black Lincoln limousine turned the corner and swerved into the wide driveway. The license plate "W-2" told him it was the backup limo. Parking near the garage door, Agent Andy Collins climbed out from behind the wheel. He wore a shoulder holster over a white shirt with rolled-up sleeves. Collins was heavyset, middle-aged, and balding. Garrison thought he looked tired. Collins walked to the garage lock box and inserted a key. There was a creaking sound as the metal security door began rolling upward in its track. Collins got back behind the wheel of the limousine and drove inside the garage. The door remained open.

Garrison crept to the edge of the door and peeked inside. The garage agent walked out of his glassed-in office and stood eating an orange and watching Collins park the limousine at the service bay. The garage was a dank, four-walled cavern housing shiny-black armored limousines, sport utility vehicles, and four-door sedans, all parked in precise, slanted rows facing the walls.

Garrison's heart rate and breathing increased. All his planning and contemplation were over. This was it. All or-nothing. If he failed, both he and the President were finished.

As Collins and the other agent chatted, Garrison darted inside. Staying low, he turned right, and moved along the wall for a few feet. Then he slipped between two black Mercury Mountaineers to wait.

Minutes later, Collins and the garage agent walked into the office.

Garrison watched as two Secret Service mechanics standing near the hoists went through the vehicle-safety checklist. The procedure took about ten minutes. When they were finished, they headed toward the office. Garrison crossed to the facing wall. Staying low, he scurried to the rear of the newly serviced limousine. Using his Secret Service master key, he opened the trunk. He crawled inside among the emergency equipment and closed the trunk lid. He could open the lock from inside by feel—a technique he'd practiced diligently in Secret Service undercover school.

Lying between a canvas bag of gas masks and a folded metal stretcher, he tried to relax, using his imagination to avoid thinking about how uncomfortable he was in wet shoes and trousers, concentrating instead on the positive: He'd made it into the trunk without getting apprehended or killed.

Garrison heard bits of conversation between Collins and the garage agent.

"He must have gone completely nuts," Collins said.

"The Director put out the word—shoot him on sight— if he shows at the House."

"Hard to believe . . ."

"He sold his ass out to the Aryan Disciples. He asked

for it. Orders are orders. If I see him, I'll fill his ass full of lead."

"No other way."

Garrison felt like shouting. He heard footsteps approaching the limousine. The driver's door opened and closed. The engine turned over. The limousine was moving.

CHAPTER 34

DURING THE SHORT drive to the White House, Garrison became slightly motion-sick, aggravated by the fact that the trunk smelled of motor oil, gasoline, and car rugs. He hadn't eaten in twenty-four hours.

Closing his eyes, he imagined himself back home in Bisbee, driving a 1960 Chevrolet he'd restored to mint condition, his father's old car. He'd had it painted candy-apple, metal-flake red, and he'd lowered it an inch all around by torching the springs. He'd installed a four-barrel carburetor, dual exhausts, and had the engine heads ported and milled. The Chevy was a slick machine, a polished charger, and he'd done all the work himself. He'd cruised Bisbee with pride. He wondered what his boyhood pals would think now if they knew he was hiding in the trunk of the President's limousine and was probably going to get killed by one of his fellow Secret Service agents. . . .

The limousine stopped briefly, then continued on for a few seconds. Another stop. Garrison guessed they were at the White House Northeast Gate.

The driver's door opened, then closed. He figured they must be in the Executive Office Building courtyard. The sound of Collins's footsteps came toward the rear of the limousine.

Garrison tensed. The footsteps continued on. He heard radio traffic: other agents and some White House staff members sharing last-minute details about the Kennedy Center visit. A cold fear seized him. What if, for some ungodly reason, they'd decided not to use this particular backup limousine? If so, if the limo remained within the White House compound when the Presidential motorcade departed for the Kennedy Center, Garrison would be trapped inside the White House grounds.

Someone, probably Collins, got back in the limousine and started the engine. The limousine pulled away, stopping again about thirty seconds later at what he hoped was its place in the Presidential motorcade forming along the White House South Portico. He heard footsteps and radio traffic. The right rear limousine door opened. Someone got in, followed by a second person. The door closed. It had to be Eleanor and the President.

Garrison curled uncomfortably in the trunk. He wanted to stretch his legs, but there wasn't enough room. He imagined the route along Pennsylvania Avenue to Virginia Avenue. The motorcade would be guided by a pilot car containing a police officer and a Secret Service agent. Traveling a quarter mile ahead of the motorcade, it served to make sure that the roadway was clear. Next in line was a lead car driven by a police officer and commanded by a Secret Service supervisor. Behind it was the spare limousine that, because of its tinted windows, served to confuse assassins as to the President's exact location. Behind the President's limousine was the Secret Service follow-up car: a van carrying six heavily armed agents whose mission was to protect the presidential limousine if it was attacked. Behind the follow-up car was a van filled with more agents. Their mission was to return fire in the event of paramilitary attack. The other cars in the motorcade were staff and press cars and a Secret Service intelligence car that carried two agents whose responsibility was to gather and relay intelligence information.

Garrison wanted to shout, to tell the President what was going on. But he knew that to warn him—to convince him—he had to be alone with him, face-to-face. He would wait until they got out of the car and he could make his way into the holding room, where they would be alone. Garrison told himself that he had time, that there was no way to rush it. He had to stick with his plan. He couldn't just shout to the President and get arrested hiding in the trunk of the limousine. Then it would be over for sure. He willed himself to remain calm.

Garrison felt a bump and assumed the motorcade was pulling into a driveway, probably the one at the Kennedy Center that led into the underground garage.

The limousine came to a stop.

He heard footsteps next to the car and the right passenger-side door open and close, then the right rear door open. Eleanor and the President were climbing out.

A woman greeted them, and the sound of their footsteps moved away from the limousine as they walked inside. Garrison knew the limousine would remain where it was and Collins would stay with it. With the sound of the commercial radio in the front seat of the limousine being turned on, Garrison reached for the trunk lock. He pulled back on the latch. He knew that there would be little movement of the car as he got out due to the limousine's reinforced undercarriage.

Hearing no footsteps or voices, Garrison opened the trunk about two inches and peeked out. There was no one nearby. He put on the uniform hat and slid out of the trunk. Squatting to remain out of the camera view, he quietly shut the trunk.

He stood and walked briskly to the service entrance. He was aware of a surveillance camera mounted on the wall of the Kennedy Center loading dock near the limousine. He hoped that the Secret Service supervisor responsible for monitoring the security television screens in the Kennedy Center Secret Service Command Post would miss him as he made his way inside. He knew this was possible because the surveillance camera's view was facing the front of the limousine and the trunk area wasn't in direct view of the camera. Also, with the supervisor having multiple screens to watch, there was a good chance a brief movement of the trunk opening and closing would not attract his attention. All he would see was a Uniformed Division officer cross the black-and-white screen.

Inside, Garrison turned left and made his way to an elevator, where he pressed the button and waited. Two women were coming down the hall in his direction. He knelt to tie his shoe so they wouldn't see his face. They passed by. He stepped inside the elevator and pushed a button. The door closed. The car descended one floor to the basement. He exited and hurried along a zigzag hall-way that he knew was used only by stagehands and Cen-ter musicians.

Entering a storage room, he closed the door and turned on the light. He picked up a wooden bench and placed it underneath an air-conditioning duct. He spent the next fifteen or twenty minutes using the screwdriver blade on his pocketknife to remove the duct's metal-grid cover. Hiding the cover under a large trash can, he re-turned the bench to its original location, and then turned off the light. Anyone entering the room wouldn't see anything amiss other than the missing duct cover.

Returning to the duct opening in darkness, he grabbed the edge with both hands and pulled himself inside. The duct was smaller than he thought. Slowly squeezing himself out again, he dropped to the floor. He removed his bulky uniform jacket, stashing it in a corner. Hoisting himself back into the opening again, he made his way forward, coughing from the thick layer of dust lining the constricted passageway. His arms were tight against his sides. He could barely move. A wave of claustrophobia came over him and he began to panic, fearing he would pass out and die, to be found days later when some ticket holder complained to an usher that the odor of rotting flesh was emanating from the air-conditioning system.

He pressed his mouth into the corner of his shirt and forced himself to breathe evenly. He lost track of time as he inched along slowly until he reached a ninety-degree turn to the right. If he remembered correctly from the advance security work he'd done at the Center, it was at this point that the duct crossed the edge of an employee locker room that hadn't been used in years.

He managed to pull his pocketknife from his trouser pocket, and began cutting the tape over a seam in the duct material. Breaking through the duct was harder than he'd anticipated. Perspiration ran into his eyes. With his hand trapped next to his body, he moved the blade back and forth, the duct swaying with his exertions. Suddenly, there was a sharp tearing noise. He was falling. He struggled to grasp something. The section of the duct he was in dropped through the acoustical board ceiling, and slammed violently to the locker room floor, the fall knocking the air out of his lungs. Gasping for breath, he crawled from the duct section. He was in the corner of the room, next to a bank of metal lockers.

Staggering to his feet, he crossed the room and put his ear to the door. He waited. Nothing. No one had heard him. Exhaling with relief, he checked himself in a wall mirror. His face and his clothing were covered with soot. Having brushed off his clothing and used his shirttail to wipe his face as best he could, he opened the door and peeked out.

He turned the doorknob and opened the door about an inch. Down a hallway to his right some Secret Service agents were engaged in conversation. Garrison closed the door and stood for a moment, going over in his mind the details of the Kennedy Center security plan he'd worked on during a previous Presidential visit.

Garrison pulled Flanagan's two-way radio from his belt. He pressed the transmit button. "Wintergreen to Thirteen Kennedy Security Room."

"Go, Boss."

"I just saw some agents near Hallway Four Adam. Have them stand by at the tactical car."

"Roger."

Moments later, the agents received the requested radio message on the Kennedy Center radio frequency and headed down the corridor. Garrison picked up a chair. He opened the door and walked down the hallway a few feet to an air-conditioning vent. Placing the chair under the vent, he stood on it and pulled off the vent cover.

He was tackled from behind and thrown to the floor. He struggled. An agent put a gun to his head as two others held him.

CHAPTER 35

DURING THE FIRST intermission of *Long Day's Journey into Night,* the President yawned and stood to stretch. To him, the actors' words had been meshing together in a mishmash of melancholy and depression. He preferred musical theater to drama. His idea of an enjoyable night out wasn't watching the thrashing of a dysfunctional family. He had enough problems meshing together in his head. Eleanor stood to stretch. He thought the play was depressing, but he would not bring it up with her. She was already acting out of sorts, and no good would come from bringing up a downbeat subject.

"I want to go to the holding room," she said.

"Some of the party people will want to chat—"

"The hell with them. I'm making a phone call to China."

"Then I'll stay here and you go."

"No. The phone call is from Beijing. The cultural affairs person. I may need you to get on the line with me for a moment to convince them that I am representing your interests."

"Oh, for God's sake—"

"Please."

He shrugged. "Very well."

She took his arm as they moved past the other guests.

"I've had a migraine headache all day," Eleanor said as they walked out to the hallway. Two agents followed.

"I noticed you fidgeting in your seat. I thought it was the play."

"So depressing."

"Family situations can get like that, can't they?"

"Is that some kind of a personal dig?"

"Aren't we sensitive. The headache. Have you talked with the doctor?"

"I have pills, but they don't seem to do any good," she said coldly. "I just hope I can make it through the rest of this play."

They entered the elevator with the agents, who looked uncomfortable and avoided eye contact. The doors closed. The elevator descended. They got out and followed other agents to the holding room. An agent opened the door for them.

"Russell, do you remember what you told me that day we were sitting on that lovely verandah in St. Bart's?" she asked when they were alone.

"I remember the view—"

She glanced at her wristwatch.

"We'd been lounging there in the sun for hours. Your exact words were: 'It's the two of us forever, baby.' You used to call me baby. Then you said something very sweet. You told me that you would never disappoint me and that you would always be there for me. It was what I'd always wanted to hear."

"We were a beautiful couple, weren't we?" the President said.

She reached up and touched his face gently.

"You used to touch my face like that all the time, Eleanor. I miss it."

"We were a sexy couple, all right."

"You're making me wish you didn't have a head-ache," he said.

"A quick screw for old times' sake? How merciful of you."

"There you go again," he said grimly.

"Does *she* say things like that?"

"Can't we at least try to be civil to one another?"

"We've come a long way together. You were my man. I loved you. I used to dream about us being in the White House."

"They should have given you a part in that damn play."

There was a silence, and he wondered what it would have been like to marry a woman less demanding, one who wasn't so emasculating. Maybe things could have worked out, he told himself. But that was all over now. He had but one life to live, and the rest of it wasn't going to be with her.

"I know why you won't look me in the eyes," she said. "You can fool your Cabinet members, the entire House and Senate, the Joint Chiefs of Staff, and the American people. But you can't fool your wife. You used me. It was nothing but a means to an end with a piece of ass thrown in. You seduced me because I had something you wanted."

"Eleanor, why do you persist in this self-torture?"

"Russell Jordan, President of the United States. What a damn joke. You're a nothing. A big zero. You'd be nothing without me."

"None of us are perfect, Eleanor."

"That sounds like a preface for some speech. Some of that insincere blather you're so good at spouting."

"You're a very demanding woman, Eleanor."

"I'm the woman you needed."

"True. But things would have been a lot easier if you hadn't rubbed my nose in it every day since we got married."

She gave him a glare he'd never seen before. She was looking through him.

"Is the truth that difficult to accept? When you look in the mirror, does it hurt to know that you couldn't have made it to this place without me? All I asked in return was to be your partner. But I guess that was too much."

"Drop it, for Christ's sake. Let's end all this."

She glanced at her wristwatch.

"It's ended," she said.

There was a tone of finality to her words, like the last remark made from the window of a train as it pulled away from the station; the final shout from the last fan at the end of the ninth inning.

"I'll be right back," she said.

"Where are you going?"

"The rest room."

"Okay."

"Do you feel all right? You're acting a little strange."

There was a knock on the door, and then it came open. It was Agent Squires.

"Mr. President, we have a security problem—"

"Don't bother us," Eleanor said.

"This won't wait."

"Go away!"

"What is it?" the President said.

Squires walked in and closed the door.

"We just apprehended Pete Garrison. He claims there is a bomb planted somewhere in this building that is set to go off at 9:15."

"Where is Wintergreen?"

The door came open. Wintergreen rushed in. Squires grabbed his arm.

"Mr. Director, Garrison says there is a bomb—"

"I'm aware."

Wintergreen turned to Jordan.

"Mr. President, this building is bomb free. But to be extra safe, I think it best that you remain here for a few minutes while we search the Presidential box."

Squires got a pained look on his face.

"What's wrong?" Jordan said staring at him.

"Garrison said that Director Wintergreen planted the bomb."

Eleanor furrowed her brow. "Surely you don't believe your own Director could be involved in anything like that."

"Wintergreen was here after the bomb dogs had finished," Squires said. "Garrison said Agent Flanagan is also involved. And I can't find him. He also said the First Lady was behind it. I recommend that we evacuate the building."

"Bring Garrison here," Eleanor said.

"Why?"

"I'll get the truth out of him."

"If there is a bomb—"

"Russell. Tell him."

"Do as she says, Agent."

"Is that an order?"

"Do as she says. I'll straighten this out myself."

Squires departed.

"What the hell is going on, Eleanor?"

"Garrison is trying to confuse everyone. You'll look foolish if you go running out of here and this turns out to be a false alarm. The press will have a field day. It'll be like the time President Nixon canceled a trip to New Orleans because of uncorroborated threat information. He regretted it until the day he left office. Don't let them do this to you. It would be a humiliation."

Jordan stared at her and, for the first time, he saw a different person than the one he'd married. He saw their deal, their connection, and he saw everything that they had done to one another, and his knees suddenly went weak.

Squires pushed the door open. He and two other agents had Garrison between them, handcuffed.

"Mr. President, the First Lady paid Larry Wintergreen to kill you," Garrison said. "She had him plant a bomb here."

"Sit down, Pete," Eleanor said condescendingly. "I'll call a doctor for you. You'll feel better after you talk to him."

"It's almost 9:15," Garrison said. "Give the evacuation order! Your life depends on it!"

"If Eleanor knew there is a bomb here, why would she be with me right now?" Jordan asked.

"Because it would look odd for her to have remained at the White House. She was covering herself."

Jordan turned to Eleanor, and then looked coldly back at Garrison.

Eleanor glanced at her wristwatch.

"Did you see that?" Garrison shouted. "She just checked her watch. The bomb must be set to go off in here. It's right here in this room!"

Eleanor's eyes were wide. "He's insane."

The red phone rang. Squires picked up the receiver.

"Agent Squires . . . yes. Okay." His jaw dropped and he dropped the receiver. "That was Agent Kallenstien. Martha Breckinridge just told her Flanagan was the one who tried to kill her."

Squires dropped the phone and faced Wintergreen with his hand on his gun.

Eleanor moved toward the door.

"Stop her," Jordan said.

She reached for the door handle. Squires grabbed her arm.

"We're all going to stay right here until the intermission is over," Jordan said.

Eleanor blinked rapidly, her eyes on Wintergreen.

"Do something!" she shrieked hysterically.

Wintergreen reached for his gun. Garrison kicked it out of his hand.

"Evacuate the building!" Squires shouted into his microphone.

Eleanor pulled the door open and ran. Wintergreen ran after her.

Squires shoved the President into the adjoining room. Garrison and the other agents followed.

A sudden, blinding flash of light and a detonation

crack flattened them on the shuddering cement floor. Shredded chucks of plaster and wood blew outward from the holding room with such force that across the street at the Watergate apartment units, windows and mirrors cracked. In the next second, spent debris and glass could be heard falling. Shouts came from inside the auditorium. Fire alarms sounded.

As fire and smoke billowed from the holding room door, Squires asked the President if he was okay. He said he was. Squires helped the President to his feet.

"Stay close to us," Squires said. "We're getting the hell out of here."

The President turned to Squires. "Remove his handcuffs."

Squires complied. Automatic sprinklers began spraying from above. The other agents shoved debris away from the door.

"Find her, Garrison," Jordan said. "No one is to know."

"I understand."

Squires and the other agents rushed out of the room and down the hall with the President. Garrison began looking through a demolished hallway and main lobby that was filling with smoke as frightened playgoers were running from the theater.

Garrison pushed his way through the crowd following the rubble-strewn hallway. He figured Eleanor and Wintergreen must have run toward the stairwell leading to the garage where the spare limousine was parked.

To his right, next to the wall adjoining the holding room, he saw a hand sticking out from under a shredded door. The explosive charge emanating from inside the holding room had blown out a wall and door. Eleanor and Wintergreen had been killed by it, their bodies lying askew among the debris. They'd made the wrong turn. It had just been bad luck. Garrison shoved the debris away, freeing her. But she didn't move. He knelt by her. She was ashen, her lips colorless. As people screamed and ran past, Garrison touched her cheek and her eyes opened.

"Pete?"

"Help is coming."

"I hate him. . . ."

"Don't talk," he whispered gently.

She coughed, sputtering blood. She met his eyes, and the corners of her mouth turned up slightly.

Her eyes remained frozen open.

CHAPTER 36

GARRISON WENT TO the White House and briefed the President, who was visibly shaken. He remained in the Oval Office with him as the White House Chief of Staff and the Attorney General arrived. The President told Garrison to remain close by. He did so, leaving the Oval office for a few minutes to go downstairs to the Secret Service command post, where he went to his locker and changed into a fresh suit.

During the rest of the night, the White House was a flurry of activity. As the news of the bombing spread worldwide, military drivers sped around D.C. transporting Cabinet members and other close confidants of the President to the White House. When they arrived, Garrison led them to the Oval office, where the President held a short meeting, soliciting advice on how to proceed. The announcement of the deaths of both the First

Lady and Director Wintergreen was made by Presidential Press Secretary Elmore Banks at three A.M., causing all the television anchorpersons in the country to rush to their respective broadcast stations.

At five A.M., the White House stewards brought breakfast to the President's advisors. The President asked Garrison to join him in the State Dining Room. Garrison followed him inside, and the President asked Garrison exactly what he'd said to Joe Kretchvane about the conspiracy. Garrison recounted his conversation in detail.

The President picked up the phone.

"This is the President. Get Joe Kretchvane on the line." He set the receiver down. "You will apologize to Kretchvane and tell him that you were working undercover against Flanagan. Tell him you were following my orders. Then put me on the phone."

The phone rang.

Garrison spoke with Kretchvane, gave him the story as the President had requested, then handed the phone over.

The President and Kretchvane spoke for a half hour. Then the President returned to the Oval Office.

An hour later, Garrison led the President down a shiny corridor to the White House Press Briefing Room. Opening the door a few inches, he peeked inside. Every seat was filled and people were sitting on the floor, standing along the walls. At a podium backdropped by a deep blue curtain with a White House emblem in the middle, Press Secretary Elmore Banks, a balding well-fed man who'd been with the President since the first campaign, shuffled through some papers preparing to speak.

"If everyone will be quiet, please," Banks said. The murmuring in the room diminished. "A preliminary joint FBI and U.S. Secret Service investigation of the bomb incident at the Kennedy Center has been completed. It has been established that the explosive used was military-grade C-4, the same type of explosive material used to bomb the Ronald Reagan Federal Building. We believe that the target of the bomb was President Jordan. When the bomb detonated, the First Lady and the President were in what is referred to as a 'holding room,' where the President was making some official telephone calls during the intermission. The explosion killed both the First Lady and U.S. Secret Service Director Larry Wintergreen. So far, no suspects have been developed, but the modus operandi is believed to be similar to certain terrorist groups that are known to the government. There will be no public statements made by the task forces that are investigating, and a blue-ribbon commission has been appointed by the President to assemble all the data and make required policy from the incident. National Security Advisor Helen Pierpont will chair that commission. The investigation itself will be conducted by agents of the United States Secret Service."

"Are you saying this is the work of the Aryan Disciples?" asked reporter Carolyn Ude from the *Los Angeles Times*.

"There are a number of similarities between this bombing and previous Aryan Disciples bombings, and it has been determined that one low-level Secret Service official, Gilbert L. Flanagan, may have been involved in planting the bomb. We are quite certain that he was the only Secret Service employee involved. But, as I said, an investigation is under way. It wouldn't be appropriate for me to comment further at this point."

"Joe Kretchvane is reporting that a reliable government source told him that Flanagan was the only government insider involved and that he may have been co-opted by the Aryan Disciples. Is that true?"

"I don't want to either confirm or deny such information at this stage."

"Wouldn't there have to be Secret Service involvement for a bomb to have been planted in an area secured earlier by the Secret Service?"

"That would be a safe assumption. The preliminary investigation indicates that Secret Service agents found the device shortly before the detonation occurred. Director Wintergreen lost his life trying to get the First Lady to safety. I'm not going to go any further right now because I don't want to taint the investigation."

Photographers jockeyed for position in the front row, shoving and pushing each other as Banks blinked at a barrage of camera flashes. Then he glanced toward Garrison and gave a nod. "At this time, the President will make a brief prepared statement. Ladies and Gentlemen, the President of the United States."

Banks moved back a few feet.

Moving past Garrison amid the sound of a hundred camera clicks, the President walked to the podium. A hush came over the crowd. The President took out a note card and placed it in front of him.

"Good morning, ladies and gentlemen. The flag of our nation stands at half-staff and I bear the greatest personal loss of my life. I wish to remind all of you, my fellow citizens, that the United States of America—our democracy, our institutions, and our Constitution—are bigger than any crisis the country has ever been forced to endure. No matter what happens to those who hold political office, our nation's principles as a shrine to freedom remain intact. We are, truly, a nation of laws, not men. Let the word go out to our enemies: No amount of violence, not even a hundred such cowardly acts, can cause us to fear you. In her death, Eleanor Hollingsworth Jordan, a great American and a loving wife, and a fighter for freedom, has vanquished you."

The President cleared his throat, and then took a sip of water. Garrison thought his eyes looked watery. "We also mourn the loss of Director Lawrence Wintergreen of the U.S. Secret Service, a man who gave his all to fulfill his sworn duty. . . ."

After the press conference, Garrison and the President walked to the Oval Office. The President stopped at the open door. He looked tired and chastened and there was a deep melancholy in his eyes.

"Pete, I'm appointing you as the new agent in charge of White House Detail."

"Thank you, Mr. President."

"No matter what happens, I'll expect Eleanor's role in all this to remain between you and me. Forever."

"Of course. But there is one thing—"

"Yes?"

"To do a good job, I'll need my own people."

"Such as?"

"Agent Martha Breckinridge would make an excellent addition to the White House Detail."

"Consider her promoted."

Inside the Oval Office, a telephone rang. The President ignored it for a moment as he studied Garrison, meeting his gaze directly before walking to the desk and picking up the receiver. Garrison closed the door quietly.

He walked downstairs to the command post. A shift change was in progress. Agents checking weapons, going over rosters and security surveys, signing in and signing out equipment. There was a hush as they noticed him. The agents moved to him and shook hands one by one. Moving on through the office, winding his way through the maze of desks and chalkboards, Garrison accepted more greetings.

Later, Garrison departed the White House in an unmarked car. The sky was a bright azure backdrop to a band of clouds, bright white and fleecy, illumined from within. For the first time in weeks, the humidity had dissipated and there was a steady, cool breeze. Passing by the guard booth at the Northeast Gate, he looked back. He'd viewed the scene a hundred times: the ancient elm trees bent over to the sidewalk from the White House lawn, a circle of red tulips surrounding the fountain. Along Pennsylvania Avenue, tourists were busily posing for and taking photographs.

Garrison told himself that, for all its intrigue and venality, Washington, D.C., was still a place of hope. He knew that during the War of 1812, the British had burned the White House down to the ground. But things had returned to normal. He walked by Blair House, where, in 1950, White House Detail agents had been in a gunfight with terrorists who tried to assassinate President Harry Truman. But old Harry never missed a beat. Maybe that's what it was about D.C. that made it different—its permanence. Through riots, demonstrations, assassinations, war, and corruption, Abe Lincoln still pondered, the Marines still kept Old Glory at the top of the pole, and the tourists continued to file past the Vietnam Veterans' Memorial, holding their children by the hand.

Garrison stopped at Margit Holakoui's flower shop. After introducing himself as the newly appointed White House Detail Agent in Charge, he purchased a dozen red roses at the White House discount price.

Carrying the flowers in his gun hand, he got back in the car and headed for Prince George's County Hospital to visit Martha Breckinridge.